Praise for Charles Jaco's first Peter Dees novel, *Dead Air*

"As frightening and unforgettable as a scud missile attack on the dark desert landscape of the mind."
—KINKY FRIEDMAN
Author of *Blast from the Past*

"The feel of reality, the excitement of fiction . . . This is one fine book."
—BOB COSTAS

"A real page-turner . . . A fabulous and smart novel."
—MARY MATALIN

"Chilling . . . Jaco's book is part fact, part fiction. . . . Jaco escorts the reader into the grit of battles in the sand with a good sense of detail."
—*St. Louis Post-Dispatch*

"A crisp, no-nonsense debut that sends intrepid reporter Peter Dees from Haiti to Kuwait as the U.S. gears up for Desert Storm . . . Timely . . . Engaging."
—*Publishers Weekly*

By Charles Jaco
Published by Ballantine Books:

DEAD AIR
LIVE SHOT

Visit the author's Web site at
www.charlesjaco.com

Books published by The Ballantine Publishing Group
are available at quantity discounts on bulk purchases
for premium, educational, fund-raising, and special
sales use. For details, please call 1-800-733-3000.

LIVE SHOT

Charles Jaco

BALLANTINE BOOKS • NEW YORK

A Ballantine Book
Published by The Ballantine Publishing Group
Copyright © 1999 by Charles Jaco

All rights reserved under International and Pan-American Copyright Conventions. Published in the United States by The Ballantine Publishing Group, a division of Random House, Inc., New York, and simultaneously in Canada by Random House of Canada Limited, Toronto.

Ballantine and colophon are registered trademarks of Random House, Inc.

www.randomhouse.com/BB/

Library of Congress Catalog Card Number: 99-91023

ISBN: 0-345-42186-8

Manufactured in the United States of America

First Edition: December 1999

10   9   8   7   6   5   4   3   2   1

FOR MELISSA

Mi vida, mi corazón
Amor es fuerte

The only qualities essential for real success in journalism are ratlike cunning, a plausible manner, and a little literary ability.

—NICHOLAS TOMALIN
Special Correspondent
The Sunday Times (London)
Killed 17 October 1973, by a
Syrian rocket while covering
the Yom Kippur war

CHAPTER 1

The figure in the rear seat never considered killing anyone in broad daylight unless it was absolutely unavoidable. It was simple prudence, really. Oh, someone *had* died during daylight hours before. But that had been in a basement, and quite by accident, when the twin electrodes from an old field telephone—and hadn't it been a bitch to find *that* piece of antiquated junk?—were attached to a squirming man's molars. The mouth had been clamped shut and the phone's hand-cranked generator spun a dozen or so times. A bloody froth spewed from the man's mouth before he shuddered and his heart gave out.

The figure in the backseat idly stroked the silencer that made the pistol look like a length of black pipe with a handle attached. "So you want to snatch him if he's disagreeable?"

The driver didn't say a word. The bearded man sitting beside him in the front seat grunted. "There is no reason to kill him at all unless he threatens to betray us. No killing unless he threatens my life, which I sincerely doubt. If he is merely, as you say, disagreeable, then yes, we remove him from the premises."

The fat raindrops landed on the windshield of the idling Ford with a series of succulent plops. A stray series of clouds blown in on the early morning easterlies from the Bahamas skidded overhead. The three men behind the Crown Victoria's tinted windows could barely hear the rustle of dry palm fronds shivering in the breeze over the hum of the air conditioner and the muted chatter from a Miami Spanish-language radio station.

"This is ridiculous," the man in the backseat said. "No one in Key West gets up at six A.M."

"This one does," replied the man with the beard. The upholstery softly crinkled as he turned to face the man in the rear. "This one, he likes his coffee."

Halfway down the block, a gust of wind blew a plastic grocery sack across Thomas Street and plastered it against one of the trellises that framed a six-by-eight-foot front porch, painted white and attached to the front of a wooden cottage whose boards glowed with a fresh coat of coral-colored exterior latex. The shade almost matched the tangle of bougainvillea flowers perched on the ends of thick stalks that covered both trellises, shielding the porch from the street. Between the porch and the freshly painted bright white picket fence was a stack of ten sheets of drywall, each four-by-eight, wrapped snugly in thick clear plastic.

* * *

Peter Dees stepped onto the porch, scratched his bare chest, and blinked at the humidity that hung over the street like a mildewed shower curtain. The rain had come and gone quick as a paycheck. He bent over, picked up the Keys edition of the *Miami Herald* and padded back inside, wiping the moisture from the paper's plastic bag on his paint-stained gray athletic pants. He walked across the newly varnished hardwood floor into the spare bedroom that had been converted into an office. Half the wall between the office and the master bedroom was missing.

Dees checked the glowing digital clock mounted just above the oversized computer screen. Six-ten. He stepped over three bundles of soundproof wall tiles, walked to a thin microphone mounted on the edge of the large mahogany desk, and said, "Telephone."

With a hum, the computer awoke from its sleep mode. The screen hissed, flickered, and displayed the telephone menu.

Dees cleared his throat, and a large blue question mark appeared in the center of the screen. The voice recognition program didn't have coughs, sneezes, grunts, or sighs in its memory. Dees said, "Telephone. Call Jacob."

The screen displayed Jacob Williams's name, address, and telephone number, and a small map indicating his house, five blocks away in Bahama Town. Dees unwrapped the newspaper and scanned the front page while the speaker warbled with the sound of a telephone ringing. The two right-hand columns below the fold detailed the news conference he had covered yesterday. The headline read NEW EXILE GROUP PLEDGES MORE ACTION. He scanned the lead paragraphs. "A sugar millionaire and a legendary exile hero have joined forces to form an anti-Castro organization that pledges more militant action against the Cuban dictator."

Dees stopped reading, since he knew the news conference by heart. He flipped the paper over. CASTRO DYING? the three-column head in the upper right corner blurted. The subhead was in boldface, but still more subdued than the all-caps screamer: CANCER REPORTS CIRCULATE IN MIAMI, HAVANA.

For the third time in as many years, reports are circulating that Fidel Castro has advanced cancer. Sources within Havana's dissident community call it colon cancer, while Miami exile leaders say they have been told "on good authority" that Castro suffers from the advanced stages of prostate cancer. This report is being taken more seriously than past rumors, however, because of concern in official Washington. Yesterday, State Department official Edward Davis . . .

Dees wrinkled his brow. Hell-lo. He reread the sentence.

Yesterday, State Department official Edward Davis told the House National Security Committee of reports that friction is increasing between the pro-Castro hard-liners and the soft-line moderates inside Cuba's Central Committee. He also noted that the top official from the Cuban Interests Section in Washington had been called home to Havana. "We believe all these events are related to reports that President Castro may be seriously ill," Davis told the committee.

A sleepy voice rumbled from the computer's speakers. "Yeah?"

Dees faced the microphone and put down the newspaper. "Jacob. Peter Dees. Check the time lately?"

There was a rustle, like sheets being wadded, and a clatter, like an alarm clock picked up and dropped. "Shit, man. Sorry. Sorry. I thought we said seven."

"We said six. We motivate and we can get this thing finished today. One more wall and it's done. And remember, my friends show up at four this afternoon, so we do some sundown fishing if the weather holds."

"Yeah, yeah." The Bahamian-accented voice sounded more awake. "Marine forecast's good and I got the boat gassed. Tee and me'll be there in half an hour. What we say, five for the whole day?"

Dees laughed. "We said four hundred, including renting your boat this afternoon and the work here. By the way, why'd you steal the Sheetrock?"

The speaker just hummed.

"Jacob?"

"What'd you mean?" The voice sounded hurt.

"The shipping tag on the bottom of the bundle of drywall? It says 'Island Development Company, Stock Island.' Why'd you rip off drywall from those new town houses going up by the golf course?"

"Overruns. They got too much and I got a deal. Besides, when you get scruples about stealing from some booshey assholes who play golf in pink pants?"

Dees grunted. The blue question mark floated on the screen again. "Jacob," he said clearly, restoring the screen display, "bring me a receipt, all right?"

"The guy I buy them from, he don't give receipts. And he don't take returns, either. Says barter is the last bastion of unfettered capitalism."

"What'd you trade him?"

"Don't ask, don't tell."

Dees smiled. "Remember, one of my friends is an FBI agent and his wife works for INS. My other friend's a TV cameraman, so he could take your picture and you'd end up on *America's Most Wanted*. Okay?"

The voice sounded hurt again. "Hey, I don't have a record in this country."

"Lucky us," Dees said. "And have Tee bring the color chips so we can paint the bedroom and the new wall."

"Right." The speaker clicked off.

Dees picked up a T-shirt, slipped it on, walked into the bathroom, and brushed his teeth. He looked in the mirror, and saw that sections of his sandy hair had been flattened by the pillow, while the brush-cut over his forehead poked up like he'd stuck his finger in an electric socket. A few brown goatee hairs that needed trimming stuck out at odd angles.

His T-shirt's message was repeated on the front and back— PERIODISTA NO DISPARE—meaning, "Journalist. Don't Shoot." Dees had a collection of them that said the same thing in French, Serbian, Hebrew, Arabic, Russian, Portuguese, English, and Mandarin. On the wall, the small framed blue, white, and red Yugoslav flag made the bright white bathroom seem cheery, despite its shredded, burned edges and the comma-shaped streak of dried blood that bisected the white stripe.

Dees picked up the newspaper and walked to the front door. He made sure it was unlocked in case Jacob and Tee showed up while he was gone, and walked into the sauna on the street. He headed down Thomas Street and had just turned right on Fleming when the big blue Ford began to move forward slowly. Dees crossed Fleming diagonally at Duval, looking both ways though there were no vehicles or people for four blocks in any direction.

The Ford idled at the corner as Dees strolled down Duval. He sidestepped a smashed Corona bottle in front of the Hard Rock Cafe. He looked up at the three-story mansion with floors and porches and beams fastened tightly by pre–Civil War shipwrights, built originally for an entrepreneur who had made a fortune lighting false signal fires on the Atlantic side of the island, near the reefs. The fires had lured schooners and sloops and barks onto the reef, where scores of hollow-eyed men would be waiting, straining at the longboat oars and claiming salvage rights on whatever cargo might have been intact among the snapped, groaning spars and the screaming, drowning sailors.

Dees turned right onto Greene as the car behind him slowly rolled down Duval. He strolled across the patio and into the Cuban Coffee Queen Café. He ordered *"Tres cafés con leche para llevar"* in Spanish, even though Maria, who had owned the place for years, had finally surrendered to the forces of gentrification and sold it to an Anglo businessman. The new owner had gotten rid of the peeling Formica, greasy beans, and Budweiser sign with the beer logo superimposed over a sputtering blue neon outline of Cuba, replacing them with new walls and ceilings stained to look like Cuban mahogany, and new tile floors, and nouvelle cuisine.

Dees took the three coffees outside, balanced on a cardboard tray, and sat them on a patio table. He plopped into one of the plastic chairs, snapped open the newspaper, and took a sip of the sweet, frothy liquid. The color photo on the bottom of the front page of the *Herald* showed a man with short white hair and a beard, his hand linked with a slim man with slicked-back hair in a business suit, their arms raised in unity, smiling broadly in front of a Cuban flag. The caption read, "Sugar magnate and Republican activist Manuel Cabrera (left) unites with exile legend Ramon Vargas announcing a new anti-Castro group."

Dees had opened to the jump page and was continuing the article when the chair next to him creaked. He peeked over the top of the paper at a fountain of henna-streaked black hair tied together in the middle with a yellow bow. " 'Morning, Tee. Didn't hear the truck."

"New muffler, *bebé*," a falsetto voice said. "My Bahama stallion finally fixed it. You want to look at these paint samples and move the damn paper so I can get my coffee?"

Dees folded the *Herald* and put it on the table. The topknot of orange-streaked hair was attached to a head with a chiseled chin, sharp brown eyes, and pockmarked cheeks smoothed over with makeup. Ripples of muscle lay just under the surface of the shoulders that strained at a red halter top.

As one manicured hand dropped two strips of cardboard dotted neatly with six spots of paint, the other clutched one of the large cardboard cups and brought it to a pair of glossy lips. "Me," Tee said, "I like the first sample. It goes best with that grass-cloth wall over the bed and all the African stuff in there."

"Some of it's Asian," Dees said, looking at the paint spots. "Some's Latin. It's just mostly brown and tan."

He took a sip of coffee and nodded. "That's it, the first one. You need to take that decorating talent up to Miami and make some real money."

Tee snorted. "I take what I get in Cayo Hueso, man. But my Cuban *hermanos* up there? Too macho, too political, too repressed. Those crazy Miami Nazis call me a *maricón* and a he-she, what time they're not talking about going back to Cuba. I mean, shit, look at this here."

He tapped one of his mauve nails on the *Herald*. His voice became prissy, dripping with scorn. "Oh, Fidel's dying. Yeah, and he's been dying every year, three times a year, since I was a baby. Brigade X gonna free Cuba. Everybody gonna go back and get their mansions and *fincas* back. Everybody actually had an estate down there who claims they had one and Cuba's gotta be the size of Brazil."

Tee laughed, put the cup back onto the tray, and picked it up. "Gotta take the coffee back to Jacob. I'm gonna get us some of those *pasteles*, maybe *mango y queso*. You want?"

Dees shook his head no. As Tee started to walk inside, he turned and looked down the street. "Guys in the Crown Vic friends of yours?"

Dees looked down at the paper and said, "Been tailing me since I left the house. Either that or shy tourists who want my autograph."

Tee laughed. "That's what you get for being mister-famous-television-star and a white guy living on the edge of choco-latte city. Visibility."

He shashayed inside as Dees turned his attention back to the paper. Dees was aware of movement in his peripheral vision.

* * *

As the front passenger door of the Ford opened and the air-conditioning escaped into the humid air outside, the man in the rear seat slid to the right and sighted the pistol on Dees's right eyebrow.

I don't like you again, he thought, and smiled.

CHAPTER 2

Dees heard breathing and looked up from his newspaper. The man standing over him had gray hair and a stubby gray beard. The effect was as if a spray gun loaded with half-inch gray and white hairs had taken a few even passes across his skull. He wore a white half-sleeved guayabera, the left sleeve pinned shut just above where the elbow should have been.

"Mister Dees?"

Dees looked up and nodded. "Mister Vargas."

The silence between them was broken by the squawking of a flock of wild parakeets as they skittered overhead, flashing yellow and green against the milky sky. Finally Vargas cleared his throat. "May I sit?"

Dees extended an open palm toward a chair.

Vargas sat heavily and chuckled. "You know, since you have interviewed me before, I was surprised you used such overblown language to describe me. You do not ask a single question during our press conference, then I turn on GTV and hear, what was it? Ah, yes, 'Vargas is still admired in Little Havana for his reckless courage. But many wonder if this one-armed warrior in winter is more Don Quixote than conquistador.' Really, now. Purple prose, nò?"

The right corner of Dees's mouth rose in a lopsided smile. "It's why I subscribe to the Cliché of the Month Club."

"And was it necessary to use animation?"

"Only because you didn't take a movie camera along in 1975."

The story on the Brigade X news conference had given Dees the excuse to use forty-five seconds retelling the story that every schoolchild from Calle Ocho to Coral Gables knew by heart. Ramon Vargas, son of a mid-level United Fruit Company manager, had joined Fidel in the Sierra Maistra. He left Cuba in 1960, his revolutionary fervor tempered by the reality of the *Fidelistas* political turn to the left, and returned in 1961 at the Bay of Pigs.

Over black-and-white video of the invasion and parades of prisoners hauled from Playa Girón, Dees's script said the legend began when Vargas was captured on the beach by an old classmate, who made sure he was only minimally tortured before being repatriated in 1962. But then—and here was where animated maps and a series of still drawings came in—the legend became epic in 1975.

Vargas, alone, had piloted a fifteen-foot outboard on a moonless night across a hundred miles of the glass-flat Florida Straits and into Havana harbor. He killed the engine and tugged at a pair of oars, sliding past the Morro and in among the jumble of Soviet freighters and oil tankers that crowded the industrial harbor. Less than a hundred yards from the spot where the battleship *Maine* sank in 1898, he pulled the skiff next to a tanker filled with crude destined to be turned into diesel by the belching refinery on the other side of the harbor.

On the floor of the boat, he had a seventy-pound magnetic mine, packed with plastic explosive in a shaped charge designed to direct the force of the blast through the hull and not into the water. But Vargas had been vague about the interior geography of a six-hundred-foot Soviet tanker. So when he leaned over the gunwale and stuck his arms into the greasy, black water, instead of clamping the mine next to one of the storage tanks that held nonexplosive crude, he attached it to the steel plate just outside one of the ship's almost-empty fuel tanks.

He still didn't know why the mine went off too early. He had planned to be out at sea, motoring back toward the Keys, when the plastic explosive came to life. Instead, he was barely a hundred yards away, straining at the oars, when the mine detonated and ignited the fumes that filled the fuel tank. For ten seconds, the fireball lit everything from Regla to the statue of the Christ of Havana overlooking the harbor in hot yellow light. The tanker heeled hard over to starboard, snapping the mooring cables that held it to the dock, and settled on its side in the gummy silt on the harbor bottom.

Vargas remembered being lifted from the boat and pushed upward by a hot, invisible palm before he blacked out. A spinning piece of desk-size metal sheeting from a hatch cover became an airborne scalpel and severed his left arm just above the elbow joint. A miracle, they whispered in both Havana and Miami, that he hadn't bled to death before he was fished from the harbor. This was where the stories made Vargas invincible.

Vargas was brought to a general, the same classmate who had captured him at the Bay of Pigs. The general, so the stories went, couldn't bear to execute his valiant old comrade. So as a parting gift before he shipped out to Angola, he saw to it that Vargas received the best medical care, and was kept in a prison hospital until 1979, when Jimmy Carter arranged for his release along with several dozen other political prisoners. As an epilogue, the storytellers added, Vargas was now a hero, and the general died under mysterious circumstances when he returned from Angola and was implicated in a vague plot against Fidel.

Dees had closed his piece with a stand-up, saying that Vargas, not an especially religious man, lit a candle once a week for the dead Cuban general. And it was this sort of blood tie to the homeland, Dees concluded, that fueled the militant exiles as much as politics.

" 'Friendship and betrayal,' " Vargas quoted, waving his hand in the air, "that is how I believe you ended your story? 'Friendship and betrayal are the wood and oxygen of the exile's passionate politics. All it needs is a spark to ignite.

And Vargas and Cabrera believe Brigade X is that spark.' Most poetic, Mister Dees."

He leaned across the table. "You seem to be a fair man. I can not tell from your coverage of Cuba whether you favor Fidel or we *contracommunistas*."

Dees took a sip of his coffee. "His time was over years ago. You lost and you can't get over it."

Vargas looked sour. "I will not argue the philosophy of freedom with one who is so mistaken. But I am not here to talk, except to make you a very interesting offer."

He opened his mouth, then closed it. His eyes grew wide. Dees followed his stare, and cracked a smile. Tee stood in the café's doorway, chomping loudly on a flaky pastry, a blizzard of paper-thin crust flying in all directions. Tee wiped his mouth with the back of his hand when he saw Vargas's glare, winked, and sashayed to the table.

He extended his hand with an exaggerated limp wrist and warbled in a falsetto, "*Enchanté*."

Vargas stared at the hand like it was a rotting fish. Dees said, "Ramon Vargas, Tequila Mockingbird. Tee, Ramon Vargas."

Tee withdrew his hand and looked Vargas up and down. "Oooh. Very butch."

"Tee," Dees said, suppressing a chuckle, "I'll be back at the house in less than an hour. I need to talk here for a while."

"Okay." It was the falsetto again. Tee turned to Vargas. "Kiss, kiss, spank, spank."

Vargas's eyes followed Tee's hips as they swiveled toward a battered Chevrolet pickup. He turned to Dees as the truck ground into gear and pulled away. Before he could speak, Dees said, "Why have you been following me?"

Vargas furrowed his brow and nodded in the direction of the truck. "What was that? Do you, ah . . ." His hand waved in the air. "Do you have a taste for that sort of thing?"

Dees folded the newspaper and sighed. "Tee's the friend of a friend. And it's not 'what,' it's 'who.' You've insulted him, you've answered my question with a question, and you're pissing me off. I think that's enough for today. A pleasure."

He scooted his chair back and stood. Vargas pushed himself to his feet and held out his open palm. "Please. I am sorry."

Dees heard two soft clicks, and saw both the driver's and right rear passenger's doors begin to open on the Crown Victoria. Vargas's head snapped to the right. He shook his head side-to-side, once. Both doors paused a quarter of the way open, and closed, almost in unison, with a pair of substantial thuds. Vargas gestured toward the table with his hand. "Please. *Siéntese.* I am most sorry. And I also apologize if my security precautions offend you. Please?"

Dees stared at the car, then sat.

Vargas settled into the plastic chair and shrugged, revealing a whipcord of muscle running across his shoulders. "Anyway, I have, as I said, an offer. You remember what we said at the Brigade X announcement?"

Dees drained his coffee. "*Más acción, menos charla.* More action, less talk. Let's see, where have I heard that before?"

"We are not like those geriatric fools," Vargas said, barely moving his lips. "They can play commando in the Everglades all they wish, but we have what they do not. Money. And me."

Dees laughed. "The money's from a man who keeps dodging Federal indictments for treating his field hands like slaves. And you may be the second most famous Cuban with a beard, but that means what?" Dees spread both his palms open.

Vargas snorted like a large dog and said, "It means this. Fidel is dying, no?"

Dees shrugged. "No, or maybe yes. Exiles have been burying Castro for years. So either they were wrong or he's got a damn good embalmer."

Dees couldn't tell if Vargas smiled or grimaced. "This time, though, almost for certain. We have information the Cuban military is on alert, so finally this entire rotting socialist structure may be ready to fall. It perhaps just needs a small push, no? No television has ever seen a commando raid on Cuba, true?"

Dees shook his head. "Bad out-of-focus black and white stills from twenty years ago is about it. All anybody knows is when Radio Havana complains or exile radio in Miami brags about it, or the Feds actually bust somebody for violating the Neutrality Act."

Vargas nodded vigorously. "The Neutrality Act. We also have much to say about that. But we wish you, alone with a cameraman, to come and show the world we mean what we say. We wish you to witness the next blow for freedom."

Dees absently kept count on his left hand. One—the pinky straightened—exile attacks against Cuba from American soil were against Federal law. Two—the ring finger straightened—most militant exile groups were comic opera outfits, but some actually *did* manage attacks in Cuba. Three—the middle finger straightened—those attacks were usually not commando raids, but terrorist bombs, usually planted for maximum effect in hotels and shopping areas. Four—the index finger straightened—the Cubans had shot down planes or sunk boats that they even suspected might be on some kind of raid. If rumors of Castro being on his deathbed were circulating in Cuba like they were in the States, the Cuban military was probably more trigger-happy than ever.

And five—the thumb straightened—no reporter had ever witnessed one of the attacks.

Dees stared at his thumb. It twitched slightly. He looked at Vargas. "I went on an Israeli commando raid into south Lebanon once. I went on an IRA raid on a British garrison once. Both went for military targets, and civilians still got killed. But those were real wars more or less, and this? Not even. You intend on a military target?"

Vargas shook his head. "I am afraid I cannot compromise security by—"

"No guarantee, no coverage," Dees said quickly. "No civilians. Purely military?"

Vargas paused, then nodded. "No Cuban civilians, a legitimate Cuban target. You have my word."

"And when the Feds come looking for you after the story airs?" Dees continued. "Don't tell me anything you don't want them to know. You know they'll know it was you. And you know you'll face Federal charges."

"Ah that." Vargas smiled, his gold left bicuspid glinting in the rising sun. "We will have more to say about that later also."

Vargas nodded. "So we understand each other." He dug in a pocket and produced a business card, blank except for a Miami telephone number. "I got your pager number from your voice-mail greeting at the GTV office in Miami. I will page you sometime in the next few days, maybe sooner. When you receive the page, call the number. You will probably have less than four hours. Understood?"

As Vargas stood, Dees heard the soft *thunk* of the Crown Vic being shifted from Park to Drive. He bent over as if to tie one of his ragged running shoes. He remained bent over as he said, "Mister Vargas, please tell your friend in the backseat that silencers are illegal under the U.S. Code, and having one waving in my general direction makes me nervous. I have a .32 caliber pistol in my hand now, snub-nosed but very effective. Have him put it away so we can all play nice."

Vargas barked a laugh. He quickly pointed a finger toward the rear of the car, used his thumb and index finger to flash the universally recognized sign for a pistol, and made a cutting motion with his flat palm.

The figure in the rear seat sighed, and put the pistol on the floor, behind the driver. The car pulled forward. As the figure in the back scooted to the far side, Vargas opened the door slightly, turned, and laughed again. "You seem to be a man of many talents, Mister Dees."

Dees straightened up. "They'll give concealed licenses to just about anybody in this state. Besides, it's Florida. Even the houseplants have guns."

Vargas got in and the car pulled from the curb. Dees watched it disappear, memorizing the license plate. He strolled back to the house, pausing on Thomas Street to admire the cottage before he went inside. Years of covering wars and disasters had left him with an unwanted kind of X-ray vision. He mentally peeled away the roof and walls of every structure he saw, imagining what its skeleton and innards would look like if a hurricane took off the roof or a bomb blew out the walls.

He paused and stared at the cottage he had spent so many weekends remodeling, and it began to look like the exploded view on an instruction sheet for assembling a child's toy at Christmas. He could see the fresh roofing shingles removed, revealing the thick plywood sheathing of the roof itself, secured in place by nails and four-inch screws every six inches. It had taken him and Jacob the better part of a month of weekends to secure that roof so that only a direct hit from a category four or five hurricane would even have a chance of taking it off.

A large black man wearing a paint- and plaster-stained white T-shirt walked onto the porch. The shirt's fabric barely held his prosperous Buddha belly.

"Hey. It's about time. Gimme a hand with the rest of the drywall."

"Chill," Dees said. "I need to make a phone call." He walked into the office, leaned toward the microphone, and said, "Telephone. Pedro. Pager."

"Hey," Jacob said. "How come you don't just dial the damn phone?"

"New toy," Dees said. "I'll probably get sick of it in a week."

The screen popped to life with Pedro Marco's eleven-digit pager number. The speakers crackled with Marco's voice-mail greeting, repeated in English and Spanish. At the tone, Dees said, "Pedro, Peter. I know you're visiting your kids, but call me before you head down. We may have a good one. I want to talk to you before I call Phoenix."

For the next five hours, Dees helped nail the drywall snug into position and glued the soundproof tiles to the office side as Jacob finished the drywall on the bedroom side. Tee managed to get the paint and double-coat the bedroom before Jacob said, with finality, "It's noon. That's it. We use the Lord's Day to finish up, I guess."

Dees looked around with satisfaction. Except for some debris in the corners, the office was done, the ISDN, telephone, and co-ax cables all neatly arranged in tight cylinders around the baseboard, the tiles deadening all sound so the broadcast microphone could be used from any part of the room. As he handed Jacob four hundreds, he noticed Tee had swept the front room and kitchen floors. "For the company you're having later," Tee said.

Dees said he'd meet them at the dock at five, good for two, two and a half hours worth of fishing. Jacob nodded gruffly. "I'll clean the boat. Don't want your FBI friend to see anything that might lead to questions about my other line of work."

He gave Dees a bear hug. The pungent wave from his sweaty shirt caused Dees's nostrils to twitch. Tee gave Dees a peck on the cheek. As they walked down the sidewalk, Jacob tenderly placed a paw in the back pocket of Tee's jeans. Jacob paused at the street, and opened the passenger door of the rusted blue Chevy pickup. Tee got in and smiled.

Love, exciting and new, Dees thought as he clicked the mahogany door shut. His telephone began to warble as he turned back inside.

Dees grabbed the front room's cordless from its cradle and clicked it on.

"Dees."

"Hey, *hermano*," crackled a voice through hissing static. "Sorry it took so long. I shut down the pager when I'm with the kids and just now thought to turn it on and retrieve your message. *Qué tal?*"

"Give me a land line."

"What's up?"

"Need to talk on a hard line. Where are you?"

"Miami. I haven't started down yet."

"Find a phone and call me collect."

Marco laughed. "Shit, that's why GlobeStar Television gave me a phone card. Whoops, here's a pay phone."

The line went dead. A minute later it rang again. Dees answered at the computer. This time the connection was relatively crisp. Marco said, "So what's up that you're worried about somebody eavesdropping on a wireless?"

Dees sat in the padded desk chair, put his feet on the desk and faced the microphone. "Vargas wants us to go with him on a commando raid on Cuba. Don't know if he means just an attack from the ocean or landing a party ashore. I haven't told Phoenix yet. You willing to do it?"

There was barely a pause. "If you have to ask, you don't know me after all this time, but thanks for asking anyway. Shit yes. I'll have to check out my night lens and get the waterproof bags in order, and I'll have to make sure I've charged every battery I've got. You think we'll need the body armor?"

"Sure, if we can swim in it," Dees said. "He'll beep me sometime in the next few days, he says. It could even be today. But when he calls, we've got about four hours. They could launch from anyplace, but probably no further north than Miami, and you can't go any more south than Key West."

"Hell, I better forget fishing altogether. Lemme pack and that way we're good to go," Marco said. There was a pause. "You know we'd be breaking the law? You know we could get killed?"

"You know you talk too much? We haven't been killed yet."

Marco laughed. "Gassed in Saudi, yeah. Shot at in Kosovo, sure. Shelled in Chechnya and Bosnia, uh-huh. Chased out of Sudan, shot down in Salvador, arrested in Indonesia. But not killed. No sir."

Dees said, "Here's the drill. You pack. When he calls me,

I'll beep you with a nine-one-one to my wireless or the house or wherever I am."

Marco said, "Later." The phone went dead.

Dees got a cigar from a box on the desk, bit off the end, dug in his pants for his Zippo, and said, "Phoenix, foreign desk." The screen flashed the number, along with the GTV letters superimposed over a globe, encircled by letters spelling out the word "new" in eleven languages. It was the logo of the new GlobeStar Television, as opposed to the old GTV, which had almost gone out of business after the Gulf War, thanks to Dees's revelations that a subsidiary of GTV had sold chemical and biological weapons to Saddam Hussein. GTV founder McKinley Burke had disappeared inside Cuba, and GTV had finally been rescued by a group of Phoenix venture capitalists.

The speakerphone growled, and a slightly accented voice said, "Foreign desk. O'Bannon." Ricardo O'Bannon was Chilean, and ran the day-to-day operations on the overseas side of the network.

"Ricardo, Peter."

"Hey, man. Thanks for the quick turnaround on the newser yesterday. I know you special correspondent types are supposed to work on your own stories, but . . ."

"But since they nuked the Miami, Atlanta, and Mexico City bureaus, I'm it between the Ohio River and the Panama Canal. Yeah, you're welcome. Got a hot one. GTV may get an exclusive on a commando raid on Cuba."

"*What?* When did it happen?"

"It hasn't yet. I have an engraved invitation." Dees paused. Someone was knocking on the front door. He turned to the microphone. "Hold on. I'll be back in a second."

The voice from the speaker was impatient. "We need to talk about this! Wow! Peter?"

Dees walked toward the door and said over his shoulder, "Hang on."

Rich Peterson was tired of being told he looked like a

smaller version of an interior lineman. He had roughly the same proportions, but carried them on a five-foot-eleven frame. His curly, reddish-orange hair was cut close enough so that all he had to comb was an unruly cowlick in the front. A tanned woman with dark chestnut hair stood just behind him, wearing stretch khakis and a short-sleeve denim work shirt, and holding a picnic basket.

"Open up," Peterson rumbled. "Federal Bureau of Investigation."

"Industrial Workers of the World," Dees replied, "and it is open. Ah, the Federal mind, able to grasp the obvious almost instantly."

"Screw yourself." Peterson smiled. He opened the screen and stepped aside, letting the woman, his wife, Janie, come inside first. She kissed Dees on the cheek and looked around appreciatively.

"Just needs decorating," she said in her smoky voice. In the time he'd known her, Dees had never heard her speak anything but English in that sensual, husky growl. "Kind of New England Mediterranean, sort of what an Anglo like you would live in. Us Cubans, we'd put in more tile and stucco. Here, Key Lime pie." She extended the basket.

Dees led them into the kitchen, put the basket on the huge bottom shelf of the new refrigerator, and looked inside. "Plenty of Corona for later. I've got orange and grapefruit juice if you want. The coffee maker's still in Miami."

Peterson looked around. "We'll just ogle. Great work, man."

Janie said, "Is your can still in the same place?" but didn't wait for an answer as she strode toward the bathroom door.

"Peter! Peter, you there?" It was the speakerphone. O'Bannon had apparently placed his end of the call on a speakerphone, too, and a chatter of voices echoed through the house like a loud AM radio. As Dees strode toward the office, one of them said, "What'd you mean a commando raid on Cuba? Shit, does anybody else know . . ."

Dees walked into the office, gently kicked the door shut with his foot, picked up the wireless phone from its charger, clicked it on, and turned off the volume on his speakerphone in one continuous motion. "Ricardo," he said, walking to a corner of the room and trying to whisper. "This is a bad time to be talking about this. Are we interested? . . . Yeah. Yeah. Marco's ready. Just get a truck from Uplink World or somebody and have it on standby. When we leave, I'll call. When we get back, I'll call and let you know where we are. Just have the truck meet us, and we can field edit and feed in a few hours. . . . I have no idea. It could be anyplace, the whole north coast's got military installations. . . . Yeah, I know, if Castro's heading for room temperature, they'll be trigger-happy. Just keep it quiet until I call. . . . What? . . . Thanks. But you can't kill an honest man."

He clicked the phone off and opened the door. Peterson was holding two beers, looking down at the floor. "You lay these new?"

Dees shook his head even though Peterson had his back turned. Peterson reached behind him with one hand. Dees took the Corona and said, "Dade County pine, original equipment. I think it's extinct or just about, but the stuff wears like iron."

Peterson turned, took a swig of his beer, and squinted. "A commando raid on Cuba? Are you in the process of finding out something I should know about?"

Dees met his gaze and sipped his beer without blinking. "Probably. And you weren't supposed to hear that."

"Come on. We get along just fine with the Cubans, off the record. They help us on drugs, they help on money laundering. They even threw that S.O.B. ex-boss of yours in jail, so we don't like to see commando raids launched from U.S. soil. And if Castro really is dying this time they're nervous. And you know it's a violation of—"

"The Neutrality Act," Dees continued, "and I'm not going

to say any more. Otherwise . . . you ever lied to me in all the time I've known you?"

"You know better than that," Peterson said, glancing down again to admire the floor. "Of course I have."

He looked up at Dees and glanced toward the porch. Dees nodded and stepped outside. Peterson followed, closing the door behind him. Dees said, "Look, I know you'll have to tell your bosses what you heard, but—"

Peterson held up his palm and sipped the beer. "Yeah, yeah, you've got a job to do, I've got a job to do. We've been down this road before. I want to talk about Janie."

"Trouble?" Dees said, hoping not. He had thought Richie and Janie were a good couple ever since he had first met them four years ago.

Peterson sipped his beer again and shook his head. "Not that kind. You ever think of kids?"

All the time, Dees thought, kids with their innards blown out or bellies distended from starvation or eyes bugging in terror as their village burned. He shook his head. "Not much. I like them well enough in the abstract, like pets and houseplants."

Peterson pulled on his beer. "Fuck you."

"For what? Am I missing something?"

"Maybe one of these days somebody from Cali or Istanbul is a little luckier than I am. There's always that, all the time, never as much time left as we think. There's more to life than the job, you know?"

Dees stared at the street. "What'd you want to talk about that you're having so much trouble talking about?"

Peterson absently rubbed the sweat from the back of his neck. "Kids," he said sheepishly. "I decided I want to have kids, and she says relax, there's plenty of time, but there never is."

Dees thought for a moment. "Janie's a weird Cuban. Marries an Anglo and won't speak Spanish, for starters. But she's a woman, and a Cuban woman, so I guess when her biological alarm goes off it'll wake the dead."

"You think?"

"Just a guess, and from me it may not be worth much. No kids, no pets, no houseplants, and a sister and two nieces two thousand miles off, so I'm not the Christian Coalition poster boy for family values. It's a guess."

Dees pulled on his beer. "You'll probably do okay as a daddy," Dees continued, "for an evil agent of the American empire, and she'll want to play Mommy one of these days. Just make sure the kid knows the three brother combinations with the highest—"

"Home run totals," Peterson said offhandedly. "You don't even remember you got me with this four months ago at a bar, do you? Jeez. Number three, Ken and Clete Boyer; number two, Vince, Dom, and Joe DiMaggio; number one, Hank and Tommy Aaron."

Dees extended his bottle. Peterson clacked the bottom of his bottle on the top of Dees's, causing foam to roil up, hiss over the top, and slowly trickle down the sides. Dees blew off the foam and took a sip.

Peterson opened the door, walked back into the front room, and turned to Dees. "You know I'll have to report what I heard on the phone."

Dees followed. "Have the Feebs try not to call too early in the morning."

"Fellas," Janie said from the doorway. The light from the kitchen window created a halo around her short hair, making her light olive skin seem even darker. "Testosterone poisoning again, guys? Let's go fishing."

Dees and Peterson looked at each other. Both shrugged simultaneously.

Ten minutes later, they were unloading the picnic basket and a large cooler from Peterson's Jeep at the Key West Bight. The slips were crowded with bobbing boats, most of them needing paint and caulk. The rich snowbirds and their multi-million-dollar motor yachts wouldn't start to come down for another two months, so the harbor belonged to eighteen-foot

Fiberglas hulls stained with yellow patching, or to twenty-two-foot sloops with wind generators, mildewed sails, and at least one terrier on deck, or to thirty-five-foot commercial and sport fishing inboards, most with streaks of rust cascading down their hulls.

The *Junkaroo* rolled in light chop at the end of a pier. Jacob, resplendent in a new, bright yellow short-sleeve shirt and white trousers, checked the three medium-size rods clamped in stanchions. "Hey, welcome aboard. So where's the other guy?"

Dees helped Janie aboard and stepped onto the gunwale, then onto the deck. "Pedro couldn't come. Jacob Randolph, Tequila Mockingbird, Richie and Janie Peterson."

Tee was wearing a light blush, translucent lipstick, jeans, and a green halter top. He shook Peterson's hand. "Pleasure. Peter's told us a lot about you two. Just in case he never mentioned it, I'm a transvestite, but I'm harmless."

"Me, too," Peterson said. "Harmless, I mean."

Janie kissed both Tee and Jacob hello, and said, "I'm the sane one of this trio. It's what I get for marrying an Anglo."

Jacob laughed and pointed a finger at Dees. "Sane you're not if you have anything to do with him."

Tee undid the lines and Jacob gunned the diesel slowly, guiding the *Junkaroo* out of the bight mouth and into the channel, turning to port and motoring slowly past Mallory Dock. Within thirty minutes, they were landing grouper at a rate that caused Jacob to stop the fishing after forty-five minutes so he could have time to fillet the catch and put the boneless white meat in plastic bags filled with fresh water. You can freeze it that way, he explained, with no freezer burn on the fish.

The cooler of Corona was empty and the larger white cooler was filled with firm white slabs of fresh grouper as the sky began to streak pink and orange.

The boat sloshed past the jugglers and fortune-tellers and tourists who jammed Mallory Dock to watch the orange sun settle into the Gulf. Janie and Peterson stood at the stern, facing the pastel light, their arms around one another's waists, his large head tilted to the left, resting atop hers. Tee stood behind Jacob, hands on his shoulders, as he steered the *Junkaroo* gently toward the bight.

Dees sat on the fish cooler and drained the last of his beer. He sighed, contented. Then his pager began vibrating.

CHAPTER 3

Dees's palms began sweating as soon as his pager hummed in his belt. By the time he saw Rich and Janie off, his feet began tingling. He phoned the Miami number and was told a speedboat was leaving from Key West. He had phoned Marco, packed his own computer and electronic gear into a waterproof duffel, and waited. His hands joined his feet in a burning tingle that seemed to send small electric shocks through his body. They were familiar symptoms, felt a couple of dozen times before. They meant he was about to cover the kind of story that ran a moderate to fair chance of getting him killed.

When Marco arrived at the cottage, Dees hoisted his duffel in the back with the camera equipment and gave him directions. They didn't exchange another word until well after the black Donzi had cleared the old light station near the reef. Keeping quiet until the story was unfolding in front of them was a habit they had developed over the years. If they talked too much before a story, they might start asking "what if." And if they asked that too many times, they might decide not to go.

Now, a few hundred yards off the Cuban coast, Dees ducked behind the small gunwale, next to Marco, as the cameraman panned the coastline with his night lens. Bullets smacking the water caused small geysers to erupt in front of them. Without taking his eye from the viewfinder, Marco whispered, "What if those cocksuckers sink us?"

Dees said, "I guess we swim."

* * *

The bullets zipped overhead with a conspiratorial *pssst*, like someone trying to get their attention. Dees could hear them over the speedboat's growling idle, along with the musical *plinkplinkplink* as they splashed into the rolling Caribbean off the port side. He was surprised he could make them out over the engine's rumble, the shouts of the men surrounding him, and the thump of his own heart.

"Pendejo!" the driver shouted, trying to keep the Donzi motionless in the rolling sea. "Do it quickly! I cannot outrun a patrol boat's cannon!"

A tall man, thin, with an oily unkempt beard and lunatic black eyes, laughed. "*Los rojos* do not even have enough gas for their boats, and we have more than enough time. I am correct, *Señor Periodista*?"

"Verdad," Dees replied in Spanish, "but only if you don't shoot that thing through the bottom of the boat first."

The driver threw back his head and laughed. The thin man scowled and turned toward Dees. Before he could say anything, Ramon Vargas spoke. "Emilio, *Señor* Dees is our friend and our guest. More respect and less talk, eh?"

Marco steadied himself, making sure the rain cover was snugly attached to the camera's body and that the lens cap was tight on the thermal night lens. Vargas walked unsteadily across to him and balanced himself against one of the rear seats in the open cockpit. "You are ready?"

Marco nodded. Vargas turned to Dees, who was standing now, scanning the coastline with a pair of night vision binoculars. He saw the same foggy green image that would show up on video shot through the night lens. Every thirty seconds or so, winks of light would appear along the coast, followed by the *glupglup* sound as individual rounds hit the water.

"They're not trying too hard," Dees, still staring at the coast, said to Vargas. "Small arms won't travel this far, and if they've got a .30 or .50 cal popping rounds at us, they're only doing it a few at a time."

Vargas whispered to him, "And you? You are ready?"

Dees lowered the binoculars. "For what? Drowning? Being eaten by sharks? Maybe getting shot? Or was it ten years chopping cane on the Isle of Youth once we're caught that you're referring to?" He raised his voice. "And why whisper? They know we're here."

Vargas laughed. "And here I thought your main problem was with Emilio. He is okay, just a little excitable."

Dees looked at him. "Excitable people get killed faster, which may be all right, but they get people around them killed faster, too, which is not all right. You ever think of feeding him some Valium?"

Vargas laughed again. "Might spoil his aim."

Marco flipped a switch on the camera and listened with satisfaction as the Sony surrounding a cassette of digital tape hummed to life. He removed the lens cap, steadied himself against the port gunwale, and pushed in tight to the coastline. He picked up a pair of winks in the darkness and pulled the shot back. It revealed Emilio leaving his cockpit seat, bending over, and removing a cylindrical object that seemed to weigh a couple of dozen pounds from the hold beneath the deck. Emilio grunted and snapped the hatch cover closed. Another grunt, and the cylinder—four and a half inches in diameter, two feet, five inches long—was heaved onto the flat stern, above the vibrating engines.

Emilio unfolded a tripod that had been secured flat against the front of the cylinder. It clicked into place. He unfolded another tripod from the rear and locked it. He lay flat on his belly, closed one eye, and looked through what appeared to be a fat, short telescope attached to the top, almost the same diameter as the tube below it. As Emilio fumbled with the sight, squinting and trying to focus, Marco panned slowly from the tubby cylinder to the coast. More winking lights appeared, and *plinkplink plopplop glupglup* sounds became more frequent in the water.

Dees, standing toward the bow so as to be out of the shot, tugged at Vargas's shirt. "What the hell is that?"

Vargas kept his eyes on the flashes along the coast. "A version of what you call the Dragon."

Dees turned his eyes toward the black horizon. "And I suppose I'd be wasting my time if I asked where you got an antitank missile?"

The winking lights on the flat coast glinted off Vargas's gold tooth. "An incredible waste of time."

Marco shot cutaways of the bow and coastline, then pushed in as tight as he could to the horizon, pulling back to the figures in the boat. He swung the camera down and taped Emilio as he fiddled. Dees glanced at what looked like an olive-green length of sewer pipe and tried to remember what he knew about the thing. The M-47 Dragon, first cousin to the TOW antitank missile, designed to be carried by infantry, although if Emilio's experience was any indication, not too easily carried, and definitely not available at the local surplus store. It had a range of . . . what? Dees drew a blank.

"*Alcance*?" Emilio yelled.

Vargas replied quietly, still watching the coast, "Eight hundred meters, *más o menos.*"

That was it, Dees finally remembered. A range of a thousand meters on the outside.

"Head into the swells," Emilio shouted again. "Stabilize. Hold it steady!"

The driver gunned the engine, then cut back on the throttle, turning the Donzi slightly to the right. "This is as stable as it gets, unless you want to swim ashore and shoot the fucking thing from there!"

There was a *piiinnngg* as a slug glanced off the tip of the bow. A bright light suddenly flashed on inside one of the tall buildings near the coast. Emilio squinted through the sight again and more or less aimed at the light as the boat rode the gently bouncing waves. Vargas suddenly shouted, *"Fuego!"*

Emilio cackled, shouted, "Luuuccy! I'm hooomme!" and jammed a finger onto the Fire button.

With a *whooossh*, the twenty-nine-inch-long missile was shoved out of the tube by a launch charge. Sixty tiny thrusters popped to life as three curved fins at the missile's rear locked in place, spinning the small rocket like a drill bit. Marco panned with the camera, following the streak across the water as Emilio tried to keep the sight locked on the light inside the high rise. The boat's bouncing shoved the sight up and down, affecting the missile's guidance. The rocket wobbled, but continued scooting fifteen feet above the water, accelerating to over two hundred miles an hour.

Marco had lost track of the pale green streak that threaded across his viewfinder. An orange and yellow flash bathed the dark coast in artificial light for a few seconds, revealing a string of tall buildings overlooking a strip of sand lined with beach umbrellas. Marco twisted the lens with his left hand, pulling the shot back until the viewfinder showed a roiling fireball that seemed to be climbing the side of a high rise.

A large oval object spiraled in front of the blast, reached the top of a narrow arc, and fell out of sight. The fireball faded, replaced by a glowing blaze at the building's base. A few seconds later, the thunderclap of an explosion rolled across the water. "Hooahh!" Emilio laughed, pounding his fist on the stern.

Dees, still staring at the coastline through his night vision binoculars, saw what looked like a propane tank arc upward and disappear next to the building. I think I know that hotel, he thought. They'd hit the barbecue grill and tank on the patio. He reached out blindly with his left hand, grabbing air until he clutched Vargas's pinned sleeve and gave it a jerk.

"You son of a bitch!" Dees yelled. Vargas looked at him uncomprehendingly. Marco opened his left eye, his right still glued to the viewfinder. He saw Dees's gesture, pulled back, panned, and framed Dees and Vargas. Dees released Vargas's sleeve and pointed toward the coast. "That's Varadero Beach! You're shooting at tourists!"

Vargas seemed to consider it and said calmly, "They have been warned about taking vacations in a war zone."

"War zone? *War zone?*" Dees was becoming hoarse. "It's a fucking beach resort!"

Vargas looked toward Marco. "Now is not a good time to be videotaping."

Dees turned around. "Keep rolling!" He turned to face Vargas again. "You said no civilian targets! You said military targets!"

"I said legitimate Cuban targets," Vargas snapped. "And this is a legitimate target. Every penny these tourists spend props up Castro and his repression! So by going after the agents of repression, we go after legitimate targets! Castro alone keeps Cuba propped up! He is dying! It just may take one push to shove the whole rotten edifice down! This is the push!"

Vargas turned away. Dees said, "Undo the stick mike. Short stand-up."

With his left hand, Marco undid a small Velcro strap that held twelve feet of coiled microphone cable. He unscrewed a clamp, loosening the camera microphone encased in foam windproofing that doubled as a hand microphone. Dees took it, uncoiled the cable, and braced himself against the starboard gunwale, the glowing fire in the distant background.

Marco, looking through the viewfinder, motioned with his left hand. "Move to your left. One step. Okay, one more. That fire's dying, you better go."

Dees angled his body slightly, turning his head and looking straight into the lens. He took a breath. "Bridge coming in three, two, one. Despite assurances . . . Shit. Assurances. Bad word. One more in three, two, one. These commandos believe attacking foreign tourists at Cuba's most popular beach resort will scare tourists away, and cost Cuba badly needed cash. They think that will destabilize Cuba even more, especially as rumors fly about Castro dying. But even though this vessel is under fire from Cuban coastal defenses, the tourists in these hotels don't have guns. And firing a rocket at unarmed civilians fits almost everybody's definition of terrorism."

Dees paused, staring into the camera. After two beats he said, "Okay. Shoot whatever moves."

Vargas looked at Dees, spit into the water, and shouted, *"Arriba!"* The Donzi's twin Chrysler V-8s thundered to life. Emilio barely had time to roll into the cockpit, pulling the empty launch tube with him before the boat's nose aimed at Ursa Minor. The boat began to pick up speed and seemed to want to launch itself toward the velvet sky. The low, sharp bow leveled itself and began to fly across the Florida Straits. Marco shot the bouncing stern through the churning spray.

Far to their rear, Dees could barely see the fire, still burning.

CHAPTER 4

Dees braced himself against the roll and slap of the ocean off the Donzi's hull, riding the bouncing deck like a surfboard until he reached the polypropylene-lined duffel bag sitting snug against one of the three forward seats, shielded by the windscreen from the flying spray. The driver ignored him as Dees reached inside, and pulled out one of a half-dozen tightly packed bundles. Each bundle was encased in a heavy waterproof plastic bag, sealed and folded, then secured by a thin, flat bungee cord.

Emilio merely glared, but Vargas watched with interest as Dees unhooked the cord, unzipped the hook-and-eye fastener on the bag itself, and pulled out a folded laptop computer. The computer's slick black metal case shed the water and spray as if it was waxed, dripping beads of moisture onto the deck. Dees walked back to the fantail and Vargas, intrigued, heaved himself from his seat between Emilio and the driver. Emilio started to rise, but Vargas shoved him back into his seat and pointed straight beyond the bow. Emilio, his beard sopping with moisture, nodded, and turned his attention back to the blackness in front of him.

Vargas staggered to the rear, and found Dees sitting on the hatch cover, connecting what looked like a large, black radar detector to the computer by a thin cable.

Dees flipped open the computer and turned on the power. Vargas could see the keyboard was encased in pliable plastic, which sealed it from the elements. With a soft hiss, a

CD-ROM drive popped from the computer's side. Dees inserted a silver disk, and the drive closed with a hiss and a click. The screen glowed to life, displaying a phosphorescent multicolored map. The screen filled with the Florida Straits, Miami barely visible at the top, Havana at the bottom. Dees flipped a switch on the attachment, which was about the size of a sheet of typing paper folded in half, and waited.

"You are doing what?" Vargas yelled over the engine roar. "Attempting to see if we are violating the speed limit?"

"GPS," Dees said. Vargas furrowed his brow. Dees, staring at the screen, explained. "Global Positioning Satellites, the civilian ones. Military satellites would give us a more accurate position, but they're encrypted. This'll tell us what we need to know within, say, four hundred meters. The Pentagon's satellites could pinpoint us to the centimeter, but what the hell. Ah, here we go."

A glowing white dot appeared in the middle of the computer's light blue Straits. Dees moved the roller until the cursor was above a screen icon, then punched a key. A readout appeared: 81-30-15W, 23-58-09 N, 55.76. Vargas leaned in closer. "And this means precisely what?"

"It means we're at longitude eighty-one degrees, thirty minutes, fifteen seconds west, latitude twenty-three degrees, fifty-eight minutes, nine seconds north, with a land speed of 55.76 miles an hour," Dees said. He moved the roller, creating a line of dashes in front of the glowing dot. "A few more seconds and I'll get the course."

Spray hissed across Dees's face as he stared at the screen in front of him. Vargas hovered over his shoulder, fascinated. Dees looked up and saw the eastern horizon slowly being lit by a presunrise glow. He moved the cursor and tracked the course of the glowing dot in the screen's center. He saw the heading, 015, and extended the dashed line to where the boat would end up if it maintained the current course.

He cupped his chin in his hands and stroked his mustache

and goatee, then looked up at Vargas. "You know," he said, "this night's just full of surprises."

Vargas only laughed.

The Dreamsicle-colored horizon was spreading to starboard, the sky fading from the color of a fresh bruise to pale orange with streaks of yellow and blue. Dees shut down the computer, secured it inside its bag, and, as he walked forward to put it back in the duffel, said to no one in particular, "Why'd we decide to skip going back to Key West?"

The driver seemed not to hear. Emilio swiveled his head, made a growling sound, and turned away, staring at the dissipating darkness. Vargas merely stared at Dees. Dees turned to Marco. "Switch to the daylight lens. Let's do an interview."

Marco unfastened the thermal lens from the camera body, shielding it from the spray with his torso. A large green plastic case held the day lens. Marco lifted it, placed the night lens in the foam cutout inside the case, and clicked the normal lens onto the camera. He powered up the camera and turned. Dees was already holding the stick microphone in one hand, and an unfolded reporter's notebook in the other. He held up the note pad, and Marco zoomed in on it, clicking the white balance switch on the camera's side. A white balance ensured that white, and therefore all other colors, would come out correctly on the tape. Marco had only forgotten to take a white balance once, under fire in Bosnia. Since they were under Serb artillery attack at the time, Dees assured him GTV could live with bluish skin and a pale green sky. But Marco had taken a penknife and cut a tiny patch of skin from his left index finger. It healed into a tiny scar on the finger Marco used to click the white balance switch, and feeling the scar with his thumb always reminded him to white balance. Dees had concluded that Marco was nuts and swore never to work with any other cameraman.

Marco nodded. "Got it."

Dees turned to Vargas. "So we're heading to Marathon,

maybe Big Pine Key. You can tell me why now or later. Meantime, let me get this interview with you done so we can wrap up this story about a rocket attack on a beach umbrella."

Vargas looked sour. "It is much more than that, Mister Dees. It is not a joking matter."

Dees held the microphone in his left hand. "I'm not laughing, and we're rolling. Tell me about what happened last evening."

Through the viewfinder, Marco could see Vargas staring straight at him. "Do me a favor," Marco said, still looking at the viewfinder image. "Talk toward the microphone, not the camera lens. Staring straight at the camera makes it look too much like a hostage video."

Vargas turned his head slightly, and Dees repeated, "What did you and Brigade X just do?"

Vargas nodded. "Brigade X has staged the first of what will be many attacks against the Castro dictatorship. We want the world to see what we do. Castro has enslaved his people, our people, for decades. We now declare in this moment that we will not rest until Cuba is free."

He seemed satisfied, and paused. Dees said, "This attack was on a resort used by tourists. What do you gain by attacking civilians?"

Vargas smiled thinly. "Tourist dollars from Canada and Spain and elsewhere allow Castro's government to continue the repression of his own people. We have warned the embassies of all these countries that allow their citizens to help prop up Castro that these tourists are in a war zone. What if tourists went to Vietnam in the sixties? Or Afghanistan in the eighties? They have chosen to take the risks. We do not intend to harm them but we do intend to cripple Castro's economy."

Marco pulled back slightly, from a tight close-up to a medium shot that revealed Vargas from the waist up. "You're violating American law," Dees said. "The U.S. isn't at war with Cuba. The Neutrality Act says it's a crime to launch attacks from American soil against any country with which the U.S. isn't at war."

Vargas turned his head and spat into the blue-green water. "Ah, the Neutrality Act. We will not hide, we wish the world to see what we are doing, which is why we are allowing this on the television. We will not run. When we return to Florida, we will have Federal agents waiting to meet us."

Marco looked up from the viewfinder, stared at the smiling Vargas, and returned his attention to the camera. Dees looked puzzled.

Vargas smiled. "We will take this craft to Cudjoe Key. You know the place, I would imagine. We have notified your FBI and the Customs Service, and their agents will be waiting for us. We will surrender peacefully and then we shall demand a trial and we shall defy the government of the United States to find a jury that will convict us.

"We will hand ourselves over to the authorities and we will make our case in the courts, but more importantly, in the court of public opinion. And now there will be more. Much, much more. Castro is dying, and so is his Communist nightmare."

The engine's growl dropped an octave as the boat slowed. Dees saw land growing larger, Cudjoe Key marked clearly by the small, unmanned dirigible floating at the end of a tether several hundred feet above the ground. It had originally been designed to carry radar equipment as it was towed at the end of a several-hundred-foot-long tether behind a Navy frigate or Coast Guard cutter. The look-down radar was supposed to scan the ocean's surface, below what ground-based radar could detect, looking for drug-smuggling fast boats or planes. Stripped of the radar and nicknamed Fat Albert, the dirigible was unreeled every night, and signals from TV Marti were bounced off its reflective skin and sent toward Cuba. Miami exile money and political influence had pushed the State Department to establish Radio Marti, which had successfully beamed news and anti-Castro programming into Cuba for years. TV Marti had followed. But because of Cuban jamming, and because the average TV set in Cuba was an ancient Czechoslovakian model barely capable of receiving Havana stations, the signal hardly made it a few hundred yards past the Cuban coast before fading into hash. But pressure from the exiles kept it in operation, so each evening Fat Albert was hoisted aloft, and shortly after every sunrise it was reeled back in on the secure U.S. government reservation that took up the western half of Cudjoe Key.

The aerostat was still up, so Marco zoomed in on it, then pulled back slowly to reveal the island, which seemed to float on the flat water like an egg in a frying pan. He heard a splash to his right, turned, and saw a pod of three dolphins swimming even with the boat, ten yards to starboard. He focused on their backs as two of them arched their gray dorsal fins above the water. The third flipped on her back and swam, belly up, toward the boat. The camera followed her as she moved, bow to stern, her snout out of the water. She suddenly flipped over and dove as the two others turned and followed, chattering with an *eheheheh* sound before they disappeared with a splash.

Dees heard a thump, turned, and saw Vargas grasping Emilio's right hand with his own. Emilio clutched a pistol, a military-style automatic. His eyes were bulging, and his breath wheezed through his hairy nostrils. Vargas was speaking to him softly, almost whispering. His breathing became easier. He finally flashed a smile that revealed a mouth full of yellow and brown teeth, and jammed the pistol back in his waistband.

Vargas came over to Dees and sat heavily on a rear seat. "He thought they were sharks," he said sadly. "He was a *campesino* before he came to the United States, and he knows nothing of the sea. I explained that *los dolfinos* mean *buena suerte* to the mariners."

Dees leaned over and reached for the duffel bag. "Good luck's hard to find these days, sort of like good help."

He glanced toward Emilio, whose back was turned. He saw his head bob forward as he seemed to smell his fist with one nostril, then the other. Emilio's head shook violently. He squared his shoulders, laughed, and swept his left arm outward, tossing what looked like a small test tube overboard.

Dees swiveled his head and looked at Vargas. "Hey! Hey! Do you know what—"

"Not now, not now!" Vargas shouted back, wheezing as he clutched the empty Dragon launch tube by the sight, and heaved it surprisingly easily over the stern into the Donzi's churning wake. Vargas walked toward the bow without a word. The boat rumbled slowly under the Overseas Highway Bridge that linked Sugarloaf and Cudjoe keys, also providing the border between the Atlantic and Gulf of Mexico.

The Donzi made a long, looping turn through the channel to starboard. Ahead, Dees could see four dark cars parked haphazardly along the shore of the Cudjoe government reservation. He counted twelve figures. Four were in suits, which marked them either as Feds or idiots in the subtropical humidity, and he recognized one of them.

The other eight wore black T-shirts, lumpy from the body armor underneath, and dark bloused pants. Marco pushed in as far as he could with the lens and motioned Dees over to look through the viewfinder. Dees saw that two of the T-shirted figures had what appeared to be riot control shotguns held toward the ground, and six others carried M-16s. Two of the riflemen were flat on the ground, aiming at the boat. The others were arrayed, three on a side, around the wooden dock that sagged into the water.

Marco pulled the shot back, framing the tableau against the island's musty green. He pulled back even more, revealing the backs of the three men in the bow. The driver continued to stare straight ahead. Vargas and Emilio seemed to be arguing, and Emilio turned, briefly, to glare at the camera before turning his attention back toward the dock. Maybe, Dees thought, it was cocaine, maybe animal tranquilizer, but whatever had been in the vial Emilio had chucked overboard now seemed to make his eyes bulge, like a pair of golf balls trying to pop out of his skull.

"Looks like you got what you wanted," Dees said to Vargas's backside, "if that includes being a bull's-eye."

One of the suits, the one with red hair that looked orange in the harsh light, raised a bullhorn to his lips. *"Hombres en el barco! Manos arriba! Manos arriba! Ahora!"*

Vargas yelled back, "We speak English!"

"Then put your hands up!" the voice said through the bullhorn. "Now! Get your hands up or we shoot! Get 'em up! Now!"

Dees waved both hands above his head, cupped them to his mouth, and yelled "Hey Richie! Richie!"

Rich Peterson, a white shirt streaked with sweat under his dark blue suit, held his left hand near his head to shield out the hot glare of the sun. He began laughing. Without using the bullhorn, he yelled "Peter? Jesus Christ! I fucking figured as much."

Dees was now sitting on the fantail that enclosed the boat's engines. Marco was still rolling. The viewfinder showed the three backs and, just beyond, the approaching dock and the armed agents.

"On assignment!" Dees yelled back. "Try not to kill me, okay?"

The black agent standing next to Peterson said to him, "Peter? Peter Dees? The guy from GTV?"

Peterson nodded. "He's the one I told the SAIC about, the one who might have something about a commando raid on Cuba? Always keeps his word, which doesn't happen too often in his business. He took my wife and me fishing down in Key West yesterday. He's worked with me on a few laundering cases. He'll help us, maybe."

Curtis Stevens, the black FBI agent freshly transferred to Miami from Chicago, looked at him quizzically, and Peterson said quietly, "He's a good man. Might want to tell the guys not to shoot him or his cameraman."

Stevens absently brushed his mustache. He took the bullhorn. "Do not aim at the man in the rear! He's a journalist! Do not aim at the man with the camera! They're friendlies! Target the three in front!"

Emilio turned and glared at Dees. He hissed, "Friendly?"

"I'm friendly with everybody," Dees said. Then, in broken Spanish, he said, "They have guns. It is necessary for you to raise your hands now. They are very dangerous."

Peterson turned to a man in a dark suit behind him. "Briscoe, get some cuffs for our guests."

Agent John Briscoe said, "I'll get mine outta the car," and walked toward a gray Chevrolet sedan. When he got to it, he opened the back door and rummaged through the backseat.

Peterson meanwhile cupped his hands to his mouth and shouted to the boat, "*Despacio*, gentlemen. *Muy despacio*. Get your hands up and move very slowly and no one gets hurt."

The driver clicked the throttle levers into the neutral position and put both hands in the air, letting the boat drift toward the dock. Vargas, standing just to the driver's left, had his hand up. At the far left, Emilio held his left hand in the air.

Through the viewfinder, Marco saw Emilio's right hand come up, holding the pistol. What happened next was a blur.

"Put it down!" Stevens screamed.

Dees yelled, "Get the fucking gun!" as he started to move toward the bow. Marco moved backward in the boat to frame the entire scene.

Vargas, shocked, turned to his left. He lunged downward with his good arm just as Emilio leveled the pistol and fired.

Peterson was reaching for the pistol in his shoulder holster when he staggered, a confused look on his face. He stumbled backward, almost toppling over, then his head jerked forward and he fell like a spastic puppet, facedown.

As Peterson was falling, Briscoe sprinted from the car,

crouched, and fired. Every other gun on the shore opened up at once. Dees later guessed that a blast from one of the shotguns sheared off the top of Emilio's scalp, tossing a scored lump of flesh with hair attached onto the fantail where he'd been sitting. Reflexively, Marco whip-panned downward, aiming at the chunk of skin and hair, then leveled the lens again toward the carnage in front of him.

Emilio's body twitched and jumped as M-16 slugs tore through it. One bullet went through Vargas's hand, leaving a flap of flesh hanging between the thumb and forefinger. The Donzi's low windshield cracked, splintered, and exploded.

With a howl, the driver jumped feet first into the water on the right, his hands still over his head. The Gulf was barely five feet deep, and the driver, who stood five-feet-six, bounced up and down off the sandy bottom on the balls of his feet to keep from inhaling seawater. His hands still held straight up, he yelled, "No! No! No!" as he bobbed above the surface, then glugged underwater, then reappeared at the surface.

Vargas stood stock still, raising his bloody hand in the air without a word as the shooting continued. Dees, fighting his instinct to cower on the deck, stood up, his hands in the air. Marco gently set the camera on the fantail, still rolling, and stood up, putting his hands up.

"Don't shoot!" Dees yelled. "Don't shoot! Richie! Richie? Jesus Christ, Richie!"

"Cease fire!" Stevens screamed, his hand trembling as he held his nine-millimeter pistol. "Cease fire, goddammit! Call for a chopper! Get a doctor!"

The shooting stopped immediately. Stevens ran to Briscoe, who had been trying to administer mouth-to-mouth to Peterson, and was now poised above him, both arms pushing into the fallen agent's chest, shoving down with a steady rhythm. He took his index and middle finger and felt Peterson's carotid artery. He put his ear next to Peterson's mouth and nose, listening. He looked up at Stevens and shook his head, once.

Two of the T-shirted agents had waded into the water and

were roughly pulling the sputtering driver to the shore. Emilio, soaked with what appeared to be gallons of blood, lay on his back, his rotten teeth bared in a hideous grin. Vargas turned and glanced at Dees.

Dees felt his arms tremble, still above his head. "If they don't kill you, I might," he said through his teeth. "You son of a bitch. You lousy lying son of a bitch."

The camera, on its side in the stern, was still rolling.

CHAPTER 5

Somewhere in the faint distance Dees could hear snatches of music in the sodden breeze. A tape player, he decided, on one of the pleasure craft chugging slowly under the Overseas Highway Bridge. He strained to hear above the roar of the helicopter as the body was loaded into the rear. The blades stirred up the sand into a beige cloud as they spun faster and the chopper rose, heeled to the left, and sped toward Miami.

The wind shifted, obscuring the music for a moment in the jumble of random traffic sounds from U.S. 1. The breeze turned again. Jimmy Buffett. What else? he thought. He made out fragments of lyrics. "People get by and people get high," the speakers warbled, "in the tropics they come and they go." There's an elegy, he thought. One body, one widow, one cliché. What a trinity.

He sat in the sandy dirt, his back resting against the left front tire of one of the FBI sedans. The duffel bag and the contents of each of the waterproof sacks inside were spread in front of him, along with his wallet, keys, two pens, a water-soaked reporter's notebook, and one Gloria Cubana cigar. Marco sat next to him, staring at the camera, tapes, and portable Panasonic digital edit pack arrayed in front of him. He was breathing through his mouth, softly.

Dees leaned across the array of small cables and equipment and grabbed what looked like a small laptop computer, except for the small telephone receiver cradled on one side. He reached again, and snagged the slightly larger laptop and some small cables. He took a short length of telephone cable with a clip at each end and used it to connect the two devices. Marco glanced at the assembly, closed his eyes, and said, "They're not gonna like that. They told us to shut up and stay put."

"I am shutting up," Dees said, flipping open the top of the smaller device. Instead of a computer screen, it revealed a plastic panel with fourteen raised plastic ridges running horizontally across it. "I won't say a word. I'm just going to type."

Marco's eyes were still closed. "Why not use the cell phone instead? That sat phone'll cost, what? Five bucks a minute?"

"Three," Dees said, unfolding the plastic panel to face the sky and rotating it until a green light on the bottom winked. "Take a look at the cell phone and see if you can figure out how to use it."

Marco opened his eyes and looked at the small Nokia phone, lying on the ground with a jagged hole drilled through where the keypad used to be. He closed his eyes and leaned back again. "Ouch, must've taken a slug. Got another one?"

"Yeah," Dees said, powering up the laptop. "A Startac back at the house. So we use the good old Thrane and Thrane. If I don't get a note in the Heads-Up file in the GTV mainframe, those numbnuts might go on the air with this if they hear it from the AP or somebody else. I need to make sure this doesn't hit air until Janie and the rest of Richie's family's notified. So, I'll just . . . oh shit."

Marco opened one eye. Dees said, "Battery's dying on the sat phone. Lemme see, yeah, here it is."

Dees grabbed a length of power cable. He plugged one end into the tiny satellite phone, and held the other in front of him. "Now we just need a cigarette lighter. I wonder if the Feds even have them in their cars anymore."

He reached above Marco's head and tugged on the black sedan's door latch. The door was locked. Dees sat again, turned, and stared at Marco. The cameraman, eyes closed again, said, "No."

"Come on," Dees said. "I know you always carry it, right next to that Swiss Army tool."

"No," Marco repeated. "They'll throw me in jail. No."

Dees sat, his back against the front tire, and stared out into the water. He squinted. "They may throw us in jail anyway. But if I don't tell Phoenix what happened, and that they need to sit on it, they may put something on the air before Richie's family finds out. How'd you like to find out about one of your kids getting shot by seeing it on the tube?"

Marco opened his eyes, and blinked. "Goddamn it."

He reached into his pocket and pulled out what looked like a long, thin pocket knife. He opened it, twisted his body, and inserted the two-inch-long serrated piece of metal into the sedan's door lock. Within seconds, Dees heard a soft click. Marco withdrew it, folded it shut, stuck it back in his pocket, and resumed his previous position.

Dees said, "Move over."

Without opening his eyes, Marco scooted until his back rested against the rear door. Dees, crouching, gently opened the front door, leaned inside, and secured the bulbous end of the cord into the sedan's cigarette lighter plug. The ban on smoking in Federal vehicles meant they'd gotten rid of the lighters themselves, not the lighter's power source.

Dees closed the door carefully so as not to crimp the power cord. The green light at the base of the tiny satellite phone glowed brightly. Dees typed in the number of GTV's in-house mainframe, hit Send, and waited. There was a soft screech as the computer's modem accessed the number. Dees wiped a bead of sweat from his nose. Time was the problem now. The satellite phone transmitted data at 2,400 baud, one-twentieth the speed of his laptop attached to a land line. For what seemed like hours he watched the screen flicker and grant him access. He watched his own fingers appear to move underwater, slowly tapping the keys, entering the Heads-Up file. Heads-Up was an internal GTV file for important information, whether it was meant to be broadcast immediately or only used for background.

When an entry was completed, a luminous orange strip appeared across the top of every GTV computer in every network department in every part of the world, flashing the words "Heads-Up-URGENT." Anyone who opened the Dees entry read:

> NOT FOR AIR REPEAT NOT FOR AIR—INFORMATION ONLY.
> NOT for broadcast. FBI agent killed in Florida Keys. Shootout with Cuban exiles. Exiles fired rocket on Cuba. Dees has exclusive video of attack, shootout. Will feed ASAP. Do NOT use story until Dees feed, even if reported by other news agencies. Dees, Marco in FBI custody. Will advise on feed time from truck in Keys. NOT FOR BROADCAST.

Dees waited. He looked up, and saw the Feds huddling with each other, using their cell phones to call someone higher up the food chain, or combing the ground for evidence. He and Marco were being completely ignored in the maelstrom of activity around them. His pager began vibrating in the sand, kicking up a small shower of grains. Slowly, the computer screen flashed with incoming messages. He opened the first. "O'Bannon, Foreign Desk," it read. The message tiptoed onto the screen, one letter at a time. "Shit. All okay? Advise your needs soonest."

Another message crept across the display. "Board," it began. Dees blinked. That meant it came from someone on the board of directors. It was the only identifier in GTV's software that didn't require a name as a prefix. "Demand details. Must air ASAP. God help you if anybody cuts our throats on this. Demand you file story NOW."

The screen began to flicker softly. The connection was

beginning to fuzz out. Dees replied to O'Bannon first. "All okay. Sit tight."

By the time he began his reply to the second message, four more, all with "board" IDs, were queued, waiting to be read. Dees typed slowly. "Can't do. Satellite phone dying. Urgent you NOT BROADCAST. Will contact you soonest."

The screen was now pulsing, growing bright, then fading. Suddenly, it blinked out. Dees heard the car door behind him slam. He looked up. Agent Curtis Stevens held the plug in his left hand. Dees looked up, returning the agent's languid stare. Stevens was almost ebony black, medium height, with a small mustache. He was the type to disappear in a crowd in almost any large city, which had made him valuable at undercover work in Chicago. He had helped the Bureau take down four top leaders of the Gangster Disciples and their interstate cocaine network before bringing his expertise in organized crime and domestic terrorism to Miami.

"Well," he finally said, "I was going to bust you for having an illegal Cuban cigar. But adding the theft of Federal DC current raises the ante. What d'you think you're doing?"

"Making sure my idiot bosses don't put a word of this on the air until you've notified Richie's wife and his folks," Dees said. "I'll pay for the electricity. And the cigars are made at the El Credito factory on Calle Ocho a couple of miles from the Federal Building."

Stevens squatted on his heels. "How long did you know Peterson?"

"Four years," Dees said. "Long enough to swap beers at Tobacco Road. I met him when I got a line on some Colombian and Panamanian bankers on Brickell Avenue cleaning large amounts of cash. Turns out Richie was working the case. I kept it quiet until they were busted, and he let me in on the arrest."

Stevens reached over without losing his balance and picked up Dees's wallet. He thumbed through the cards and

IDs laminated in plastic. "So you own a gun and you live in Key West."

"Not yet. I'll be moving there once I get my place finished. I've been working on it a couple of years, about the same time I've known . . ." Dees paused. "Knew . . . About the same time I knew Richie. I shoot enough to keep in practice. I floss regularly and used to be a Methodist before I became a Druid."

Stevens furrowed his brow and stood up. "Being a smart-ass with me isn't going to help much seeing as how you're a principal in the murder of a Federal agent."

Dees looked up tiredly. "I've already told you I'll help any way I can. Why not back off?"

"And if I don't?"

Dees rose, wiped the seat of his pants, and shrugged. "Then I won't tell you there's an M-47 rocket launcher floating about a half mile out and that it probably won't sink, since it's fiberglass. And I won't tell you that while you've been playing J. Edgar you've been standing in a fire ant nest."

Stevens looked down. His right shoe was covered with the tiny, wiggling ants whose painful bites raised small pustules. He muttered "Shit!" and jumped backward, rubbing the ant-covered shoe against his pants leg.

Marco snickered. Stevens swiped each shoe against his pants again. He paused and seemed to study the small army of black specks. He took two steps away and said, "I deserved that. Fair enough. Anything else you can help us with so I might forget you've been transmitting information from an FBI crime scene?"

Dees looked at Marco. "Power up the edit deck. Dub everything."

Marco cocked his head. "Everything?"

Dees nodded. Marco grunted, got up, and placed what looked like a large laptop computer on the hood of the car. Unfolding the large screen revealed a pair of rectangular ports. Below them a rollerball cursor and a series of switches and buttons were arrayed where a keyboard would normally have been. Marco dug into the duffel and pulled out an unlabeled tape box. He put the small digital tape into one of the ports and hit the Rewind button. By the time the tape was cued, he had unwrapped a fresh tape and inserted it gently into the right port.

The liquid crystal display screen popped to life as Marco hit the Record button. It opened with a night lens shot of the Donzi being loaded at a small harbor on Stock Island. "Less than a mile and a half," Vargas chuckled on the tape, "from the Key West Naval Air Station." Stevens watched, fascinated.

"When are you going to tell Janie?" Dees asked.

"I'm going to her office from here," Stevens said, not taking his eyes off the screen. "How long'll it take you?"

Dees looked at the dancing phosphorescent images on the screen. "What, an hour on this tape?"

Marco wiggled his flat palm in the air. *"Más o menos."*

Dees pursed his lips and nodded. "Not a word from me until I hear from you that Janie knows."

Stevens stared at the screen again. "I thought you guys never gave up your complete videotapes or notes or anything like that without a subpoena or something."

Dees ran a hand through his matted hair. "We usually don't. Or they usually don't. Richie was a friend of mine, and—"

"This guy does what he wants," Marco interrupted, squinting at the screen, boosting the brightness level a shade. "If it's the right thing, he'll end up doing it sooner or later. Beats the fuck out of me why."

Stevens stared at the back of Marco's head. The cameraman didn't take his gaze off the screen. Finally Dees said, "I need to borrow your phone, to call for a satellite truck."

Stevens, still staring at the screen, reached into his inside coat pocket and pulled out a wireless phone. "You promise you won't feed this story until you hear from me?"

"Sure," Dees said, clicking the phone's power button. He called Phoenix, asked for O'Bannon, and told him to get an uplink truck to a small public fishing area with a flat dirt parking area about two miles north of Cudjoe. O'Bannon said it would take about two hours.

After the dub was finished, Stevens took the tape and said, "I suppose you heroes need a ride."

As Dees and Marco repacked their duffel bags, Agent Briscoe stomped to the driver's side door of the car, glared at Dees, unlocked it, and got inside. As he walked away, Dees could hear the solenoid clicking under the Ford's hood.

"Fuck!" Briscoe shouted. "The battery's dead!"

* * *

An hour and forty-five minutes later, Stevens stopped his blue government-issue Chevy in the parking area next to the Atlantic. The clouds had thinned and the sun danced off the water. The refracted light made the jet skiers look like they were zooming across an ocean of diamonds. Marco pulled two duffel bags from the backseat, grunted "Thanks," and began to walk toward a tan Volvo truck. It looked like a large delivery truck except for the two-meter-wide white satellite dish that was slowly unfolding from the roof.

Stevens turned to Dees. "Thanks for the tapes. I'll page you as soon as I've told Janie. Anything else?"

Dees nodded. "Yeah. Emilio. Putting a doper on one of these is crazy, even by exile standards. It doesn't sound right, so just let me know—"

"Why?" Stevens said matter-of-factly. "I can't tell you anything about a Bureau investigation."

Dees's hand paused above the door latch. "I'll tell you what I find out, which is not something somebody in my business usually does, but Richie's a special case. So let's trade."

Stevens shook his head. "I can't promise anything. This may end up involving national security for all I know. It already involves the murder of an agent. But I'd be interested in anything you find out."

"One way street?" Dees said again, opening the door and getting out. He leaned his head inside the car. "Not much of a deal. Look, we can talk later. Just contact me when Janie knows."

Stevens nodded and Dees closed the door. The car kicked up a small cloud of powdered dust as it pulled away, coating Dees with a gritty film. As he approached the stairs and door that led to the edit bay inside the truck bed, the door swung open and Marco popped his head out. "No digital edit, just feeding. I'll have to edit on the portable deck. And Phoenix is on the phone."

Dees climbed the three metal stairs and stepped inside an enclosure the size of a large L-shaped bathroom. Four edit decks—two for broadcast Beta videotape, one for three-quarter-inch tape, one for the newest generation of digital tape—were embedded in the gray carpeted wall to Dees's right. By extending his arms, Dees could have touched the left wall, which was also carpeted and filled with toggle switches, buttons, and dials that controlled the uplink satellite dish, the power and frequency of its signal, the generator that powered the entire truck, and the hydraulic jacks that folded down from the wheel wells and leveled the truck. To the right, the short leg of the L was filled with a small bench and table, a work space that was definitely a luxury in a satellite truck.

A thin, small man sat on the bench. Strands of hair were combed from just above his left ear across the top of his head. They looked like they had been glued in place. He wore a clean white T-shirt with the Apollo 11 photo of the blue earth on it, and the words UPLINK WORLD underneath.

He saw Dees, smiled, and stuck out his hand. "Hi, I'm Darrell Holloway. I'm sorry about only having one digital machine, but the other one's on order. Your desk said they wanted me on G-four-twelve ASAP, but they want to hear from you before they book the time. We've got Cokes, water, juice, and some halfway decent tuna salad sandwiches in the cooler, so just help yourself, and let me know whatever you need." He smiled again, nodded, and went back to reading a dogeared paperback copy of *Siddhartha*.

Dees punched in the Phoenix number on the wall-mounted cell phone. Marco could hear the yelling from the other end as he set up the Panasonic edit deck on the waist-level shelf, and pulled Dees's laptop computer and printer from another duffel, setting them up next to the pile of three digital tapes.

Marco put a fresh tape into the right-hand slot on the edit deck. He could hear more loud chattering from the phone, but couldn't make out the words. "No," Dees said tiredly. "No, no, no. We don't go on the air until the family's been told, period. Because I gave my word, that's why. So it's what, eleven Eastern now? Book the bird for one Eastern, 1800 GMT. Yeah, it's hot shit. Not a word? Okay. Yeah, you've got the number."

Dees hung up and dropped into a small desk chair next to the one Marco sat in. He powered up the computer and said, "Okay, we'll open with a live shot, probably out by the water, then we cut the shootout for me to V.O. After the voice-over, back to me live, then to the raid package."

Marco nodded. For the next hour and a half, he shuttled tapes back and forth in the left-hand port, first using a series of edits to create a one-minute-thirty-second tape of the shootout on Cudjoe. Dees hammered out a script on the computer, and recorded it. Marco laid the audio onto another fresh tape, then began putting in pictures to match the underlying narration. It was twelve-thirty, with four shots left to lay in, when Dees's pager went off.

He clicked the phone receiver off the wall and punched in the number. Steven's voice answered, on a cellular phone. "Yeah?"

"Dees."

There was a pause. "His brother knows and his parents, but it's been a bitch finding the wife. She was checked out to Key

Largo. We finally got her by phone a few minutes ago. She made us tell her, so she's a mess, I think. She's driving back to her office. We got a doctor there with some sedatives. That's the whole family, so when's the rest of the world get to find out?"

Dees looked at his watch. "Probably in about half an hour. Know anything more about Emilio?"

There was a long silence.

Dees said, "Hello? You there?"

"I'm here." Another long pause. "I've been called over to the autopsy. There's, ah, something. I'll call you back."

The line went dead. Marco turned. "Got the last shot laid in, it comes in at three thirty-seven. Too long?"

Dees shook his head. "Let's take a look."

The piece began with the rush of nightscope-green water across the Donzi's bow, and ended with a shorter version of Peterson's death. Dees watched it and shuddered. "Okay, let's set up for the live shot. Darrell, could you coordinate with Phoenix?"

"You betcha," Holloway said.

In twenty minutes, they dragged cables from the truck, attached them to Marco's camera, and locked in on the tripod. Marco attached a three-foot-diameter disk of silver nylon to a light stand and angled it so that it caught the overhead sun and bounced it back up into Dees's face.

Marco turned toward the truck. "Darrell. We got IFB?"

"Dialed up," a voice from inside the truck said. "And we're up."

Dees clicked the knob on the Walkman-size metal box clipped to his belt. Immediately he heard ". . . in the Keys. Control to Dees in the Keys, turn on the goddamn IFB."

Interrupted feedback was a combination of the audio programming actually on the air and commands from the control room. Dees finished pinning the small lavalier microphone on his shirtfront. "I'm here. Sorry for the delay. How long to air?"

"Three minutes."

"Okay, here's the setup. I go live, then toss to a V.O. We roll from here. Then back to me live, then I toss to the package. Then back to me live. Package runs three thirty-seven."

"We got it. Here's the lead-in. 'A United States Federal agent is dead following a commando raid on Cuba by a group of militant anti-Castro Cuban exiles. Special correspondent Peter Dees has this live, exclusive report.' The live chyron'll read 'Florida Keys.' We got the shot list and chyron inserts for the package from here. The anchor's Melissa Mancini. Got it?"

Dees flashed a thumbs-up at the camera. "Darrell in the truck," he said into his mike, "you got the cues to roll the V.O. and then the package?"

"Yep," a voice said in his earpiece. "Right here in front of me."

"Thirty seconds," the control room voice said. "We're giving you air."

Dees heard an ominous series of musical notes from a synthesizer, with a faint computer-generated kettledrum in the background. A resonant male voice said, "This is a GTV Special Report from the world's news voice," and the music faded. A female voice crackled in Dees's earpiece. "This is Melissa Mancini at the GTV newsplex. A Federal agent is dead and several people have been wounded following a commando raid on Cuba by a group of anti-Castro Cuban exiles."

Dees heard the control room say, "You're in the split," meaning his live image appeared on one side of the screen while the anchor's face appeared on the other. The female voice continued, "GTV Special Correspondent Peter Dees joins us live—" Dees nodded slightly to the camera. "—with this report. Peter, what happened?"

Dees took a breath. "Melissa, it started last night when a group of exile commandos attacked a tourist hotel in Cuba. Those kinds of attacks launched from U.S. soil violate Federal law. The exiles claimed they had planned to challenge that law in court by surrendering to FBI agents. The FBI had been notified by the exiles that they planned to give themselves up. We were aboard the commando boat about four hours ago when it returned to the Florida Keys. Then the shooting started and a Federal agent was killed."

Holloway punched the Play button in the truck and the videotape images of Peterson and the rest of the Federal agents appeared, lining the shore. On the tape, the camera mike picked up Peterson yelling, "*Manos arriba!* Get your hands up!"

Dees looked down at the small TV monitor on the ground, its screen angled toward him, propped up on four empty tape boxes. He said, "That's Miami FBI agent Richard Peterson." The video switched to a wide shot of the cockpit, agents in the distance. As Vargas turned his head, Dees said, "That's Ramon Vargas, a longtime anti-Castro militant. The man next to him with the black beard we only know as Emilio. We don't know the name of the boat's pilot."

As the boat sidled up to the leaning dock, the camera jerked to a forty-five-degree angle as Emilio pulled his pistol and fired and Vargas leaped for it. The image righted to show Peterson, in a wide shot, stagger backward. Then with a *brrat brrat brrat,* the M-16s began chattering and the image zoomed dizzily toward the sky, then jerked down in time to catch a spray of red from the crown of Emilio's head. From the bouncing framing of the slightly out-of-focus shot, it merely looked like he was being spritzed with cranberry juice.

In a small arc, the shot followed the driver as he jumped into the water and bounced up and down with his hands up. It pulled back to a steady shot of Vargas's and Dees's backs, their hands up. Marco had the presence of mind to steady the shot and then rack focus from their backs to the line of helmeted and black-body-armored figures on the shore. Dees whistled, low, at the smoothness of the shot. There was a quick cut to a medium close-up of Peterson's body as Stevens and Briscoe rolled it faceup. Briscoe bent over and began applying mouth-to-mouth. The video switched to the line of agents again. One of them yelled, "Put the goddamn camera down! Now!"

The video ended with a shaking shot of sky and the Donzi's steering wheel, tilted on its side at a ninety degree angle, the result of Marco having immediately taken the camera off his shoulder at the agent's order and laying it, still rolling, on its side.

Dees looked straight at the camera even before a voice in his earpiece said "You're on." The screen showed Dees and the flat Atlantic water over his shoulder. He said, "Ramon Vargas and the boat's pilot are in custody. An autopsy's being performed on Agent Peterson's body." Dees felt a lump rising in his throat.

He cleared his throat, smoothly said, "Excuse me," and continued. "This could become an international incident. A commando raid is launched from the United States against a civilian target in Cuba. American authorities were notified at some point. Were they notified in time for them to warn the Cubans? Meanwhile there'll be anger in Washington at the killing of a Federal agent, apparently by one of the exile commandos. Will that undercut support for the anti-Castro movement in Congress? No one knows.

"And what about tension inside Cuba from this attack, especially with reports that Fidel Castro may be dying? Again, no one is sure. What we do know is that the Miami-based exiles staged an attack last night, one that ended in tragedy."

Dees paused one beat for effect. "We went along on that commando raid last night. We were told the attack would be against a military target. We were lied to. Here's that story."

He turned his head slightly to look at the monitor just as Holloway pushed the Play button. As the ghostly green night-scope image of the Donzi pushing off from the Key West dock appeared, Dees's narration began. "Brigade X is a newly formed anti-Castro exile group. Their motto is 'Less talk, more action.' They hope to prove it this evening with an attack on Cuba. An attack launched from American soil."

It was all there—the preparations, the nightscope-illuminated splashes in the water, the rocket launch, the return fire from the Cubans, the explosion, Dees's stand-up, Vargas's interview, the Cudjoe shootout. Like all TV, it was reality made even more intense by compressing time, in this case fourteen hours stuffed into two and a half minutes.

The tape ended. Holloway switched from the video player to the live camera and whispered into his headset microphone, "You're hot."

Dees took the cue. "We have no word on any casualties from the attack on the hotel in Cuba. Agent Peterson was a ten-year FBI veteran. He leaves his wife, a brother, and his parents. Funeral arrangements are pending. Melissa?"

A pause. "Peter, has anything like this ever happened before?"

Dees shook his head. "No. Exile groups have staged commando raids off and on for years. The FBI has stopped several before they even began. But there's no instance we know of where a Federal agent has even been hurt."

The female voice said, "We've just been told the Cuban government is claiming two Canadian tourists, a husband and wife, were injured in the attack."

Dees nodded and said, "That probably means Canada will become involved now, too. Melissa?"

"Special Correspondent Peter Dees," she said in the earpiece. "We now have Correspondent Jaime Lopez from our Havana bureau on the phone."

Dees heard a raspy, strained voice say, "Here in Havana, official reaction has been swift. . . ." when the programming IFB went dead and he heard voices from the Phoenix control room.

"Hot shit, man!"

"Jesus! Great!"

"They want more, Peter! Next live at three Eastern. And feed a lock-out so we can air the attack package separately."

Dees did seven more GTV live shots over the next six hours. He and Marco reedited the Cuba raid story with a new stand-up to close it. He did nine live shots with GTV affiliates. By the time Holloway buttoned up the truck and drove Marco and Dees back to Key West, Marco was sandwiched in the middle of the truck cab's seat, mouth open, snoring. It was close to midnight when Dees got out, thanked Holloway, and tried to persuade Marco to spend the night on the couch and leave for Miami in the morning.

"Thanks but fuck it," Marco said groggily. "I'll get some coffee at 7-Eleven and just go home. I want to sleep in my own bed."

Dees watched as Marco's GMC disappeared down the street. Dees shed his pants and shirt as he walked to the bedroom and flopped on the bed, facedown. He closed his eyes, but they kept popping open. After a few minutes, he said, "Goddammit," walked to the computer, and said, "Telephone. Rich. Peterson. Home."

The screen hummed and displayed a Kendall address, along with a color photo of a sunburned Peterson and Janie, laughing, she gingerly holding the tail and he clutching the business end of a thirty-inch barracuda. The caption beneath read, "Moby 'Cuda."

The phone rang four times. A fuzzy voice said, "We're not in. Please leave a message," followed by the same greeting in Spanish, followed by a warbling beep. "Janie. It's Peter. I'm sorry. I was there. Give me a call when you—"

There was a clatter, followed by a tired, breathy voice. " 'Lo? Peter? That you?"

Quietly, Dees thought. The dead can only whisper, so we best do the same. "You need anything?"

The voice was as flat as dead-calm water. "Richie's family's coming. There were some other Feeb wives here but I shooed them off. Nice pills the doctor gave me. Pink. I love him. If I say it enough you think he'll come back?"

Dees felt sour bile rising in his throat. "I can be up there in a couple of hours."

The sound from the other end of the phone started as a moan and exploded into a scream, angry and short. The line went silent. Dees said, "Janie? Janie?"

There was a ragged sound of inhaling and exhaling from the other end. Now she sounded like she had a bad cold. "The Bureau won't leave me alone. They're sending more people over to stay with me in a few minutes I think. Funny. They didn't want to tell me he was dead over the cell phone, but I made them. Maybe if I hadn't made them . . . I don't know, I don't know anything. I'm tired, Peter, and I just want to sleep. Okay? Sorry."

The line went dead. Dees just stared at the screen and whispered, "Yeah, me too."

He fell back on the bed and was asleep within minutes.

He awoke with a start. He thought his own snoring had done it, but it was the vibrating pager on his bedside table. He grabbed it. The illuminated readout said it was seven-ten A.M. The number below belonged to Curtis Stevens.

Dees swiped the cordless phone from its charger and punched in the number. Stevens answered and said, "You don't answer your phone?"

Dees glanced at the computer. The orange telephone message light was blinking. "Must've been zonked," he said, rubbing his hand across his face. "Still am. 'Zup?"

"I went to the autopsy," Stevens said flatly. "We froze every frame of your tape. I've been up all night. The tape didn't show us much, but the autopsy did. Emilio was hopped up like a nervous Chihuahua, mostly meth and a little coke. Peterson was shot twice . . . once in the back of the head."

Dees held the phone, silently.

CHAPTER 6

It was a 1991 Mustang painted flat gray, with a large dent in the center of the driver's door and another, smaller one in the right front fender. It had been a Florida Highway Patrol car until it was rolled twice chasing a pair of fifteen-year-old convenience store robbers down the turnpike between Pompano Beach and Fort Lauderdale. Dees had bought the remains for nine hundred dollars, and poured another six thousand into it at a garage on the Tamiami Trail. The garage was run by a cheerful Haitian from Port-de-Paix who had learned his trade by repairing cars damaged in transit. The transit in his case involved cars stolen in Miami and loaded onto container ships for sale along Haiti's north coast.

The entire Ford police package—muscular V-8, heavy-duty brakes, shocks, and suspension, reinforced undercarriage and overbuilt transmission—had been rebuilt. Dees had it painted nondescript gray, and left the dents in the door and fender to complete the urban assault vehicle look.

It was a ritual every time he headed north to Dade County, even to the GTV office in North Miami. Dees made sure the snub-nosed .32 was snug in the ankle holster, and checked to see that his concealed carry permit was in the glove compartment and his firearm's owner ID with concealed certification was in his wallet. He rolled down the windows, started the surprisingly quiet engine, and drove past strip malls and tourists on motorbikes, across the Stock Island causeway, past mangrove flats and wooden shacks perched wearily next to condo developments where each unit sold for half a million, minimum.

The September heat shimmered off the moist pavement, but he still kept the windows open and the air-conditioning off, the humidity encasing him like a cocoon. He selected the CD of Solti conducting the Chicago Symphony in Beethoven's Seventh from the menu programmed in the dashboard controls, and let it carry him from the bridge lined with bored fishermen at Sugarloaf Key to the biker bars on Key Largo. One Seventh and the first movement of the Eroica later, he was in Homestead, topping off the gas tank amid the cheap construction that had sprung up following Hurricane Andrew's devastation. He steered the Mustang up the turnpike and east along the 836 toward downtown.

Pulling into a parking lot on Miami Avenue, he unstrapped the holster and shoved it under the driver's seat. He set the alarm, and walked to the new Federal Building, asking for agent Stevens and being directed to the fourteenth floor. Stevens was waiting for him as the elevator opened. He extended his hand. "Thanks for coming. I see the metal detector didn't go off."

Dees grasped the offered hand and said, "With a steel spine and a lead butt, I don't know why not."

Stevens laughed, and motioned for Dees to follow him down the hall. The agent opened a side door, and Dees followed him into a windowless room. Two men sat amid the monochromatic gray carpet, pale gray walls, and gray metal chairs surrounding a large oval wooden table.

Stevens nodded toward them. "You've met agent Briscoe. And this—"

Before he could finish, the other man, fortyish, clean-shaven, with sandy hair fashionably tousled on the top but sharply razor-cut at the ears and neck, stared at Dees through round, tortoiseshell-framed glasses and said, "If we didn't need you, you would be prosecuted."

Dees stared back at him flatly. "I love being needed, but

you're sure it's not just girlish infatuation? How've you been, Ed?"

Stevens stared at Dees, then at the other man, then back at Dees. "You two know—"

"Ed Davis and I go back quite a ways," Dees said.

"You violated national security then and you're doing it now," Davis said, never changing his expression.

Stevens folded his arms across his chest and spoke to Davis. "You asked for him to be here. Am I going to get some background? I have an investigation to run and I don't need distractions."

Dees, uninvited, walked to a small side table and filled a foam cup with steaming coffee. He pulled out a chair, sat opposite Davis, took a sip, and said, "Tegucigalpa, city of lights, city of magic. You want to tell him about it?"

Davis's voice was flat. "Not especially. I asked for you to be here in spite of it."

"Somebody better tell me something and quick," Stevens said impatiently.

Dees looked down into his coffee. "Have a seat," he said, and told the story in less than five minutes. He left out the details that picked at the edge of his brain like birds at a feeder, the smell of entrails blown from a living human being, the buzz of bullets through the jungle canopy that sounded as harmless as bb's, the crash and splinter as wooden crates full of weapons parachuted into a jungle clearing.

It was 1987, Dees told them. He had sneaked inside Nicaragua as a stringer for AP radio to travel with Contra guerrillas. Two weeks later, he had slipped back into Honduras, clutching a muddy business card. The card had been given to him by a Contra commander two hours before a Sandinista ambush left him disemboweled and howling in the clearing where the supplies had landed.

The *comandante* had told him this was the card of the man who had helped arrange the weapons flights. "Your Congress has outlawed this sort of help for we freedom fighters," he was told, "but this man has helped us a great deal." It was not an official State Department business card. It looked like the work of a job printer someplace. It merely read: "Edward Davis, United States Embassy, Tegucigalpa."

So Dees requested an interview with Davis, who, he was told, was one of the embassy's Nicaragua experts, recently posted on TDY from the States. During the interview, Dees produced the business card and asked Davis why his card was in the possession of a Contra commander, since the Boland Amendment made it illegal for the United States to arm or train the Nicaraguan rebels.

Davis denied knowing how the card got inside Nicaragua. He denied any knowledge of any airdrops. And he grew tired of Dees's persistent questions, so that twenty minutes after the interview started, Dees found himself on the street, escorted there by a pleasant-enough Marine guard.

Dees finished his coffee and looked at Stevens. Davis was glaring at him, and Briscoe looked bored. "So," Dees said, "I filed the story, which ended up with GTV offering me a job, and Ed . . . well Ed had to do some explaining before a couple of closed Senate committees."

Stevens flicked his mustache with an index finger. "I hate spy shit. I never even liked James Bond movies. So why is Dees here and how badly is this going to interfere with my investigation?"

"*Our* investigation, agent," Davis replied smoothly. "I'm here to help, not interfere. And Mister Dees is here because he's well thought of by all sides of this Cuba mess. We need him."

Dees poured another cup of coffee and sighed. "All right, somebody has to be an adult here and it might as well be me. You're here because of Cuba, I'm guessing. Stevens and Briscoe are working on the murder of a Federal agent. I'm here because Richie was a friend of mine. So who wants to fill in the blanks?"

Davis looked like he had indigestion. "Agent Stevens?"

Stevens remained standing. "Turns out Rich had two bullets in him, one .45 and one nine millimeter. The .45 came from the meth head. The nine was from the rear, a head shot, burrowed in and didn't exit. John?"

Agent Briscoe was built like a linebacker, six-three and 220, Dees guessed, with a small scar on his right cheek and a belly that was starting to roll over the top of his dark brown trousers. In a monotone, Briscoe said, "I was removing extra handcuffs from our vehicle. When I looked up, Agent Peterson seemed to be pitching backward. He fell forward, away from me. I didn't hear any other shots."

Stevens continued, "We don't know why or who, but Mister Davis has some theories."

Davis took off his glasses and stared through the lenses into the overhead fluorescent light. He cleared his throat, still looking at his glasses. "Mister Dees. Peter. I can call you Peter, can't I? Peter, your passport number is 077530268, and it expires July twenty-second, three years from now. You've had this one seven years and have, let's see . . ."

Davis paused and looked at the ceiling again, his hands still folded like a choirboy's. He looked back at Dees. "You've been to Albania, Argentina, Bahrain, blah blah blah, and Zimbabwe. Seventy-two visas, so I bet it's the size of a paperback book, but since you knew about the commission of a Federal crime and failed to report it, it should be suspended. Without a passport, I would imagine someone in your line of work would be, how should I put it? Completely fucked?"

Davis never raised his voice, never emphasized any words. The monotone made everything he said sound both automatic and ominous. He folded his hands on the table. "And then there's the matter of Federal charges, and if I were you, I'd stand on freedom of the press, which is what I'd imagine you would do, but I'm not sure your employer is in any mood to provide you with, what? Maybe a half-million dollars worth of legal defense if it came to that? They missed earnings projections by five cents a share last quarter and the stock's taken a pounding. So, Peter, I am prepared to help drop the full faith, credit, and majesty of the United States government on your head like a hammer on a nail unless you agree this is all off the record and you agree to give us some help."

Dees sipped his coffee and nodded slightly. "Off the record. Help depends on what I hear."

Davis returned the nod. "Officially, United States policy is that Castro is the Antichrist. Unofficially, Cuba cooperates with us quite a bit on everything from money laundering investigations to drug trafficking intercepts, weather forecasts, air traffic control, search and rescue, a number of other housekeeping items. You know and I know and the Cubans know that Cuba isn't a national security threat anymore. But we are under certain pressures to maintain the fiction that it is. And everybody in Miami knows what those pressures are."

"Not me," Stevens said. "I just got into town."

"You'll love Miami," Dees said dryly. "It's so convenient to the United States."

Briscoe snickered. Dees ignored him and said, "Short course. Miami exile groups kick in millions to political campaigns, mostly Republicans, but some Democrats, too. They can still muster votes. They hate Castro. Every President since Kennedy figures it this way—the exiles control the Miami vote. As goes Miami, so goes Dade County. As goes Dade, so goes Florida and a few dozen Electoral College votes. It may not always work, but no way Florida would ever go for a candidate who wanted to get chummy with the Cubans. So it's about power, votes, and money."

"And," Davis said disapprovingly, "about the genuine desire for freedom in Cuba among the exiles and the Cubans themselves."

Dees sipped his coffee with an ironic look toward Davis, who continued, "There are also national security concerns. We have to be prepared for the day when Castro is no longer in power. And we're informed that day may be sooner than we thought."

He turned to Dees. "This is where, unfortunately, you come in. And I must say I don't care for your flip attitude."

"I only laugh to keep from crying," Dees said with a straight face. "And I'm starting to guess where I come in."

"My guess is you should be in jail, asshole," Briscoe said heatedly. He had leaned his metal chair back on its rear legs. He now leaned forward for emphasis. The front legs hit the linoleum with a clack. "Your stunt got an agent killed."

"Briscoe," Stevens said sharply. "Enough."

Davis cleared his throat again. "When the FBI got the call from Brigade X that the commando raid on Cuba was under way and that they planned to surrender on Cudjoe Key, we called the Cubans. We try to warn them about things like this. Their response was, ah, interesting.

"They told us they knew the raid was coming. And they volunteered that Vargas is one of theirs."

Dees felt itchy all over. "What? Meaning that Vargas is DGI?" The Directorate General of Intelligence served as Cuba's FBI and CIA rolled into one.

Davis nodded. "Possibly. They said he was gathering intelligence on the anti-Castro movement and that they would greatly appreciate it if he would be repatriated to them. We of course refused."

"So either they're telling the truth," Dees said, thinking out loud, "and they've given up one of their intelligence agents. Or they're lying to discredit Vargas when it leaks in Little Havana. But does any of this have anything to do with Richie's murder?"

"It may," Davis said. "Let's assume word leaked. Maybe there was a Cuban agent waiting someplace once we refused to give Vargas to them. Maybe the agent was aiming for Vargas and missed. Or maybe Peterson was killed by the Cubans to stir up trouble between Washington and the exile movement, and distract us from reports of Castro's dying."

"Or maybe," Dees said, "word leaked and it was an exile fruitcake who believed Vargas was a traitor to the exile cause. Maybe he was a bad shot. Or maybe it was somebody paid by one of the money launderers Richie sent away and they got wind of the surrender and figured it was a chance to even things up."

"But why did what's-his-name," Stevens asked, "you know, the one in the boat who kind of looks like Charlie Manson?"

"Emilio," Dees said.

Stevens nodded. "Right, Emilio. Why did Emilio shoot? Why would they take a chance on somebody so methed-up he tried to shoot dolphins? He's the only one we know for a fact shot agent Peterson. Any connection?"

Davis smiled wolfishly. "That's where Mister Dees—oh, I'm sorry. Peter—that's where Peter comes in. There's only one person we know of who can travel freely to the exiles and to Havana and find out what's going on. He's the only person we know of trusted by just about everybody on all sides."

"Except me," Briscoe growled.

"I share the agent's lack of enthusiasm," Davis said. "But we use the tools we have at hand. And Peter here, I would imagine, would be willing to do it anyway, since he says he's here simply because of Agent Peterson. Isn't that right, Peter?"

Dees felt vaguely nauseous. Maybe, he thought, it's the coffee.

*   *   *

The casual observer might have thought that the trim black man in the light gray suit and the stockier white man wearing a black polo shirt, khaki trousers, and a tan linen sport coat were ready to come to blows. The observer would have been wrong, but not by much.

Dees walked next to Stevens, weaving his way among sidewalk stalls selling everything from *coco frio* to counterfeit designer T-shirts. Conversations in Spanish swirled around him, as the owners of discount electronics and clothing stores accused the street vendors of hurting business and humping their own mothers, and the vendors replied with a spirited defense of free markets and charged the store owners with impotence.

Dees turned and faced Stevens, raising both hands in a gesture of hopelessness and almost smacking the nose of a Honduran who was selling a pair of absolutely guaranteed Gucci sunglasses, four bucks a pair.

Stevens walked to a street corner. "So? Are you going to help or not?"

Dees stared into the distance, not looking at Stevens. "When's Richie's funeral?"

"Tomorrow afternoon. Four."

Dees leaned against the corner streetlight. "I need to talk to Vargas."

The agent shrugged. "Who doesn't?"

Dees absently wiped a trickle of sweat from the right side of his face. "You can do it. Just sign Vargas out to the Igloo and let me talk to him. You have some sort of spy mess, I need to find Richie's killer, and you can get me access to Vargas."

Stevens took off his sunglasses. "How'd you know about the Igloo?"

Dees cracked a smile. "Who doesn't? Richie arranged an interview for me there once. Nasty money launderer. Washed forty mil clean and blew up one of his rivals in Cali. Problem was, his rival's family was in the car, too. So he runs here and turns himself in on laundering charges. He figured it was better than sitting in Colombia and waiting for *his* car to blow up."

The Igloo was an over-air-conditioned spare room in Miami's old federal courthouse. A frigid jumble of old filing cabinets, chairs, and tables, it was, officially, a storage area. Unofficially, it was where agents brought prisoners from the new Federal detention center for questioning. Since the twenty-story detention center was attached to the old courthouse, transferring prisoners was relatively simple.

Stevens put his sunglasses back on. "So if you know the Igloo, you know the hoops I'd have to jump through to get Vargas there for you."

"You'd have to get an AUSA to writ over the prisoner," Dees said. "Then said Assistant U.S. Attorney hands the paperwork over to the Marshal's Service. The agents show up with ID and copies of the paperwork and check the perp out. It all takes about seventy-two hours, right?"

Stevens nodded. Dees continued, "You know and I know if you get a writ from whoever's stuck as duty AUSA, and if you walk the paperwork over to the U.S. Marshal's yourself and make it plain this is national security while you're being charming, you could probably get him signed out, what, this afternoon?"

Stevens put his hands on his hips. "And cutting corners like that could put my johnson in a meat grinder. You're asking me—"

"To do nothing remotely illegal or even improper."

Stevens waved a hand. "I'm not arguing that. But what you're asking me to do is trust you."

"Um-hm," Dees said, looking absently across the street. Between a jewelry store and an electronics shop, a plywood board leaned against a no parking sign. The yellow, hand-painted lettering read: RED STRIPE, JAMAICAN MEAT PATTIES, CHECKS CASHED.

"Come on," Dees said, stepping into traffic, moving his hips like a bullfighter to avoid being hit by the zipping parade of cars and delivery trucks. "Let's eat."

Stevens watched as Dees disappeared into a twenty-foot-wide entranceway that opened the entire width of the restaurant to the street. By the time the agent worked his way through traffic, Dees was perched on a torn, red upholstered stool at the gray Formica counter. The counter ran perpendicular to the street, fifteen feet back to a jerry-rigged wall. The wall had a square, about the size of a small window, cut through the wallboard at shoulder height, dividing the restaurant from the kitchen. An oily smell floated through the opening.

Dees sniffed. "Ah, plantains."

Even though sunlight poured in from the street, two fluorescent bulbs hummed above the counter. Stevens looked around. The place was empty except for four tables, some faded Air Jamaica tourist posters, and a lanky counterman with his dreadlocks crammed inside a black hair net, giving his head the look of a lumpy pillowcase.

Stevens sat next to Dees and clicked his sunglasses on the counter. "What—"

Dees held up a finger. "Not what, who. Theodore Ras Hinton, Curtis Stevens. Mister Stevens is with the Federal Bureau of Investigation. Mister Hinton is the owner of this establishment, member of the Greater Miami Chamber of Commerce, and elder in the Church of Jah, Triumphant."

Hinton narrowed his eyes, looked at Stevens, and nodded, the dreadlocks shifting uneasily under the hair net. Stevens didn't move, didn't blink. Dees seemed not to notice. "Two of your excellent Blue Mountain coffees," he said, "and two red dots."

Hinton nodded again, smiled slightly, and after wiping his hands on his apron, reached under a heat lamp, lifted out a pair of small plates, and put them on the counter with a clatter. Each contained a tan, bulging half-moon of crispy dough, folded flat along one edge, crimped with a fork along the curved edge. Each was dark and flaky in the center, retreating to beige at the edges. In the center of each half-moon was a red dot.

Stevens stared at his plate. Dees said, with satisfaction, "The dot's hot sauce."

Stevens stared at the patty, then languidly at Dees. "I'm here for a reason?"

"Like Saul of Tarsus struck down by Jah on the Road to Damascus!" Hinton said suddenly. He bent over and stuck his head between Dees and Stevens, bobbing his head and its looming dreadlock avalanche for emphasis. "We all need epiphanies so we may sanctify ourselves in the image of Ras Tafari, Lion of Judah!"

He straightened and nodded again, a tsunami of braided hair lunging forward and straining against the hair net. Dees smiled and used his fork to cut the pastry, exposing the steaming meat, onion, and raisin filling. As he chewed, small beads of sweat appeared on his forehead. He took a sip of coffee, looked at Hinton, hovering nearby, and nodded toward Stevens.

"He wants to know if I can be trusted," Dees said between bites.

Hinton leaned forward again, planting his elbows on the counter between the two men. Stevens toyed with his meat patty suspiciously, and looked at Hinton, who returned the stare. "If I trust anyone in a-Babylon," Hinton said, "it's this man. He saved my life for no reason except that it needed saving."

Stevens raised his eyebrows. Hinton continued, "I tell you it was election time in Kingston, what, five years ago?"

"Six," Dees said, taking another bite and sweating some more.

Hinton pursed his lips. "Six, then. I'm no political man. I'm walking down a sidewalk on election day, have my hair up in a bundle, in a red cloth, didn't think anything about the colors of a-Babylon on election day."

"Colors," Dees explained, taking a sip of coffee. "One major political party's colors are blue. He was wearing red—"

"In the wrong neighborhood," Hinton continued. "Suddenly I'm attacked by a whole mob of rude boys wearing blue. I tell them I care about the word of Jah, not the words of any political man. They beat me. This white man here is driving by, stops, and saves me. Simple."

Stevens, listening, stuck a forkful of meat pie in his mouth. He had almost finished chewing when the heat rolled down his throat. He swallowed, and began to breathe through his mouth. Hinton furrowed his brow as sweat began to trickle down Stevens's cheek.

Dees finished the last of his patty. "Cleanses the system."

"Yah, so," Hinton said with the trace of a smile.

Stevens took a gulp of water but was still breathing through his mouth. He managed to swallow, looking at Hinton, then at Dees. "So why did you—"

"Because he is a righteous man as Jah has commanded all of us to be," Hinton said quietly. "A most righteous man except he thinks he has free patties for life."

Hinton smiled broadly, nodding forcefully again so that Stevens felt himself in the path of a possible dreadlock avalanche if the hair net gave way. "So do I trust him?" Hinton said. "Most emphatically so."

Stevens shifted his eyes toward Dees. "So the brother says I should trust you because you jump into trouble when you don't need to?"

Dees shrugged. Stevens sighed and said, "So if I trust you, you can keep that hyperactive sense of justice regulated until we solve this?"

Dees was noncommittal. "So, I get to see Vargas?"

Stevens wiped his lips precisely and put his sunglasses back on the bridge of his nose. "I'll try tomorrow. I'll page you to let you know."

He got up and left without shaking hands.

* * *

The early morning sea breeze seemed like vaporized syrup, its humidity making Dees feel like he was trying to breathe in a shower. His pager went off as he was loping slowly along the sidewalk between Ocean Drive and the Atlantic, getting in a workout before the Rollerbladers came out. It was seven A.M.

He had spent the night sleeping on a fold-out couch inside the two-room GTV offices on the second floor of a strip shopping center in North Miami. When Dees first came to Miami, a year after Desert Storm, the bureau had been made up of ten people, and the offices were in a skyscraper in downtown Miami, the turquoise reflected from Biscayne Bay bathing every office and edit room. But after the new board of directors took over, costs were being cut to the bone, so everyone except Dees and Marco had been fired, and the bureau had been moved to the lowest-rent space GTV could find and still not run afoul of the health and building codes.

Dees had driven to South Beach, parked near the News Café, and was only ten minutes into his morning run. He punched the number displayed on the pager into the keypad of the tiny wireless phone clipped to his running shorts. It rang once.

"Stevens."

"*C'est moi.*"

"Ten this morning. Be outside the Igloo."

"Thanks."

"Took some doing. Hope it's useful." The line went dead.

At ten o'clock, Dees was leaning against a pale green wall in the courthouse. A minute later, Stevens and Briscoe came around a corner. Vargas was between them, able to take strides of about thirty inches before his ankle chain snapped taut. He wore an orange jumpsuit with FDC—Federal Detention Center—stenciled in black across the back. His hand was manacled in front of him, a short chain looped through the spare cuff attached to a longer chain around his waist.

Vargas looked up, saw Dees, and smiled ruefully. "Had I been tied together this tightly in Havana harbor, perhaps my arm would not have blown away."

Dees remained immobile against the wall, glancing down at the foot chain, then at Briscoe. "Strictly necessary?"

Briscoe nodded his head. "For a shooter who helped kill a Federal agent, yeah."

Vargas appeared to be about to speak, but Dees beat him to it. "He tried to stop the shooter. He was unarmed."

Briscoe merely sucked on his lower lip and unlocked an unmarked door. It opened onto a room with two metal eight-by-three tables, a jumble of metal chairs, and a dozen three-drawer filing cabinets. They stepped inside, and Stevens closed the door.

"*Mucho frío*," Vargas said, smiling. "I remember the ninth circle of Dante's hell was frozen like this."

Dees looked around. "Abandon hope all ye who enter here."

Briscoe looked puzzled. "Huh?"

"Educated men," Stevens said dryly. "Let's leave 'em alone."

Stevens reached in his pocket, withdrew a key, and un-snapped the single cuff around Vargas's hand. He looked down briefly at the ankle manacles and shook his head. "Sorry, no can do."

Without a word, Stevens and Briscoe left the room. Vargas's hand was bandaged, and the left sleeve of the jumpsuit was pinned over his missing half-arm. Dees said softly, "You doing all right?"

Vargas shrugged. "It is a bit difficult to eat with this wounded old claw. But it is my good luck that the food here is terrible in the first place, so I do not miss much."

Dees saw the gold tooth glint when Vargas smiled. He thought that Vargas looked a good deal older than he had two days before. Dees said, "Do you trust me?"

Vargas was silent for several seconds. "We do not agree on much. But you are honest and seem to be fair and I know the work you have done."

Dees said, quickly, "You're in trouble. I may be able to help. I don't care about your revolution, or counterrevolution, or under-the-counter revolution. I have a dead friend and his widow and that's all that concerns me. So I need answers."

Vargas leaned back in his chair. "Emilio. He seems to have given in to panic and killed your friend, and for that I am very sorry."

"He was snorting methamphetamine on your boat, maybe some cocaine, too."

Vargas opened his mouth, then closed it. Finally, he said, "No, no. I would never have allowed . . . I never knew of . . ."

His voice trailed off. Dees spoke gently. "When'd you meet him?"

"Less than a year ago. He was a *balsero* and had, I was told, been in the Cuban armed forces, so he knew how to use certain of the weapons we had. He came highly recommended to our training facility."

"Recommended?" Dees asked. "By who?"

Vargas stroked the bridge of his nose with his bandaged hand. "By someone Brigade X trusts a good deal."

Dees sighed. "They tell you you're going to be charged with espionage?"

Vargas laughed again. "Since when is violating your Neutrality Act espionage?"

"It's not," Dees said. "But combine that with a Cuban spy as a principal in the murder of a federal agent, and you have a very good case for the Federal death penalty. They have that now, you know."

Vargas sat like a statue. Dees continued, "Havana gave you up. You DGI?"

"Maricones!" Vargas spat. "They are trying to discredit our movement, they—"

"Save it," Dees interrupted. "The Feds will charge you with espionage and with conspiracy to kill an FBI agent. Even if you're found not guilty, which I doubt, you'll be finished with the exiles. And some of them might even try to kill you, especially when they get their juices running on talk radio. Which is all a shame now that it looks like Castro's on his last legs."

Vargas considered it, looked straight at Dees, and said, "Manuel Cabrera."

Dees cocked his head to one side. "So what? Everybody knows he's the cash behind Brigade X."

Vargas looked satisfied. "Cabrera and Cano de Oro. Gold Cane."

Gold Cane sugar's distinctive golden yellow boxes, bags, and tiny sugar packets were familiar in supermarkets, convenience stores, kitchens, and restaurants in eleven southern states. Vargas continued, "Cabrera, as you know, owns all of this Gold Cane. *Bueno.* He informed us that he was able to use his connections to convince an ex-soldier skilled in various weapons to get on a raft and risk coming to Miami. So Cabrera arrives at our training camp with Emilio and says he is here courtesy of our friends in Havana."

Dees's eyebrows arched. "Whoa. What friends in Havana? And if this is going to be one of these nonlinear exile conversations, go slowly, okay?"

Vargas grunted. "*Despacio, claro.* Cabrera has much influence in Cuba and has spread money around over the years, eh? He knows many reformers, some inside the Central Committee. When Cabrera bribes them to look the other way when Emilio's boat leaves, he also suggests we meet with some reformers to talk about investment after Castro."

Dees toyed with his goatee. "Met them where and how?"

Vargas's eyes crinkled. "Here in Miami. They flew in on one of the daily charter flights. They sneaked in simply as relatives of Cubans here in Miami, with legitimate-looking and utterly forged exit visas. We meet with one woman, one man. We talk about investment. We find more details about discontent on the island."

Vargas's tooth glistened in the overhead light. "So Cabrera says he has a plan. So I convince these Cubans that I am disillusioned with capitalist life, and might wish to act as agent, spying on exile activities in Miami. So they fly home and spread the word that I can be convinced to betray the anti-Castro cause.

"I make a call to the Cuban United Nations mission in New York. I fly to New York to meet secretly with the *Fidelistas* there, and tell them this Cabrera is a pig and that I have realized the exiles in Miami are nothing more than fascists and am willing to use my position to funnel information to the hard-liners. I will actually give them enough harmless information so they will trust me. They, in turn, will give us more information on what is *really* happening in Cuba."

Dees rubbed his temples with his fingertips. "Do you know this sounds stupid?"

Vargas shook his head, once. "No, I do not, not to me or any of us who are Cuban. You *norteamericanos* will never know, so to you it sounds stupid. But we live every day of our lives with loss, with souls split into two parts, one part here, another there. We live with ghosts walking the streets with defeat and hope together on each street corner, with the past being present, even in the future."

Vargas stared at his hand. Dees looked puzzled. "If the Cubans had known about your attack on the coast, they would have been waiting and arrested us for propaganda purposes."

"They knew," Vargas said simply. "Dollars funneled from Miami to Havana can work wonders."

"Fine," Dees sighed. "Back to Emilio."

"As I told you," Vargas said, "Cabrera introduces him to us a couple or three months ago. He said he could be helpful. But it was my mistake to trust him, since Emilio had many unstable tendencies."

"It's worse than that," Dees said. Vargas looked puzzled. "The agent who died was shot twice, once by Emilio, once from the back."

Before Vargas could answer, Briscoe opened the door and stuck his head in. "Time's up. Let's go."

Vargas screeched his metal chair backward across the concrete floor. "Maybe you should speak to Cabrera."

Dees rose and said, "Maybe I should."

Vargas nodded.

Dees walked out as Briscoe, Vargas, and Stevens retreated down the hall. He walked outside through three blocks of cloying humidity, got in the Mustang, reached under the driver's seat, pulled out the cell phone, and punched in Stevens's pager number.

The phone gurgled less than five minutes later. "Dees here . . . Yeah. Thanks for the Igloo session. I need another favor and you'll have to trust me on this, again. Use whatever grease you've got with the AUSA who has the case. Try not to file any charges against Vargas, just hold him as long as you can. I think I'm on to something, but you'll have to work with me. See you tomorrow at Richie's funeral?" Dees nodded as he held the phone. "Right. Thanks."

A late afternoon thunderstorm began to move in from the Everglades, turning the western sky ebony. Gray sheets of rain were illuminated on the flat horizon by streaks of lightning. Dees drove toward the turnpike. Home James, he thought. Time to pack for a few days. The rain was going to make it a long drive to Key West.

He looked in the rearview mirror. Downtown Miami had completely vanished in the pounding rain.

CHAPTER 7

Dees slept until ten the next morning. Stepping onto the front porch to retrieve the newspaper, he was surprised by the lightness of the air as sea breezes swept away the humidity and surrounded him with the smells of clean saltwater, Confederate jasmine, gardenia, and fresh limes. A curious sea gull hovered, motionless, in the wind currents above the street.

He went inside and phoned the paper delivery service, post office, and police to let them know he'd be gone for a few days. He called the housekeeper, who came by once a week, and asked her to drop by daily to check the place. He packed the small duffel bag with khakis, polo shirts, socks, and underwear, and put the dark blue wool and polyester blend suit into a suit bag, along with a starched white shirt, a blue tie with tiny white dots, dark blue socks, and black tasseled loafers.

He loaded the bags into the Mustang's trunk, came back inside, and flipped on the Weather Channel's tropical update, just to check on what had been a quiet hurricane season. The Atlantic and Caribbean were clear, but a fist-sized blotch of red and purple thermal-imaged clouds on the screen just off the African coast caught his attention. He was thinking they were, maybe, ten days to two weeks out as he had the computer dial the GTV foreign desk.

"GTV. O'Bannon."

"Hey Ricardo, it's Dees. Is Jaime busy in Havana?"

O'Bannon sighed. "Funny you should mention it. The Havana bureau's dark for now. Lopez got strep or something and decided he couldn't get the treatment he needed in Cuba, so he flew home to Mexico. His voice is shot. Why?"

Dees tried to sound nonchalant. "Just wondering about a follow-up on the raid on Cuba and this mess in the Keys and whether or not Castro's dying. How's about Marco and me head to Havana to get the Cuban react to the raid and snoop details on what happens if Castro actually *is* croaking for a change."

"What're you, psychic?"

"Psychotic, maybe. Why?"

Dees heard O'Bannon say, "No dammit, the London feed's not on transponder twelve, it's on fourteen. Jesus. Sorry, Peter. Anyway, the Cubans themselves called us here and they wanted you to come down. They say they've got no problem with you because you're fair."

Dees laughed. "And I suppose my being the one who covered an unprovoked attack on their country and gave them plenty of propaganda when the exiles killed a Fed had nothing to do with it."

O'Bannon chuckled. "Actually, it had everything to do with it. But you won't need Marco. They've got a shooter there, a Cuban, Juan something or other, and you'll use him. Can you leave in, what, three or four days?"

"Shouldn't be a problem."

"Yeah, well, don't speak too soon, son. You may not like the spin they want you to put on Cuba."

In the years Dees had known O'Bannon, he had never heard the Chilean use the word "spin" before. "Spin? Who?"

There was a pause on the other end of the line. Finally, O'Bannon said, "The board of directors ran some focus groups and—"

"Focus groups?" Dees hooted.

"It gets better," O'Bannon said. "They found interest in international news has shrunk to the point of disappearing, so they want everything now with a personality spin, sort of people in the news."

Dees kept quiet, so O'Bannon continued, "They want you to shoot for a profile on Castro—you know, the lion in winter while he's still alive, rumors he's been married several times, fathered children all over the island, that sort of thing."

"So GTV's going tabloid?" Dees asked.

"That's what the surveys show people want. We had a big meeting here on it yesterday. The board figures we've got four satellite services providing hard news, but nobody's going twenty-four/seven with people-driven news."

"*People*-driven?"

"Yeah, that's their phrase. More of this is coming, we think. Anyway, just use the bureau shooter, he shoots solo, and there's no editing or feeding, just shoot and hand-carry the tape back. You can send us raw tapes with time codes and scripts."

"Sounds okay," Dees said. "I'll take the daily Miami charter, just have the tickets sent to me here."

"Very good," O'Bannon said, "and I'll put their, um, story suggestions on paper and send them with the tickets. I'll have to cover my ass on this. And by the way, we'll have maybe a dozen cases of equipment for you, more or less, at the Miami airport to take into Havana, along with all the paperwork."

"Why?"

"The Havana bureau whined long enough, so we're sending in reconditioned edit decks, new mixers, cables, and cases of food and toilet paper. The whole thing. You mind just getting it off the plane in Havana and making sure it gets to the bureau?"

"I may charge extra," Dees said. "Just kidding. Thanks."

Dees hung up, switched to the computer, and listened as the modem came to life with a screech and a squawk. A half-hour search produced fifteen references to Manuel Cabrera, the most recent a six-month-old article highlighting Cabrera's speech at a Republican fund-raiser in Coral Gables that drew seven senators and ten congressmen, along with four hundred people willing to pay three thousand dollars a plate for overcooked pork and access.

Dees shut down the computer and flipped a switch on a small gray box hooked between the telephone and wall jack. Before police raiders had put them out of business permanently for selling eavesdropping devices, the staff at the spy equipment shop in Miami had assured him it would register a false caller ID on the receiving phone.

First, he called directory assistance in Manhattan and got the main number for the Cuban mission to the U.N. He then programmed the number into the keypad on a black metal box, so that the caller ID on any telephone on the other end would register the New York number.

He walked to a kitchen cabinet and pulled out a sunshine-yellow box of Gold Cane Sugar and turned to the back. Gold Cane Sugar, Inc., he read. Lappahoosa, Florida. He called directory assistance for that area code, got the main number for Gold Cane, punched it in, and asked for Mister Cabrera's office.

"Executive offices," the lilting voice on the other end said. Jamaican? he thought.

"Manuel Cabrera, please."

There was nothing on the other end for several seconds. "I'm sorry," the voice said coldly. "I didn't catch the name."

"*Permiso,*" Dees said. "I am calling from the United Nations, in New York. This is a matter of the utmost urgency."

More silence. Maybe, Dees thought, they get paid by the minute. "And what is the nature of this emergency?"

"Urgency," Dees corrected. "Mister Cabrera has an urgent call from the United Nations."

Dees wondered if it was possible to hear a smirk. "I'm afraid you will have to submit any message in writing to—"

"And I am afraid," Dees interrupted, "that it will go very badly for you personally and your company if Mister Cabrera does not receive the following message within the next thirty seconds. This is an urgent call from the United Nations in Manhattan. That is all you need to know, unless of course you are a member of the diplomatic corps who happens to be answering telephones."

Dees heard the faint pulsing of a phone put on hold. Twenty seconds later there was a click.

"Yes?" The voice was deep, clipped.

"Mister Cabrera?"

"Yes. What is this?"

Dees took a breath. "I know all about your deal with the Cubans at the U.N. I know all about Brigade X. I was there during the raid. I witnessed the shooting. My name is Peter Dees. I'm a journalist. Your name keeps coming up with the Cubans, the State Department, and the FBI. I thought we might need to talk. I'll be in Lappahoosa tomorrow morning. Why don't we meet?"

"Why do you not tell me what you want?" The voice was a modulated growl.

Dees said "An interview."

He could hear a soft chuckle. "And why, Mister United Nations?"

Dees picked a ballpoint pen off the computer desk and began clicking it. "Because with what the Cubans tell me, your next call could be from the FBI or the U.S. Attorney's office, maybe the State Department, maybe the Labor Department to shut you down domestically and the Commerce Department to make sure you're out of business internationally. You're implicated in espionage, and in the murder of a Federal agent. If your version doesn't match the government's, maybe I can help you stay out of jail and in business."

The chuckle disappeared. "I have nothing to say."

Dees sighed. "Okay then, be sure to wave your handcuffs at me when Federal agents haul you away. I'll be somewhere in the middle of the pack of journalists with cameras. Since Gold Cane's private, you don't have to worry about shareholders, just about what all those good folks who buy your product will think when they hear about a dead FBI agent. There's plenty of other sugar out there for them to buy."

Silence followed, and Dees leaped to fill it. "Just talk to me and you get your story out first. Maybe Uncle Sam's the bad guy, persecuting an honest businessman. How about eight o'clock tomorrow morning? Just me, no TV camera, no pictures."

There was a soft grunt from the other end. "Eight o'clock but not at my office. Here is where to go."

Dees scribbled the instructions on a legal pad. He said "Thanks" as the line went dead with a click.

Dees shut down all the electronics, set the office window air conditioner to low, collected the laptop computer, newly printed files on Cabrera, and his keys. He loaded it all in the car, set the house's motion sensor and door and window alarms, and locked up.

As he walked back to the car, he noticed there were now three sea gulls floating in a V-formation above the trees and rooftops. As he prepared to start the Mustang, Dees thought he heard them laughing.

* * *

The rain blew in fine sheets outside the church, turning the bright emerald palms and grass a dark, moldy green. Fat drops used the two-story-high, stained-glass window as a target. Its halves were angled like the bow of a ship, so that if you stood inside, there was a twenty-foot-tall Jesus to port and a slightly smaller Virgin Mary to starboard.

St. Francis the Redeemer had been new in the heady Jackie Gleason fun-and-sun-capital-of-the-world days of 1960. The Kendall parish had grown poorer over the years with each successive wave of immigrants who were just slightly more impoverished than the wave before. Water stains on the wall beneath the Blessed Virgin's feet showed how stressed the maintenance budget had become.

Thanks to an accident on U.S. 1 just south of Homestead, Dees arrived two minutes after the service started. He deftly changed into his suit in the parking lot, and picked a seat in the next to last pew on the left, the bride's side, he supposed, if this was a wedding rather than a ceremony commemorating Richie's marriage to the hereafter.

The priest talked about duty and honor. An FBI supervisor from Washington talked about Richie's exemplary record. The pews were packed with law enforcement officers from almost every jurisdiction within 150 miles of Miami. As the mourners stood with the final invocation, Dees saw the widow rise and start to walk slowly away from the coffin, down the aisle, toward him. She wore a black sleeveless dress cut just below the knees. She had a strong neck for a woman, and her bare arms showed glowing muscle tone from her daily workouts. Her black hair was pulled back in a severe bun that accentuated her sharp cheekbones.

Janie walked regally, her posture erect. She stopped opposite Dees and stared at him with dark brown eyes. "I'm sorry I spaced on your call, but with—with—"

She looked slowly left, then right. She mouthed the words "Oh, Rich," soundlessly.

"Oh, Rich," she finally managed to whisper. "He's gone, Peter."

A single teardrop oozed languidly across her lightly applied makeup, leaving a faint trail behind, like a satellite photograph of an ancient riverbed curling smoothly through fine-grained sand.

"Janie," Dees said quietly, so quietly that for a moment he wasn't sure she'd heard him. "I'm sorry. What can I do?"

She bit her lip and shook her head. "Just tell me why it happened. That's all. I love him so much."

"Can we talk?" Dees asked. "You feel up to it?"

Janie nodded, and said, "Just let the grieving widow do her duty. I'll see you under the overhang out front."

She turned and strode into a crowd of concerned faces. Dees waited until the bodies thinned out, then walked outside to the angled canopy that shielded parishioners from the ele-

ments while they waited for their cars. Dees wanted a cigarette but had quit a year before, and didn't think this was the
most appropriate place to light the cigar in his coat pocket, so
he jammed his hands in his pockets.

"Nicotine withdrawal?" Dees turned to face Curtis Stevens
and nodded. Stevens said, "If I was a cop, I'd bust you for fidgeting like a crackhead."

"And if you were a cop you wouldn't need my help. Sorry,
didn't mean that. I'm a little grumpy." They stared at each
other while the rain drummed its fingers on the roof. "Thanks
for your help. What's up with Vargas?"

Stevens cocked his head. "Better I ask what's up with you."

Dees shrugged. "What d'you know about Manuel Cabrera
or Gold Cane Sugar?"

"Why? This involve him?"

"Maybe, maybe not. Right now just a couple of names."

"We and INS busted some middle level Gold Cane execs
four years ago for alien smuggling," Stevens said. "We had a
little to do with it in Chicago because of a connection with a
Mexican middleman from Rogers Park. Seems Gold Cane's
legal quota of Jamaican field hands wasn't enough and they
got caught fiddling the papers for a bunch of Hondurans imported to cut cane. We convicted the middleman but the Gold
Cane execs got a walk from an Orlando jury. And even a
gringo like me knows how rich and connected Cabrera is."

Dees played with the keys in his pocket. "About Vargas.
How long can you hold him without charging him?"

"Maybe a week. Maybe more."

"So what would it take to drop all the charges?"

Stevens looked surprised. "Between him and the U.S. Attorney and his lawyer."

"He doesn't have a lawyer. Do me a favor?" Dees asked.
"Drop a hint to the U.S. Attorney that we can keep information about Uncle Sam's back-channel cooperation with Castro
out of open court. And we might be able to net some even

bigger fish than Vargas. Hypothetically, just ask them what sort of cooperation gets all the charges dropped."

Stevens looked at the rapidly thinning crowd of mourners. "I can ask, but what's going on? You all of a sudden a jailhouse lawyer?"

Dees shook his head. "No, just keeping my word. Tell you what, I'll call you Tuesday. Any way you can keep Vargas safe in custody for a while?"

Stevens cocked his head again. "First you want the charges dropped. Now you want him kept in jail, so somebody won't whack him?"

"Just until we figure out who killed Richie and who's behind all this."

Stevens dug for his own keys. "Okay. Tuesday then," he said, and walked away.

Dees turned, facing the rain sweeping across the parking lot in waves. He had just decided the itchy suit was too much wool and not enough tropical blend when he felt a tap on his shoulder.

Her aquiline nose, high cheekbones, pulled-back hair, and black dress made her look like an alabaster bust of Nefertiti, Dees thought, maybe the best-looking *balsera* ever to get off a raft as an adolescent.

Her eyes were rimmed with red. "Is it as simple as they told me, Peter? Just a lunatic who got in a lucky shot?"

Dees leaned against one of the metal columns supporting the overhang. "Maybe. I'm taking a look at it."

"So what does that mean?"

"I'm not sure myself. Janie, what did they tell you?"

She sighed. "Just what I said. Some insane person opened fire and happened to hit Rich."

Dees rubbed the bridge of his nose with his thumb and index finger. "That's the truth, or part of the truth. The shooter in the boat was hopped up on meth. Richie was also shot in the back of the head, from behind. I don't know who did it or why and don't know why the crazy Cuban opened fire. But I'll find out."

Her head jerked, once, galvanically. "Shot in the . . . shot in the back? *In the back*? Rich? What—"

He interrupted. "I'll find out. It's the kind of thing I'm good at. You staying here?"

"Yes, maybe. I don't . . . I just don't . . ." Her voice trailed off. She blinked, hard. "I just don't know yet. Rich is being cremated and then there's the insurance and the paperwork and the mortgage insurance and I have to pack his things and—and I just don't know. Then there's my job. Besides, I'm a *cubana,* so where else do I go? New Jersey? Or maybe back home if Castro *does* die?"

Janie worked for Immigration and Naturalization, a perfect liaison with Cubans upset over tight new Federal procedures that actually shipped some Cubans back to Havana. Dees laid his right hand softly on her shoulder. He fished with his left in his coat pocket, pulled out a business card, and placed it in her hand. "If you need me, punch in the pager number. Otherwise, I'll—"

She exhaled, heavily. "I know. You'll call. What're you going to do?"

"Not quite sure. I'm driving to Lappahoosa tonight and may know something tomorrow."

She looked puzzled. "Lappa-what?"

"One horse town near Clewiston, except the horse died years ago."

An awkward silence hung in the sticky air. She pecked him on the cheek and said, "I have to go. Thank you."

Dees turned and sprinted through the rain to his car. Three blocks away, he pulled into a Circle K and changed in the bathroom into a polo shirt and khakis. He got a cup of coffee, got back in the car, and lit a cigar.

He was about to start the Mustang, then decided against it. He sat, wreathed in blue smoke, listening as the rain made a hollow sound on the roof.

* * *

It was nine P.M. and still raining when Dees turned off the turnpike and headed west, toward Clewiston, Lappahoosa, and the verdant sugar canefields that satisfied most of the world's sweet tooth. Dees planned to overnight in Lappahoosa before his meeting with Cabrera, hoping the extra hours might buy him some information if he hung around town and talked to some people.

He pulled onto a two-lane state road, barely visible through the gusting rain. It ran like a sinewy black snake through dark green cane stalks, each taller than a man, shoving to within ten feet of the asphalt. The cane was harvested mostly by Jamaicans, a work force supplied by an immigration bill called the Jamaican Exemption that the sugar industry had pushed through Congress. It guaranteed that Jamaicans in excess of normal immigration quotas could be let into Florida for the cane harvest only.

Because of cheap labor and mammoth volume, the merry yellow packets of Gold Cane had muscled their way onto tables across a third of the United States and half of Latin America. Decades-old sugar price supports that had been jammed through Congress guaranteed that companies like Gold Cane could cut their prices to obscenely low levels for short periods, just long enough to bankrupt the sugar industry in the Caribbean, one island at a time. Cuba was the only country left whose economy was fueled by sugarcane.

Dees was thinking of the islands he had visited where abandoned stone towers from the rotting sugar mills dotted the landscape like so many Easter Island heads, pockmarked tombstones to a ruined industry. A flash of light in the rain-streaked rear windows caused his eyes to snap to the rearview mirror. Two pairs of headlights had suddenly appeared, side by side, on the two-lane road where there had been no traffic visible seconds before.

As Dees lightly steered with his right hand and unsnapped the ankle holster with his left, he considered that they had either been following with their lights out or had peeled onto the highway from one of the access roads that trailed off into the cane fields. He put the .32 caliber snub-nosed revolver between his legs, and flipped open the center console, feeling for the box of cartridges. The Mustang's five-liter turbocharged eight cylinders could have howled down the road at over a hundred miles an hour within six seconds. Instead, the car began to slow as Dees took his foot off the accelerator. As he rolled down the driver's side window, he was glad the air bag had been disconnected.

Both sets of headlights approached rapidly, the pair behind the Mustang growing larger faster. Dees waited until they almost filled the rear window before pushing down on the accelerator slightly. The car responded immediately, picking up speed so rapidly that what should have been a teeth-shaking rear-end collision became a jarring nudge. As the car behind him retreated from his rear bumper, a black Lexus slid silently up on his left. Both passenger windows began to roll down silently as Dees's car was punched again from the rear.

The Mustang fishtailed slightly on the wet pavement. Dees accelerated a little more and gently eased the front tires back in line. He gripped the Smith & Wesson in his right hand as he looked to his left and saw both Lexus windows open. He glimpsed what looked like a small cannon framed against a massive black head.

As the barrel of the sawed-off shotgun angled toward him, Dees pulled up the pistol and thrust it, stiff-armed, out the window, turning to face left long enough to pull the trigger twice before returning his eyes, briefly, to the ruler-straight pavement shining in his headlights.

He heard tires screech as the Lexus slammed on its brakes. The headlights following him receded suddenly, then winked out. An access road with an asphalt lip was approaching on his left. He turned in suddenly, stopped the car with a jolt, shut off the lights, slapped the Mustang into reverse, backed onto the highway, and put the .32 in his left hand. He aimed at the spot where he guessed both vehicles had stopped and gunned the engine.

The steering wheel was slick with sweat under his right hand as he picked up speed and counted one, two, three, four, five. At six, he jammed his knees against the steering wheel, reached down to flip on the brights, and grabbed the wheel again in time to see the Lexus and a small brown truck, side by side, driving away with their lights out less than fifty feet in front of him.

He could hear the truck's wheels scream as they skidded to the left, then turned hard to the right, ducking behind the Lexus and shooting across an asphalt apron and onto one of the muddy access roads where the rear-wheel-drive Mustang would have a hard time following. The Lexus, directly in front of him, began to pull away. Dees strained to make out the plates. The county name at the bottom was obscured by the plate's frame, but he glimpsed the number AXL-446, just as a shower of sparks shot across the hood of the Mustang. Someone, he decided, was shooting at him with an unsteady aim from the Lexus, glancing slugs off the hood at a shallow angle.

The wind sang in his ears, and the hairs on his arms stood straight up, as if suddenly charged with electricity. He raised the pistol and found, to his surprise, that his left arm was hardly shaking at all. He pulled the trigger four times, aiming at the rear window. Two shots punctured it cleanly and the third went wild before the fourth shattered the window and caused fist-sized shards of glass to drop like chunks of ice from a gutter on a warm winter day. As the Lexus continued to speed away he thought, Okay, that's six shots. He killed the lights and slammed on the brakes.

He stuck his head out the window and listened as the hum of the other car quickly disappeared. He sat, sucking in air through his mouth with a slight whistling sound. He opened the revolver, slapped the spent shells into his palm, and stuck them in his pocket. He reached in the cartridge box and reloaded, surprising himself that he was only shaking enough to drop one shell.

Cautiously, he put the Mustang in gear, turned around, and drove a mile on the deserted road before switching the lights back on. He stopped in Clewiston, went into a mildewed Holiday Inn, registered under the name of Judah P. Benjamin, and paid in cash. Then he went back to his car, drove it to the almost empty rear parking lot of a Day's Inn two blocks away, and locked it.

He walked back to the Holiday Inn, ordered a double Johnnie Black at the bar, carried it to his room, and dialed Curtis Stevens's home number. "It's me," he said. "I need a favor. I need to find out about a license plate registration as soon as possible."

"Trouble?" Stevens asked.

"Other than somebody driving around with a missing rear window and nine-millimeter skid marks on my hood, not too much, no."

He sketched what had happened and gave Stevens the license number. "Just call back here and ask for Judah Benjamin."

"Who?"

"Treasury Secretary, Confederate States of America, and the only Jew in Jefferson Davis's cabinet. Let me know."

Half an hour later, the phone rang. "Got it," Stevens said. "Alpha X-ray Looie four-four-six is registered to Gold Cane Holdings, Incorporated, as a leased vehicle. Reported stolen this morning."

Dees said thanks, jammed a chair under the doorknob, stuffed the pistol under his pillow, and tried to sleep.

CHAPTER 8

The house squatted like a huge red brick toad above the sodden cane fields, elevated on a packed earth pad five feet above the black muck that had been covered with strips of dark green sod. Two sitting cement lions, paws draped over a pair of generic cement shields, rested on top of brick columns that anchored a spiked iron entrance gate. Dees noticed the lions had mildew growing under their eyes.

The gate clattered open, sliding on small rubber wheels. Dees steered the Mustang up the circular asphalt drive. A black man built like a sumo wrestler stood at the bottom of the brick stairs leading to the front door. A head the size of a small infant sat atop a pink guayabera.

Dees parked the car, got out, and started up the stairs when a hand resembling a smoked ham was planted on his chest. The huge head shook side to side.

"No, mon. Gotta check you out first."

Dees was glad the revolver was secured inside the locked glove compartment. He looked down at the hand on his chest, then looked up. "Must be hard to use a sawed-off shotgun with a hand that big. You have to pull the trigger with your pinky?"

Without a word, Dees was picked up under the armpits by a pair of mammoth hands and propelled back against the car. The Jamaican expertly frisked him, starting at the ankles and working his way up. He grunted, satisfied, and stepped back.

Dees stared at the giant head. "You ever think of renting out billboard space on that thing?"

The Jamaican's eyes narrowed, giving him the look of a surly jack-o'-lantern. "I searched everything except your smart mouth. Maybe I'll look inside and take care of that fancy tongue of yours."

Dees was telling himself it was time to be calm, not witty, when the door to the house clicked open. A man with black hair moussed straight back from his forehead stepped out. His cream-colored linen pants contrasted with a black short-sleeve, open-collared guayabera. Dees glanced at his tan, woven slippers. Dees had an almost identical pair, thirty bucks from Manolo's Shoe Wear House. But these on the porch had a small oval metal tag just underneath the tassels, meaning they were made by Vittorio somebody-or-other and retailed at designer boutiques on South Beach for eight hundred dollars.

The Jamaican waddled up the steps and whispered in his ear. The man's dark-eyed gaze settled on Dees. "Come in, Mister United Nations."

Dees climbed the steps until he was eye-to-eye with the man, whose face was taut and tanned, without a wrinkle, blemish, or blackhead, at least any that Dees could see. He looked through the open door into the house's dark interior and said, "Before we go inside, someone tried to kill me not far from here last night. They were driving a Lexus registered to your company. The one with the gun looked like that small mountain there."

The man sighed. "You are rude, since we have not even been introduced yet, but that seems to be an occupational hazard for some Anglos, hm? And if Joseph ever did set out to kill someone, he would most assuredly do it."

"Then let's start over," Dees said, extending his hand. The man took it. Dees noticed he was trying to squeeze his hand hard, but it wasn't having much effect. "I'm Peter Dees, and I assume you're Manuel Cabrera. And I can't help you if I'm dead."

The man shrugged. "Too many people here lead a sorry existence, and they turn to drugs like this crack or this methamphetamine. There has been much violent crime over this past year and we have had several vehicles stolen lately, including a Lexus yesterday. I have nothing to gain by having you dead, even though, as I said, you are very rude. And I only knew you were supposed to arrive here this morning, so how could I know you were coming last night? And as you said, I am Manuel Cabrera."

Cabrera turned without a word and walked inside. Dees trailed behind, followed by Joseph, who blotted out the sun completely as he squeezed through the doorway. They walked through the marble-floored foyer and through a dark room that Dees figured was thirty feet to a side, with a projection TV and stereo equipment and speakers that covered almost the entire far wall.

They emerged into a room flooded with light from a dozen floor-to-ceiling windows. A series of overhead fans turned lazily above the dark rattan chairs and tables. The backs and arms of the chairs were padded with chocolate-colored leather. Stretching to the horizon outside, a green sea of sugarcane waved lightly in a rare morning breeze. The effect was like standing on the glassed-in bridge of a ship plowing through a bright green ocean.

A trim man, clean-shaven, with a short, military-style haircut, sat in one of the chairs. He started to rise, but Cabrera waved his cane. "Sit, sit. Orestes, this is the man I spoke of. Mister Dees, Orestes Diaz."

With a *whoompf* from a leather cushion, Cabrera sat. Dees nodded. "Major. A pleasure."

Diaz's eyebrows shot up. "You know of me?"

Dees noticed that Diaz seemed pleased. "Who doesn't? Major Orestes Diaz, credited with four South African jets shot down in Angola. Gets upset when the Cuban commander in Angola comes home and is executed by Fidel, supposedly for drug trafficking. Defects to the U.S. by flying a MiG-21 from Havana to Key West. You flew below coastal radar, so the first anyone knows about it is when you fly over Duval Street waggling your wings for permission to land. You embarrassed the hell out of the U.S. military because they didn't spot you."

Diaz smiled. "It showed me what I did not want to believe, that your government is too soft to deal with the butcher in Havana, that your traitors in Washington and even in Miami have—"

"Orestes," Cabrera interrupted quietly, "we can talk of *la causa* later. Now, we listen."

He turned and smiled wolfishly at Dees, who leaned back in his chair and said, "As I told you, the Cubans gave you up to the U.S. government. The Cubans say you're DGI and that you met with them at the United Nations and agreed to spy for them. The Feds have been cooperating with Havana on—"

"Traitors!" Diaz hissed. "They cooperate with the monster in Cuba! How many Communists must there be in your government? How many Cubans must die before—"

"Orestes!" Cabrera slapped his palm on the chair's arm. "*Basta!* Enough. You were saying, Mister Dees?"

Dees noticed Diaz was sweating, despite the air-conditioned breeze circulated by the ceiling fans. He continued, "The Cubans are cooperating while the FBI figures out why the man you recommended to Brigade X killed a Federal agent. So it looks to them like you can be charged with espionage and conspiracy to commit murder. The dead agent was a friend of mine. I just want your story and to find out why he died, that's all."

Cabrera drummed his fingers on top of the chair. "Is that what this is about? Friendship?"

Dees looked out at the waves of green sugar, and said, "Please don't patronize me like I'm a Boy Scout knocking on your door. You know the maximum-security Federal prison where they keep convicted spies? It's in Colorado. You might see the sun one hour a week if you're lucky. So yes, it's about friendship, and maybe about keeping you out of prison if you can tell me what you know."

Diaz started to speak, but Cabrera held up his hand. "What is it you wish to know?"

"Let's start with your recommending Brigade X use Emilio and why he started shooting."

Cabrera sighed. "A distant cousin of mine, but not distant enough, I am afraid. He is a simple man, maybe a bit simple-minded also. I—we—needed someone with updated skills in current weapons of various kinds. I used my, um, influence to convince him to desert his army duties and come here on a raft. Actually, it was more of a motor launch, and there was plenty of food and water. He hated Castro, as does my entire family, so I thought . . ."

His voice trailed off. Dees said, "You thought he could be helpful and maybe not get in the way too much?"

"Exacto," Cabrera nodded. "I do not know why he started shooting."

"Did you know he was on methamphetamine and cocaine? I saw him snorting on the boat. He even tried to open fire on some dolphins."

Cabrera blinked once, like a lizard sitting on a leaf. "I merely thought he was a useful idiot who hated Castro and maybe drank too many *coladas.* You know the story of my family, no?"

Dees shook his head. "No, just what I've read. You came here as a teenager on the Mariel boatlift in 'eighty and here you are today."

Cabrera laughed sharply. "A man in my position keeps a good deal quiet. I am the exile success story, I am a *patrón* of the exile movement, *bueno.* You are a fan of *el beisbol*?"

Dees looked up. "I grew up wanting to be a pitcher for the Cardinals."

Cabrera beamed. "Ah, *Los Cardinales*. They have much to do with my story, you know."

While Diaz fidgeted, Cabrera told Dees an abbreviated version of the story. His father had started life in Oriente Province, the eldest son of a shipping supervisor for a U.S. sugar outfit and a mother who was a bookkeeper for the company. His father's passions had been swimming, which he had practiced daily in the pool at the club, and baseball. In his teen years, his father had idolized Enos Slaughter, whose daring dash from first to home on a single in the seventh game of the 1946 Series had enabled his father's beloved *Cardinales* to beat the Red Sox.

A run like that, his father had told him at least once a year, took *cojones* and showed that one could achieve anything one wanted in life if one was willing to take the risks. *Audaz*, his father had said, paraphrasing Frederick the Great, *siempre audaz*.

Audacity in sports had led to his father's athletic scholarship at the University of Havana. He had gone on to law school, discovering common sporting and political interests with a tall, charming fellow law student named Fidel Castro Ruz. Fidel was expelled, and the elder Cabrera almost was, too, for taking part in an anti-Batista student strike. When Castro and a ragged group of rebels stormed the Moncada Barracks, Cabrera's father had served as a cocounsel at their trials. During Fidel's years in the Sierra Maestra, his father had represented anti-Batista students and labor leaders. Many of his clients had ended up dead, regardless of the verdicts.

The U.S. finally decided that Batista was more trouble than he was worth, and convinced the dictator to accept an offer of exile. So Castro, Cabrera said bitterly, was able to ride on top of a tank into Havana without firing a shot. His father ended up with a position in the new government's Justice Ministry. But revolutionary justice meant the expropriation of his father's *finca*. The papers had crossed his father's desk, and he immediately objected. He was fired and moved to a shabby "people's apartment" in Santiago, where he and his wife and son lived for two years before Manuel was born.

One day in 1978, his parents received word that his older brother had died in Angola. His father had deteriorated inch by inch, until his heart finally gave out a year later.

A week afterward, his mother put on the dress she had worn to her eldest son's funeral, and the pearls her husband had given her for their twenty-fifth wedding anniversary. She had adjusted her formal white gloves, walked to a busy street corner, and thrown herself in front of a bus.

"And that," Cabrera said, lips barely moving, "is *nuestra historia*, the story of all of us, millions of us, not just myself. The rest of it—my coming to the States, my fortune, Gold Cane—is merely, as you would say here, window dressing. Castro and his monsters are traitors to Cuba, traitors to their own people. So that brings us here."

He glanced out at the cane that stretched into the distance. "I do not grow this because I love the way sugarcane looks. I grow this because it is profitable. The Cubans are becoming, as you say here, savvy marketers since the Soviet Union went *pfft* and stopped supporting the Cuban cane crop with outlandish prices. I made it a point to approach them with an offer, along with someone you have already met."

Dees furrowed his brow. Cabrera merely stared and said, "He was in the boat with you? The esteemed freedom fighter Ramon Vargas? The one who told you all about me?"

Dees felt a tickling in the back of his throat, and returned Cabrera's stare. "I know Ramon Vargas. All he wants to do is talk about freedom for Cuba. But your friends at the U.N., the Cubans? They're another matter, especially when they talked to the FBI about you."

Cabrera sighed. "As you wish, then. Vargas buys the confidence of the Cubans at the U.N. by telling them about the Brigade X attack. If this attack takes place, as he has promised, they are to call a telephone number and repay Vargas with, ah, certain information."

Dees massaged his forehead. "So the hard-liners in Cuba knew this attack was coming? Because Vargas told them? With your blessing?"

"Claro."

"But then an FBI agent gets killed and complicates things?"

Cabrera looked at Diaz again, and nodded. "I am afraid so. The telephone call I was to receive after the attack to fulfill their part of the bargain was to be a briefing on the dynamic within the Cuban Central Committee month-to-month. As you know, it always shifts. But that information helps marketing strategy. If the reformers gain the upper hand, I can expect sugar output to be curtailed as they attempt to diversify their economy, thus raising prices. But the hard-liners, they still believe sugar is their salvation, so if they gain the upper hand, production will rise and prices will be depressed, at least temporarily. So I use guile to find out."

Cabrera nodded with satisfaction. "As King Lear said, 'As if we were God's spies.' "

"You know what he said right after that?" Dees asked quietly. Cabrera stared without blinking. " 'And we'll wear out, in a walled prison.' "

"Of course," Cabrera said, once again barely moving his lips.

"All fascinating," Dees said without enthusiasm, "but it still leaves me a little short on why the FBI agent was killed."

Dees looked from one to the other. He looked at Joseph, who stood by the door, silent as cancer, and stared back with red-rimmed eyes. All he heard was the *swish-swish-swish* of the overhead fans.

Cabrera glared at Diaz again, then turned to Dees. "But the telephone call I receive tells me what we agreed to, and more, I am afraid. It confirmed some of my fears. You see, the hard-liners really *do* have many agents in the United States, including your friend Ramon Vargas."

Dees exhaled once, deeply, but didn't say a word. Cabrera

continued, "Why do you think I used Vargas to gain entry to meet with Castro's people at the U.N.? Because he is the great exile hero? *Pfah*. Rather, because he *is* in *reality* a Cuban spy, and he was, how would you say it? My foot in the door."

"And there was someone else also," Diaz said quickly, the words bouncing off each other. "Someone else was waiting for your commandos to land, someone the Cubans paid to create an incident by killing one of your FBI agents."

"Your friend," Cabrera said softly, " he was shot in the back by a Cuban agent."

Dees felt dizzy, even though he was sitting down. Only a handful of people knew about the back shot, and they were making sure nothing about it showed up in the media. Dees kept his left arm draped languidly across a chair arm and his right cupped on his chin. "No," he lied, "I didn't know that. How do you know?"

He thought Cabrera looked at him suspiciously. "I hope it is, um, not too much of a shock. And I know because I know. A tautology, my Jesuit professors would call it. Where I know and how I know and who I know it from are none of your business."

The silence that followed seemed as sticky as the shimmering air outside. Through the windows, Dees could see thousands of cane stalks standing stiffly at attention. Every trace of a breeze had died under the glare of the overhead sun. Cabrera folded his hands on top of his stomach, as if in prayer.

"Joseph," he said, staring at Dees. "Our friend is leaving now. Please go to the front and open the door for him."

Joseph turned his back and walked, rolling side to side, disappearing through the door that led to the hallway that led to the foyer that led to the front porch. Cabrera grunted and rose. Dees stood. Cabrera reached up and squeezed Dees's shoulder. "That is my story, Mister United Nations. I am not a spy, merely a patriot. I want my country to be free of certain influences before it sinks to the level of this country."

Cabrera nodded toward the doorway. "That one, and all these Jamaicans. Just like in Cuba, *los negros* started out in the fields and now they help run the Castro apparatus. Here they run your cities and destroy them. They are animals, worse than animals. That is one among many things I hate this Castro for. Those who fled here, the early refugees, the doctors and lawyers and architects and professionals? Those who made Cuban society function? All white. And now?"

He laughed bitterly. "And now Cuba collapses, and the blacks, they help run the evil there. That is why, here, they know their place, and stay there."

He released the shoulder. "I am simply a businessman with an interest in business and in freeing his *patria* from a dictator. I have done nothing remotely illegal. How can you help me?"

"I'm not sure," Dees said, trying to sound bored. "Would you be willing to tell the FBI or the U.S. Attorney what you've just told me?"

Cabrera shook his head. "No. But I have given you much information that may help you find the truth, so I would assume you will tell them for me that investigating me would be a waste of time. Please."

He gestured toward the door. They walked to the front door, where Joseph stood, glowering. Cabrera said, "And I assume I am now a source of yours, so you will tell no one, as you promised?"

"You can assume that," Dees said. "I won't tell anyone unless it gets in the way of finding out who killed my friend, and why. Then, I can't make any promises."

Cabrera looked placidly at Joseph. "Please get me one of the parakeets. A small green and yellow one, I believe, in the cage in the dining room."

Joseph walked away, returning a few minutes later with the struggling bird held gently, it seemed, in his fist.

"Ah, bueno," Cabrera said. He took the struggling bird in both hands, stroking its head. He looked directly into Dees's

eyes and, with a soft crunch, twisted the bird's head. He smiled and jerked hard, pulling the bird's head off. Tiny flecks of blood trailed across his guayabera. Without breaking his stare, Cabrera dropped the body onto the tiles.

"Joseph," he said. "When you have a moment, I seem to need a clean shirt."

Cabrera chuckled and turned, closing the door behind him. Dees got the key from his pocket and looked up at Joseph. "You know he thinks you're nothing but a field hand? He stopped just short of calling you a nigger."

Joseph squinted and said, "The conditions I choose to work in are none of your business. And I better never see you again."

Dees walked to the car, got in, started the engine, and pulled away slowly. A lightning bolt miles in front of him sizzled across a patch of black sky. He looked in the rearview mirror. Joseph had disappeared.

* * *

It was a little before five in the afternoon when Dees pulled the Mustang into a downtown Miami parking lot, locked it, and walked toward the Federal Building. Stevens was waiting for him on the street.

"When somebody calls me as hot under the collar as you were," the agent said, extending his hand, "I figure it's best to meet them in public in case they go nuts. What happened?"

Dees ignored the hand and said acidly, "Who knows besides me Richie was shot in the back?"

Stevens let his hand fall to his side. "Just the Bureau's forensics people, headquarters in D.C., the State Department and Davis here, Briscoe, you, me, and whoever you've told. Why?"

Dees took a deep breath and exhaled slowly, trying to drain the tension from his body. It wasn't working. "I told the widow, because I figured she should know what I'm working on. And we have a leak someplace, either that or Cabrera's the luckiest guesser in the world. He knows about the back shot.

Told me so. Claims it was a Cuban agent who was waiting there for the surrender."

Stevens whistled, once, low. "You believe him?"

Dees shrugged. "*Quién sabe*? He says the Cubans knew about the Brigade X raid in advance, and let it go off so they can get a propaganda bonanza from it, plus they were bribed a little. Davis ever mention anything like that in all his back-channel chat with Fidel's boys?"

Stevens shook his head. "No. All he said was that the Cubans claim Vargas is working for the DGI."

They stared at each other. Dees fished in the pocket of his tan sport coat for the palm-sized cellular phone. "Vargas keeps coming up, and I need to talk to him again, I think," he said, holding the phone out to Stevens. "Can you call the AUSA or somebody and get me back in there?"

Stevens took the phone and punched in a number. "I'll just call the Marshal's office directly. See if I can speed up— Yeah, hi. Curtis Stevens, FBI . . . Oh hi, Fred. Thanks for helping with the Vargas paperwork the other day. . . . Yeah. Say, I need to check Vargas out again. Any way we could speed up the—"

Stevens stopped talking. He pressed the receiver tighter to his ear, and shot a sideways glance at Dees. He began to chew on his lower lip. Finally, he said, "You sure? . . . What's the name? . . . Who? . . . Never heard of him. From where? . . . What? . . . How long ago? . . . Shit. Don't go anyplace, I'll be right over."

He snapped the phone shut, handed it to Dees, and began to stride away, across the street. Dees palmed the phone and caught up to him. "What's up?" he said as they stepped onto the sidewalk in front of the Detention Center.

Stevens turned. "Vargas is gone. He was checked out this morning to the Igloo and the Marshals haven't seen him since. Some agent from D.C. checked him out. They didn't worry because the log indicated he'd be signed out for most of the day."

"D.C.?" Dees said. "You know about any agent from—"

"No," Stevens said, "I don't. I need to get up there. Stay here."

Dees shook his head. "Sorry. Sign me in, okay? I want to know, too."

Stevens sighed. "Stay here for now. Give me the cell phone number. I'll call when you can come up."

Dees pulled a felt-tip pen and reporter's notebook from his pocket and scrawled down the number. Stevens disappeared inside. Fifteen minutes later, the phone beeped. "Come on in," Stevens said. "There's a pass at the desk."

Dees got the small yellow badge with a black V stamped on it and rode the elevator to the sixth floor. The Marshal's office was as new as the rest of the center, but looked old and damp; probably, Dees thought, from the moss-green paint on the walls. Stevens met him and led him to an interior office. He shut the door. A thick black ledger book sat on the desk.

"I commandeered an office for a few minutes," Stevens said. "The Igloo hasn't been used all day. An FBI agent showed up, and he had the badge, the ID, and a writ with the embossed seal, the whole thing. The Marshals don't know him, but hey, he's from D.C., right?"

Stevens stepped to the desk, and opened the ledger. "So here, an Agent Victor Fleming signs him out. Vargas had been signed out to the Igloo before, so who's suspicious? They say Fleming was a small guy, five-six or so, breathy voice like he had bronchitis. He gave them an office extension in the Miami office where he could be reached. Guess what?"

Dees said, "I have no idea."

Stevens leaned across the desk. "The number he gave is Peterson's old extension, with his voice still on the voice mail. We check D.C. There used to be an agent Vic Fleming, but he retired in 1967 and died in 1979. That's it. Nobody over by the Igloo has seen anybody use it for days, and nobody says they noticed a short FBI agent and a prisoner in an orange jumpsuit. Fucking incredible."

Stevens straightened, and tapped the logbook with his finger. "And check this out. Look here."

Dees walked around the desk and peered at the ledger. Stevens jammed his finger on one line. "Here it is. Signature, name, Peterson's extension, prisoner's name, destination 'Igloo.' Time out 1045, time due back 1930. And over here, in the corner, look at this."

Printed in tiny letters with a ballpoint pen were the letters "gwtw." Dees stared, and made a low, growling "Umm-hmmhmph" sound. "Nice," he said.

Stevens furrowed his brow. Dees tapped the ledger. "Victor Fleming was a Hollywood director from the thirties and forties. Guess what movie he's best known for? GWTW?"

Stevens's jaw sagged. "Wonderful. *Gone with the Fucking Wind*. Just wonderful."

He twitched slightly, as if he'd been shocked. Dees could hear the faint hum of the agent's vibrating pager. Stevens stared at the number on the display, and punched the numbers into the desk phone. "Yeah, Stevens."

He didn't say a word for perhaps ninety seconds. His shoulders sagged as he said, "I'll be there in half an hour. Establish Federal jurisdiction now. . . . What? . . . I don't give a fuck! This is a Federal case so tell the BSO to back off!"

He hung up the phone. "A body's been found in the 'Glades off Alligator Alley about five miles west of the toll plaza. Briscoe's there with the Broward Sheriff's office. He thinks it's Vargas."

As they rode down in the elevator, Dees said, "What I'm about to ask isn't nearly as shitty as it sounds. If there's a bigger story here than Richie's murder, it's on the record. Nothing goes on the air until all of this is unraveled, which may be never."

"Too tired to argue," Stevens said. "I'll get a car from the garage. Meet me on the corner in five minutes."

Four minutes later, a dark blue Chevrolet Caprice pulled

up to the corner and turned south on Miami Avenue. Dees followed in the Mustang. It took them thirty-five minutes to navigate the entrance to I-95, drive to Fort Lauderdale, head west on 595, and zip through the toll plaza of what was still called Alligator Alley but had been widened so that now it was, at least according to the signs, Interstate 75.

Five miles later, Dees saw an EMS van, three Broward Sheriff's cars, and an unmarked Federal sedan parked nose-to-tail along the narrow right shoulder. They were parked over a culvert where a five-foot-diameter pipe ran under the highway, allowing the 'Glades to drain and allowing passage for one of the maybe dozen surviving Florida panthers that tried to survive in the shrinking wetlands. Briscoe leaned against a six-foot-high chain-link fence, built the length of the highway to keep the panthers from becoming road kill.

He was talking to Stevens. And Davis. Briscoe rocked himself off the fence and onto the balls of his feet, almost as if he were about to take a step in Dees's direction. He didn't. "You tried to pump Cabrera for information and gave up Vargas to get what you wanted. Just to get a fucking story, like all you scumbag reporters."

Briscoe started to move, but Stevens put a hand across his chest and said, sharply, "That's enough! Briscoe, I'm in charge, in case you forgot, so just do your job. Dees, tell me you didn't tell Cabrera about Vargas."

"No. Cabrera told me Vargas was a DGI spy. I didn't say anything."

In the silence that followed, Dees pretended to be studying the sky. He looked from Stevens to Briscoe to Davis, and said, "Cabrera seems to be the key to all this, doesn't he? Here's a bright idea, and forgive me if you've already thought of it, but why not haul Cabrera in and sweat him?"

Briscoe shot a glance at Stevens, who looked at Dees and said, "We already made a phone call. John?"

Briscoe looked like he was sucking a lemon.

Stevens repeated, "John?"

"I called," Briscoe mumbled quickly. "Some Jamaican said he was gone, not available. I haven't had a chance to go to his place yet and check it out."

"I had the airports checked on the way out here," Stevens said. "A flight plan was filed in Lauderdale for Gold Cane's jet, Cabrera and a passenger named Diaz flying to Freeport, wheels up for the Bahamas probably a couple of hours after they talked to you."

Dees scratched his goatee. "So why me? I suspect Cabrera, you suspect Cabrera, all God's children, well, you know. So why all the games? I'm being straight."

"Mister Dees," Davis said, wiping his glasses with a handkerchief, "in a case like this all of us are paid to be suspicious. Myself, I'm suspicious that you're compromising a national security investigation, but I'm willing to forget that. You're going to Cuba, yes?"

Dees swatted a mosquito feeding on his neck. "How'd you know?"

"Don't you even watch your own channel?" Davis asked sardonically.

"Not if I can help it," Dees said. "So I guess they're promoting the upcoming blah-de-blah from our Peter Dees in Havana where he'll reveal yak yak yak?"

"Something like that," Davis said. "So as I said, I'm willing to forego any pleasure I might otherwise get from personally canceling your passport if you travel to Cuba and tell us about anything you find. I'll regretfully make sure this misunderstanding is forgotten."

Dees looked at Stevens, who shrugged. Dees said, "I'm not spying for anybody. If the Cubans know something that helps me find out what happened, fine. Anything else you find out like everybody else, by watching GTV."

Stevens finally spoke. "No more games, I promise. Just help us, okay?"

There was a *whoosh*, then a soft growl followed by a gurgle as an airboat with two sheriff's deputies and two EMS technicians pulled up. A body, covered in a white sheet, was bound to an aluminum gurney by three straps. Stevens walked over to the airboat and spoke to the deputies. Briscoe and Davis followed. Dees pulled a cigar from an inside pocket, bit off the tip, thumbed open a well-worn brass Zippo lighter, and sent a blue cloud of smoke into the air as he walked over.

Stevens looked up from the body. "Seems a boatload of tourists out to look at alligators found it early this afternoon on a hummock, with fire ants all over it."

He nodded at an ambulance attendant, who pulled the top of the sheet back. Among the oozing fire ant pustules on his face, a piece of skin and skull the size of a quarter was missing from the upper right quadrant of the head. Dried blood on the bristly gray hairs showed where the shot had entered the left temple. The two white-uniformed EMS workers covered the head with the soiled sheet, picked up the gurney, and slid it into the back of the van like a pizza sliding into an oven. "What the fuck," Stevens said tightly. He slammed the side of the van with his fist, three times. "What! The! Fuck!"

The driver started the van, and gunned the engine, leaving a cloud of fine white dust behind. Dees walked over to Stevens. "Notice he was naked? No manacles, no cuffs."

Stevens just stared at the disappearing van. "Somebody didn't want the body found too fast and an orange prison jumpsuit'd look like a neon sign. Guess they didn't figure on tourists, huh?"

Stevens walked to the Caprice as the Broward Sheriff's cars pulled away. Without looking at Dees, he said, "Call me when you get back, unless they've transferred me to Guam by then."

He scattered gravel for ten yards when he pulled away. Dees stood alone on the shoulder, staring at the sawgrass. A faint breeze stirred, rubbing the sharp, tough blades together. It sounded, Dees thought, like the swamp was hissing.

* * *

The gurgling jets in the small hot tub filled his ears with foamy warm water and a dull humming sound. Dees had considered driving three hours on a two-lane highway in the dark and rain back to Key West. Then he considered spending another night on the lumpy fold-out couch in the bureau's back room. Then, on a whim, he made a phone call and found he could get a large room at the Mayfair in Coconut Grove at an off-season rate. He had a grouper sandwich and two Sam Adamses from room service, lit a joint, turned on the TV, and settled into the tub, lying flat so that only his nose, mouth, eyes, and the smoldering ganja were above water.

He looked at the Weather Channel forecaster circling his hands around a crimson blotch in the Atlantic, sloshed his head up, reached for the remote, and turned up the sound. ". . . as large as Gilbert in 1989 or Andrew in 1992 or Mitch in 1998 at this stage of development. The storm has gone from tropical wave right through tropical depression to tropical storm all within thirty-six hours. But remember, this has been a quiet season. It's September and we're only on our fourth named storm. This one is David." The forecaster gave it the Spanish pronunciation Dah-veed. "It'll be another forty-eight to ninety-six hours before David comes close enough to the Caribbean or any other land mass to be a threat of any kind. But stay tuned, since this storm is gathering strength and speed faster than usual."

Dees clicked the sound off, climbed out of the tub, and checked the time. Eight-thirty. He requested a five A.M. wake-up call from the desk, fell asleep, and dreamed he was lost in a forest of sugarcane stalks as big as redwoods.

When the phone rang, he stretched, reached for the receiver, thanked the recording, and hung up. After a pot of coffee from the coffee maker on a side counter, he called the air freight number at the Miami airport and found that thirteen various-size cases of broadcast equipment had arrived from Phoenix, bound for the afternoon Havana charter. Export forms were in order, and a copy would be waiting for Dees at the charter flight desk. The hotel health club opened at six, so Dees went upstairs and spent half an hour with the free weights, barely able to complete three repetitions of twelve lifts pushing 160 pounds on the bench press.

He showered, ordered breakfast, ate, and called Janie. He was mildly surprised when she answered. She said she'd love to see him on the way to the airport. By the time he checked out and loaded his bags into the Mustang, it was almost nine o'clock. He didn't have to be at the airport until noon for the mid-afternoon charter. It took him forty-five minutes to arrive at the coral-colored two-story stucco house in Kendall, identical to every other house in the Coral Palms development except for the paint job.

He was aiming his finger for the doorbell when the plain white door swung open. Dees looked up and felt his mouth fall, slightly, before he closed it.

"Come on in," Janie said. "With your mouth opening and closing like that you look like a guppy."

Her hair was razor-cut, short on the back and sides, longer, jet-black, and slightly spiky on the top. Dees stepped into the gray-tiled entranceway and stared again.

She smiled, kissed him on the cheek, and ran her hand across the top of her head. "Catharsis. I had to do something, and this seemed to be as good a something as any."

She took him by the arm and led him through the hallway to the dining room. Spread out on the table were Peterson's FBI ID in a black leatherette case, his badge, a half-dozen manila envelopes bulging with papers, and a stack of FBI stationary and memo pads.

She sighed deeply. "Packing things up to go back to the Bureau, all of his files, the stationary, the remains of Richard Trevor Peterson's service to his country."

Her eyes began to fill like overflowing saucers. She turned. "Not a hell of a lot."

Dees took her in his arms and patted her back. He used his thumb to wipe the corners of her eyes. She looked up and sniffled, "Enough already, *basta*. Richie's family went back to Minneapolis, which is just as well, since I need to get on with . . . with . . ."

"Life?" Dees said. "The thing itself."

"Or a rough approximation," she said, pulling herself away, straightening her shoulders, and turning toward the enclosed cement patio visible through the seven-foot sliding glass doors that led from the dining room. "There's fresh O.J. out back."

They walked through the sliding glass doors and onto the screened-in patio. She collapsed into one of the black aluminum chairs designed to look like wrought iron, pulled a Salem from a pack on the table, and lit it. She inhaled deeply and coughed.

"Damn," she said, her voice suddenly husky and a full octave lower, "these things do a number on my lungs. Now I'll sound like Marlene Dietrich for an hour or two."

The morning light reflected off the small swimming pool, dappling the patio and Janie's face with moving patches of light. Dees sipped his juice. "I'm going to Cuba. There may be some answers there."

She raised her eyebrows and ran an index finger absently around the rim of her glass. The only sound was the stiff rustle of brown palm fronds outside the screen. "You think running around outside the country will help find Richie's killer?"

Dees drained his juice and stared briefly at the pulpy remains at the bottom of the glass. "Because the answer may not be in this country. It's bizarre, is all I know."

She still stared. He continued, "The shot from Emilio, the guy in the boat? That would have at least wounded Richie badly, but it might not have ended up killing him. The second shot from behind was a head shot, small caliber, not much of a wound."

Her eyes widened. He reached across the table and squeezed her hand. "Sorry."

"I'm a Feeb's wife," she said softly. "Widow now. I should be used to hearing this sort of thing, and I'm the sorry one for cracking like this."

Dees squeezed her hand again, and sighed. "The second shot definitely did kill him, but I don't know who fired it, or why, either."

"So why Cuba?"

"Because maybe somebody in Cuba can help fill in the pieces. If it was somebody sympathetic to Castro, a hard-liner looking for trouble, maybe somebody there might know. Or maybe somebody'll have some hints if it was a nut case anti-Castro shooter, or maybe none of it fits together and I'm wasting my time."

Her eyes became hard. "And then if you find out, what do you do?"

Dees shook his head. "Haven't thought that far ahead. If they're in Cuba, I guess try to extradite them, and if they're not, track them down."

"What about what's-his-name?" she asked. "You know, the one that they arrested after Richie was shot? The big exile hero?"

Dees looked over the top of his glass. "He's dead. Some-body got him out of the Federal lockup and popped him. Found the body late yesterday."

She breathed through her mouth. "Body?"

"Somebody stashed him in the 'Glades but not well enough."

She nodded. "So that's what they were talking about."

Dees looked puzzled. She laughed. "Sweetheart, being part of the extended Bureau family gives you a subscription to the coconut telegraph. I got a couple of sympathy calls last night and this morning from other wives, and both of them were worried silly about something they wouldn't talk about that could torpedo the breadwinner's career, so I knew some-thing had happened."

Dees looked at his watch. "I have a plane to catch."

They walked through the glass doors, past Peterson's artifacts in the dining room, through the front door into the white-hot sunlight. He gave her a hug and she kissed him, very lightly, on the lips. She said, "Do me a favor."

"Name it." He pulled out his sunglasses and put them on.

She reached up, pulled them off, and stared at him, the hard look back in her eyes.

"If you find out who killed Richie?"

"Yeah?"

"Kill the bastard."

CHAPTER 9

Every day except Thursdays, a creaking Haiti TransAir 727 charter flew one round-trip between Miami and Havana. Coming to Miami, it carried Cubans who had obtained visas to visit relatives in the United States. Flying into Havana, it carried Cubans on the return trip home, Cuban-Americans visiting relatives on the island, academics, relief workers, diplomats, and journalists, pretty well exhausting the list of Americans legally allowed to visit Cuba.

A guitar and conga drum trio serenaded the sweating passengers as they stepped onto the steaming tarmac at José Marti Airport. Dees wondered how long it would take them to strike up the unofficial Cuban national anthem when, almost on cue, the band struck up *"Guantanamera."*

"Soy un hombre sincero," the guitarist warbled. You betcha, Dees thought, we're all sincere men. Questions kept running through his head like an annoying Top Forty tune. Why have a druggie like Emilio on a commando raid? Who shot Richie in the back? Who killed Vargas? Who's the spy? Cabrera? Vargas? The American with a goatee standing in the middle of swirling chaos at Havana's airport?

"Dees! Dees! *Oye,* GTV!"

Dees looked up and saw a short man wearing a Mets baseball cap and sweat-stained, short-sleeved plaid shirt, waving at him from the other side of a rope line set up outside the Customs area. Next to him, a good three inches taller, stood a woman with luxurious black hair cascading onto the shoulders of a bright yellow sleeveless dress. She looked down at the man, who pointed toward Dees.

She said something to the uniformed soldier at the end of the rope line. He nodded, and unsnapped a catch on the rope. She strode through the Customs area, nodding perfunctorily toward one of the agents whose eyes were devouring her brown legs, and walked up to Dees. In crepe-soled flats, she was still only a few inches shorter than Dees, who was six feet even.

"Peter Dees?"

Her chocolate eyes had faint flecks of green in them. Dees held out his hand. "And you are?"

Her handshake was firm, businesslike, and brief. "Gloria Bravo, with Radio Havana and Minrex."

Minrex—*El Ministerio de Relaciones Exteriores*—was Cuba's State Department. She turned her back and began walking away. Dees picked up his two bags and followed. She sliced through passengers and soldiers like the prow of an icebreaker. She nodded over her shoulder toward Dees without breaking stride as they double-timed through the last Customs checkpoint.

During Dees's previous trips to Cuba, the government-appointed fixers who had met him at the airport had fidgeted like used-car salesmen, cajoling and pleading their way through bureaucrats and soldiers. Dees decided that either Gloria Bravo was as connected as she was cool, or else she outranked everyone at the airport. The rope line parted, and Dees, along with the short Cuban who had first hailed him, trailed in Gloria's wake across the terminal.

She stopped, and turned. "Juan, you can get the car."

"Hold it," Dees said. He sat his bags down with a plop. He held out his hand to the short man in the baseball cap. "Call me archaic, but let's exchange some pleasantries first. I'm Peter Dees."

The man smiled. He had the faint hint of a scar above his

left eye, and a thin mustache. "Juan Gato, the bureau's cameraman. But you can call me Jack the Cat."

Gloria wrinkled her nose with impatience. Dees turned to her. "And Ms. Bravo, thanks for your help, but you're here because . . ."

He let the thought trail off. Gato laughed and said, "The esteemed *Señorita* Bravo is our guide, our benefactress, our fixer, our analyst, our spy."

Her eyes snapped right and bored into Gato, who seemed to shrink a little under their glare, the smile still frozen on his face.

"Coordinator," she said softly. "I coordinate the activities of foreign journalists visiting Cuba. And it would be very helpful, Juan, if you coordinated the car and all of that equipment waiting in the baggage area."

"Sure, sure, right now," Gato said, and scooted away. Dees had seen less terrified looks on men about to be shot.

Dees thought that if she wore a power suit and carried a cell phone, she could pass for a stockbroker or high-priced attorney. Even in the tropical sheath cut five inches above her tanned knees, she exuded authority, the effect spoiled only by the dirt underneath several of her fingernails. Soap was in short supply in Cuba, along with toothpaste, toilet paper, razors, shaving cream, feminine hygiene supplies, food, gasoline, and clothing, which was why Dees's tan duffel was half filled with personal grooming supplies for trading.

"So how did I rate you?" Dees asked.

She looked puzzled.

He continued, "I've had minders before—"

She scowled.

"Oh, sorry," Dees said sardonically. "Coordinators. I've had coordinators from Minrex before, but never one who walked through airport security like she owned the place, and never one who worked for Radio Havana, too. So how did I rate you?"

She looked bored. "We have some special interest in you.

Your eyewitness account of an attack on our country means we now must show you the consequences of the counter-revolutionary bandit's actions."

Dees whistled. "Very good. Where's that from, the tourist's guide to North Korea?"

She cracked a half smile. "A bit much, I admit. You tell me what stories you wish to cover, then, but I also have some suggestions on showing the impact of these attacks and of the embargo."

Dees nodded, deadpan. "Remember, *nunca una propaganda*."

This time, she laughed out loud, then covered her mouth, embarrassed at reacting to the bad pun on the decades-old propaganda slogan—*nunca una aspirina*, not even an aspirin. It was meant to dramatize the effects of the U.S. trade embargo on the average Cuban. But it had become an ironic commentary on Cuba's desperate scramble for hard currency. Dees knew that if you had dollars, you could get not only aspirin, but cheese puffs, candy bars, soda, stereos, and cellular phones at the shopping centers that catered to diplomats, foreigners, and Cubans lucky enough to have U.S. currency instead of the worthless Cuban peso.

But for the average Cuban who stood in a long line clutching a dog-eared booklet of ration coupons and a wad of Cuban pesos to buy a monthly allotment of rice, flour, and dented canned goods, the consumer cornucopia that tumbled from Panama's Colon Free Trade Zone into the diplomatic shops was as out of reach as the North Pole. *Nunca una aspirina*.

Dees heard a horn beep. He turned and saw Gato behind the wheel of a DeSoto, originally white above the swooping strip of punctuating chrome, pumpkin-yellow underneath. But time, salt water, neglect, and shortages of paint had faded both into the more-or-less uniform yellow of bad teeth. Dees strode to the front passenger door, opened it, and motioned Gloria inside. She cocked her head, raised her eyebrows, and said, "Thank you."

Behind them a small Lada truck, a flatbed model with a

scarred white cab, was idling, tossing clouds of acrid smoke into the air. The bed was piled with gray hard-plastic equipment cases, two of them measuring at least four-by-four-by-three feet. Gato waved a sheaf of papers in his hand. "Got the carnets right here. No sweat with Customs, but you'll have to reimburse me for the *propinas* I gave to the boys here at the airport for loading and the tips I'll have to hand out at the hotel to get all this shit into the office. Oh yeah, the car. Minrex had a Lada for us but it's not running. GTV has a car under contract, but Lopez goes home to Mexico City and tells them to take the week off. So I borrow this from my cousin."

Dees tossed his two bags into the rear seat and climbed in. " 'Fifty-five?' "

Gato stared at him, then smiled, shaking his head. " 'Fifty-four. I modified the engine to run on diesel, which you can still get more of around here than regular gasoline."

"Must've been a bitch to drop the engine and replace it with a diesel."

Gato laughed. "I said modified, not changed the engine. It's still the same hunk of beautiful Motor City iron."

It was Dees's turn to shake his head. "That's impossible. You can't modify a gas engine to run on diesel."

Gato made a sound like a snort. "Yeah, impossible. That's why three dozen people I know did the same thing. It's Cuba, *hermano*. Nothing's impossible. I'll show you sometime how I manage to recharge flashlight batteries. And not that *gringo* ni-cad stuff, either. Just regular old flashlight batteries. See, I run a trickle charge through them, not more than a half amp, then I—"

"Juan," Gloria said icily. "Drive please."

Dees said, "Yeah, I'd love to see that. First, let's get me checked into the Havana Libre, then I'd like to take a run to Varadero and see what damage the attack did."

Gloria nodded. "And do you know what they hit?"

Gato laughed and said, "A propane tank for the barbecue

on the patio. Blew it up and scared the *mierda* out of some Canadian tourists."

Gloria turned to Dees. "Do you know what we are calling it?" She showed a mouthful of even teeth. "The Bay of Roasted Pigs."

A 1949 Mercury ground by, its body revealing brush strokes where it had been covered with flat black house paint, its small rear window and sloping metalwork making it look like a giant armored beetle, its rusted muffler making a sound like ragged .50 caliber fire. I have carried Communists and gangsters and Hollywood stars, the engine rumbled, and I have survived revolution and embargo and hurricanes. I am Cuba.

The DeSoto picked up speed, crawling past a camel, the Ministry of Transit's name for a pair of semi truck trailers welded together with a low U in the middle. Large windows had been added, along with an upper deck. Passengers boarded at the U, then walked up stairs to sit on benches, like on any other Third World bus. The entire thing was pulled by a semi, hauling three times the passengers as a normal bus but using half the fuel. A girl no younger than fifteen, no older than nineteen, stared frankly at Dees out a window. With a brief, elegant gesture, she brushed a strand of dark hair from her eyes, and winked.

The DeSoto creaked on its springs and turned, becoming a time machine as it rolled unsteadily between potholes disguised as small craters. Havana was a fly trapped in translucent amber, a preserved fossil turned to rock. Except for Argentine Chevys and sputtering Ladas, every car on the street predated Kennedy's assassination. The city was an old woman who had once turned heads and broken hearts as she danced until dawn and drank double *mojitos* with Meyer Lansky and Gary Cooper. She was poor now, and rum was rationed, and even if she had some, there wasn't any ice.

But she still had her wink and a sense of faded style. A pair of plump middle-aged women in faded housedresses leaned out their third-floor windows, laughing. A shirtless, sinewy young man disappeared from the waist up inside the engine compartment of a red '59 Pontiac convertible, salsa banging from its cracked radio speaker. A skinny man in a faded white shirt sat in a kitchen chair on a street corner, closing one eye as he carefully restrung a scarred guitar with a set of precious new strings. He looked up at Dees as the DeSoto ground to a halt at a stop sign.

"Gringo?" he said.

"Si."

Gloria pursed her lips. The old man looked down at the guitar, then looked up again. *"Canadiense?"*

Dees shook his head. *"No. Norteamericano."*

As the car began to chug away, the old man smiled and shouted, "Hey! Damn glad to have you back!"

Dees was still chuckling as they pulled in front of the old Havana Hilton, long since renamed *La Habana Libre*. A hunched, white-haired man in a faded green bellman's uniform stood near a rack of dented bicycles. Dees unlatched the rear door of the DeSoto and stuck out his head. "Professor! *Oye*, Professor!"

The old man walked over slowly, then clasped both of Dees's hands in his own. *"Amigo,* it has been what then, two years?"

"Almost three, I'm afraid. Professor Fuentes, this is *Señorita* Bravo and—"

"I know, I know," Fuentes said with a wave of his hand. "And the Juan Gato who makes a nuisance of himself since your GTV opened its bureau here. And who could not know *Señorita* Bravo from her reports for Radio Havana?"

Her expression didn't change. "Charmed. Please help Dees with his bags while I attend to the hotel."

She walked off without looking back at Dr. Ricardo Fuentes, former philosophy department chairman at the University of Havana, and bellman for the past twenty years. It was his life sentence of proletarian reeducation for suffering from a lack of revolutionary fervor. Dees grabbed a nearby luggage cart and threw the bags onto it. He looked down at Fuentes, and at the spine that seemed to curve more than he remembered.

"So, Professor, how goes the society of philosopher kings?"

Fuentes's laugh sounded more like a cough. "Actually, it is less Aristotle and more Kant these days. I remember you as a facile young man, so you tell me, what does the *Critique of Pure Reason* have to say?"

Dees struggled to get the cart's worn, uneven wheels up the incline toward the door. "That we only know the world through our senses."

"Correct as far as it goes," Fuentes said. "Our experience allows us to extrapolate from what our senses tell us. And what can we extrapolate from this charade around us?"

Dees pressed a twenty dollar bill into the old man's hand. "My senses tell me you're probably one of the richest men in Havana, what with two decades worth of tips in dollars."

Fuentes slipped the bill easily into his pocket. "Oh, there are probably several hundred men in this city with more money than me, mostly Spanish investors and government officials. But I, on the other hand, must be careful not to show too much prosperity. So I am careful not to gain weight even though I can buy more than enough food, even the occasional black market lobster."

Fuentes took the cart from Dees and began wheeling it through the glass doors into the lobby. "This capitalism is a sweet revenge," he said softly. "My old colleagues at the university go hungry often as not. I have a full stomach every night and a Japanese color TV and toilet paper soft as a kiss. It is no wonder the great Gabriel García Márquez loves Cuba. He does not even have to exaggerate to have the grotesque."

Dees reached out to shake Fuentes's hand. The old man pulled him close and in a raspy whisper said, "*Cuidado.* I hear your arrival has been much anticipated. There is more unrest we hear of in the Central Committee, which is not so new. But there is a great deal of talk on the street now about a crisis between *los duros* and *los suaves*. They jockey for position now that Fidel may be passing."

Dees said, quietly, "What's it mean for you?"

"For me, not much. I have dollars, far more dollars than even you suspect. But this latest raid along the coast, and the involvement of the legendary Vargas, and maybe the end of Fidel? This has raised the temperature. And who can tell if civil war will erupt if *el jefe* does die? Both sides have been smacking their lips over your arrival. You are the propaganda for one side, maybe both."

"Or neither," Dees said flatly.

Fuentes hacked out a laugh again. "As you say, but I now see you have some guests that I suspect you will have to talk to."

Dees turned and saw Gloria, with Gato fidgeting by her side, talking to two men. Both wore short-sleeved white guayaberas, and both had almost identical gray and white beards that extended three inches beyond their chins. Dees turned back, but Fuentes had disappeared into the maelstrom of people at the reception desk.

As Dees walked over, Gloria made no attempt at introductions. All of them squeezed silently into an elevator, built for self-service but attended by a bored female operator who guarded the buttons. She punched the sixth floor button, and they slid upward.

The elevator stopped with a shudder. Gloria strode down the hall, opened a room door with a key, and walked in. The two strangers squeezed in behind her, pungent with sweat and traces of cigar smoke. Since a thick Cuban accent is to Spanish what a Highland brogue is to English, Dees had to strain to understand what one of the fraternal twins was mumbling to Gloria.

"He wishes to know," she said, "what you—"

"Are doing here," Dees said. "I picked up that much."

Dees cleared his throat and spoke in Spanish to the nearest beard. *"Lo siento, mi español es muy malo."* That got their attention, and Dees forged ahead in Spanish. "But if you will forgive my grammar, we can speak directly. I am here as a journalist to investigate Cuba's version of this recent attack."

Before the first man could speak, the second waved his hands across his chest. Through his beard he snorted, "No, no, no!" and began speaking to Gloria in guttural colloquial Cuban that left Dees mystified.

She looked confused, and said, *"No comprendo."*

The first man ran his fingers from his mouth to the tip of his beard in exasperation, and chimed in, speaking even faster than his colleague. Gloria turned to look at Dees and nodded. "Okay. He wants to know your real reason for coming, and what sort of spying you will be doing for your friends, the bandits, and how you propose to spy to find out about the murder of your friend, the American Federal agent."

Well, Dees thought. Well, well.

* * *

Manuel Cabrera was wearing a tropical version of an English hunter's outfit, lightweight twill pants stuffed into thick-soled, knee-high leather boots, topped with a pressed, short-sleeved khaki shirt. A Glock rested in a hand-tooled shoulder holster. He got out of what appeared to be a small mover's van and stood at the rear, arms folded, as Joseph unclamped the latch and raised the segmented rear door with a clatter.

The five men inside blinked in the harsh daylight. Joseph motioned with a huge arm. "Okay, okay, out here now. Smartly!"

They climbed out, rubbing their arms and legs, trying to get the circulation moving again after a two-hour ride. To their right, a small shack with an attached screened patio sat a few dozen feet from a large cinder-block building. A light breeze tugged halfheartedly at a flagpole and the Cuban flag fastened to the top before giving up. Joseph walked away.

Cabrera walked in front of the men. The oldest, he guessed, was twenty-five. All Jamaican, all well-muscled. Cabrera nodded. "As I told you, I selected you five because you are my hardest workers. Out there—" He gestured at the sawgrass and scrub that stretched behind him. "—out there, someplace, is the foundation of an old house. I need you to find it because of some, um, title difficulties I have with this land. I need to know exactly where it is. The first one to find it, also as I mentioned, gets one thousand dollars, cash."

The five black men looked at one another. One wet his lips with his tongue. Cabrera turned and motioned with his arm at ten Hispanic men, all dressed in green camouflage, standing next to the shack. "My staff here has been too incompetent to find the remains of the old building. Some of them know of my thousand dollar offer to you, and may try to find the remains first. If you see any of them out in the field with you, you are to yell as loud as you can. I will make sure only one of you receives the money. Joseph."

Joseph walked back from the general direction of the cinder-block building, holding the handles of three machetes in one fist, two in the other. Without a word, he handed each man one of the blades. Another breeze failed to move a hair on Cabrera's head.

"Take these," he said, "to cut through the grass. Remember, a thousand dollars. Go now."

The men looked at one another again, then walked, bunched together, toward the flat greenery that stretched to the horizon. "Spread out," Cabrera shouted after them. "You cannot all share the money. It goes to one man only."

Two of the men began running toward the scrub. After a brief pause, the other three followed, fanning out. Cabrera walked to the men beside the shack. *"Cinco minutos,"* he said, continuing in Spanish, "and after that, you can follow. They are armed, and they have been warned to watch for you. It is broad daylight and these are young men in excellent physical condition. If you can do your job in conditions like these, night activity in *la patria* once we finally arrive should be no problem. But I will kill any man who fires an unsilenced weapon. *Sigilosamente y silencio, eh?*"

Cabrera turned to Joseph, who stood beside the truck, and said, "So tell me, why did you select these five men? You know what is going to happen."

Joseph stared into the distance, watching five shirts slowly disappear toward the white hot horizon. "The two tall ones, they disrespected one of my uncles, called him an old man. The other three, just part of the posse they hang with. I don't like any of them."

Cabrera nodded toward the shack. The ten men disappeared within seconds. He looked back at Joseph. "Dislike is as good a reason as any."

A soft beep came from inside Cabrera's right front pocket. He pulled out a tiny wireless telephone. "Yes, *dígame.*"

He stared at the ground as he listened. Joseph saw movement in the tall grass maybe two hundred yards away. A machete flew briefly into the air. Joseph smiled thinly as Cabrera said, "No . . . I said no. He already has ten thousand of our money. . . . What?"

He cupped one hand over an ear, still looking at the ground. In the distance, Joseph saw one of the black men begin hacking wildly at the tall grass around him before he suddenly disappeared, both hands flying in the air. A sound like a soft handclap reached Joseph's ears. Cabrera seemed not to notice.

"Only, and I mean *only,* if he agrees to take a seat on the Foreign Relations Committee, where he can do us good. . . . What? . . . No, we can arrange it. Tell him that, and tell him this thirty thousand is all we can afford this time. We have other campaigns to fund, not just his. What else?"

As he nodded at the ground, Joseph held a massive hand across his brow and watched as another man's head flew backward and his feet jerked off the ground, disappearing in the sawgrass. Another soft handclap, this one fainter than the first, then silence.

"Umm, all right, tell them we offer three-fifty for their entire plant. . . . Yes, I know. But they either take our offer or face receivership. Tell them I am willing to cut my prices so much that they will be begging me to buy them out in two weeks for a fifth of that price. *Luego*."

He clicked the phone off in time to look up and see the fourth man jumped from behind, bent backward, and killed with one quick movement of a knife across the throat.

"Damn," Cabrera said. "The one that's left, he will see them if they jump from the grass like that."

He'd barely finished speaking when the remaining man began to scream. "Good heavens," said Cabrera, walking double-time into the sawgrass. Joseph stayed put.

As Cabrera tromped through the grass, the Jamaican saw him, and screamed again. "Mister Cabrera! That man, he killed Justin! Shit! Mister Cabrera!"

He began to run wildly toward Cabrera. Suddenly, one of the camouflaged figures popped up from the grass in front of him. The Jamaican screamed again, and swung the machete at the camouflaged man. The man howled as he quickly turned away, spreading a spray of pink and red from between his fingers. The Jamaican screamed once more, raising the machete.

Cabrera broke into a trot, unsnapping the Glock as he moved. He raised the pistol and fired, a surprisingly thin, sharp sound. The Jamaican's right knee exploded.

In three steps, Cabrera was standing over the cowering Jamaican, who held his hands over what remained of his right leg. Cabrera snapped his fingers, and one of the camouflaged men handed him a pistol with a silencer attached. Cabrera fired three handclaps into the prone man's head. He took two more steps to where the other man lay, groaning, covering his slashed face with his hands. The nine other men in camouflage formed a semicircle.

Cabrera looked around at all of them. "He shouted. We are agreed?"

Nine heads bobbed. "And if one of us shouts inside Cuba, no matter what, all of Brigade X's men could die, we are also agreed?"

Again, nine quick nods. Cabrera aimed the pistol, quietly said, "Go with the angels," and fired.

He looked around. "His family?"

One of the other men cleared his throat. "A single man. A mother and sister."

Cabrera shook his head. "Pity. They receive fifty thousand dollars each, cash. He died in a robbery. Place the body in some nigger neighborhood, no ID."

Cabrera walked back to the truck. Joseph was in the cab, listening to the radio. A lilting flute solo filled the truck as Cabrera got in and closed the door. He looked at the radio, then at Joseph, who said, "Soft jazz. Soothes the nerves. Lotsa noise out there."

Cabrera sighed. "Too much. I am afraid we will need to find five more young men you do not like."

Joseph nodded and started the truck. Cabrera pulled the wireless phone from his pocket and punched in a number. "It is I. Please call INS. Tell them five of our Jamaicans have run away and we have no idea where they have gone. Fill out all the proper paperwork, please. By the book."

Joseph turned up the air conditioner. It whistled softly as the truck headed north.

* * *

"*Espía*," said the first beard over his shoulder.

"*Espía*," The second beard nodded in agreement.

The door rattled and clicked shut behind them. Gloria leaned her back against the door and breathed deeply. "They really truly believe you are a spy. So who are you anyway, *chico*?"

"More to the point, who are they?" Dees asked as he lifted his duffel bags onto the small bed. He piled polo shirts, khakis, sport coat, deck shoes, socks, and underwear onto one side of the bed. On the other side, he arranged six cans of shaving cream, six packs of disposable razors, twelve bars of scented soap, and assorted tubes, boxes, and cartons containing everything from sanitary napkins to toothpaste. From the very bottom of one of the duffels, he pulled three packs, four rolls each, of premium, ultrasoft toilet paper.

"Coño," the cameraman whispered. "I've been wiping my ass with old copies of *Granma* because it's softer than the toilet paper."

Dees tossed a four-pack into Gato's lap. "Here, I don't need a cameraman with a chapped butt. And like I was asking, who were they?"

Gloria stopped staring at the toiletries on the bed and walked to the window. "They are assistant secretaries for ideology in the Central Committee. They have been with Fidel since the attack on the Moncada Barracks in 1953, which is why their breed is called *los históricos*. They have what you might say is a very strict idea of Marxism."

"Crazy fucks," Gato chirped, still squeezing his gift. "They think it's still 1962 and Fidel's staring down John Kennedy and fighting off *los gusanos* at the Bay of Pigs."

Gloria stared out the window, brushing a fly away from her face with a surprisingly delicate wave of her index finger. "My father was like them, in the old days. You know he fought at the Bay of Pigs? He was the one who captured the great Ramon Vargas."

Dees cocked his head. She continued, "My father, Fidel, Vargas, all were at the university at the same time. My father once told me it was the biggest surprise of his life to capture his old classmate on the beach."

Dees stopped sorting the piles of gifts onto the shelves over the bed. "How did they know about the dead Federal agent in Miami?"

"I have no idea. They only told me they suspect you because you were on the raid and therefore you must be a spy and anything you do will be counterrevolutionary. They did not explain the source of their information."

Dees stuffed a plastic laundry bag with toothpaste, tooth-brushes, toilet paper, shaving cream, deodorant, razors, and feminine hygiene supplies. "Let's get started to Varadero. Here."

Gloria stared at the bag, then looked at Dees coldly. "I do not want a *bolsa* of patronizing gifts from the great *gringos* like I am some sort of Tiano and you are a *conquistador.*"

Dees put the bag on the bed and shrugged. "Suit yourself, but I'm not going to use them, and somehow I don't think a gift of Colgate and Charmin to a professional colleague is going to convince Fidel to give me the keys to his office, assuming he lives that long."

Gato snickered. Dees motioned for everybody to leave. As Gloria brushed by him, she took the sack. Her eyes met his. "Thank you," she said.

They rode the elevator to the lobby. As the doors opened, Dees said, "Let's take the inland roads to Varadero so we can get B-roll of someplace besides Havana. We hit Varadero, then we go to the Tropicana tonight on my dime."

Gato looked delighted. It was Gloria's turn to nod, with the hint of a smile. With the same walk she'd used at the airport, she cut through the crowd at the reception desk and talked briefly to a clerk, who nodded attentively.

"Reservations made," she said simply, walking past Dees and toward the car.

He climbed in the backseat and fell asleep, shielding his eyes from the mid-afternoon sun. An hour later, the car hit a pothole, shaking Dees awake. He sat up, rubbing his eyes, and saw cane and banana plants stretching to the horizon to his right and climbing the sides of the coastal hills to his left.

"Madruga," Gato said over his shoulder. "Nice town, and we can shoot some B-roll wallpaper here."

Faded pastel buildings lined the highway where packed dirt lanes intersected with the pavement. Facing the side streets were tightly packed clapboard houses, some wood brown, some lightly washed with sun-bleached tropical colors. Two scruffy yellow dogs stuck their noses through a collapsing wooden fence to watch the car roll to a stop.

The only other vehicle in any direction was a two-toned Lada police car parked in front of the office for the Committee for the Defense of the Revolution. Every small town and big city neighborhood had its own CDR. Members ranged from police and interior department officials to the town busybody and the neighborhood gossip, which came in handy, since innuendo fueled the CDR as much as official police reports. Counterrevolutionary activity was a charge that covered everything from dissident pamphleteering and black marketeering to suspicious prosperity.

Gloria got out and walked down the cracked sidewalk to talk to the CDR officials, while Gato got his camera and tripod from the trunk. "My old man came from a town like this," he said, adjusting the camera. "Palmira, over in Cienfuegos. Told me under Batista, kids died from TB, rickets, that sort of shit. In comes Fidel, *ba-bing*, you got doctors and clinics and teachers in every bullshit town. And the *campesinos*, like my old man, stayed put in the villages after the revolution, didn't come running to the city for a better life. So you didn't get slums popping up overnight. Ah, beauty, nice shot."

Gato shot pans, zooms, and static shots of everything from a young girl crossing the highway to building facades. Gloria emerged from the CDR office, two middle-age men and an older woman in her wake. One of the men, wearing olive-drab military fatigues, pumped Dees's hand. The other, in an off-white guayabera, smiled and nodded. The woman, white-haired and bony, waved an index finger in the air, speaking rapidly.

"I picked up *'defendemos la revolución'* and that's about it," Dees said, shooing everyone away from Gato so his shots wouldn't have excited chatter for a soundtrack.

Gloria crossed her arms, smiled, and said, "They want you

to know they have no bad feelings for Americans. They just want to defend the gains of the revolution."

"Anybody willing to go on camera?"

After rapid-fire arm-waving negotiations, the woman was selected. Her name was Victoria Soto, she said, she was sixty, she had lived here all her life, and—

"Alto, por favor, habla despacio," Dees said, laughing. He continued in halting Spanish, "Wait for the camera. And tell the truth. I have trouble believing a young woman who claims she is sixty."

She blushed as she absently brushed a hair away from her tanned face. Gato framed the shot and handed Dees the microphone. Slowly, in Spanish, Dees asked, "What do you mean when you say you are defending the revolution? From who?"

"From those who would take away the gains of the revolution," she said firmly. "Here, look, see?"

She shyly pulled up her loose frock to reveal a line of scar tissue and rock-hard pale purple flesh that ran from just below her right knee to just short of her ankle. "Gangrene," she said. "I was a teenager when my leg was cut deeply by a machete as we harvested cane. We were poor and had no way to get to Havana and there were no doctors or nurses around here. My father told me—" She made a hacking motion with her flat palm. "—he thought about cutting it off to save my life."

Dees said, *"Y después?* After Fidel, what?"

She lowered her dress. "I am scarred and I walk with a limp because there were no doctors. I stopped attending school when I was twelve, for why did a girl need to know mathematics or literature? I went back to school when I was twenty, thanks to the revolution, and I became a teacher, thanks to the revolution. If the *mafiosi* and the criminals return after Fidel, why then we become like Russia. No more free schools, no more free medicine, no more clothing for the people, just the criminals and the capitalists, just like Batista when I was a child."

Dees said, "And what if someone disagrees with you? What if someone says Fidel and socialism must go away?" Gloria shot him a sharp look, and Dees pretended not to notice.

The older woman frowned. "Then they are counter-revolutionaries and must be dealt with. We must try to convince them they are wrong to oppose the people."

"But what about their freedom to speak?"

"It is nothing compared with the freedom of eight million Cubans to exist."

Another five minutes of conversation was along the same lines, so Dees said good-bye, with *abrazos* and handshakes all around. As they drove away, Gloria turned toward Dees in the backseat. "Was it really necessary to ask her that?"

Dees looked out the window. "The only stupid question's the one you don't ask. Yes."

They rose in silence through Matanzas and up the narrow highway toward Varadero, a peninsula that stuck into the Florida Straits like a crooked finger, beckoning vacationers to use its strip of European- and Canadian-built hotels.

Gato dutifully videotaped the blast marks spread in a five-foot star pattern at the base of the Playa Cubana Hotel. Dees interviewed the Spanish general manager, who said in impeccable English that it was an outrage that such an attack could be staged from American soil against a hotel partly owned by a Spanish corporation and filled with Canadian tourists. After all, he asked, are not Spain, Canada, and America supposed to be allies?

He tried to deflect further probing about ownership from Dees but finally said yes, under the Cuban Joint Ventures Act, the hotel was fifty-one percent owned by the Cuban government, which received fifty-one percent of the profits while all the operating expenses were borne by the Spanish.

More interviews with hotel employees who witnessed the

explosion, plus some shots of pale Canadians frolicking in the ocean, added up to a full day as far as Dees was concerned. As they drove down the peninsula back toward Havana, a wave crashed against the rocks, tossing spray that refracted light from the setting sun into a misty rainbow that momentarily surrounded the car.

Two hours later, at five minutes after eight, Dees sauntered out of the elevator at the hotel and found Gato in the lobby, wearing a clean shirt with a small tear in the right armpit. He stood beside Gloria, who was wearing a loose white cotton dress slightly shorter than the one she had worn in the afternoon.

"So," she said, "you are late, and another polo shirt and khaki pants? *Mala moda, chico.*"

"I figured if there was anyplace I could arrive on Cuban time, it'd be Cuba, and I try not to be a slave to fashion." He noticed that her fingernails were clean.

Twenty minutes later, the car rattled to a stop in front of the Tropicana. Once a playground for mobsters and oligarchs, it was now a tacky parody of its former self. Hemingway, Batista, Barrymore, Lansky, Joan Crawford and Desi Arnaz, Clark Gable and Jean Harlow, had once stuffed themselves into tuxedos and cocktail dresses and sipped *mojitos* under the giant banyans that framed the outdoor stage. Now, sunburned tourists and bored diplomats dressed in everything from guayaberas to beach sarongs jammed the tables to see the floor show and drink watered-down cocktails, each costing as much as the weekly food allotment for the average Cuban adult.

The tuxedoed *maitre'd*—Christ, Dees thought, a pencil-thin mustache—spread his arms. "Ah, *Señorita* Bravo. We have a wonderful table for the three of you, no sharing with tourists."

Gato and Dees looked at each other. The banyan canopy ruffled slightly in the breeze as they were ushered to a table next to the stage. Dees looked up, and could see the Little

Dipper through the branches. They had just taken their seats when a waiter sidled up and deposited six *mojitos* on the table. Gato greedily grabbed one and gulped down the mixture of club soda, rum, sugar, and bruised mint. "*Coño*, these actually have booze in them."

As Gato swallowed the second drink, Gloria made a brief gesture with the index and middle fingers of her right hand. Two minutes later, four more drinks arrived, two each for the cameraman and Dees. He glanced at Gloria, who said, "They know me here."

Dees put down his glass. "Is all this because you're who you are or because you're your father's daughter? The connections everywhere, I mean."

She looked at him from the corner of her eye. "I am perfectly capable of achieving things without the memory of my father, thank you."

The rum and humidity sent small drops of sweat trickling down his back. He studied the twenty-foot-tall diving platform on one corner of the stage. She cracked a thin smile. "Why do men sweat so much when they drink? And then they think they are charming and want to tell you their life stories?"

"I'm more interested in yours," he said. "The Radio Havana part I've figured out. A lot of other government-run radio and TV does the same thing, using government officials on the air, I mean. But what do you do at Minrex?"

She paused. "Assistant secretary for political affairs, Department of the United States and Canada."

Dees leaned back in his chair. "They don't give that to newcomers. Where were you before?"

"Our embassies in Argentina and Mexico," she said offhandedly, "and a few months at our mission at the United Nations in New York."

Dees furrowed his brow. "You know many people at your U.N. mission?"

"Maybe a few still, but that was four years ago. Why?"

"Because the great Ramon Vargas was trying to sell himself to your mission as a spy. And your DGI claims he actually *was* a Cuban government double agent."

He tried to gauge her reaction. There was none, except for beads of sweat forming on her upper lip. He continued, "You ever hear of Manuel Cabrera?"

She wrinkled her nose. "*El gusano grande?* Who does not know that one? He owns half the sugarcane in Florida and controls seventeen percent of the world market, which would be closer to thirty percent if he and the bandits return and he takes over our sugar industry, which is what he wants. But back to Vargas, why would he be talking to our United Nations representatives?"

Might as well toss a grenade into the septic tank, Dees thought, and see what sticks to the walls. "Your U.N. mission, like I said, claims Vargas is a spy for your government. Cabrera says the same thing. So does the DGI. Vargas claims he was offering himself as a spy, but was actually spying on the Cuban government for the exiles. It was all Cabrera's idea, he claims."

She opened her mouth to speak when a brassy blare of trumpets blowing a conga chart announced the master of ceremonies, a square-jawed man in a white dinner jacket.

His microphone popped and rumbled as he announced, "*Bienvenidos a La Tropicana damas y caballeros, mesdames et messieurs, herren und damen,* ladies and gentlemen!"

As he paused for breath, Gloria leaned close to Dees's ear. "We will talk more after the show."

A line of taut dancers in animal print bikinis paraded onto the stage, followed by a line of conga drummers in loincloths. It was part Vegas, part modern dance, part allegory about a female slave's struggle against the Spaniards. It ended with the heroine executing a soaring swan dive from the top of the diving tower into the arms of two male dancers. Only their arms were between her body and the stage floor.

Next came a line of leggy chorus girls in sequined G-strings, each wearing a small chandelier as a headdress. A dozen or so tiny lightbulbs in each chandelier glowed, powered by frayed extension cords that trailed for yards behind each woman. They seemed to be able to avoid tripping over the cords without looking down, despite three-inch heels and stage smoke from a snarling dry ice generator.

After over an hour of dancers, musicians, jugglers, acrobats, and chorines, the chorus line began to mambo, inviting the audience to join them. *"Oye, mami! Socialismo o muerte!"* Gato shouted as he scrambled up the stage steps unsteadily and began to gyrate, a black dancer in front, a blonde behind.

Wiggling between them, he looked down at Dees and shouted, *"Oye, gringo!* How's this for a Cuban sandwich?"

Dees smiled. Gloria leaned close again and said, "We need to talk, and this is not the place. Juan will be just fine without us."

She motioned to a waiter, whispered to him briefly, and got up, walking purposefully toward the entrance. Dees caught up with her, and found her at the DeSoto with a Tropicana employee behind the wheel. She sat next to the driver. As Dees got in the backseat, she said, "He will return to the club to get Juan home safely. Be sure you tip him."

After a few minutes, the car entered the Havana Libre driveway. As Dees dug in his pocket and handed the driver an American twenty, Gloria hopped out of the car and went into the hotel. The driver grinned, winked, and drove into the darkness.

She was waiting by the elevator, and they rode in silence to his floor. She walked inside the room, sat at a chair by the window, pulled back the curtain and opened the rusting frame, and said, "I need a cigarette."

"Sorry, I only have cigars."

She shrugged. "As you might say, what the hell."

Dees clipped the end from a Churchill and held his lighter

while she puffed the oversized cigar to life, holding it between her thumb and the middle and index fingers.

She tried to blow a smoke ring as Dees lit his own cigar. She studied the ragged plume of smoke and said, "You say my government claims this Vargas is actually a spy who works for Cuba. How could this be? What sort of spy attacks the country he works for, and why is this any of your business?"

Dees blew a jet of smoke in the general direction of the Morro fort that towered above Havana harbor. "It's my business because any information I get may tell me why people keep getting killed." He leaned forward. "The FBI agent who was killed was shot—"

"By one of the exiles," Gloria interrupted.

Dees locked his green eyes on her face. "Let me finish. The FBI agent was shot by the exile, but probably not fatally. What killed him was a shot in the head from behind, some sniper someplace. I need to know if your government knows anything at all about who may have shot him and why."

He paused to let the words sink in. She started to speak, but he held up his hand. "There's more, then we talk. So my friend was shot down from behind. Number two, the great Ramon Vargas is dead."

She gasped, and opened her mouth. Dees said, "Again, just let me finish. Vargas was in an American Federal prison in downtown Miami. Someone disguised themselves as an FBI agent and took Vargas away and then killed him. One, who killed the FBI agent? Two, who killed Vargas? Three, was Vargas a Cuban agent? Those are the questions."

"*Tres preguntas difíciles,*" she said quietly. "And you would do what with all this information, tell your Federal law enforcement friends?"

Dees half yawned. "I'm just after the truth. If the Cubans help find the shooter, then Cuba looks good. Just the truth, that's all."

Dees twisted the top from a small plastic water bottle and

offered it to her. As he opened one for himself, she said, "You have something in your medical kit for *la mala*? My stomach. The cigars, maybe."

Dees nodded and walked into the bathroom, which actually seemed to have been retiled sometime in the past decade. The powdered barbiturate she put into his water bottle dissolved almost instantly. Dees came out and handed her a tiny bottle of Pepto-Bismol. "Here. Drink it all and you should be fine."

She took the small bottle and drained it, then took a sip of water. Dees upended his water bottle. Bubbles gurgled inside. Gloria smiled and glanced out the window. "You should be very thirsty after a day and night like this."

"You bet," he said. He sat the bottle on the floor and blinked his eyes. "Tired, too. Maybe some fresh air over there by the win—"

He started to stand, then stumbled, knocking the plastic bottle over. He sat heavily on the bed, smiling a dopey smile. "Whoo, guess the *mojitos* were pretty stiff. Don't wanna be rude, but I'm passing out, so see you later, I guess."

She nodded, and said, *"Buenos sueños."* He was snoring in seconds, lying on his back, his right arm tossed limply across his face. Silently, she rummaged through his duffel bag, probing with her hands. Dees kept snoring as she withdrew her hand and got up, quietly latching the door behind her.

In the lobby, a whispered conversation with the night manager produced a telephone. Ten minutes later, a Lada sedan and a driver were idling out front. She got in and in fifteen minutes was in front of an anonymous gray ten-story concrete building on the edge of downtown, built with Soviet rubles and workmen twenty-five years before.

She used her key to open one of three glass doors, and nodded at the sleepy-eyed soldiers on duty. She walked up a set of stairs to her right. On the second floor, she emerged into a cavernous hallway. To the right were Information Ministry offices, including Radio Havana. To the left were suites occupied by a DGI counterintelligence section disguised as a trade analysis office, the Interior Ministry, and Minrex's Department of the United States and Canada. She turned left.

CHAPTER 10

"Tell you what," Gato said, wolfing down his second plate of beans, eggs, and chorizo in the hotel dining room, "that Bravo chick, man is she connected. She got somebody to drive me home last night 'cause I was too fucked up to see. Hey, pass the bread."

Dees felt surprisingly alert, despite the hangover. "Yeah, well-connected. Do you ever eat at home?"

"Not much. See, I got dollars but I'm also a Cuban, which means not a lot of choices and not a lot of food, but you come here, you crazy *yanqui*, and I can eat like a tourist. *Oye señor, más café por favor.*"

Dees watched Gato sop the last traces of food from the plate. "What d'you know about her?"

Gato shrugged. "Not much except she's connected. She's a propaganda specialist is my guess, and everybody knows her old man."

"Just pretend I'm not everybody."

Gato sighed contentedly and lit a cigarette as he savored his coffee. "I turned forty-two last year. When I was an eighteen-year-old dickhead full of revolutionary fervor I got drafted and shipped to fucking Angola. So I'm dropped in, and Cubans and Ethiopians, East Germans, Russians, and Hungarians are all fighting Jonas Savimbi's UNITA troops and the South African army. They're paid for by your Uncle Sam, and they want to destroy Angola's economy by blowing up the oil refineries.

"The refineries are operated by Texaco and Shell, so there we were, the big bad fucking Red menace protecting capitalist oil refineries against attacks from the South Africans who were paid for by Washington. Go figure." Gato hungrily eyed the leftovers of Dees's fruit plate. Dees pushed the plate toward him.

"Ah, *muchísimas gracias*, capitalist pig. So there were three big heroes in Angola. First the top man, General Arnaldo Ochoa. Guy's in charge of fifty thousand troops and he takes mess with the men and leads them personally in attacks, out front on the point. Shit, *qué hombre*.

"Then there's Major Orestes Diaz. Blew a half-dozen South African planes out of the sky. And then there's our girl's *papi*, General Guillermo Bravo, outflanked some South African general named van der Kock or some shit like that and captured the general and his whole staff and a dozen tanks."

Dees sipped his *café con leche*. "Some heroes. Fidel executed Ochoa. And Major Diaz defected. So you've got one hero who flew a jet to Florida and another hero who earned a firing squad when he got back. One defector, one dead."

Gato stubbed out the cigarette and held up two fingers. "Two dead. Ochoa was executed by Fidel. And Bravo died last year in a car crash, which may have been just as well since he was real close to Ochoa."

Dees nodded as Gato popped a gooey slice of papaya into his mouth. If you believed Fidel, General Ochoa, the hero of Angola, came home besotted with drug-smuggling profits from the war zone. Castro claimed Ochoa continued his trafficking in Cuba, so the general was tried, convicted, and shot. If you believed the men who had served under him in Angola, Ochoa came home to Cuba with a base of loyal support that threatened *el jefe*. In either case, Ochoa had been executed.

Dees looked at Gato. "So Gloria's old man died in a car crash, huh?"

Gato rolled his eyes. "Yeah, but who knows? When we're lucky enough to have cars and gasoline, we drive like ass-holes, so maybe. Then again, a lot of people close to Ochoa ended up demoted, or dead, so *quién sabe?"*

A waiter limped from the kitchen toward a table full of Spanish tourists. He saw Gato, smiled, and nodded. Gato waved.

"See that one? Angola vet. So are the cab drivers, construction workers, the guys hanging out on the street corners, and about half the people on the army's general staff. There was a time when they were fighting for their lives, and Ochoa was there with them, always. Some are fried from combat, some are wounded, some get AIDS from the Angolan girls. They fight for the glory of international socialism and come home and find their families are fucking starving, and then General Ochoa, their hero, he's lined up and shot."

Gato finished the last melon ball on the plate. "They remember, *primo*, and they're not too happy with Fidel. Me, I think this Bravo chick remembers, too."

"So what d'you think happens next?" Dees asked. "Who wins, the hards or the softs? What happens when Fidel—"

"Shhh," Gato said, looking around. "You know what you mean and so do I and so do the fucking microphones in your breakfast plate. Don't talk about it in public. It makes me nervous. I am just a simple man," Gato said ironically. He looked at his cigarette. "Political opinions are as unhealthy as these things."

He leaned across the table and whispered, "Me, I think the fix is in. Castro dies, okay? And the mob comes back and this place turns into Vegas. Hell, we already got *putas* back walking the streets. Or maybe the people will get fed up with no food and no shoes and they'll go nuts in the streets, which means the army vets and general staff from the Angola days take over and we get a slow, easy transition to the mob.

"Or maybe Fidel dies and his *maricón* brother Raul takes

over. People will get fed up, and Raul will fall, and the mob still comes back. Man, you *gringos* and the Cubans in Miami get their claws back in and you watch how fast we get roulette and Big Macs and drug smuggling. Some company takes over sugarcane, another takes over telephones, another gets the medicine and hospitals, so pretty soon we got prosperity and capitalism and you'll die if you get sick without insurance."

Dees watched Gato slurp his coffee, and said finally, "Do you hate this country or love it?"

Gato put the cup down with a clatter. "Come on, let me show you something. We got almost an hour before she's supposed to meet us."

Gato and Dees got up and walked through the lobby, into the bright sun. They double-timed south along Calle L, eventually coming to a sharp curve in the street across from the University of Havana's library steps. The seated statue of the Alma Mater stared flatly at the rows of pockmarked apartment buildings rolling down a hillside to the backside of the harbor. Gato motioned Dees toward a row of crumbling gray three-story apartment buildings that faced the university.

"Top floor," Gato said over his shoulder, "if the stair doesn't collapse with us. Watch your head."

Dees ducked his head under the patched plaster ceiling and followed Gato up the creaking wooden steps, worn smooth by five generations of shoes, boots, sandals, and bare feet. On the top floor, custard-colored light filtered through a pair of dirty windows. Gato rapped with his knuckles on the left side door on the top landing.

The door cracked open, and a short man with pockmarked skin stared out suspiciously, his tongue flicking across his lips like a lizard. Gato smiled insincerely and pressed his palm against the door, forcing it open. The man with the lizard tongue made a halfhearted effort to keep it shut, stepped back, and stared sourly at Gato, then at Dees.

"*Buenas,* Lázaro," Gato said in Spanish. "The captain here?"

The man nodded toward a dark hallway that ran the length of the airless, narrow apartment. "*El loco* is down in his room, as always."

In a smooth motion, Gato put his hand around the smaller man's throat and shoved him into the rotting French doors that opened onto a narrow cement ledge that might have been called a balcony by someone with a taste for hyperbole. The lizard tongue flicked again as Gato squeezed harder, smiling his insincere smile. "You can call him the captain, you can call him *Señor* Gato, or you can even call him Rafael if he gives you permission. But I swear you ever call him *el loco* again and I will cut you into tiny pieces, *comprende?*"

Lázaro bounced his head up and down quickly. Gato released his grip and motioned for Dees to follow him down the hall. The second door to the right was open. The walls were a gray-green with large splotches of pale white plaster smeared across badly patched cracks. Pulsing light came from a table lamp that hummed and crackled in a corner. The only color in the room was spread across the wall to Dees's left. A series of tourist posters had been taped together to form an uneven mosaic of blue sky, turquoise water, green palms, and a leering waiter serving a magenta drink to a dark-haired beauty with perfect teeth who smiled uncertainly at the camera. The tattered cover on the small cot was tucked in perfectly, military style, at the corners.

A man with thinning, neatly trimmed white hair sat erect on a corner of the cot.

He wore laundered and pressed khaki slacks and a short-sleeved yellow shirt that looked as if it had been starched. He wore a black patch over his right eye. A rectangular hole had been cleanly cut in the wall behind the cot, and what looked like a relatively new 5,000 BTU air conditioner hummed quietly, connected to an electric outlet screwed to the wall.

Dees's eyes followed the galvanized metal tube that held the electric cable. It ran outside the door. Gato followed Dees's gaze, and smiled. "It was a matter of splicing into the main power feed for the building. You have any idea how hard it was for me to scrounge the tubing and the cable? Don't even talk to me about the air conditioner and the bribes to inspectors to ignore our power source."

Gato became grave and snapped a salute at the figure. *"Capitán, éste es un amigo mío, un gran amigo del pueblo cubano."*

The figure turned his head without moving his body. His eye seemed to shine for a moment as he nodded and smiled. The smile faded, and he returned the salute. *"Soy Capitán Rafael Gato de los Fuerzes Armadas Revolucionarias.* You cannot make me say anything to betray my country. *Patria o muerte!"*

He dropped the salute and returned his placid gaze to the posters. His hands were palms down on his thighs. Gato nudged Dees. "Look at his left hand."

Dees saw the thumb was missing. The other fingers were missing from the first joint, leaving four cauterized stumps. Dees looked back at Gato. "What happened?"

Gato didn't speak but walked to the figure on the bed, gently stroked his hair, bent over, and whispered something in his ear. The man nodded, once, never taking his eye off of the Kodachrome beach five feet away. Gato motioned for Dees to follow him as he walked through the front room, glared at the man who had opened the door, and stomped down the claustrophobic staircase without a word.

Outside the front door, he stood squinting in the sunlight, staring a moment at the Alma Mater. He wiped the back of his neck with his hand and turned to Dees. "You want to know if I love or hate this place? That's why I hate it. My brother— that's my brother—he commanded a . . . what'd you call it, counterinsurgency? *Sí,* counterinsurgency, a company in Angola. Savimbi's troops captured him and sliced his hand up, but he didn't say shit and he escaped and walked a week through the bush. General Ochoa gave him a medal, the Order of some shit or another."

Gato grabbed a loose cigarette from his shirt pocket, jammed it in his mouth, and tried to light it with a match whose flame danced as his hands shook. The tube of tobacco finally glowed. Gato flipped the match into the street with an angry flick of his wrist. "So he's a hero, right? He's a fucking hero of the fucking socialist revolution. And he's a little spooky, okay? He's had his fingers cut off, and he's kept in a cage like a dog for two months, okay? But he never says shit, so he's a little weird after all that, but he can function. So . . ."

Gato took a deep nervous drag on the cigarette and exhaled a billow of smoke. He sniffed. "So he comes home after the war. Guess what, Ochoa's on trial for being a drug trafficker. Now remember, this guy is God to his men, okay? They all figure if there's anybody who can take over after Fidel, it's Ochoa, and Fidel knows it, too. So Ochoa's executed, and everybody who was ever close to him is picked up for suspicion of counterrevolutionary activity."

Dees looked into the distance, then back at Gato. "Including your brother."

Gato nodded sharply, took another drag of the cigarette, and tossed it into the gutter. "Including Rafael. He's picked up at his barracks, fucking disappears, I mean disappears, and I can't find him for a year. A year? No, more like fourteen months, I guess. Then one day I get a notice that Raffie's being released, so I borrow a car and scrounge gasoline and go get him in front of some prison buildings in Camaguey."

Gato and Dees walked toward the hotel, silently. Dees finally said, "What happened?"

Gato stopped and faced Dees. "What happened?" he whispered. "What happened was what you saw back there. He gets in an argument with a guard, they tell me, and the guard puts out his eye with a bayonet. That sounded, like you might say, fishy, but hey, what am I gonna do about it, you know? His hair's turned white and now he's a zombie. I barely knew who he was when I picked him up."

A deep sigh seemed to rattle Gato's body. "They tortured him and let him go when they figured they'd made a mistake, so now my big brother the war hero's a piece of meat with air-conditioning and some posters of Varadero to stare at. And me? I love my country so I want to fuck these people that run it. I'd like to hurt them bad."

Suddenly Gato smiled, a vacant, almost cruel smile. He clapped Dees on the shoulder. "But hey, what am I gonna do, you know? I'm just a fucking cameraman. Let's go."

As they approached the hotel, they saw Gloria standing out front, wearing a white blouse and black skirt. She stared at her watch, then at them impatiently. She walked over and said tersely, "Juan, get the car please. We have a number of inter-views arranged. Peter, can we talk, over here?"

She turned and indicated the low wall that circled the hotel. Gato looked at Dees, shook his head, and headed down the block. Dees walked to Gloria, sat on the wall, and patted the cement next to him. "Take a rest."

She sat. He stared for a moment before he said, "No bombs, no pornography, no counterrevolutionary material. I take it everything else in my bags was in order."

She opened her mouth, then closed it. Dees said, flatly, "The angle of incidence equals the angle of reflection. The mirror in the bathroom reflects the mirror next to the bed, which reflects you spiking my drink. So I blow air bubbles into it, you turn away, I knock over the bottle so you don't no-tice I didn't drink. I leveled with you and you just end up pissing me off."

She cocked her half smile. "You know it is my job, and you are, as you say, a big boy. You know how this all works."

The bleating horns, belching buses, clattering bicycles, and shouting pedestrians formed a cocoon of white noise around them. "Listen," she said softly, "I have done what you might call some investigative reporting. Vargas was an agent for my government, spying on the more radical exile factions. He was also, it seems, an agent for your government, doing the same thing. Spying on the exiles, I mean."

He squinted at her through the gray-green bus exhaust. She continued, "You might as well know, *chico,* I have met with Cabrera and Vargas. I was part of the reformer mission to Miami."

Dees made a sound like he was sucking on a toothpick. "Must've been a neat trick getting out of the country, since everybody knows who you are."

"Umm. There are more of us than you know. Friends in television makeup turn me into a gray-haired woman with a missing front tooth, others at the airport make sure all the exit papers were properly stamped, still others in the Customs Service pass the gray-haired grandmother through when she returns two days later."

"My headache's getting worse," Dees said. "Maybe it's the bus exhaust. Maybe it's you going through my bags, and then telling me all this. You could go to jail for this. Or you could wind up like your father."

"You are a reporter," she said, wiping a cinder from her eye, "and we want the world to know that the Communist monolith is a myth, that there are many of us here who want reforms, urgently. But if your embargo stays in effect, the hard-liners will win and this island will dissolve into chaos when Fidel passes. The military is quietly going on alert, just in case, so time may be very short."

Dees looked down Calle L at a rusted, blank movie marquee that hung drunkenly over the street. He said, "Take it from the top."

"Well, then. I traveled to Miami to meet with this Cabrera and the great Vargas. My disguise was good enough so that I am still unknown to the hard-liners. Above suspicion, you might say?"

She sighed. "But my compatriot did not, um, fare so well. He is back here but I know for a fact orders are being processed for his arrest. Nothing has happened yet, though, and I suspect that is because he is paying off some officials. Also perhaps because many of his former students think so kindly of him."

Dees looked at her sharply. "Mind telling me who?"

She laughed. "I believe I just did. There are several things you need to remember. *Primero*, I do not know who killed your friend. *Segundo*, Vargas was a double agent, working for Cuba and the U.S. government. *Tercero*, Cabrera cannot be trusted. *Cuatro*, this Diaz, the defected pilot? He is crazy with hate over Angola and the purge that followed. *Quinto*, we—I mean they, the hard-liners—seem to have another active agent in Miami, and it seems he also works for your government. All I know is he is called *la tortuga*."

"The turtle?"

"The tortoise," she corrected.

"All sorts of people would want Vargas dead," he said. "You, for one, since he double-crossed you. The hard-liners for another, if they found he was working for the U.S. at the same time. The U.S. government, for another, if Vargas was spying for the Cubans. And maybe my friend got in the way? And maybe the bullet he took in the head was actually meant for Vargas?"

She shrugged as Gato pulled the car to the curb. "I have told you all I know," she said, "except that your stay here ends tomorrow. Your Weather Channel says Hurricane David may come through in three, four days. The airport is being closed early just in case."

"Tomorrow? But I have two more—"

"No you do not," she said, motioning for him to get in the car. "Even the search for the truth stops for a hurricane."

Dees looked up. Only high, thin cirrus clouds barely moving from northeast to southwest across the pale blue sky gave any hint there was anything out there east of them.

The wispy clouds continued their lazy paseo the entire day, through six interviews and stops for B-roll. The spokesman for the Interior Ministry said socialism might have surrendered in Europe, but not here, while the Minrex spokesman said Cuba wanted normal relations with everyone, including the United States. The university specialist documented how the U.S. embargo had hurt the average Cuban. The snaggle-toothed woman waving her ration book at a corner store said the sacrifices she made for the revolution were worth the pain. A sour-faced young man nearby opened a paper bag to show his allotment of a torn sack of rice and three dented cans. "There's your revolution," he said as he stalked away from the camera.

All three were sweaty and sunburned as they pulled back to the hotel. It was almost dark. "Maybe we go out again tonight?" Gato asked expectantly. "I mean since you've gotta leave so soon."

Dees shook his head. "Sorry, man. I've got to get these videotapes upstairs and pack and I have to see someone this evening. Next time."

They embraced with three sharp claps on the back. Gloria hugged him and whispered, "*Cuidado, chico*, especially if you are going where I think you are."

"Meet me early tomorrow," he said, "so we can talk before I fly out."

He took a half-dozen videotapes in his arms and walked inside. Once in his room, he packed his clothes and the tapes in one duffel, and filled the other with the remaining toilet articles. He checked his address book for a notation he had written three years before. Half an hour later, after two wrong turns quickly corrected by orienting himself toward the hotel's tower, he arrived at an old wooden house, sagging in the humidity.

A family of five had once occupied its dozen rooms. Now fifteen people, five families more or less, used its kitchen and one bathroom. The gray paint on the rotting stairs had disappeared years before. The white boards that once girded its three stories were faded into a combination of damp pale yellow and soot gray, in the few places where paint remained at all. The rest of the wood was a mottled tobacco color spread like a melanoma around the dirty windows.

To the right of the entrance hallway, Ricardo Fuentes sat in a tattered green stuffed chair next to an end table in the center of what had once been the mansion's sitting room. He was reading by the light of a bare bulb in the lamp beside him, listening to a small cassette tape player fitted with a pair of plastic speakers. Dees furrowed his brow. Ballads. He picked out Gloria Estefan's warbling voice with, yep, Jon Secada singing harmony. Exile music from Miami was illegal in Cuba, regardless of the content.

Dees's shadow, cast by another bare bulb in the hallway, flowed through the open door and across Fuentes's book. The old man looked up, surprised. Dees leaned against the door frame. " 'Evening, Professor. Something you picked up in Miami?"

Fuentes looked cross, put his index finger across his lips, and nodded his head toward the aluminum-legged kitchen chair next to him. As Dees sat, Fuentes said, in a hoarse whisper, "Electronic samizdat. And please be careful about what cities you mention too loudly."

He put the book he had been reading on his lap and spread his arms with a thin smile. "This room comes from veneration of my age, much like tenure. I really should give it to the couple upstairs with two children, but I have a very difficult time with stairs these days. Besides, there is something absurdist about a large room such as this with a fireplace in the tropics that appeals to me."

Dees sat on a duffel on the floor next to the armchair. Fuentes craned his neck to look inside, and saw toilet paper, shaving cream, razors, toothpaste, and deodorant. "Hm," he said, "many thanks. These are things my dollars could buy, but I choose to be, how you might say it? I choose to be low-key about having money. It is healthier for me that way."

Dees looked around the large room, sealed off from what used to be the dining room by a sheet hung from a cord. "Professor, I need—"

"Shhh." Fuentes held up his hand. He glanced toward the wide entranceway from the hall.

"*Señora* Limonta," he said, raising his voice, "you could sit here and join us except that I have not invited you. It must be difficult to listen through the wall, but if you insist, try not to breathe so hard."

Dees heard a sound like a bull snorting before it charged, and looked up in time to see two thick, dark ankles stomp up the stairs. Fuentes smiled thinly. "A true revolutionary, that one. She is afraid that if she fails to protect the gains of the revolution, she might actually have to work for a living someday. She reports me regularly for counterrevolutionary thought, which, one supposes, is better than having no thoughts at all."

Dees heard scattered voices drift in from the street. Sharp-edged shadows from the bare bulb looked as if they had been drawn on the uneven wall with a ruler. In the distance, a clattering bus gunned its engine and slowly faded away.

"These are not the walls of Troy," Fuentes said, looking around the room, "but I feel you are a Greek bearing gifts with some other purpose, hm?"

"Just call me Achilles," Dees said flatly. He leaned closer to Fuentes. "I know you sneaked into Miami with Gloria and talked to Vargas and Cabrera. I know Vargas went to the hard-liners at the Cuban U.N. mission and turned you in. And I suspect you've been bribing your way out of going to jail, but I'm not sure how much longer you can manage it. The hard-liners who showed up at the hotel knew the dead FBI agent was my friend. But the only thing I don't know is the only thing I really give a shit about. Who killed him and why? You have any answers or just more glib chitchat?"

Fuentes made a sucking sound through the gap between his two front teeth. He stared at the chipped tiles on the fireplace, and finally said, "You wish, then, to blackmail me?"

"I wish, then, for the truth," Dees said sharply.

Fuentes nodded absently. "As do we all. My trip to Miami was, it seems, the last gasp of patriotism in a foolish old man. My effort to achieve something by acting as a liaison for reform-minded former colleagues at the university has cost me dearly. As you pointed out, the great Vargas and his millionaire friend betrayed me, and I have been depleting my resources passing about pesos here and dollars there to keep me out of prison. I feel, though, that my money and my luck may run out about the same time."

Fuentes paused, and stared at the fireplace again, as if looking at it hard and long enough could transport him back in time, before the tiles were chipped and neglected, before the great house was subdivided. A deep, rattling sigh became a wheeze, then a series of short, hacking coughs. The old man looked up sheepishly. "Pardon me. It seems even memories are too much for my body to bear. No, my friend, I do not know who killed the American agent in Florida, nor do I know why he died. I am sorry."

Voices from the dark street outside grew louder. Something bounced off the wooden porch with a clatter, followed a second later by the sound of glass shattering just outside the window.

"*Hmpfh,*" Fuentes snorted. "More bottles and rocks. I do believe *Señora* Limonta has arranged for my friends from the Rapid Response Brigades to come calling."

Dees got up, walked through the doorway into the foyer, and stepped to the open door that faced the splintered porch. Fuentes shuffled slowly behind him. In the darkness, Dees could make out a dozen or so figures on the sidewalk, staring at him. They seemed to be mostly young men, with three women in the crowd.

Fuentes brushed past Dees and stepped onto the porch. "For almost fifteen years," Fuentes muttered without looking up at Dees, "these *brigadistas* make the rounds from the CDR offices on even the suspicion of the wrong kinds of ideas. I am sure they do not know of the trip to Miami, or else I would have been injured by now, maybe worse."

He raised his voice. "*Hola, compañeros.* Why are you here again?"

"Fuentes!" one of the men yelled. "Your neighbors must know you are not loyal to the revolution!"

"As you have told them at least once a month, *hermano*," Fuentes shouted back. "Go away now so people who work for their rice can sleep!"

A shower of street debris arced toward them from the street. Dees started to step between Fuentes and the cascade of stones when a small bottle flew from the crowd and hit the old man above his right eye.

He let out a yelp that sounded like a small dog being kicked, and began to fall. Dees grabbed his shoulders and eased him down onto the porch. The clatter of rocks against the wood stopped. Dees put his ear next to Fuentes's mouth, and listened. Satisfied that he was breathing, Dees squinted as he saw a small trickle of blood from just below the eyebrow.

Fuentes opened his eyes and said weakly, "I believe we should go inside now. I have some iodine inside. If we ignore them, they will go away."

"Don't move," Dees said. "Just lie here for a minute."

As Dees stood up he scooped a baseball-sized rock inside his left palm. He kept his arms at his sides as he walked down the steps and covered the five paces between the stairs and the sidewalk. The man who had been yelling smirked, thrusting his arms apart, palms up, and nodding his head in a what-are-you-going-to-do-about-it gesture. Dees stopped two feet from him, smiled, and shrugged his shoulders. The man sneered so that his scraggly mustache turned up at one corner, and had just started to turn to say something to a short black man to his right when Dees delivered an upper-cut into his throat. He made a liquid, choking noise and dropped to his knees.

The short man to Dees's left cocked his fist back just as Dees swung the palm holding the rock in a roundhouse blow and drove the jagged stone into his right ear.

The black man staggered to the left, clawing at the ear, dark blood oozing between his fingers as he howled. Dees felt a searing pain in his left hip and cocked his head in time to see a woman in a dirty white T-shirt finish her follow-through with a baseball bat.

He staggered to his right, dropped the rock, and managed to clutch her hair with his left fist. He swung her around until the top of her head collided with the rusted wrought-iron fence that framed the old mansion's front yard. She shrieked, dropped the bat, and flailed at the top of her head with both hands. Dees pivoted to his right as another man, reeking of alcohol, stepped forward and raised a soda bottle like a club. Dees's right fist shot out, closing the man's mouth with a sharp click. The man dropped the bottle and stumbled backward.

Dees felt something—rock? fist? club?—hit him behind his right ear. He staggered forward and felt something else slam into the back of his head, driving him down into the dirt between the sidewalk and the street. He was using his arms to shove himself off the ground when a kick to his stomach drove all the air out of him. He fell heavily again, and was guessing he had been kicked in the head as a blinding pain shot across his skull, right to left. His face felt wet.

He could feel the vibration from his body shuddering, but

was unaware of any pain from the kicks and rocks. Suddenly, it stopped. Sleep, he thought. I'll take a nap.

He thought he heard a familiar female voice telling someone she was going to shoot them just before he passed out.

CHAPTER 11

He was able to breathe easily, even though he was swimming underwater. It's dark, he thought, so either I'm swimming deep or it's night. Every so often, a frisson of light would shiver across the surface above him, like a searchlight skittering across the water. A boat? Voices settled down from the surface. They must be having a picnic, he realized, since they were talking with their mouths full of mashed potatoes. Nope, it must be beans and rice, he decided, since they're all speaking Spanish.

"*Chico. Oye, chico.* Hey, Teofilo Stevenson, wake up. You think you are Mike Tyson or somebody?"

He blinked, opened his eyes briefly, then squeezed them shut. A woman in a white lab coat spoke very slowly and distinctly, in English, as she placed a stethoscope on his chest. "Bruised ribs. A slightly bruised kidney but not serious. A mild concussion and six stitches in the back of the head. Serious bruising but no fracture of the left radius. And one very bloody nose."

"Thank you, Doctor," Gloria said. "Can he leave?"

"As long as he does not get drunk again and fall down a flight of stone steps." The doctor stared at Dees, then walked out.

Dees tried to raise his head. "Huh?"

Gloria pushed his head back down on the pillow. "A nighttime tour of the Morro Castle arranged by Minrex for foreign journalists, remember? You got drunk, created a scene, and fell down thirty Spanish stone steps and landed in a bed of sharp rocks."

He took a breath and realized a cylinder of gauze was jammed into his right nostril. He started to remove it, and she slapped his hand.

"Have enough sense to leave it in, please, even if you do not have enough sense not to cause an international incident. We leave quietly, since three of the people you introduced yourself to are here also. One severely lacerated ear and concussion, one whiplash and concussion with injury to the top of the head, and one possibly serious injury to the, ¿cómo se dice?" She indicated her throat with a finger.

"Voice box? Larnyx?"

"As you say. Why did you hit a dozen *brigadistas*?"

"Three." He held up three fingers unsteadily, studied them, then raised his pinky. "Four. I think I hit four."

"Oh shut up and let me get you out of here."

Dees swung his legs over the side of the bed and sat up. His forest-green polo shirt was splattered with blood. There was a bruise on the meaty part of his right forearm just below the elbow, a purplish-black throbbing stain the size of a fist. He ran a finger along the thin line of stitches in the back of his head and winced. He stood up slowly, gripping the bed. "Fuentes? What happened to the professor?"

She put her arm around his waist and helped him move toward the door. The warmth of her hand on his aching kidney felt good. "He is fine. I apologized to him."

Dees stopped. "You what?"

With a soft shove, she started him moving again. "Apologized. I told that *mentirosa* upstairs from him that she could be sent to harvest cane if she ever calls the brigades again. And the one who started it all, the one who threw the first rock, has been, ah, chastised."

Dees looked at her from the corner of his eye. "So why the lie about falling down the steps?"

She gave him an exasperated look. "To avoid having you

arrested this evening. It seems that some in the *duro* faction would want an incident like this. Imagine, *yanqui periodista* takes part in a raid on Cuba and then attacks *brigadistas* while defending a counterrevolutionary. So they would love to arrest you and use you to show the *gringos* cannot be trusted, even if they are journalists."

Dees steadied himself. "So do I have time to soak in a hot bath before I'm declared the number one enemy of the people?"

She opened the door to a Lada sedan and shook her head as she helped Dees into the front seat. "No. If they are unable to arrest you, then none of this ever happened, officially. But the word on the street will spread that an old man fought off some brigade hotheads. The old man becomes a sort of folk hero and the brigades lose a little credibility.

"This is a good thing, but it will only happen this way if you are not arrested. So you are leaving the country tonight. Air Canada flew in a special charter to get out tourists ahead of any hurricane, so you are flying to Toronto in, oh, about four hours."

They drove in silence to the hotel, where Dees ignored the stares of the desk staff as he limped through the lobby. He took a brief, tepid shower. He slowly put on a fresh polo shirt and khakis, collected his duffel, paid the bill in cash, and got back into the car.

As they drove through the deserted streets, she said, quietly, "I may have helped you too much. I still have many friends, but the hard-liners will want many answers about this evening and about you revealing that Vargas was one of their agents."

"So why do all this for me?"

He thought her lip quivered, but it might have been the flickering dashboard light.

"Cuba is doomed if we do not act. If we do not open to the outside world, there will be bloodshed and chaos when Fidel dies, and then the right-wing gangsters from Miami return.

To prevent it, we have to discredit the hard-liners. Your friend may have died because he got caught between the factions here."

She looked at him sideways, and said, "And I find you—*¿cómo se dice?*—sexy, at least for a *yanqui*. Ah, *bueno*, the airport. Please do not say anything while I get you onto your flight."

As she breezily bullied and cajoled them through various checkpoints, Dees caught her staring at him three different times. As they walked across the tarmac to the plane, he bent over and whispered, "You find me sexy because I'm a *gringo* who can get you off this island?"

She smiled, leaned toward him, and quietly said, "Do not be an asshole. I find you sexy because you are an honest man, which is even rarer in the States than here, *verdad*?"

As he started up the ramp to the plane, she discreetly patted his butt.

* * *

"And as this thermal image from space shows, the winds are intensifying. You can see the eye here is very well defined, as David remains stalled, gathering strength. The latest coordinates are twenty-five degrees eight minutes north, seventy degrees two minutes west, which you can see is north of Hispanola and Puerto Rico and west-northwest of the Turks and Caicos."

Dees stared at the TV screen as the Weather Channel tracked the stop-start progress of the storm. Gale force winds were lashing the north coasts of Haiti, the Dominican Republic, and Puerto Rico. Mammoth waves were already gouging away the beaches in the Turks and eastern Bahamas.

Dees had used a two-hour layover in Toronto to air-freight the videotapes and his notes to GTV in Phoenix. He had used the three-hour drive from the Miami airport to Key West to outline three rough scripts in his head. Arriving home and fueled with coffee, aspirin, and cigars, he wrote the scripts, fed them into the GTV mainframe, and then sent the voice tracks via the switch. He was preparing to call Curtis Stevens when the phone rang.

"Peter. Ricardo here on the foreign desk." There was a pause, and muffled conversation on the other end of the line. "Peter? Someone here wants to talk to you."

"Pete? Pete Dees?" It was a well-modulated voice, with the mellifluous quality of an insurance salesman trying to pitch an annuity. "The board likes your stuff but it lacks a little sex appeal, you know?"

"The board? Who is this?"

"Oh yeah, you've been busy. Dunlap, Jack Dunlap. I'm the new executive producer for dayside. The board of directors ran some focus groups and found news is skewing too old, like I think Rick here told you earlier."

Dees had never heard anyone call Ricardo "Rick" before, and no one called *him* Pete except his sister. He let the silence hang in the air until the voice finally said, "So I understand Rick told you we wanted some personality profiles of Castro before he dies. Why don't we have them?"

Dees said, "I shipped the story about him fucking goats. You didn't get it yet?"

There was another pause. When the voice spoke again, it had lost all of its mellow resonance. "You're over thirty, you're white, you're male, and you're covering the kind of things we're cutting back on. This is the new news, in case you've been under a rock someplace. Sizzle, personality, heroes, villains, victims, sex."

The voice became sonorous again. "Hey Pete, I've always thought the best way to manage people is to tell them what's positive. So let's start again, okay? So what do you have to say that's positive?"

"I hope your tanning gel doesn't give you cancer," Dees said cheerfully.

There was a clatter on the other end, like someone had tossed the telephone on the desk. Dees could hear muffled voices again, louder than before. O'Bannon got back on the line. "Nice going. I think you've just made a very powerful enemy."

"He can stand in line and take a number," Dees said tiredly. "Where did he come from, anyway?"

"Marketing. I'll try to calm him down. Meantime, the national desk wants to know about availability for live shots in case the hurricane gets close."

Dees sighed. "I'm reachable. Just page me."

Dees hung up, and over the next hour, filled four boxes he kept in an unused closet with insurance papers, photo albums of both his family and various assignments, and three drawers worth of files. He carried them to the car, then packed a duffel with clothing and equipment, securing them inside a half-dozen heavy plastic waterproof sacks.

He called Stevens and arranged to meet at eight P.M. at the News Café on South Beach. Dees drove the car full of boxes to the La Concha Hotel. Fifty dollars and a box of Cuban cigars got him an interior storage closet on the seventh floor, well away from any windows. He drove back to the cottage, unlocked the waist-high storage area attached to the house, and made sure the generator inside was filled with gasoline, and that heavy extension cords, a shovel, two sacks of quicklime, and three spare cans of gasoline were tightly secured inside.

Dees pulled the corrugated aluminum storm shutters from a shed in the backyard. An hour later, every muscle in his body ached as he finished screwing the last of the shutters into the tracks that ran above and below every window and door. Except for sunlight streaming through the glass panel in the front door, the entire house was dark.

He carefully removed a scarred cigar box from the corner of the hall closet. There was just enough marijuana inside for one fat joint. He rolled it into a cigarette paper with a practiced technique, lit it, and filled the bathtub with scalding hot water. He dozed off and on in the tub, occasionally adding more hot water by using his toes to turn the faucet. The weed and the hot water made the ribs, kidney, and bruised arm feel better. He got out of the tub, dried himself, dressed, looked around the inside of the house, stepped outside, and fastened the last shutter to the front door. He then tossed the screwdriver into the backseat and headed toward Miami.

Three hours later, Dees checked into the Mayfair, then drove to South Beach. The valet parker's eyes lit up when he slid into the driver's seat and felt the eight-cylinder rumble through the steering wheel. He looked up at Dees, who nodded. The tires squealed as the car leaped into traffic on Ocean Drive and made a sharp right onto Eighth.

Stevens was waiting at a table next to the bar, on a tiny balcony above the street-level outdoor tables. The agent looked Dees up and down.

"What happened to you? That arm looks like somebody hit it with a baseball bat."

"The penalty for being politically incorrect," Dees said. "I slipped and fell. I found something out, but you won't like it."

Stevens leaned across the table. "Look, the pressure on this is getting serious. Davis is yelling at me on behalf of State. The Bureau's turned up the volume from D.C., Peterson's dead, Vargas's dead, and the National Security Council wants some answers. On top of that, I have an office to secure in case Miami gets hit by the hurricane, and I don't get much sleep these days. D.C.'s starting to take the reports of Castro croaking pretty seriously, so the temperature's rising, fast."

A Corvette with green neon tubing on its undercarriage lit up the pavement as it growled by. A dark-haired Rollerblader glided through a crowd of doughy tourists, the muscles on his bare shoulders rippling as he flexed.

"Remember, I said you won't like it," Dees said. "My sources say Vargas was a double agent working for the U.S. and the Cubans. They also say there's another Cuban agent around here who may have had something to do with Richie's death. He's called *la tortuga,* and he works for us and them."

A soft breeze rustled the stiff palm fronds hanging from a

nearby tree. Stevens sat back in his chair and seemed to study something in the distance. Dees walked to the bar, got two pints of Bass, and sat back down. Stevens took a sip without looking at the glass.

"Vargas," he said, "working for both sides? And another double agent here?"

Dees nodded and said, "If that turns out to be true, maybe we can solve at least one murder. If we find out who *la tortuga* is, I bet we find out who killed Vargas, and maybe get some hints about why Richie was killed."

Another humid breeze sent cocktail napkins flying off the tables below them like a flock of small, frightened birds. Stevens drained his pint. "What do you do now?"

Dees finished his own ale. "Get some sleep, and check on Cabrera again tomorrow morning, weather permitting, and assuming he's back from the Bahamas."

Stevens got up. "I'll beep you as soon as I know something. Since I can't tell the fucking double agents without a scorecard, this may take a while."

Dees watched him leave. He stared south, past the neon and rollerblades, toward Havana, and wondered if Gloria might be looking north beyond her own coast. He wanted to smell her breath and her skin and her hair. He got up and walked to the curb, waiting while the valet pulled up with the Mustang.

"Whew," the valet said as Dees slipped a five into his palm, "you could get hurt driving this thing if you ain't careful."

Dees noticed the scored marks on top of the hood. "Yeah," he said, "lucky thing I wear my seat belt."

* * *

The fog evaporated off the blacktop like a fading memory as Dees approached Lappahoosa. Even the open air had a hint of mildew and rot. Clouds of tiny gnats thickened the air above the drainage ditches on both sides of the road. He drummed his fingers on the steering wheel. Cabrera had to figure that the Feds had tried to contact him because of Dees, which was not the best way to make Cabrera favorably disposed to talk to him again without having a bullet put through his head first.

He drove past a dented Dodge pickup, its rusted tailgate open to display dozens of plastic bags full of lumpy brown material. The sign said BOILED PEANUTS. A rail-thin man in a John Deere baseball cap sat on the open tailgate, watching Dees with sunken eyes.

Dees pulled the car to the shoulder and got out. He remembered his mother's stories of his grandfather sitting by the Arkansas roadside during the Depression, selling rattlesnake skins or walnuts or anything else he was able to forage to people driving between Little Rock and St. Louis. The man nodded, waving at the gnats with his hand. Dees nodded back and picked up one of the Baggies, the soft peanuts filling it like so many small, brown tumors. He thought of the taste of boiled peanuts, and winced.

He looked over at the figure on the tailgate. "How much a bag?"

"A dollah," the man said. "Six fer five."

Dees tried to ignore the gnats that were trying to burrow into his brain through his eyes and ears. "Not much business?"

The cap shook back and forth. "Lessen, you count 'em Jamaicans workin' the fields. 'Em coloreds seem to like boiled goobers."

Dees pulled out a twenty and put it in a weathered hand. The man looked at it suspiciously. "Ain't got change fer that."

"Don't need change. At the special price, I figure that's twenty-four bags."

The man stared at the twenty for a few seconds before stuffing it into his jeans. "Brother, 'at's more'n I sell in a day, sometimes two. You eat many a them?"

Dees watched as two dozen of the Baggies were stuffed into a brown paper grocery sack. "I love 'em. I can eat three, four bags a day."

The man squinted as he handed Dees the bag. "Ain't from around here?"

"Passing through." Dees looked down the highway at the cane fields that stretched as far as he could see on both sides of the road. "Gold Cane own everything around here?"

The man snorted. "Includin' the road if'n you listen to 'em. Big colored fella was here no mor'n half hour ago, drivin' one a them fancy Jap cars with dark winders. He told me to get my cracker ass off'n their property. I said 'ese roads 'n' shoulders is public property. He said if I'se here when he comes back, he'd kill me, even flashed one'a 'em itty bitty twelve gauges with a pistol grip. Looked like a toy in 'at fat hand a his."

Dees absently rubbed his left foot against his right ankle, reassuring himself that the pistol was still there. He turned and looked down the empty, steaming highway toward Cabrera's house. "Anybody with him?"

The man squinted again. "You askin' a lotta questions."

Dees dug in his pocket and pulled out three more twenties. "Like I asked, anybody with him?"

The man smacked his lips. "Saw a feller with short hair, white feller, hair cut short like he's a soldier or the like. Saw somebody in the back, couldn't see who through 'em dark winders. They's by here, like I said, no mor'n half hour ago. Drove off toward 'at big brick house 'at rich Cuban feller lives in."

Dees handed over the twenties, which disappeared into a jeans pocket. "Hope business gets better."

The man cracked a grin, showing a mouthful of perfect acrylic teeth. "Brother, business ain't been this good in months."

Dees nodded. "I need a favor. Is there a Circle K or 7-Eleven up the road anyplace?"

"Jest an ol' Quicky Mart 'at went outta business an' Velma Perkins bought it. Velma sells sodys and cigarettes to 'em Jamaican boys."

Dees walked to the Mustang, dropped the sack of peanuts on the passenger seat with a sodden plop, and picked up the cell phone. He called directory assistance, got the number for the Quicky Mart, and programmed the number into the phone's rapid dial. He explained to the man how the phone worked, and showed him how to punch the star key followed by 7 to get the preprogrammed number, then said, "Now let's call Velma."

Ten minutes later, Dees was at the Quicky Mart. Velma, short and shapeless beneath a faded blue flannel housedress, smiled, exposing two missing front teeth, and said, "Glad to help Vernon out."

So that's his name, Dees thought. He microwaved a barbecue sandwich, had an orange for dessert, and washed it down with a bottle of Gatorade. He talked to Velma about fishing, the price of gasoline, and hurricanes. He listened to the AM radio's Voice of Lappahoosa tell him Hurricane David was now a category-four storm that had grown not only powerful, but huge. It now covered more area than even the giant Gilbert had in 1988. It had started to wobble slightly southeast, heading toward Miami or the Keys or maybe even Havana.

Dees felt a chill and thought about Gloria again. He ate another orange, and talked with Velma about her two sons, one in the Navy in San Diego, the other with an MP unit in Bosnia.

Finally, a little after six o'clock, the phone rang. Velma nodded at Dees, who took the receiver. He listened, nodded, and said, "I'll be there in ten minutes."

It took him less than eight to pull alongside where Vernon had parked his truck on one of the cane field access roads that intersected with the main highway leading from Cabrera's house. Vernon said with satisfaction, "They's gettin' ready to leave and go someplace. Saw 'em packing the trunk when I drove by and called you."

Dees shook hands with him, palming two more twenties.

Vernon took the bills and put them in his jeans without look-ing at them. He got back into the truck and moved forward, allowing Dees's Mustang to pull in behind him, shielded from the highway by the tall cane.

A few minutes later, a black Lexus hissed by on the as-phalt. Damn, Dees thought, how many does he own? Vernon pulled the battered Dodge onto the road behind it, as Dees followed several car lengths behind. Within a few miles, the Lexus turned left onto the main highway, heading east toward the turnpike. Dees waved at Vernon as he slid past and turned left, a little more than a mile between him and the Lexus.

It was growing dark as they turned south on the turnpike. The Lexus's headlights snapped on as Dees prayed that some-body's bladder was full. An hour later, Dees smiled as the Lexus pulled into the Pompano Beach service plaza. He slid the Mustang into a far corner of the parking lot, and watched as Joseph and Diaz got out and Cabrera emerged from the backseat.

Before they even disappeared inside, Dees took the thin screwdriver from the backseat and held its tip over the flame from his cigarette lighter. He tried to look nonchalant as he walked over to the Lexus and shoved the heated screwdriver tip into the right taillight lens. In less than thirty seconds, he was back inside the Mustang, watching. Five minutes later, the three men got back into the car and drove off, a tiny white beam winking from the middle of the red taillight lens.

Just like a little star, Dees thought. Twinkle twinkle little rat, how I wonder where you're at. An hour later, the Lexus turned off the turnpike extension and headed west on the Tamiami Trail. Dees followed, staying three-quarters of a mile back, mixing with traffic as they drove farther into the Everglades. Eventually, all other traffic disappeared, leaving the Mustang trailing the Lexus by over a mile. Suddenly, Dees saw the taillights turn left.

He drove past where the Lexus had turned without slowing down, and saw the taillights turn right in the far distance down a rutted sand and loam road. A hundred yards ahead, on the other side of the highway, Dees saw a mass of pipes where the shoulder doubled in width to accommodate a pumping substation that kept 'Glades water flowing into drainage ditches and canals.

He turned the Mustang around and parked with the right side of the car snug against the pipes. He locked the car, and set the remote alarm with the tiny keypad attached to his keys. He started walking, the combination of sharp limestone pebbles and crushed shells crunching under his feet, and turned right onto a sandy track freshly rutted with tire imprints. He hugged the right side of the road, trying to conceal himself in a line of scrub bushes and melaleuca trees that ran parallel to a drainage ditch next to the road. Every few minutes a gust of wind whistled through the scraggly trees. Clouds scudding in from the east would obscure the moon for minutes, then disappear, causing the light from the three-quarter moon to flicker off and on like a short-circuited fluorescent light.

Dees's eyes were growing used to the light. A hundred yards or so in front, to the right, he saw a low building, looking like a horse paddock that had morphed into a house. In a flicker of moonlight he saw a screened-in porch attached to the left side. The Lexus and another car were parked in front, just beyond a tall flagpole planted in the middle of a roughly circular drive. A ripped Cuban flag snapped in the breeze.

The Everglades west of Miami had been dotted with various exile commando training camps since the Bay of Pigs fiasco. As long as the scruffy, aging commandos stayed on private property with registered weapons, the Miami-Dade police generally left them alone. It was only when a stray shot would zip across a highway and into a house, horse, or car that the police showed up, sometimes to issue just a warning, sometimes walking away with handcuffed exiles and crates full of illegal weapons and ammunition.

Dees crouched by a fence post that anchored a rusty metal gate, wide enough to let a car pass and still open. He crouched low and loped to the rear of the Lexus. A solitary frog croaked in one of the sodden ditches that surrounded the property. He took five quick steps to the rear of the second car. He could hear voices in Spanish, merging with the sounds of frogs, crickets, and the wind through the sawgrass and melaleucas.

The voices became more distinct. He recognized Cabrera's voice, and Diaz's rapid-fire, almost breathless voice. He didn't recognize the third one, a breathy voice speaking without any discernible accent. Dees peeked over the trunk, and saw four figures behind the screens on the porch. One had his back to Dees. Cabrera and Diaz were facing Dees and the other figure. He saw a huge shape shift behind Cabrera, and guessed it was Joseph, standing in the shadows.

A stack of hay bales was piled haphazardly twenty yards ahead of Dees. The bales were about fifteen feet from the porch, but still mostly in darkness because of the feeble light from the screened-in porch's two bare overhead bulbs. Dees looked up and saw another line of clouds, moving fast, beginning to obscure the moon. He put his back against the rear bumper and noticed he was leaning against a dark Crown Victoria, similar to the one Cabrera had used to follow him in Key West.

As he tensed waiting for the moon to duck behind the clouds, he glanced down at the license plate. It was white, like the standard-issue Florida plates. But this one read U.S. GOVERNMENT across the bottom. He froze. The sky was now completely dark, but Dees still didn't move. He was preparing to glance down at the plate again to try and memorize the number, but looked up and saw the clouds about to pass. He sprinted from the bumper to the hay bales just as the moon peeked out again, bathing the flat landscape in light the color of skim milk.

Dees closed his eyes and took a deep breath, shifting his thoughts from English into Spanish. He strained to listen.

"Este es muy malo," he heard the voice he didn't recognize say. "With our contacts you should have gotten a Foxbat, perhaps a Flogger. But a Frogfoot?"

Dees heard a palm slap onto a table, then Cabrera's voice. "Ah, your contacts, a very good joke indeed. Your contacts with *los serbianos* were next to worthless. And it was my money, do not forget."

"And what?" he heard Diaz say excitedly. "You think I cannot outfly your pathetic coastal defenses in a Frogfoot? I took on the best the South Africans had and defeated them! I could have destroyed the naval station at Cayo Hueso before the idiots even knew I was there! I can—"

"Basta!" Cabrera said. "We are all aware of your capabilities, Orestes. I am sure our friend here meant no disrespect to you."

Dees's mind raced in the silence that followed. Soviet-era aircraft had been nicknamed decades before by the U.S. military. H was for helicopter, like the Hind, Hip, and Hook. B was for bomber, like the Badger and Blinder. F was used to designate fighter aircraft. Dees thought back to Afghanistan, when the Sukhoi Su-25 had riddled entire villages and concentrations of *mujahadeen*, blasting people, animals, and buildings into barely recognizable pieces.

The Su-25, nicknamed Frogfoot by the Pentagon, had been the Warsaw Pact's version of the A-10 Warthog tank killer. It was a single-seater, subsonic, designed to take a pounding from bullets, cannon, and even small rocket fire, and keep flying. With an experienced pilot nestled in the titanium bathtub that surrounded the cockpit, the Frogfoot was devastating against ground targets. But with a novice at the controls, the relatively slow Su-25 could be brought down by concentrated ground fire. Dees had seen three of them come down in flames after encounters with Afghan rebels armed with CIA-supplied shoulder-held Stingers.

The unfamiliar voice said, "I was led to believe our friends in Belgrade had something more modern in mind."

Cabrera laughed. "Even ten million dollars in cash and another million in, as you might say, gratuities, can only buy so much. But there is, as you may say, a clearance sale special here. Firstly, we receive the Frogfoot and exactly which ordnance, Orestes?"

Diaz's staccato voice chopped the words into bite-size nuggets. "One thirty-millimeter cannon, twin barrels. Eight wing pylons, maximum load forty-five hundred kilos. Eight air-to-ground missiles, three incendiary, total weight four thousand kilos."

Dees heard Cabrera's edgy laugh. "Plus one very small suitcase containing a Spetznatz atomic demolition munition with a yield of one kiloton. It would seem that former Soviet general who said dozens of these were missing was not so wrong after all. So you really have no reason to complain, since this investment of eleven million procured us merchandise worth five, six times that much, perhaps more."

Cabrera continued, "But now that the cargo has been unloaded, we need to worry about moving it out of harm's way in case our ally David becomes our enemy."

The unfamiliar voice spoke. "A nuclear warhead is slightly insane, perhaps?"

The plywood floor inside the porch shook as someone, apparently Cabrera, stomped a foot down, hard. Cabrera's voice rose. "I have paid you! I have paid eleven million fucking dollars, plus shipping from the Adriatic to the Caribbean, plus bribes from Serbia to the Bahamas! I have paid you over a million! I have paid others nearly that! Insane? This enterprise's total indebtedness to me is in excess of fifteen million dollars! And I and you could profit over a hundred times that from one small explosion that could level, maybe at most, five square blocks!"

Another long pause gave Dees time to listen to the frogs. Nausea tickled his chin. He fingered the strap on the ankle holster. He paused, and tried to figure the odds of holding all four of them at bay while he got on the phone and called the

FBI. He settled on heading for the cell phone in the Mustang as soon as the moon went dark again.

The voice Dees couldn't identify spoke again. "So everything is in Freeport?"

The laugh again. "I am afraid we have moved a little too quickly, even for you. When David began to move south, we moved everything to one of the out-islands behind the storm's projected track. Our people should have already assembled everything on a small airstrip on David's lee side."

"A drug smuggling airfield?"

"Let us merely say it was used for other commodities. Here, let me show you where."

Dees heard paper rustling, and guessed it was a map being unfolded. The frogs and crickets and wind all went silent at once, so he could hear what sounded like a pencil thumping on the table.

"Here. Orestes and I will fly there, perhaps tomorrow."

Dees heard the soft click of a disposable lighter, and smelled cigarette smoke. The unfamiliar voice said, "And the Bahamas Defense Force?"

Cabrera said, "Their country is mostly water, and they are too busy preparing for David's arrival and the aftermath. The local officials on nearby islands, on the other hand, are most susceptible to, um, gratuities."

There was another pause. Dees thought he heard someone whisper, but couldn't be sure, since a gust of wind was once again whistling through the trees. He thought he might have heard a screen door creak, but it might have been the quivering branches rubbing against a tree trunk.

The unfamiliar voice said, "So when does the attack take—"

"We will talk more of that," Cabrera interrupted, "in a moment or two."

Dees leaned against the hay bales, listening, but heard only silence. He looked up, and saw the moon was about to disappear behind the clouds. He turned again, preparing to peek over the bales, when he noticed that while everything else was still washed in pale light, he was in shadow. He thought that maybe the moon was about to disappear again.

When he turned to look up, he saw Joseph towering over him like a skyscraper with gleaming white teeth.

"You better do something about them sinuses, fancy mouth. I heard you breathing."

A huge fist slammed into the side of his head. The moon went dark.

over the bales, when he sensed that, while everything else was still wide, Lomate lights began to glow. He thought

CHAPTER 12

His head felt like someone was trying to inflate a balloon inside his skull. Whatever Dees was lying on was hard and uniform—probably, he guessed, the shack's plywood floor. He kept his eyes shut and tried to ignore the feeling that his brain was about to pop through the stitches on the top of his head and blow out of his skull like lava from an erupting volcano. He felt something on his wrists and barely cracked his eyes to look. They were duct-taped together, in front of him. He remained still and listened.

"—put us all in danger." It was the unfamiliar voice. "I don't need any of the details."

A screen door a hundred miles away creaked and slammed shut. A car started and barely made a sound as it pulled across the sandy loam and faded in the distance. Several frogs started to make a racket all at once. He heard the scrape of a chair on the floor, followed by an *umpfh*, as if someone heavy was lifting himself up. The thump of footfalls vibrating through the plywood felt to Dees like a hammer smacking off the wood, sending bolts of pain through his throbbing skull.

He thought he heard a sigh. "Very well. Orestes, please start the car."

The screen door clattered again, followed by the click of a car door opening and the soft purr of a muffled engine. Cabrera spoke in English.

"We will be flying to the Bahamas. Do what you have to do and take the old truck out in back. Find his car and take it to

Lappahoosa and destroy it, and please make sure that if someone finds him, they cannot identify him. Our friend Vargas was found all too quickly, maybe cut the hands and head off this one, eh? No fingerprints, no dental records."

There was a snicker and Joseph said, "You much care how I do it?"

Another sigh. "You can shoot him or stab him or garrote him for all I care. But no torture, which I know will be difficult as much as you dislike this one, but we do not have time for you to play. This needs to be done quickly, and not here, since I do not want the authorities scraping the ground here for DNA samples. Just take him someplace and do what needs to be done. Get his car back north as soon as you can, strip it, and remove everything, including the VIN number, and then burn it. *Comprende?*"

There was a grunt in reply. "I'll take the truck then, and take him to—"

A foot thumped on the floor again. This time, the vibration hardly hurt Dees's head at all. Cabrera said, "I do not wish to know. Just do what we need and quickly, quickly."

The screen door creaked again. A car door opened and closed and the soft hum of the Lexus faded away. Dees suddenly smelled Joseph's pungent aroma as two mammoth hands gripped him under the armpits and shoved him into a kitchen chair that sat against the wall dividing the porch from the shack itself. Dees's head bounced lightly off the wall. Pain blazed through his skull and, against his will, forced his eyes open.

"Well, fancy mouth. You're awake but not for much longer, I don't think."

A gust of wind blew through the screens, ruffling a large sheet of unfolded paper on the table to Dees's right. He snapped his eyes toward the table and saw what appeared to be a navigation map, covered with lines and notations.

He looked back at Joseph, who was standing with his arms

folded not five feet away. Dees pretended to stretch his legs, rubbing his right ankle with his left foot. The holster was empty. He saw a small lump under Joseph's pale gray guayabera, and figured it was his pistol.

Joseph grinned. "So, fancy mouth, no smartass from you? Nothing to say? How about begging for your life?"

Dees felt his car keys in his right pocket, cutting into his leg. Joseph bent over, not taking his eyes off him, and picked up the small shotgun that had been propped against the wall. Dees's mind raced. If he bolted from the chair, he could throw himself against one of the screens, burst through it, and try to run for it, if Joseph didn't either shoot him or knock him cold first. He tensed, and then relaxed. He had another idea.

Joseph lightly clicked the shotgun's safety to Off. Outside, more frogs croaked in chorus as the uneven light from the cloud-shrouded moon blinked on and off. Joseph leveled the shotgun at him. "Get your arse up, fancy mouth. I'm gonna show you how you're gonna die."

Dees stood up. His head ached, but not nearly as much as he thought it would. Maybe the Rwandan army colonel who had pulled him from the helicopter wreck ten years before had been right when he said that it was most fortunate that Dees's head was not near a vital organ. Joseph shoved him through the doorway into the shack. The room was barely lit by two weak bulbs suspended from a cheap plastic imitation stained-glass shade. Keeping the shotgun level with Dees's chest, Joseph reached toward an unfinished wood shelf and pulled down a pint mason jar.

He shoved it close enough to Dees's nose so that a putrid smell drifted upward, even through the sealed lid. Dees coughed, gagging slightly. Joseph laughed. "Mister fancy mouth tough man not so tough? Yahbo, that's good. You know what this shit is?"

Dees looked toward the shelf and saw a small brown statue of a man leaning on a crutch. Oh boy, he thought. *Santo*

Lázaro, Saint Lazarus, the antisaint, a thinly disguised *Babalu Aye*, the crippled god on a crutch who headed the pantheon of deities swirling around *Santería*. The saints worshiped in *Santería* had started out as gods in West Africa, worshiped by the slaves imported by the Spaniards to work the cane fields. The slaves brought their religions with them, but under pressure from the slave owners and Holy Mother Church, camouflaged the gods carefully as saints.

So tribal religions became *Santería*, and *Babalu* became Saint Lazarus, complete with animal sacrifice where the body of the goat or chicken became a barbecued sacrament, eaten by worshipers the same way wafers and wine at Mass became the body and blood of Christ. But in some neighborhoods, voodoo was folded into the mix, so if pigs or chickens were in short supply, cats and puppies would serve nicely, and ceremonies could include incantations to incite lust, exact revenge, or turn enemies into zombies.

Joseph saw Dees glance at the Lazarus statue. "Yeah, lotsa these crazy Cuban fucks believe in this shit."

Dees stared at Joseph. "You believe in it?"

Joseph looked offended. "I'm a Jamaican, not a savage. But I do believe the shit in this bottle will kill you. You wanna know how?"

"Like I have a choice."

"Yahbo, you got that right. No choice at all." Joseph held the jar of milky liquid in his fat palm. "See, they don't exactly tell me what's in it, but I figure out most of it."

A gust of wind blew the porch door open. It hit the door frame with a sharp crack, and closed with a flimsy slam. Joseph glanced toward it.

"Weather's getting worse. C'mon, smart mouth, we talk about your funeral while I take care of business."

A beefy hand shoved Dees onto the porch. With the shotgun in one hand and the other enveloping the jar, Joseph pushed Dees through the door. The moon flashed on and off behind the ragged clouds, so that the Cuban flag snapping almost straight in the wind was lit stroboscopically, visible for just a moment before disappearing into blackness.

Joseph opened the passenger door of a rusted Ford F-150, a crack running from upper left to lower right across the windshield. He put the jar on the floorboard and motioned with the shotgun for Dees to move to the truck's rear. "You sit on that bumper or I won't care what Cabrera says about DNA evidence and I'll just blow you away right here."

He drew a key from his pocket and fumbled at a huge lock set in the door of a cinder-block storage building about ten feet from the truck's tailgate. The blockhouse was fifteen feet on a side, and the door was solid steel, set in a steel frame. There were three steps leading up to the door because the cement floor was slightly over a foot thick. The flat roof was covered with foot-square cement tiles. The whole structure was coated with thick waterproof paint and sat on an earth pad that elevated it out of the swamp. As Joseph opened the door, a gust of cool, dry air hit Dees's face.

The blast of refrigerated air made his head feel better. "An air-conditioned blockhouse. Nice," Dees said. "I wonder what a billionaire Cuban exile nuclear lunatic stores in it? Fish dip?"

Joseph just grunted, opened the door, and clicked on a light. Rows of metal shelves, each containing crates of various sizes and shapes, lined the walls. Joseph turned and snorted. "Yeah, I forgot you're a big deal war reporter. So come over here and see what this army's got."

Dees slid off the bumper and walked to the top step, the shotgun now pressing against his abdominal muscles. Each crate, whether metal or wood, was stamped with serial numbers. English lettering on some said U.S. ARMY. Others were stenciled with Cyrillic lettering.

"We got a couple more of them Dragons," Joseph said proudly. "We got three Stingers and four of the Russian kind, what they called? Oh yeah, SAM-7s. We got RPGs, we got a case of AKs. You Americans and them Russians leave so much shit lying around every corner of this earth, I just wonder how many people besides us are able to buy this shit. God bless the free market."

Joseph fumbled on one of the shelves with his left hand and pulled out the biggest machete Dees had ever seen. It looked to be three feet long and about four inches across at its widest point. It gleamed from the oil coating the blade, and from what Dees could see from the bright edge, was sharp enough to cut you if you just looked at it.

"Looks like a scimitar," Dees said. Joseph looked puzzled. "A big curved saber. The Arabs use them to slice up enemy troops or behead somebody."

Joseph grinned. "You got the idea. No hands, no feet, no head, no way to trace a decomposed body."

The shotgun waved, motioning Dees back to the truck. Joseph transferred the machete to his belt, closed the door, turned the key, walked over to Dees, and put the machete in the truck's bed. He motioned with the shotgun for Dees to climb in the passenger's seat. The duct tape was rubbing his wrists raw as he plopped onto the seat.

Joseph closed the door, and walked around the front of the truck, holding the shotgun stiff-armed, aiming through the cracked windshield at the bridge of Dees's nose. He gently felt for his car keys through his pants fabric. As Joseph moved toward the driver's door, Dees nudged the keys up his leg with the ball of his taped right hand so that, finally, the small keypad attached to the key chain edged out of the pocket.

Joseph settled in, closed the door, put the shotgun on his lap, and started the engine. It sputtered and coughed and caught on the second try. Dees looked down at the mason jar on the floor and said, "So you were going to tell me what's in this stuff?"

"Yeah, smart mouth," Joseph said, shifting into Drive. "See, you're gonna drink it. The way I figure, first the mango peel in it starts to close up your throat. You know datura? It's a real pretty fucking plant. Take some of the bark and boil it in a tea and, man, your cock gonna stay hard for two days, won't go limp. It's one of them things, what they call it?"

"A paralytic," Dees said as the truck turned left out of the compound.

Joseph nodded enthusiastically. "Yeah, yeah, right. But they boil so much of it into this shit, it stiffens all the muscles in your lungs. So, see, the mango peel's closing up your throat so you can't swallow and the datura's making you not be able to breathe. And then they mix in the puffer toad poison and the juice from the bofu toad, the one that sweats LSD?"

The truck stopped briefly before Joseph turned left off the road and onto the Tamiami Trail, heading west, deeper into the Everglades. Dees felt for the keypad.

Joseph continued, "So you drink this and it takes you an hour or so to die, choking and trying to scream and tripping your ass off. It ain't gonna be pretty, and you know what?" Joseph laughed again. "It's gonna be funny as hell, me tossing you out with the 'gators and water moccasins, you rolling around on some hummock with just you and them and the fire ants, dying. Ain't that funny, asshole?"

In the truck's headlights, Dees saw the Mustang parked to the left, by the drainage pipes, facing them. He moved his taped wrists over the keypad sticking out of his pocket, stiffened the little finger of his right hand, and depressed a button on the keypad.

The alarm on the Mustang went off with a screeching high-pitched cross between a train whistle and a siren. The Haitian who installed it had guaranteed Dees with a wink that the sound would annoy even the most jaded urbanite three blocks away, and might sterilize anyone within fifty feet. At the same time, the car's high-beam headlights began to flash rapidly. With a "What the—", Joseph leaned forward across the steering wheel, shading his eyes against the glare with a beefy hand.

Dees braced his back against the door, quickly swung both

feet off the floor, bent his knees, and drove his legs, like twin pistons, into Joseph's midsection. The air went out of the large man's lungs with a *whooomph*, as he almost drove the truck into the parked car. He clutched the wheel and pulled it to the right just as Dees kicked him again, this time aiming for the right kidney.

Dees thought he heard a muffled *snnaap*—a rib?—as he found the door latch with his taped hands. Just as he clicked it, he aimed his right leg toward the bridge of Joseph's nose with a roundhouse soccer-style kick. As his instep made contact with the middle of the Jamaican's face, Dees muttered, "Oh, shit," and shoved himself backward out of the truck, which was by now traveling at only around twenty miles an hour.

He landed hard on his right shoulder, the pain moving like an electric shock down to the balls of his feet. He rolled twice and stopped just short of the incline where the gravel dropped into a black roadside canal. He got on his throbbing knees and watched the truck's taillights swerve and then straighten out twenty yards down the highway. Holding his taped wrists low in front of him, Dees crouched and ran straight for the passenger's side of the truck.

The truck jolted to a stop just as Joseph bounded out of the driver's side door with a snort. Hidden on the opposite side of the F-150, Dees dove to the gravel and rolled under the truck. He saw Joseph's feet, encased in a pair of huge black Nikes, stand still and then begin walking into the darkness, toward the spot where Dees had jumped.

Lying on his back, Dees scooted forward until his torso was under the steaming hot muffler and tailpipe. He held his breath, pulled his wrists away from each other to increase the tension on the tape, and shoved the tape onto the heated tailpipe. With a soft sizzle and a mild tearing sound, the tape's fibers began to melt. Dees pulled his wrists apart even harder and bit his lip as the hot metal burned through the tape and began cooking the flesh on both wrists.

The tape stretched, and finally snapped. Dees scooted to his left, moving out from under the truck. He crouched, gingerly pulling shards of tape from his tender wrists, listening. Between the stiff rustle of wind through the sawgrass and the croaking frogs, he heard snatches of heavy breathing and the crunch of feet on gravel.

Dees moved to the passenger's side of the truck and looked inside. No keys. He tried to orient himself in the dark, guessing that the Mustang would be at about two o'clock from where he stood, and the giant Jamaican would be someplace between ten and twelve o'clock. He gripped his car keys with his aching right hand and began sprinting down the blacktop. His own sneakers hardly made a sound as he caught a glimpse of Joseph's back to his left. The large man was slightly bent over at the very edge of the shoulder, apparently peering into the dark canal.

The car alarm had automatically shut off after sixty seconds. Dees gripped the key tightly and slid it into the lock. The door unlatched with a faint *thunk*, but the hinges squeaked loud enough, it seemed to him, to be heard all the way to Miami.

He threw himself into the driver's seat just as an orange flash and a roar erupted behind him. But Joseph was too far away, so the sawed-off's blast dissipated. The shotgun pellets merely embedded themselves in the door's inside upholstery with a soft *poppoppoppop*. Dees slammed the door shut and twisted the key in the ignition.

The eight cylinders rumbled to life at the same moment Dees clicked the floor shift into Drive and flattened the accelerator. The car jumped off the shoulder with a jolt, spraying gravel eight feet in the air before the tires screeched, and then bit into the pavement. There was another flash and a sound like a board smacking an empty metal barrel as shotgun pellets stippled harmlessly across the trunk.

Under his breath Dees said, "Oh, give it a rest," as he cut the wheel hard to the left and stomped on the brake. The left side of the car rose higher and higher, then leveled with a creaking groan as the rear wheels skidded to the right. When the Mustang's nose was pointed in Joseph's general direction, Dees floored the accelerator again. He switched on the brights and saw Joseph standing next to the truck.

The hulking figure had the door open and was apparently preparing to heave himself inside. Dees tried to figure the angle, and reduced speed so that when the car hit Joseph, it was a glancing blow. The Jamaican spun to his right, his arm striking the edge of the door. The impact jolted the shotgun from his right hand. It flew into the F-150's left front tire and bounced off, landing with a clatter in the middle of the pavement.

Joseph's left leg crumpled as he ricocheted off the door and flopped on his belly in the gravel. Dees slid the Mustang to the side of the blacktop and leaped from the car. He ran to the center of the highway and scooped up the pistol-grip shotgun. Glancing at the small clip, he guessed that it held four shells, and hoped Joseph had filled it before firing at him twice. He looked up, and was surprised when he saw the huge man struggling unsteadily to his feet. Joseph's back was pressed against the truck so hard that the Ford's cab began to lean to the right.

As Joseph forced himself upright, the wind carried a sweet corrupted summer smell of decomposition across the pavement. Dees aimed the sixteen-inch barrel at Joseph. He yelled, "Hey! Hey! Don't move! We can still both get out of here alive!"

To his surprise, he saw his own .32 in Joseph's right hand. The Jamaican laughed thickly. "I'm still man enough to take the likes of you and your empty shotgun."

Dees hoped the darkness masked his twitching cheek. "You say empty, I say two more rounds, three if you had one chambered with a full clip. If it wasn't loaded, you'd've shot me by now. So why try?"

"I got reasons," Joseph rasped.

"You know Cabrera treats his field hands like slaves?" Dees said. Joseph just stared. "He's helped kill two people I know of, he's got a fighter jet in the Bahamas, he's got a nuclear weapon. And you're being loyal?"

"Because I got a family, motherfucker," Joseph said tiredly. "Because I got two brothers and six cousins and five uncles and they all got supervisor's jobs in the cane. More money in the season than they get in two years back home."

Dees steadied the shotgun's barrel in his left hand. "All that charity and not a thing for you?"

"Fuck you."

"Loyal and a dry sense of humor, too," Dees said. "Here's an offer for you. The Feds are going to be after Cabrera now, so he's finished. You're at least guilty of attempted murder and guilty of conspiracy to use a weapon of mass destruction. You may be guilty of murdering a Federal agent and a Federal witness."

"No!" Joseph said. "I didn't murder nobody!"

Dees sighed. "Okay, let's just say conspiracy to murder both. So far that's life without parole. We can make a deal. Flip on Cabrera. He takes the fall and you end up doing easy time in one of those country club prisons. You could take up golf."

Dees thought he heard Joseph laugh, but couldn't be sure. "Fed, huh? You got more trouble than you even know, fancy mouth. Fed? Shit."

With a suddenness surprising for a big man, Joseph jerked up his right arm and fired. Dees instinctively dove to the pavement as the massive arm was rising. He saw the revolver's muzzle flash at the same time he heard its short, sharp bark.

Dees raised the shotgun and fired at the same moment the bullet cut through the empty air above him. He was momentarily deaf and blind from the flash as he racked another shell in the chamber and fired again.

He heard a sloppy *ploopp*, like a bowlful of Jell-O hitting the floor. It was followed by a gurgle, then a flat thump as Joseph's face hit the pavement.

The moon finally came from behind the whipping clouds. It cast light like a dirty truck stop bathroom bulb, washing the colors out under a dull film. Joseph was on his stomach, his arms spread in front of him. A thick dark stain was beginning to clot on the warm asphalt.

Dees took a deep breath. The rotting smell from the swamp was stronger than before.

CHAPTER 13

The helicopter bucked and rolled in the gusty rain. Strapped into a rear seat with an H-shaped belt that secured his shoulders and chest, Dees could see the white-helmeted head of the Coast Guard pilot shake in disgust as he fought with the stick and leveled the chopper. Dees was in the left rear seat, Pedro Marco in the right, with Stevens strapped in between them. The three bounced and jerked as the helicopter flew through blasts of gray rain, followed by calm, azure skies, followed by more gusts.

Stevens jabbed Dees in the shoulder. Dees looked at the FBI agent and saw him mouthing words. Marco, looking thoughtful, cradled his camera in his lap. After a series of breathless phone calls, the three had boarded the Coast Guard Dolphin an hour before at the Opa-Locka Coast Guard Air Station, just northwest of Miami. The security team at the hangar refused to let Dees take along his duffel containing his cell and satellite phones, laptop computer, and fresh shirt and pants. They never thought to look for an ankle holster and pistol, or for the twelve extra shells attached to the holster by plastic webbing. A team of agents, led by Briscoe, had stayed behind in the Everglades to secure the blockhouse and coordinate the paperwork generated by Joseph's body. Stevens was clutching the same map that had been on the table at the commando training camp.

Dees reached over and rapped the side of Stevens's helmet with his knuckles. He swung down the microphone arm

189

attached to his helmet's left side, and shoved a small box attached to the microphone cord into the FBI agent's hand. Dees pointed to the box attached to his own mike cord and punched a button on top.

"Use the mike."

Stevens nodded and punched the button. His voice sounded like it was coming over an AM radio, hissy and clipped. "You ever been here?"

With his free hand, he was pointing at the map unfolded on his lap. His finger wrinkled the paper where a string of islands had been circled with a red marker.

Dees keyed his microphone. "The Mira Por Vos Cays. The Looking-for-You Islands. Long Cay's the only one with people, about four hundred. The southern one's Castle Island. You can see it for miles because of the automated lighthouse. The big island to the north's Acklins, maybe a few hundred people scattered on it. Mayaguana's the long, skinny one to the east, two, maybe three hundred people, and there's a small airstrip there for puddle-jumpers from Nassau."

Stevens's tinny voice came through Dees's headset. "What about old airstrips on any of the other ones?"

"I'd say plenty. Four hundred fifty miles from Florida, far enough out so antidrug radar wouldn't spot them immediately, isolated enough so the BDF would have a hell of a time finding them. These and the Ragged Islands over to the west," Dees said, his finger crinkling the map, "used to be cartel favorites for flying blow into the United States. What about the BDF?"

Stevens shook his head. "They're busy making sure everything from Grand Bahama to Eleuthera is nailed down or evacuated. One of their commanders talked to me on the phone at Opa-Locka before we lifted off. 'The Bahamas Defense Force is large in heart and small in number, Agent Stevens,' is what he said. We've got permission to enter their territory while they're dealing with the hurricane."

The helicopter shook, dropped suddenly, regained altitude,

and kept on its heading. Stevens stroked the map again with his finger. "They're a little south of the outer winds, so the weather there should still be good."

"Sir?" It was the copilot, turning to look at Stevens.

The agent pressed his microphone button. "What?"

The helicopter shuddered sharply. The shaking made the copilot sound like he was gargling. "We're going to have to land. We have a problem."

Stevens's eyes became wide under his helmet. He looked out the window and back at the copilot. "Where? In the water?"

The copilot shook his head no. The pilot's squawky voice came through the headsets. "Autec Andros this is Coast Guard Dolphin three-seven-foxtrot."

"Three-seven-foxtrot," said a distant voice, almost obscured by static.

"Autec, request clearance. Oil pressure's dropping rapidly."

"Three-seven-foxtrot, are you declaring an emergency?"

"Negative, Autec. But we may have oil pump failure soon."

"Roger that, three-seven-foxtrot. You have three passengers?"

Dees looked at Stevens. The pilot said, "Roger, Autec."

"CINCLANT's cleared you. Approach three-one-zero. Winds southwest fifteen gusting to forty. Ceiling two-zero-zero. Squawk nine-seven-six-six-three."

The copilot dialed the IFF transponder—Identification Friend or Foe—to the frequency. It would send out an electronic pulse, known as a squawk, to identify the helicopter. "Roger, Autec. Three-one-zero approach. Squawking nine-seven-six-six-three."

"All the way to the Commander in Chief Atlantic Fleet," Dees said. "When did you call CINCLANT?"

"I didn't," Stevens said. "I just called the Bureau in D.C. Once I mentioned a loose nuclear warhead, they probably called every number in their Rolodex. And what the hell's Autec?"

The helicopter bucked again. Dees looked at the control panel and saw a glowing red light. He keyed his microphone.

"Autec's the Atlantic Underwater Testing and Evaluation Center, top secret base run by the Navy and the Brits. Underwater munitions, antisub warfare, sonar, stealth submarine technology. It's on Andros, the biggest island in the Bahamas. Mahogany forests, flocks of flamingos, top secret base. The usual."

A high-pitched whine punched through the helicopter's white noise. As the helicopter jerked again, Dees noticed they were slowly losing altitude. He poked the copilot on the shoulder. "We gonna make it?"

The copilot nodded. "Ten minutes out, sir. We should."

"What the hell is going on?" Stevens said. Dees noticed his knuckles were straining against his knees.

"Oil pressure, like the man said," Dees replied. He decided to keep Stevens's mind off their decreasing altitude. "Something else you can blame on Congress."

"Huh?"

"The Coast Guard buys some perfectly good helicopters from the French," Dees explained, "great for everything from antidrug work to search and rescue. The Dauphin model, the Dolphin. But Congress says at least fifty-one percent of any aircraft flown by U.S. forces has to be American-made. So they take out the engines and the turbines and navigation systems and replace them with stuff made by American contractors.

"The nav systems are great, the engines aren't. So you keep ending up with engine failures, especially the oil pumps which seem to do everything except pump oil."

The copilot keyed his mike, and smiled. "You said it, sir, we didn't."

Stevens looked grim. He turned to the copilot. "I need to contact Autec. Tell them we need another aircraft when we land."

As the copilot radioed Autec, the wind slapped against the helicopter's skin, and the high-pitched whine grew louder. Stevens shot Dees a questioning look.

"The engine," Dees said. "It's telling us it's tired of running without enough oil."

A blast of wind shoved the helicopter sideways. The Dolphin vibrated and began to slip to the right. The pilot shook his head again and eased the nose to the left, fighting the stick to keep the aircraft level. The wind suddenly died, and blue sky appeared again. Stevens saw dark green foliage beneath the clouds skidding under them.

"Andros?" he asked. Dees nodded. The green triple-canopy bush was coming up at them fast. He could see a jumble of buildings and an airstrip in the distance.

The whining grew louder as the pilot steered the Dolphin to the left, then circled around and headed directly into the wind. "Three-seven-foxtrot, come in at one-nine-one. That should head you straight into the wind."

"Roger Autec, one-nine-one."

The wind began to lift the helicopter's nose. A soft grinding sound joined the whine in the cockpit. The helicopter shook violently as it slowly approached a thirty-by-thirty-foot slab of concrete with a large red H painted in the center.

The shaking inside the cockpit became even more violent, and the grinding noise was the same volume as the shrieking whine. The copilot said, "We're losing it."

The pilot briefly glanced out his side window. "Maybe twenty feet. Hang on. Cut power!"

"Cut power," the copilot said immediately. The helicopter dropped like a falling truck, bouncing violently on the deployed landing gear. All five men were shoved against their harnesses as the Dolphin's wheels left the ground and came down again, and again, and again, bouncing a little less each time. The Dolphin was rocking front to back like a bucking horse when the blades, which had been slowing, suddenly jerked to a stop.

Momentum was instantly transferred from the blades to the helicopter's body. The tail skidded violently to the right, then stopped with a jolt. Simultaneously, the two passenger doors slid open and the two cockpit doors swung wide. A figure dressed in a white fireproof suit and hood barked, "Get out now!"

Marco grabbed the small duffel packed with camera equipment, and shoved himself onto the concrete. Stevens shook hands with a lieutenant commander waiting at the far side of the helo pad. Dees followed. The agent trudged over to Dees and pointed toward a stubby helicopter with a spike protruding from its nose and two cigar-shaped containers on pylons above each landing gear. Two four-man crews were unbolting the cigars and placing them on wheeled sleds.

"CINCLANT says we get that one," Stevens said, jerking his thumb over his shoulder. "What is it?"

Dees squinted. "SH-2. It's an antisub chopper. Those things they're removing from the pylons are torpedoes. What'd you hear about the weather?"

Stevens looked sour. "David's moving, fast, southwest. The Navy thinks it'll move across Great Abaco. Where is that?"

Dees waved his hand northeast. "That direction. Nassau's about sixty miles from here, Great Abaco's the big island fifty miles beyond Nassau."

Stevens looked at the sky. "Close. Navy thinks it'll hit someplace between Miami and Marathon and, big as it is, be over here not too long from now. Unless it stops moving again, that is."

The young lieutenant commander walked over. There was a thin layer of perspiration on his upper lip, just below his sharply trimmed blond mustache. He nodded at Dees and spoke to Stevens. "Sir, the Seasprite's ready and CINCLANT advises because of the weather they might be able to get you some help from Guantanamo or Roosevelt Roads but not anytime soon. You're on your own for now."

The wind suddenly died. Patches of blue sky tore jagged holes in the motionless clouds hanging overhead. Glancing to the south, Dees saw more blue than gray. To the north and northeast, the sky was the color of a dirty carpet.

"We'll radio," Stevens shouted over the whine of the chopper's turbines, ducking as the four blades began to pick up speed. "We may need backup."

The lieutenant commander gave a thumbs-up. As soon as Stevens, Dees, and Marco were strapped in the backseats, the sliding doors were latched shut and the helicopter rose straight up, pitched forward gently, and accelerated toward the southeast.

A voice came through both headsets. "Gentlemen, welcome aboard the SH-2G Super Seasprite."

The pilot turned to face Stevens, who was seated behind the copilot. Under the helmet, Dees could make out green eyes with barely visible crow's-feet radiating from the corners, and a short orange-blond mustache. He snapped down his tinted visor and began to imitate the voice of an airline pilot, complete with Chuck Yeager twang. "I'm your pilot, Lieutenant Sam Wymore. On our flight to Paris this evening I'll be assisted by first officer Lieutenant Dana Hansen. Say hello, Lieutenant."

The copilot smiled as she turned to face Dees. She had an aquiline nose, peeling from a sunburn, and chocolate-brown eyes. She nodded toward the pilot. "He's crazy but harmless, sir, and a great helo driver."

Wymore's eyes crinkled as he smiled. "Do not attempt to stow your tray tables since you might screw up several million dollars worth of top secret electronics and your flight attendants will have to kill you."

"Our in-flight movie," Hansen chimed in without missing a beat, "will be 'Thelma and Louise Join the Navy.' Please enjoy the flight."

Both were laughing now, and Wymore picked up the patter. "We'll be flying at an altitude of a few feet, more or less, in our SH-2G. Our Seasprite comes equipped with sonar, radar, thermal, and sound detection equipment. It can track and kill anything that paddles, crawls, or vibrates on or under the water. It's normally configured for three people, four max, so the three of you will have to lose some more weight to fit in comfortably back there."

Dees keyed his microphone. "You two thinking about taking this act on the road?"

Wymore nodded without turning his head. "The best pilot/first officer team any airline or space program could want. She can fly anything except maybe a submarine."

"And he," Hansen continued, "has been flying something or other since he was fourteen. We're—"

"The best damn team in the Navy," Wymore said. "Sir."

"Good," Stevens said, his voice clipped. "You ever take on a Russian fighter?"

"Sir?" Wymore said.

Dees keyed his mike. "What did they tell you about this mission?"

"Just to fly you gentlemen to the Mira Por Vos," Wymore said, looking straight ahead. "We're supposed to look for an airstrip and an aircraft and report back, maybe rendezvous with another helo from Autec or maybe Gitmo or Rosey Roads."

Stevens said, "There may be a Sukhoi at the airstrip and a small nuclear device along with it, and we may have to stop it from taking off."

"Sir?" Hansen thumbed her mike switch. "This is an unarmed aircraft except for the torpedoes, which have been removed. The Su-25 has a thirty millimeter cannon, and if both the Tumansky R-13s are putting out full thrust, can cruise at six hundred miles an hour. The pilot sits in a titanium-lined cockpit that could deflect anything we might throw at it except, as I said, sir, we're unarmed."

Wymore's voice crackled through the intercom. "See, I told you she was good."

Hansen looked thoughtful, then said, "But if we powered up everything at once and painted the jet with radar and sonar and infrared and broad-band radio hash, we might be able to scramble his avionics so he couldn't take off. And if there's dirt on the strip we could stir up a rotor wash so he couldn't see to fly without instruments, and it might toss dust into his turbines so he couldn't take off anyway. Maybe."

* * *

Dees's head began to nod and he dozed, waking with a start twenty minutes later when Stevens's voice came over the intercom. "Hey, that them over to the right?"

Dees blinked and looked to the west. "Uh-huh," he said sleepily. "Those are the Raggeds. Cay Verde's the one just ahead off to the right there. The Mira Por Vos are those little ones, dead ahead. See, off to the left you can see the lighthouse on Castle Island. That land just behind it is Acklins."

Stevens strained forward in his harness. "Nothing but rocks, some of them."

Dees nodded. "Only a couple or three of them are even big enough for any kind of airstrip, and then it'd fill most of the island."

"Like that one?" Hansen's voice sounded crinkly in Dees's headset. Dees followed the line of her arm and gloved hand, pointing slightly off to the right. He saw a long, low islet overgrown with scrub except for the right tip, where what looked like a white dirt road disappeared into a thicket that grew next to the ocean.

"Runway?" Dees asked.

"Looks like it," Wymore replied. He held the Seasprite in a hover, about ten feet above the flat water, hidden from anyone on the island by the scrub. "Here's an idea. If there's a plane, it'd have to be at the very end of a short runway like that, and it's not at this end. So I'll sneak to the other end—"

"And approach them from the rear," Hansen continued. "That gives us a little more of an edge."

Stevens reached inside his dark suit coat and tugged at a strap that ran over the right shoulder of his short-sleeved white shirt. He unsnapped a hook on one end of the strap, and sat the Uzi in his lap. A clip of ammunition was inserted, with another clip taped to it, upside down, so the shooter could empty one clip, eject it, flip it over, and insert a full clip in one motion. Stevens keyed his microphone. "Let's do it. Dees, you still have your friend on your ankle?"

Dees nodded. He closed his eyes and concentrated. Back in the box, he thought. Just jam the fear back in the box. He visualized himself stuffing something that looked like a big black bed sheet into a cardboard box about the size of a beer case. The sheet flapped and twisted, like it was caught in the helicopter's prop wash, but finally disappeared into the box. He opened his eyes and blinked, once.

The helicopter nosed forward, moving a few yards above the ocean, a hundred yards from the nameless patch of scrub with a runway on it. Hansen pointed and said, "Check it out."

A thirty-eight-foot Cigarette boat, its black script logo almost invisible against a dark blue hull, was tied front and rear to thick bushes perched above the coral rocks. As they moved away from the racing boat, still parallel to the coastline, Dees shoved his face against the glass on the sliding door next to him. "Take a look at two o'clock, up the coast from the Cigarette. Is that another boat on fire?"

Marco thumbed the power switch on the camera and focused through the window. Staring at the viewfinder, he saw a grainy image of something dark and low in the water, a lazy curl of gray smoke twisting upward from one end. As the helicopter moved closer, Marco panned from the Cigarette to the dark object. He could see it was a boat, built for speed low to the water, wider than the Cigarette and with more room on deck. He focused on the three fist-size holes in the windscreen. Panning down, he saw it was painted solid black, with no registration numbers or insignia.

It had apparently settled on the bottom in about four feet of water, the nose heaved up at a thirty degree angle, the stern completely submerged. Water slopped over the gunwales, filling most of the wide cockpit with water. A dark mass of something, Marco couldn't tell what, was smoldering just forward of the windscreen. He panned up, then knew what it was that was smoking on the bow. His stomach lurched.

By now, Dees could see it, too. The body was facedown, tilted downward because of the steep shore of coral covered by bushes. The greenery below it and on both sides was flattened, as if it had been dragged from the boat and dumped. At first, he thought the branch sticking straight up above the corpse's waist had been caught in a rear belt loop of the olive-green fatigues. As the helicopter side-slipped to the right, Dees's angle changed, so he could see that the branch had sprung through a hole where the small of the back should have been.

Dees tugged on Hansen's flight suit, and pointed. She motioned to Wymore, who cautiously steered the Seasprite a few feet closer. Marco widened his shot to include the body and the boat. He pulled back to an even wider shot that framed the turquoise water and dank green shoreline. He sighed and shut off the camera.

"He took something right through the middle," Marco said tiredly into the microphone. "Maybe a grenade from an RPG. Those look like blast marks across his jacket. I think that's his stomach cooking on the bow. A phosphorus grenade, maybe."

"The vessel looks pretty shot up," Hansen said, "like they were approaching the shore and someone opened fire."

Wymore nudged the helicopter toward the far end of the islet. He glanced at the GPS readout on the control panel and said, "Autec, six-three-five."

The response was immediate. "Six-three-five."

"We have an airstrip on a small island. Seventy-four, thirty, nineteen west, twenty-two, twenty-five, sixteen north. We have two vessels in the water. One's been sunk, with a body nearby on the shore. We're checking the runway now, stand by."

Turning gently right, still a hundred yards offshore and fifteen feet above the Caribbean, Wymore poked Hansen on the shoulder and pointed. "Runway."

A strip of white earth emerged from the scrub. Stevens said, "We need to get up to take a look."

"We'll do it fast," Wymore said. "Hang on."

The chopper pitched forward slightly and shot almost straight up so fast that Marco found himself unable to lift his camera until they jolted to a stop fifty feet over the island. He said "Shit," softly, and powered up the camera, zooming in and focusing through the thick windshield on a dappled gray jet that sat at the end of the runway.

One green branch was atop its right wing, while several more straddled the fuselage near the tail. "They've pulled off most of the camouflage," Stevens said to no one in particular. "Taking off?"

The question was answered by two large puffs of dirt that erupted at the rear of two large jet exhausts just forward of the tail. The branches on the fuselage shook, and were blown straight out into the ocean. The body of the jet looked barely wide enough for one person to sit. It broadened just behind the cockpit where an engine intake was mounted on each side, then narrowed again at the tail. The two thick, slightly swept-back wings were mounted over the engines.

"What're they doing?" Stevens said, straining against his harness to lean forward. Dees saw seven figures in a clearing that had been hacked from the bushes. Four stood, three knelt. The three on the ground had their hands behind them.

Marco focused in time to see one of those standing raise a rifle. A wisp of smoke came from the barrel, and three pinpoint eruptions of dust blossomed behind the person kneeling in the middle, who rocked backward and pitched to the left.

Another man pointed toward the helicopter. The one with the rifle took a quick stride to his right, held the weapon at waist level, and fired another burst into one of the kneeling figures. This time Dees could see liquid erupt from the head before the body folded straight back.

The shooter ignored the third person kneeling on the ground. Instead, he raised his rifle toward the chopper just as it pitched forward a few degrees and began to dive straight toward them.

* * *

As the helicopter's blades spun at nearly full throttle and the twin turbojet engines of the jet began to build thrust, the five people on the ground were enveloped in a choking cloud of swirling, gritty white dust. It was powdered oolite limestone, which rose 15,000 feet from Continental shelf bedrock like a line of rough calluses to form the Bahamas' 2,700 islands and cays. Airborne dirt trapped in crevices, slowly decaying nutrients in the fossilized limestone, and the occasional rain shower provided just enough habitat for the scruffy cabbage palms, stunted Caribbean pines, and scrub brush that covered most of the nameless islet.

A circular area around the jet and the people near it looked, from the air, like it was trapped in the vortex of a tiny hurricane as the Seasprite hovered lower and the rotor wash became stronger. Dees saw the brush still atop the jet's right wing go airborne, flying into the midsection of the man with the rifle.

The helicopter was fifty feet off the ground, Dees guessed. It was close enough for him to see that the four men with guns were black, and dressed in civilian clothes. The person kneeling might have been military, wearing the same olive fatigues as the body next to the boat and the two bodies near the runway. Marco, who had been rolling through the window on the entire scene, looked up from his viewfinder as Wymore said, "Paint the jet with the works."

Hansen reached into the backseat next to Dees, and flipped four toggle switches, then punched a series of touchpads on the console in front of her. "Sonar, radars, ECM set," she said. "Painting now."

An avalanche of bone-shaking sound waves, radar pulses, and electronic hash on several frequencies washed over the jet. From the Seasprite's altitude, the sonar alone caused the tempered Plexiglas sections of the fighter's canopy to rattle and strain against their seals. Dees suspected it was also giving the pilot one hell of a headache. The combined radar and electronic countermeasure pulses were designed to fry the Sukhoi's avionics and make everything from the compass to the fuel indicator useless.

As the four standing men tried to shield their eyes from the dust, which almost obscured them, Dees noticed what looked like a large ice pack, about ten feet in diameter, not far from the jet. It lay deflated on top of some scrub. He said, "That tan thing at three o'clock. What—"

"Fuel bladder," Hansen replied, not taking her eyes off the controls in front of her. "Used to gas up in forward areas away from fuel depots."

"We're dropping down a little," Wymore said. "A little more wind and we can flatten these guys. I don't think our friend in the jet's going anywhere. He can't see a thing and his instruments are out."

"Uh-huh," Dees said, "tell that to Superman down there. He's taking off."

"Shit!" Wymore said as he heeled to the right and pitched the helicopter's nose down. But the Su-25 was already in front of them, the exhaust from the turbojets glowing like a small pair of hot yellow suns surrounded by cooler blue coronas. The distance between the pursuing helicopter and the accelerating jet grew greater, until the fighter shot off the end of the runway, tucking its twin landing gear into the belly almost immediately, picking up speed barely five feet above the water.

"He's gone!" Stevens said. "Radio the base and get us back to those people on the ground before they recover."

Wymore jerked the helicopter hard to the left and headed back down the runway in a tornado of dust. As it approached the men on the ground, Stevens's raspy intercom voice said, "How do I slide this door open?"

"Big handle," Hansen said. "Jerk it up until it locks, then shove hard left."

The helicopter was less than twenty feet from the men on the ground when the door swung open and latched. The man with the rifle swung it from the remaining kneeling figure and pointed at the Seasprite. Stevens braced the Uzi against his shoulder, cocked his head, and fired a pair of three-shot bursts. A small red geyser erupted from the rifleman's T-shirt. He collapsed in a heap.

Just behind him, a thin man wearing a blue short-sleeved shirt tossed down a pistol and thrust his hands into the air. To his left, a heavyset man whose ebony belly protruded from under his tight green T-shirt began waving his arms and yelling. The man in the blue shirt turned toward him, yelling something in reply, when the man with the belly pulled the trigger. The thin man fell flat on his back.

Stevens twisted the quick-release latch on his H-harness and jerked off his helmet. He pounded Wymore on the shoulder and pointed down with his index and middle fingers. The Seasprite dropped lower, hovering less than four feet off the ground when Stevens jumped out. Dees removed his helmet and released his harness, jerked the handle of the door to his right, slid it open, and jumped.

Marco, in contrast, dropped gingerly to the ground. He stumbled but immediately regained his feet, crouching and shielding his eyes as the helicopter regained altitude. He sprinted toward Stevens with the camera rolling. Throwing himself flat on the ground, he steadied the shot through the viewfinder just as Stevens fired off another burst, spinning the man with the pistol around completely.

Out of the corner of his eye, Dees saw something move. A man with a scruffy fringe beard emerged from the brush. He carried a rifle with an attachment on the front that ended in a projectile shaped like a teardrop.

"Grenade launcher!" Stevens yelled, and dove to the ground. The bearded man raised the rifle to his waist and launched the teardrop in their direction. It seemed to move in slow motion, jerking in the swirling wind created by the helicopter. It hit at the runway's edge, fifteen yards to the left of where Stevens had dived to the ground and covered his head with his arms.

The grenade exploded with a *whhammp*, scattering shrapnel and white limestone, which was caught in the chopper's vortex, creating a swirling cloud of grit and shredded metal around Stevens and Dees. The bearded man was reaching into his belt and attaching another teardrop projectile as Marco pulled back to the widest shot possible. The shot showed Stevens in the foreground, the kneeling figure in olive fatigues behind him, and to the left of the frame, the man with the grenade launcher.

Dees rolled to his left and reached for his ankle holster. Stevens, on his knees now, steadied the Uzi on his shoulder. As the grenade launcher was being raised, they both fired. Puffs of dust rose briefly at the man's feet. He seemed distracted by the whining bullets buzzing near him. Stevens, up and running in a crouch, fired off two bursts. Dees ran forward, then dropped to one knee and squeezed off two rounds just as Stevens emptied his clip with three more bursts.

Three of Stevens's slugs traced diagonal lines across the man's chest to the edge of his stomach, where they burrowed inside his body. As he spun to his left, one of Dees's bullets hit him between the ear and temple. Small jets of blood pirouetted in the churning air as the man spun and fell facedown.

The helicopter was hovering behind Dees, to his left. He looked at Stevens and yelled, "You okay?"

The FBI agent, staring past Dees, pointed with his left arm. Dees swung around in time to see the Su-25 pop up as if out of nowhere. It was over the ocean, just beyond the far end of the runway. As it hurtled straight toward them, Dees saw twin blinking lights just below the front of the canopy, winking like a pair of shorted-out Christmas tree bulbs.

He heard a *screaakk* like metal tearing, followed by what sounded like a cross between a shriek and a whine, followed by what Dees was sure *was* a scream just before the Seasprite exploded in a blossoming orange and black fireball. The blast started just below the rotors, behind the cockpit. All four rotors separated from the body of the helicopter. The blade assembly turned on its side, and spun jerkily toward the ground like a giant four-bladed scythe.

Dees, Stevens, and Marco glanced at each other and began running toward the cover of some bushes on their right. One blade slammed into the runway, snapped off, and whistled upward in an arc, sailing twenty feet over Dees's head before dropping into the ocean. The other blades gouged holes in the rock-hard limestone before they sliced three small pine trees in half and finally crashed down on the shoreline, half on the island, half in the water.

Dees watched a mass of flame and smoke cover the entire Seasprite except for the tail rotor. The burning wreckage had hit the runway nose first, and seemed to pause before another explosion sent a small orange mushroom cloud roiling toward the clouds. The Su-25 screamed through the cloud of flame and debris, heeled to the left, and dove below the level of the scrub, the rumble of its twin engines fading quickly.

The sickly sweet aroma of burning flesh mingled with the odors of acrid burning plastic and rubber and overheated metal caused Dees to gag. Stevens, standing up, shook his head slowly as he stared at the flaming wreckage. Dees coughed, got up, and walked over to him.

"There's nothing we can do," Stevens said, a lost expression on his face. "They're dead. The jet got away. It may have an A-bomb. There's nothing . . ."

His voice trailed off. Dees squinted and stared at the flat horizon. "Maybe they had time to radio Autec. Maybe the transponder's still broadcasting so they can find us. Maybe somebody on Acklins'll see the smoke and call for help."

The kneeling person now rocked upright. Dees said, "Hey, Curtis, give me a hand? Let's see what we've got."

Stevens nodded mechanically. He picked up the Uzi, took out the spent clip, and inserted the end of the full clip. He racked a shell in the chamber as he and Dees approached the figure from behind.

"Don't move!" Dees said.

The figure's head flipped to the side sharply, tossing the long dark hair out of her eyes.

"Oye chico," Gloria Bravo said weakly, "can't you stay out of trouble?"

CHAPTER 14

Stevens stepped forward, Uzi raised. Dees looked up. "Put it down. I know her."

Stevens just shook his head and kept the gun leveled. "How?"

Dees had been squatting next to Gloria. He got up and turned to Stevens. "Details later. Just put the gun down while we talk."

"I could talk more," Gloria said, "if you untaped my hands."

"Momentito," Dees said. He turned to Marco, and made a spinning motion in the air with his index finger. Marco nodded, picked up the camera, powered it back up, and took a wide shot of the burning helicopter. He zoomed in for a close-up of the hottest part of the blaze, held the shot steady, and pulled back slowly. He walked to his right and repeated the series from a different angle. Dees pulled a Swiss Army knife from a pocket of his photographer's vest, and easily cut through the plastic filaments embedded in the duct tape.

He gripped her elbows to help her up, and looked at the trickle of sweat running down her chest. The top two buttons of the olive drab uniform shirt were ripped off. Dees noticed that one of her breasts was outside her white bra.

She followed the path of his eyes with her own and pulled her elbows free. She tugged inside her shirt. "Yeah," she said quietly, "one of those Jamaican *maricones* grabbed a feel after he clubbed me with a rifle."

"Jamaican?" Dees said.

"*Chico,*" she said with an exhausted half smile, "interesting times."

"Who the hell are you?" It was Stevens. His eyes had lost their glazed look. He held the Uzi in both hands, level with his waist, and seemed to be considering whether to swivel the barrel and aim it at her. Marco sat on the ground and watched.

Reflexively, Dees took a half step forward, putting himself between her and the weapon. "Curtis, this is Gloria Bravo, she's a friend from Havana with—"

"From Havana?" Stevens's voice was tight.

"From Havana," Dees continued. "She's with Radio Havana and the Foreign Affairs Ministry, or so I've been told."

Dees motioned toward Marco, and faced Gloria. "This is Pedro Marco, Cuban-American lunatic."

Gloria looked sour. "And I presume dedicated anti-Communist?"

Marco studied her for a moment. "I got no politics except television, *hermana.*"

Dees nodded toward Stevens. "And this is Agent Curtis Stevens with the Federal Bureau of Investigation, and his friend Uzi."

Gloria laughed and Stevens cracked a smile. Dees sighed, relieved. "Good. I'm assuming they either radioed or Autec's monitored the transponder. Either way we should have help coming soon, assuming Diaz hasn't nuked Miami."

"You do not need to worry, at least yet," Gloria said. "Do you have any water?"

Dees shook his head. Stevens looked beyond the shoreline and said, "Maybe in the Cigarette? Then we can talk, if that's not asking too much."

All four trudged between the smoldering remains of the Seasprite and the body of the man with the grenade launcher. As Dees pushed the thorny scrub aside, he fought off a wave of nausea. Swarms of flies were circling the branch that stuck from the midsection of the body on the shoreline. Dees stepped into the Cigarette, and saw a small cooler fastened to the port bulkhead with a bungee cord. He opened the cooler, found three unopened liter bottles of water, reached inside his photographer's vest, and pulled out a red bandanna.

Gloria stepped gingerly into the cockpit, followed by Stevens. Sitting in an upholstered seat behind the steering wheel, she took the bandanna and soaked it with water. Looking around appreciatively, she said, *"Muy impresionante,"* and dabbed the wet handkerchief on the bruise over her eye. "This Cabrera even spends his money on upholstery in a speedboat. *Primera clase."*

Stevens took a long gulp of water from another bottle and poured half the remainder over his head. It rolled down his neck and soaked his filthy white short-sleeved shirt. He looked down in some surprise at the undone necktie he was still wearing. "So much for my spread in GQ," he said ruefully, turning to look at Gloria. "Who the hell are you and why am I sitting on the island with nine bodies?"

"We are, you might say, in the same line of work," she said. Dees looked puzzled. "We have also been looking into *Señor* Cabrera's activities."

"We?" Dees said. "We who?"

She paused, and sighed. " 'We' meaning my country's intelligence services, meaning the Interior Ministry security apparatus and the Central Committee. 'We,' in my case, meaning the DGI."

The only sound was the slap of tiny waves on the hull and the creak of the mooring lines against the brush. Dees had been standing. He sat heavily on the cooler, causing the boat to rock briefly. "DGI," he said quietly, shaking his head. "Why not?"

Stevens stared at Gloria, his right index finger on the Uzi's trigger guard. She stared back, just as flatly, and said, "The nuclear warhead, we think, is not on the jet. It could be in the United States someplace or even elsewhere."

Stevens sucked in air through his teeth. "We thought it was on the plane."

"It is not that kind of weapon," Gloria said, pressing the water-soaked bandanna against the bruise above her eye. "It is in, what do you call it, a briefcase?"

Dees pursed his lips. "Like they said, Spetznatz."

Gloria looked at Dees, then at Stevens, and nodded. "Yes."

Stevens narrowed his eyes. "You seem to know a lot about a renegade atomic device. And what's a Spetznatz?"

She took a swig from the bottle, and wiped her mouth. "Spetznatz was Soviet, that is to say, Russian Special Forces. They still exist, trained commandos designed to penetrate enemy territory and create chaos, also trained in, ah, unconventional warfare."

Dees squinted to his right, due north, at the flat horizon and high floating clouds in the far distance. Without looking at either of them, he said "When I was in Afghanistan, the *mujahadeen* I was running with captured a Spetznatz when they overran a company of Russians guarding a mountain pass. Two of the survivors ratted on him, and the *mujahadeen* got plenty of information by torturing him to death. They sliced off one-inch strips of flesh running from his knees to his ankles, then they'd rub salt or dirt into the pulp where the skin used to be.

"When they got around to showing him off to me, everything between his knees and ankles on both legs was an oozing mush filled with abscesses and flies. He was hanging from his wrists from a small tree. The *mujahadeen* thought it was pretty funny that he'd bitten off his tongue at the end and tried to choke on it and kill himself. Before they finished him off by sticking a rifle up his ass and pulling the trigger—"

Gloria made a soft, gurgling sound. Dees looked embarrassed. "Sorry. He'd told them about these one-kiloton briefcases Spetznatz had available. Infiltrate an enemy city, plant one, and you get a very dirty but relatively small mushroom cloud that levels a few city blocks and throws fallout all over the place. So the Soviet Union goes out of business and finds itself with Spetznatz units all over the place, armed with these things. Places like Yugoslavia."

Gloria nodded, and added, "And they are for sale, so our sources say. They claim Cabrera purchased a Foxbat fighter in Serbia along with one of the briefcases."

Stevens gagged briefly as the smell from the nearby corpse and the body parts simmering in the helicopter drifted into the boat. He took a deep breath. "So you're going to cooperate with us?"

Gloria looked at him suspiciously. "As if I have any choice now. But only if you can assure me I will not be compromised and that I will not be taken into custody."

Stevens looked down at the Uzi, and rehooked the clip on the strap, letting it hang over his shoulder. "As long as we're after the same thing."

"Bueno," Gloria said. "We, that is the security services, have been watching this Cabrera. We have linked him to several bombs that went off in Havana a few years ago, and to the Brigade X assault, and to some bribes paid to a variety of Cuban officials who were aware the attack was coming and ignored it. We also were made aware of his purchases in Serbia."

Stevens said, "And?"

"And," she said, "our best estimate is that he plans to stage an attack on the United States, set off the nuclear device, and make it seem as if it came from Cuba. We can only assume he thinks in the confusion the *yanquis* will retaliate against Cuba, Castro will fall, and he will profit from the chaos. I personally think this is foolish since the American radar and satellites will be able to confirm there is no attack from Cuba and—"

"The hurricane," Dees said quietly. Gloria wrinkled her

brow, and Dees tried not to sound exasperated. "The attack's supposed to come right after the hurricane. The hurricane's supposed to be used as cover. In that kind of confusion, nobody'll be able to confirm anything. If it's moving fast, he'd attack now. If it's stalled, he'll wait."

Gloria put her head down and slowly massaged her temples with her thumbs. "That is something we did not consider. We were sent to this island to stop the plane, but it seems they knew we were coming. Vila tried to fire back and they put a grenade through his stomach. Gonzalez and Ramirez, you saw, were executed. They knew about us. We were betrayed." She spread her palms open. "I will do whatever I can to help stop this, but we have little time."

"Shh," Dees said. "Listen."

They heard a faint hum, growing louder. Dees stood up, steadying himself on the port gunwale, looking over the top of the brush. He squinted and focused on a familiar silhouette in the distance.

"Seahawks," he said. "A pair of them. I think help's arrived."

All four scrambled out of the boat, shoved their way through the thorny scrub, and emerged onto the littered runway. Dees yelled, "Far end, away from the debris."

Marco focused the camera and rolled on the helicopters as they came closer. He walked forward two dozen paces and focused again, shifting the angle of his shot. He stopped when Dees yelled, "Hey. Let's go."

As they sprinted for the end of the limestone airstrip, Dees yelled at Stevens, "Remember, she's with us."

Stevens nodded. They waved their arms as a pair of single-engine helicopters with bulbous front ends and narrow tails hovered a hundred feet above them. As the helicopters began to land, Dees saw three rifle barrels aimed out a sliding door, pointing straight at them. Dees shouted above the rotor wash, "Smile and wave. We're the good guys, remember?"

The first helicopter sat down with a soft shudder, and a

half-dozen Marines piled out, screaming at them to get down on their stomachs. Six M-16s were leveled at their chests.

* * *

The four of them stood, soaking wet, inside a hangar office just off the Autec main runway. The wind jerked at the office door as it whistled inside the cavernous building. Mammoth sliding panels on tracks in the concrete had been rolled shut, but the winds and spray still managed to work though the gaskets.

Stevens looked down sourly at his feet, and saw he was standing in a puddle from his drenched clothes. He looked at the lieutenant commander who had seen them off a few hours before. "I never want to go through that again. We fly into a hurricane?"

It was the Navy officer's turn to look like he was sucking on a lemon. "Into a shitstorm. The hurricane's approaching category four, moving like it's drunk. Eye was stalled north of Marsh Harbor and Abaco, then it started moving due south, toward us."

"That means we need to get out of here now," Dees said. "Can we get a plane to fly around it and get back to Miami?"

The lieutenant commander glared. "Not until I get some answers for CINCLANT about two dead Navy officers and a pile of bodies on an island." He jabbed a finger toward Gloria. "And I need to know who you are."

"One of our agents," Stevens said coolly. "Tried to stop the jet on the island. This is a national security matter now, and Dees is right, we need a plane to get back to Miami, and I need a telephone that still works. Please."

The officer indicated a phone on the corner of his desk. "That one should still work if the wind hasn't taken down the uplink dish."

As Stevens picked up the receiver, he said, "And we do need to get off this island and back to Miami. Got a plane we can use?"

"Twin engine prop transport," the lieutenant commander grumbled. "We may need it to ferry some items to the *Truman*."

Dees's head snapped up. "The *Truman*? What's a carrier doing around here?"

The officer shrugged. "Radio intercepts indicate a good deal of military traffic in Cuba, more troops moving along the roads than usual, and even air force patrols have increased, which is unusual because—"

"There is not enough fuel," Gloria interrupted. "Training flights are almost nonexistent because of a severe shortage of aviation fuel."

"I don't know about that, ma'am," the officer said suspiciously, "but the *Truman* task force's been ordered to maintain a station fifty miles off the Cuban coast. This incident seems to have everybody nervous. On top of that, who knows if Castro's even still alive or not?"

Stevens was barking into the phone receiver. "Briscoe? . . . Yeah, you'll have to speak up. . . . What? . . . Okay, okay . . . Everybody all right? . . . Listen, meet me at Homestead. . . . What? . . . If it's that bad, get a Humvee from the National Guard or somebody. Just meet us there. What? . . . Speak up, what?"

He turned to the officer. "Time from here to Homestead?"

The officer shrugged. "Depends."

Stevens snapped his fingers, twice. "Let's do better than that, okay? CINCLANT and the FBI are asking you very nicely."

Another shrug. "An hour, maybe two if I can get a crew to fly and an aircraft gassed up in this mess."

"Try then, okay?" Stevens said. He turned back to the telephone. "Yeah, Briscoe? Meet us at Homestead in an hour. It may take longer, just wait. . . . What? That bad? . . . You're kidding."

Stevens held the receiver out and stared at it like it was a rotten banana he'd just bitten into. "That's bullshit. . . . What?

I can't understand you with the break-up. . . . You're kidding. . . . Okay, okay, see you."

The officer shot Stevens a sharp look and walked out the door into the hangar. Stevens stroked his mustache. "Floodwater's made a mess of pretty much everything. Homestead's got clear runways, but outer edge winds gusting to sixty and lots of debris they're clearing up. And Briscoe says Washington doesn't believe the Cabrera angle. The White House told the Bureau in D.C. that we have a national security emergency because of all the military noise in Cuba. Seems a couple of Florida hotheads are on the NSC and, well, shit, it looks like things are getting out of control. Those guys claim they know Castro's dead, or just about, and all hell may be ready to break loose on Cuba."

Gloria stared at the phone. "Is that a satellite telephone link?"

"Sounds like it," Stevens said.

Dees looked at her. "Time to call home?"

She nodded, walked to the receiver, and punched in a series of numbers. The connection broke off twice before she tried the third time and succeeded. She spoke rapidly, in Spanish. "Fernando, it is me. . . . What? . . . No, a terrible telephone line, I would imagine. . . . No, no, we failed. I was the only one to survive. The jet escaped. No! No! Listen."

Her voice took on the cool, hard edge Dees had first heard in the Havana airport. "I said listen! The Americans are working with us on this. They also want Diaz stopped. These increased military movements are just going to cause problems because there is no threat to Cuba. Do you understand?"

She paused and listened. Her eyes looked tired. "They are what? . . . No, no, Fernando, I know for a fact this is not so. The Americans know that an attack on them could be blamed on us, and they are working with me to stop it. You must make sure that—what? It is the phone line, say that again. . . . No! You are fading out. . . . What? Hello?"

She sat in the desk chair heavily, putting both palms on her forehead. "It feels like *una jaqueca*, as you say, a migraine. Or maybe it is just my reaction to idiots. The hard-liners in the Defense and Interior Ministries are spreading reports that an American attack is imminent."

She looked up at Dees. "They claim the Americans are preparing a first strike because Fidel is dying, so now the Cuban military is on its highest state of alert. And these fools . . ." Her voice trailed off. She was silent for a moment, inhaled, and let the words come tumbling out. "They say if there is any provocation they are prepared to counterstrike against Florida."

The room was silent until Stevens said, "Does anybody know how far in advance of an explosion you can set the timer in the briefcase?"

"One hundred hours," Gloria said, almost in a whisper. "Actually, ninety-nine hours and fifty-nine minutes, or so I have been told, since it is a four-digit timer."

"So it could be put in place four days in advance," Dees said, leaning across the desk. "But they'd have to coordinate it with the fighter, since they have to use the hurricane as cover. So we can assume they'll plant the briefcase at the last minute, with enough time to get away. So we can assume it hasn't been planted yet, since it all depends on where the hurricane moves, and when."

There was a whistle and a gust of wind as the lieutenant commander came back in, carrying a bundle under his arm. He plopped it on the desk with a smile. "Every flight crew volunteered. I picked the two who're the least sane and gave them a twin prop so the water won't put out any jet turbines. You leave in ten minutes, and we dug up some spare flight suits so you can dry off."

Stevens said, "Thanks."

Dees said, "Find out anything new about the hurricane?"

"The meteorological boys have a new name for it. Instead of Hurricane David, they're calling it Hurricane Norman, like in Bates, like in *Psycho.* It's moved, it's stopped, it's wiggled, it's changed direction. It's been stalled northeast of here, now it's started to move again, almost due west and a little south, so you'd better get out of here while you can. They tell me it could pass somewhere between Miami and Marathon in a couple of days, or it could speed up and cross within twenty-four hours, or slide south and hit Key West, or north into Miami, or it could sit still and flood everything."

"But it's moving west now?" Dees said. "And that could put it somewhere between Florida and Cuba in a while?"

"I guess," the lieutenant commander said. "I'm going to make sure your plane gets gassed. Get dressed, since as soon as the storm passes I'm going to be real busy with CINCLANT."

As the door latched, Dees sighed. "It's starting to become the kind of cover Diaz'll need. But he'll have to wait until it's almost past before he could fly, so we may have plenty of time, or no time at all."

Gloria looked up. "So where do you think he has gone? Can he be found beforehand?"

Dees was walking absently around the small office, looking at the various maps mounted to the wall, each encased in Plexiglas. He stopped, and rubbed the remains of grease pencil from the surface of one. He tapped it with an index finger. "My best guess is here, the Ragged Islands. There are plenty of old doper airstrips on them."

Stevens, his face to the wall, had changed from his drenched shirt and muddy suit into the flight suit. He turned to face Dees, who suppressed a sputtering laugh. Stevens glared. "Got a joke?"

"Black wing tips and a Navy flight suit?"

The agent looked down at his feet. He suddenly looked thoughtful, and said, "Why don't you file a story on this now and blow the whistle on Cabrera and Diaz? Maybe you could stop the entire thing."

Dees said, "Let's say I was able to file something from

here. What's the story? We have a lunatic in a jet who may or may not have a nuclear weapon. I get the word out about that, and every highway between Key West and Orlando will be jammed with terrified people trying to run from the apocalypse. And they'd drive right into a hurricane, which would probably kill God knows how many of them."

There were three sharp raps on the door, and the lieutenant commander's voice came from the other side. "Everybody decent? Time to go wheels up."

Both Dees and Stevens stepped into the hangar and closed the door behind them. A twin-engine propeller plane sat near the closed hangar doors. Gloria emerged from the office, wearing the flight suit and holding her soggy clothes under her arm. Marco looked at Gloria's form-fitting flight uniform and arched his eyebrows appreciatively.

They climbed into the passenger compartment, which looked like a small civilian commuter plane, and strapped themselves in. Ten minutes later, they were airborne. Out of his window, Dees couldn't see anything but swirling rain gusts and skidding black clouds. He checked his watch. Almost dawn, but there was no way to tell from the color of the sky.

He thought he might die no more than three times during the two-hour flight. The last time came an hour and a half after takeoff; as Marco pointed the camera out a round window to record the multiple bolts of lightning that spread out on all sides of the plane, it seemed they were flying through the bright yellow bare branches of some gargantuan tree.

The plane shuddered and fell, pushing all four of them up against their harnesses, the polymer and canvas weave cutting into their shoulders. While they fell, the twin engines screamed as they banked hard to the right, followed by another hard bank, this time to the left, and another bank to the right. Whatever the flight crew had been dodging apparently fell away to the rear. The rest of the flight was technically severe turbulence, but seemed silky compared to what they had already flown through.

Forty-five minutes later, they broke through the dark clouds, zipping along at six hundred feet, and touched down on Homestead Air Base's twelve-thousand-foot main runway, stirring up a hissing shower of spray from the wet tarmac. The runway and control tower were about all that remained from the days before Hurricane Andrew ripped the base apart in 1992, turning hangars into flying buzz saws of jagged scrap metal and flipping twenty-ton fighter jets through the air like dry leaves. All of the buildings, from hangars to mechanics' shops to base housing bungalows, had been demolished. Now there was a wing of Air Force Reserve fighters, and vague plans to someday turn the entire area into a civilian airport or an office park.

The engines had barely shut down when the main door was opened from the outside. A tall black major, trailed by a chunkier white captain, ducked inside. The major crouched in the aisle between Stevens and Gloria. "I'm Major Gerald Chapman, this is Captain Lou Wozniak. One of your agents is here with a Humvee. You'll need it. It's not nearly as bad as Andrew was, but it's lasted for three days, with a lot more rain. Going's rough on some of these roads. Given the high alert right now—"

"Excuse me?" Dees said.

The major looked at him expressionlessly. "The base may be reactivated, given the tensions now with Cuba. We could be getting aircraft sent down from Eglin and Patrick once the weather clears enough. We've been told to provide all the assistance we can. But with the alert and the storm clean-up, we're stretched thin."

The major motioned them outside. Led by the officers, the three walked across the taxiway. Dees noticed that Briscoe's orange flat top bristled even more in the humidity. Gray-green clouds skidded above them, and piles of palm fronds, fallen limbs, and plant debris were shoved up against a six-foot chain-link fence, almost reaching the top.

Briscoe wore a blue blazer, gray slacks, and a white shirt. He walked over, shook hands with Stevens, ignored Dees and Marco, and looked Gloria up and down. "Nice flight suit, it fits real well. Who're you?"

Stevens, with a hint of exasperation, said, "Gloria Bravo, John Briscoe. Ms. Bravo's our liaison with the Cuban government to try and stop this thing before it gets out of hand. Where'd you get the Humvee?"

"Florida Guard's been Federalized," Briscoe said, sliding into the driver's seat as Stevens sat opposite him, separated by the vehicle's mammoth console. Dees, Marco, and Gloria climbed into the rear seats. "Cuba thing's getting too hot, so everybody here is on alert. I just used Federal status as leverage to get it."

He ground the Humvee into first gear and drove it slowly off the taxiway and down a winding asphalt road leading to the main gate. Briscoe glanced over his shoulder at Dees, sitting behind Stevens. "So did dickhead give you any trouble?"

"Don't start," Stevens said. "We need to find Cabrera and a small nuclear device before this thing gets any more out of control."

"That should be no problem," Briscoe said offhandedly, looking straight ahead as he drove through the gate and reached the main road. "I've been doing some surveillance of my own and managed to trace Cabrera. About now he should be at Turkey Point."

"The nuclear power plant?" Dees said quietly. "Shit."

"Great job, John," Stevens said with a trace of relief. "How—"

"Just sweated some of his associates," Briscoe said as the Humvee plowed through three feet of standing water, crunching over countless branches and several small trees. "Found some people in Lappahoosa that apparently Sherlock back there didn't find."

Dees let it pass, and looked around at the scattered apartment and office buildings. Most of the damage seemed to be from rising water, although he did see the occasional broken window or section of roofing shingles peeled back by the wind.

Stevens asked, "What about Vargas?"

Briscoe shrugged. "The documents that got him out of the lockup were forgeries, all right. None of the AUSAs had gotten a writ, nobody issued any paperwork, and we have a composite of that phony agent, Fleming, that's circulating. Other than that, we got bupkus."

The Humvee rattled off the main highway and onto a two-lane road heading east, toward Biscayne Bay and the Turkey Point plant. The road was under anywhere from six inches to two feet of water. Stevens turned in his seat and asked Gloria, "Could a one-kiloton warhead breach the core of a nuclear plant?"

Gloria shook her head. "I have no idea."

"They couldn't get it too close," Briscoe said. "The plant's got the National Guard around it, first because of the hurricane, then this Cuba alert shit. The turn for the cooling water canals is up ahead. If somebody planted something, maybe they put it outside the security zone, by the canals, maybe?"

Stevens stroked his mustache. "Maybe, but first we need to coordinate any search with the Guard."

Briscoe squinted through the water-streaked windshield. "Part of this road's got a sinkhole up ahead. Hold on, I'll take us off-road and then back around."

The Humvee jolted to the right, plunging immediately into sawgrass that reached all the way to the door latches. Dees could hear water splashing under the tires. The Humvee jolted briefly. "Fucking log or something. I'll just take us a little further this way and cut back to the road."

The water sounds stopped as the Humvee drove onto a

slightly elevated island of muck and sand, a hummock that had drained enough to be above even the floodwaters. The vehicle tore through a stand of cabbage palms and lurched to a stop.

"Shit," Briscoe said. He immediately shut off the engine and pocketed the keys. He opened the driver's door and said over his shoulder, "They warned me this might happen. The right rear hub locks up sometimes. I got it."

He walked to the rear and opened the hatch, revealing the storage area behind the rear seats. "Hey," Briscoe yelled, his head still inside the cargo area, "all of you get out for a minute, take some of the load off the springs so I can unlock this thing."

Dees and Stevens unlatched their doors and got out of the Humvee's right side while Gloria and Marco climbed out on the left. "All of you get over here on the right side," Briscoe said, still rummaging through the storage compartment. "Lean on this thing and it'll raise up a little so's I can adjust it quicker."

Gloria walked in front of the vehicle, standing behind Stevens. Marco joined them. All of them placed their hands on the side of the cab. Stevens called out, "You want us to rock this thing or what?"

Dees placed his hands on the rear part of the cab, and turned to Stevens. "Maybe this is a new model, but there's nothing I know of back there to adjust the suspension on—"

"Hey Curtis!" Briscoe yelled. Stevens pushed away from the cab, turning to his left to face the Humvee's rear just as Briscoe swung around, both hands holding a pistol with a foot-long silencer attached to the barrel. The two *pops* were softer than a champagne cork's, and the flash suppressor reduced the light from the barrel to a brief wink.

The first slug entered the center of Stevens's forehead and was about to blow off the crown of the skull when the second bullet bored into a spot just to the right of his nose. The geyser of blood and gray matter shot from the top of Stevens's head just as the second slug splintered and stopped, embedded in the torn remains of his medulla oblongata.

Stevens's feet both left the ground at once. He bounced off Gloria's shoulder, leaving a splotch of blood the size of a softball on her flight suit, and spun to the left, landing on his back. His eyes seemed to stare in surprise at something in the gray-and-black-streaked sky.

CHAPTER 15

Dees started to stride forward, but Briscoe swiveled the pistol directly at him. "Asshole," Briscoe hissed through clenched teeth. "I'd love to do this right now, but not yet. You!" He looked toward Gloria, his pistol still on Dees. "Turn around. Back over to me slowly. You don't wiggle that cute Cuban ass now, I'll kill him!"

Gloria narrowed her eyes, turned around, and put her hands up, then walked backward slowly until she stopped next to Briscoe. He put an arm around her neck and jerked her next to him, pressing the silencer's barrel into her right temple.

Dees's nostrils flared. He looked down and saw a disk that used to be the top of Stevens's skull, about the size of a tea saucer, lying next to the Humvee. It looked like a small patch of black curly grass trying to grow through the hummock's sand and limestone.

"Hey!" Briscoe rasped. "Hey tough guy! I'm really gonna enjoy this."

"And the National Guard?" Gloria said, her voice calm. "They would probably come by and take you into custody in just a few minutes."

Dees could see Gloria wince as the barrel was pressed harder against her temple. "Fucking spics," Briscoe whispered. "Fucked up this whole state, you and your fucking politics and jabbering in Spanish. The Guard'll never hear this silencer."

Marco tensed. Dees sensed it and gently put a hand across his chest, staring at Briscoe. "You killed an FBI agent," Dees said hoarsely. "You smart enough to weasel out of the Federal death penalty for killing your supervisor?"

"My supervisor?" Briscoe snorted. "Another affirmative action case."

Dees took a half step forward, then stopped as the gun's barrel was twisted harder into Gloria's skin. Dees put his palms in front of him. "Briscoe, this is just going to get you killed. Why do it?"

Briscoe smiled. "No, it's gonna get me rich for you three, plus Stevens."

"Cabrera?" Gloria said. She made eye contact with Dees, looked up toward Briscoe, then back at Dees, then moved her eyes sharply to her left. Dees nodded once, making it appear he was scratching his nose. He looked sideways at Marco, who raised his eyebrows with a slight nod.

"I got a rich retirement, thanks to Cabrera," Briscoe said. "And you know, if all this works out, I'll be even happier because all you spics will kill each other. I watched the spics take over Hialeah until my folks had to move, so we move to the Grove and the niggers take over."

The words came tumbling out like angry passengers shoving to get off a bus. "So the coke cowboys got rich and the fucking exiles got rich and the street pimps got rich and the Bureau gets all sweet and PC and I'm stuck in the field pulling down fifty thou a year. So Cabrera needs some help and I get ten years' pay in cash, and the great thing is if his plan works, all the spics'll leave Miami and go home to a free Cuba so they can rip off their own kind for a change."

Dees suddenly dove to his left, away from the Humvee, landing on his stomach just to Briscoe's right. At the same moment, Marco dove to his right. Surprised, Briscoe pivoted with the gun to his right. He released his grip with his left arm for a moment, long enough for Gloria to reach behind her in a swift motion, lock her right arm around his head, and twist sharply at the waist. Briscoe stiffened, but still went flying over her hip. He managed to hold onto her waist with his left arm, so when he landed on his butt she was pulled to the ground. She twisted away as he hit the sandy muck, and his grip loosened momentarily.

He was still clutching the pistol in his right hand, and was swinging it around toward Gloria when Dees sprang up with a yell and planted a kick squarely in Briscoe's left ear. He rocked to his right, the gun still in his hand. Marco threw himself on top of Briscoe as Dees dove headlong toward the oiled metal, grabbed the pistol with both hands, and twisted it out of Briscoe's grip. Rolling to his knees, he aimed the gun at Briscoe's midsection.

"I can't miss," Dees said, getting to his feet, "and I'm not sure I want to. Gloria? You okay? Pedro?"

Gloria dusted herself off and absently rubbed the circular indentation above her right temple. Squatting beside Briscoe, she said, "I feel another bad headache coming on, and I am easily upset and get angry when I have a headache. Are you, then, this *la tortuga*?"

Briscoe stared at Dees, then at the pistol, then at Gloria. Marco, behind them, was hauling the camera from the Humvee. Briscoe wrinkled his brow. "Who the fuck are you? What the fuck are you talking about?"

Gloria looked up at Dees. "This one needs to be telling us what he knows, and quickly."

Dees motioned her over. "Here," he said, not taking his eyes off Briscoe. "Take this, and if he moves at all, shoot him in the balls."

Gloria smiled and took the pistol. "It is a good thing I am an expert shot to hit a target that small."

Dees opened the door of the Humvee and rummaged through the passenger compartment. From the center console, he pulled out an envelope, removed some papers, and whistled.

"Well," he said, "he didn't get this Humvee from the National Guard. Here's the title and registration. Seems Gold Cane Holdings, Inc. bought it new four years ago with a custom camo job. So it's Cabrera's, so Cabrera knows it's here."

Dees searched the backseat, then began looking through the rear storage area. "Thought this thing seemed a little cushy for a military vehicle. Hmm. Well, it's not much but we can make it do."

He approached Gloria with a length of rope and a small machete, the blade about eighteen inches long. Bending down, he ordered Briscoe, "Put your hands above your head."

He tied the agent's hands with four loops of rope and, with a grunt, dragged him by the loops over the sand and muck. Dees pulled him to the rear of the Humvee. There he triple-looped the rest of the rope around the cylindrical steel bumper, leaving Briscoe's hands tightly bound above his head and pinned to the bumper.

"What the fuck are you doing?" Briscoe demanded.

Dees ignored him and turned to Marco. "Roll on this. But keep it tight close-ups of Briscoe's face. I don't want anything else in the frame."

Marco nodded and took a white balance off Briscoe's shirt. Dees looked down at the agent. "What I'm doing is videoing your story. And since there's still an atomic bomb out there and I still don't know who killed Richie, and my lady friend here is getting cranky, I'd suggest you talk."

He looked at Gloria, who picked up the machete, squatted by Briscoe's feet, and with a deft motion, pulled off his left shoe and sock. She grabbed the foot, squeezing a pressure point until the toes splayed. She rested the machete against his little toe.

She looked straight at Briscoe. "He will suffer a great deal of pain, and I imagine I will not have to cut off more than four or five toes before he tells us everything."

"By the numbers," Dees said as Marco focused a close-up of Briscoe's face. "Who killed Richie and why?"

Briscoe shook his head. "I don't have any fucking idea. That was never part of anything I knew about, just Vargas was all I knew."

"So Richie gets shot as soon as Brigade X lands," Dees said sardonically, "and you're there. And you're being paid by Cabrera. And you don't know anything about Richie?"

Briscoe tried to muster a sneer. "Oh fuck you!" he said. Suddenly, his face contorted in pain. The wind had started to rise with increasing force, whistling through the trees, so Briscoe's scream couldn't be heard more than twenty feet away. Looking through the viewfinder, Marco could see Briscoe's face, eyes bulging, mouth open, looking in terror at his foot.

Marco clicked off the camera and turned. Blood was oozing from the stump where Briscoe's small toe used to be. Gloria held out the machete, flat. The curled little toe sat in the middle of the blade like the last shrimp on a plate. Dees reached into a rear pocket and tossed a handkerchief to her. Marco looked at Dees. "C'mon, man, we can't do this."

Dees went over to Marco and squeezed his shoulder. "If you don't want to be part of this, I understand. But you have family here? You have relatives in Havana? You know this piece of shit's willing to kill them all for a few bucks? Your decision."

Marco took a deep breath and wiped his face with his hand. "For the greater good, huh?"

Dees shrugged. "I hope to hell it is, pal. But we're running out of time."

Gloria jammed the handkerchief against the bleeding nub. "You will not bleed to death, at least not from one toe," she said. "Not even from two or three, but if I cut off all of them, then you may bleed to death, or maybe you will just be unable to walk normally for the rest of your life. It is your decision."

Marco inhaled deeply again, hit the power button, and focused on Briscoe's face. Dees looked down grimly at Briscoe. "Now let's do this right. I ask, you answer, no smart remarks. Richie. What do you know about agent Richard Peterson's murder?"

"Nothing." It was almost a sob. "I swear. I just knew I'd been paid to get Vargas released once he was in custody, that's all. I swear, I never saw who shot Peterson, I never knew it was going to happen, I thought it was just more Cuban hotheads."

"Vargas," Dees said. "Ramon Vargas, a Federal prisoner who was murdered while in custody. What did you have to do with that?"

"C'mon man," Briscoe whined, trying to jerk his throbbing foot away from Gloria, who held it tight. "You can't let this happen to me."

Dees looked at Marco and made a cutting motion across his throat. Marco shut down the camera. A half smile creased Dees's face as he knelt next to Briscoe. He said quietly, "I'm a reporter, remember? I've let it happen to a boatload of better people than you. A reporter records, reports, and watches. I watched a baby in Ethiopia die of starvation in my arms. I had one of my best friends in Bosnia get ripped to pieces by shrapnel, and write 'I love you' on a pillowcase in his own blood before he died so his wife and kids would have something from him. Maybe he figured it made dying in a mudhole mean something. I've had twelve-year-olds in Rwanda and thirteen-year-olds in Kosovo and fourteen-year-olds in Afghanistan blown to stinking shit in front of my eyes. And you know what, pal? I let it happen each time, so to answer your question, yeah, I'll let it happen."

Dees stood back up. "So if I were you I'd start telling the truth the second he turns this camera back on."

Dees nodded again at Marco, who thumbed the power

switch, and looked through the viewfinder. Dees said, "Ramon Vargas. What do you know about his murder?"

Briscoe's terrified eyes moved from Dees to Gloria. She just smiled and waved the machete. He caught his breath. "I just managed to phony up the paperwork. I ripped off an embosser for the seal on the writ to get Vargas released. I forged the signatures. I told the Marshal's office to be expecting some agent named Vic Fleming. That was it, honest to God!"

Marco pushed the shot in tighter as Dees said, "Who did you do it for?"

Briscoe took a ragged breath. "Cabrera told me he'd set it up to have someone get Vargas out. I just fronted all the paperwork to Cabrera. I never got Vargas out and I didn't kill him and I don't know who did."

"And you were paid?"

Briscoe nodded. "By Manuel Cabrera. He told me Vargas had to be eliminated."

"How much did Cabrera pay you? For how long?"

Briscoe blinked his eyes, and they settled on Gloria. She laid the machete blade, lightly, against his fourth toe. He looked up at Dees again. "Half a million over two years. I'd acted as the Bureau's liaison when the Immigration Service nailed him for illegal Jamaicans. One day he calls me at home, says he wants to meet, so we talk, he needs information on exile activity, so we talk some more and he pays me and I snoop.

"He told me he already had somebody else for Vargas, to take care of him, I mean. So he—I mean Cabrera—Cabrera just wanted the phony paperwork. See, Cabrera thinks if it looks like Cuba's attacked us, the exiles will go nuts and the U.S.'ll hit back hard, and that means Castro goes away and Cabrera gets to be sugar king in Cuba. He explained it once about paying a dime on the dollar to Cuba for their sugarcane and they'll be glad to get it, see?"

Marco leaned around the edge of the Humvee and focused

on Stevens's body. He held the shot for ten seconds, then slowly pulled back, panning down and left, to Briscoe's face. Dees continued, "We witnessed your murder of FBI agent Curtis Stevens. Why did you kill him?"

"Cabrera," Briscoe said. He sounded like he might cry. "He tells me there's another hundred thousand in it for—"

"Hold it," Dees interrupted. "Stevens called you from Autec on Andros Island. So how did Cabrera find out we were coming back here?"

Briscoe began sniffling. "Yeah, Stevens called me and then I called Cabrera about how you were all coming back. He laughed and came up with the idea about Turkey Point, since it's nice and isolated. He tells me to do all of you for another hundred thou."

"And the attack?" Gloria said heatedly. "Where? When? And this atomic bomb, what about it?"

For a moment, Briscoe's face flashed with his former arrogance, but he couldn't maintain it. "I don't know shit about that nut case Diaz and his fucking jet. Maybe if we're lucky he'll blow up Calle Ocho and take out all the spics in Miami."

Gloria's face tightened, and she steadied his toe with her thumb, using the rest of her hand to press the machete against it, like she was preparing to slice a fresh green bean. Briscoe's eyes became wide again as he struggled against the rope. Marco pushed in for a tight close-up of his face as Dees said, "You know how excitable Cubans can be."

Briscoe suddenly looked exhausted. "The day you left for Cuba and had all that TV equipment at MIA? Cabrera knew about it. He said an extra piece'd be delivered to the airport and loaded with all of your shit. I went to the airport three hours before your flight and made sure the Customs boys'd let everything through without any questions. Bureau business, I told them. Whoever delivered it to the cargo area in the first place had been there and gone. My job was just to make sure it got loaded on the plane without any questions. Cabrera said everything'd be taken care of on the Havana end."

Marco looked up from the viewfinder, puzzled. Dees looked at Marco, then back at Briscoe. "There was something Cabrera shipped to Havana in the pile of GTV supplies for the Havana bureau?"

Briscoe managed a smile through pursed lips. "You know what you and the cunt here did?"

Briscoe tried to puff out his chest, but only managed to cough. "You fucking assholes managed to deliver an atomic bomb to Cuba in a briefcase piled in the middle of all that TV gear."

Dees stared at Briscoe. Small stinging bullets of rain began to pelt the hummock. Dees didn't feel them.

Gloria blinked to keep the water out of her eyes. Her right hand still clutched the machete and Briscoe's toe in the same grip she would have used to peel an apple with a paring knife. Her left hand was balled in a fist. A bead of water rolled down her forehead to the end of her nose and plopped on the ground. She seemed not to notice.

"A nuclear bomb," she said quietly. "You put a nuclear bomb in Cuba?"

Briscoe managed to grimace and smile at the same time. "I didn't put it there; I just helped, and this asshole," he said as he jerked his head toward Dees, "delivered it. Whoever's in Cuba's the one who's planting it. I just helped get it *Shit! Arrggh!*"

Dees looked down at Gloria, who was starting to slice at another toe with the machete. As Marco shut down the camera, Dees said, "Hold it. Save the toe."

"Why?" she said without expression. "This pig put an atomic bomb in my country that could kill thousands of people, and he is proud of it. And now it is too late."

"Not yet." Dees walked to the Humvee and found the phone on the console. It worked. "It's got a ninety-nine-hour timer," he explained. "Cabrera and his gang don't know what the hurricane's going to do any more than we do. It'd have to be set at the last minute, because they probably want it to go off about the same time Diaz slips from behind the hurricane and attacks something here. So somebody in Cuba would have to set it and they probably haven't done that yet."

"We must contact Havana," Gloria said firmly, looking at the cell phone.

"Sure," Dees said, leaning against the rear of the Humvee, "except that it'd be a bitch to call Havana from here because of the storm, and there's a hurricane chewing up everybody's communications. Or we could use the military facilities down at Homestead, but by the time they debrief us and run it through channels and probably arrest you, we could have an attack on the U.S. and a nuclear fireball in Cuba. So we need to get to Cuba, which might be faster."

Dees looked down at the compress on Briscoe's toe. "Keep the pressure on it. It's clotting up. Briscoe, you in much pain?"

The agent squinted and said, between his teeth, "Fuck, yes, I'm in pain."

"Good," Dees said. He looked at Gloria. "Do something for him. Knock him out or something."

She looked up, keeping pressure on the bandanna. "How?"

"What d'you mean, how? You're the damn spy. Don't you know how to knock somebody out?"

She looked thoughtful. "I do mostly office work. I could hit him on the back of the head, I suppose."

"No!" Briscoe yelped.

"Shhh," Dees said. "Hit him on the back of the head, or pinch some pressure point on his neck, or give him the Vulcan death grip for all I care."

Marco shook his head. "No such thing as the Vulcan death grip. See, Kirk and Spock used the *threat* of the Vulcan Death Grip once, but turns out there's no such thing. But there *is* the Vulcan nerve pinch."

Dees closed his eyes, massaged his temples, and looked

like he was speaking to the ground. "Pedro, keep the pressure on that bandanna Gloria's holding. Gloria, please knock him out."

As Dees turned back to the Humvee, he heard a soft *crunch*, followed by Briscoe yelling, "Ow! Shit! Oh man, shit!"

As Dees punched eleven numbers on the phone's tiny keypad, he heard another *crunch*, then silence. The phone on the other end rang. "Hello, Theodore? . . . Peter. How'd your family come through the storm? . . . Yeah, like you say, praise Jah. . . . Me? Theodore I need a favor, a big one."

Gloria listened as Dees talked for another five minutes. He paused, listened, and finally smiled. "Like you say, bringing peace to Babylon in the name of the Lion of Judah . . . Theodore? The phone line's getting bad, it's raining harder. . . . Theodore? Stop at a pay phone on the way. Please call Miami-Dade 911. Tell them an FBI agent's been murdered. . . . Yeah, that's what I said. . . . Here's the location. . . ."

Dees gave instructions on how to find the hummock, and snapped the phone shut. He untied the rope and dragged Briscoe next to Stevens's body. Bending over, he closed Stevens's eyes with his fingertips. He bowed his head for a moment, sighed, and picked up the pistol by its silencer. With his shirt, Dees wiped the grip. He untied Briscoe, then placed the pistol in the unconscious man's hand, squeezed the fingers around it, and left it lying near Briscoe's outstretched hand. Dees dug in his pockets, and retrieved his keys.

He motioned for Gloria and Marco to get into the Humvee. He started it, ground the gears into reverse, backed off the hummock and into the water, and headed back toward the main road, making sure to bulldoze a clear path through the water grasses for Miami-Dade to follow.

As they turned onto the main road heading north, Gloria turned to Dees. "Is it Juan? Gato is the only one who supervised loading the TV equipment into the truck at the airport and the only one who unloaded it at the GTV bureau at the hotel."

"Not the only one," Dees said as the hissing wipers sluiced rain off the windshield. "Professor Fuentes helped wheel the equipment up to the office. Maybe neither of them knew what was in it."

Gloria shook her head. "Not Juan. Jack the Cat knows by heart the serial number of every piece of equipment he operates. If he found a briefcase for which he did not have a record, he would have asked you about it. He must be the contact, the one who has to receive a message from Cabrera and then set the timer on the briefcase."

After twenty minutes of steering through flooded roads and around jagged shards of metal and glass, Dees turned left, heading down a paved two-lane road into the soggy green of the Everglades. Fifteen minutes later, a one-story, windowless cinder-block building appeared to their right. Dees pulled into a small parking area covered with crushed oyster and clam shells. Gloria and Marco followed him around a corner of the building, and saw that what had looked to be the size of a ranch home as it faced the road was actually the size of four or five houses, and appeared to be a very large garage.

They walked to the far end, which opened onto an asphalt airstrip, and turned left. A gleaming white Learjet's nose faced them, sitting on a concrete floor clean enough to eat from. Various tools were neatly attached to a pegboard that almost ran the length of one wall. A set of three steps on a wheeled aluminum frame was nestled against an open fuselage door. A hollow voice came from inside the plane. "You know if they make a Hollywood movie of this, ain't no one gonna believe it."

Theodore Ras Hinton stuck his head, the top tightly wrapped in a black kerchief, through the door. His body unfolded like a pop-up greeting card as he straightened and walked

down the stairs. A small Jamaican flag, red with the black
St. Andrew's cross, was sewn to the left shoulder of his tan
coveralls.

His scraggly beard tickled Dees's cheek as they embraced.
Holding him at arm's length, Dees said, "You get a haircut
just for us?"

"Nah," Hinton said, "light trim. Me dreads fit tighter now,
better for flying. And you might be . . ."

"Gloria," she said, extending her hand. "Gloria Bravo."

He took her hand and held it, turning to Dees. "You said
you and a friend, not you and Miss America."

Gloria looked at Hinton coolly, but Dees saw her cheeks
flush. "Gloria," he said with a nod, "Theodore Ras Hinton,
spiritualist, pilot, businessman. Theodore, Gloria Bravo, a
colleague of mine. And this is Pedro Marco, cameraman
extraordinaire."

"So," Hinton said, releasing her hand and looking at Marco,
"you in the business of poisoning the minds of the unwary
also?"

Marco smiled. "Only if the pay's right."

Gloria looked confused. Dees explained, "Theodore has a
low opinion of television. Don't worry, she's in radio."

Hinton shot her a suspicious look and motioned them
toward a gleaming white table on the far side of the hangar. It
was the kind an architect might use for drawing, its top canted
at a sharp angle. An aviation map was fastened to it with a series of plastic clamps that looked like oversized clothespins.
South Florida was in the upper left, Port-au-Prince in the
lower right, and it included most of Cuba, all of the Bahamas,
the Caymans, Jamaica, and the better part of Haiti.

"If I'm going to save the world from one of a-Babylon's
devil bombs," Hinton said, staring at the map, "I need to deal
with a hurricane that is barely moving west with winds I
cannot fly through, winds extending out to here."

He took a pencil from the breast pocket of his flight suit
and drew a circle that took in everything from Fort Lauder-

dale on the north to a chunk of Andros on the east to a slice of Cuban coastline on the south. "This includes where we are right now. We can fly with a most stout tailwind to north Broward County and then cut east and then south. I have an associate of some long standing who can gladly provide fuel for us here."

He tapped his finger on Great Exuma, halfway down the Bahamas chain. "Then I could do what I must for you and fly on south to Kingston. I need to pick up some, ah, funds there to help with business repairs from the storm. What else do I need to know?"

Dees took the pencil and drew a circle fifty miles wide just north of Havana, southwest of the hurricane winds. He took the edge of the pencil and shaded an area around the Cuban coast. "We've got a carrier task force watching every plane, vessel, and flying fish in this radius. The Cuban military's on high alert, so I'm guessing at extra radar coverage along their entire coast."

"Extra coverage and complete coverage are two different things, you know," Gloria said. Hinton, Dees, and Marco turned to look at her. "Even at full alert we—I mean they— would not have the resources to watch every bit of the coast-line, especially at very low altitudes."

Hinton stared at her, then turned to Dees. "Radio she's in, you say?"

"Radio as in an import-export business that allows you a Learjet and a six-bedroom—"

"Eight. Eight bedrooms, nine baths, two pools."

"Eight-bedroom house," Dees continued, "instead of try-ing to live on what a spiritual man would make from a restau-rant in downtown Miami. That kind of radio."

"So then," Hinton said, smiling again, "we have Hurricane David and the United States Navy and the Cuban armed forces all between us and this atomic bomb. Where do you want to go?"

"Havana," Dees and Gloria said in unison.

Hinton stared at the map. "I am a servant of Jah, not Superman. I could fly to, let us say, Holguin, perhaps not that far inland, but most certainly not any more west than that. I have a feeling that Miss Bravo knows the principle at work here . . . be there and be gone before they ever know you were there."

"That's what?" Dees asked. "Three hundred miles from Havana?"

Gloria shrugged. "If you can get us there, I can get us to Havana, I think."

"I would suggest we be on our way," Hinton said cheerfully. "Miami Center did not much seem to care about my flight plan to Jamaica except to tell me I was insane for even considering it. And that will lead to lots of questions upon my return, so this time I will be returning to this wonderful country as clean as a soul washed by the River Jordan."

As they walked toward the plane, Dees said, "Maybe they were just shocked that you filed a flight plan for a change."

"Perhaps," Hinton said, climbing up the steps and working his lanky body into the pilot's seat. Dees watched Gloria and Marco navigate the steps, then rolled them into a far corner of the hangar, well away from the jet's engines. He jumped in through the plane's door, pulled himself in, then closed and latched it. The turbines had already started their soft whine. The plane rolled slowly out of the hangar and onto a blacktop runway. Hinton reached above his head and pushed a button, and a forty-foot-wide reinforced aluminum and steel door began to roll down, its bottom finally securing in a slot that ran the width of the building.

Hinton motioned Dees forward, indicating the copilot's seat on the right. "This won't do much good, Theodore," Dees said into the small microphone on the headset he had slipped on. "I don't know how to fly."

"Luck," Hinton's scratchy voice replied, "just like my luck in your saving my life."

"What?" Gloria's voice popped through the headset.

Hinton told her the abbreviated version of the story as he kept his eyes glued to a console readout. It showed cross-winds of thirty knots, gusting to above fifty. But the wind was slowly shifting from the east to the north. Dees guessed that Hinton was waiting for that brief moment when the wind was directly from their front before attempting to take off.

As the wind started to howl directly from the north, straight into the Lear's nose, Hinton shoved the throttle forward and ended the story. "That is one reason I am doing this, but not the only one. My children live on this earth also, and I will not have them caught in the middle while the forces of darkness in a-Babylon destroy each other."

The jet shuddered and picked up speed rapidly. Gloria spoke into her microphone, staring at Dees. "*Chico*, I thought you were just crazy. Now I think you are just Don Quixote."

"Saint George," Hinton said, looking straight ahead as the jet suddenly nosed up and climbed quickly. It entered the dirty gray clouds and began to shake violently. It shook up, down, left, and right in hard jolts before it blasted out of the clouds and emerged into what looked like a low-ceilinged room stretching into infinity, lighter gray clouds providing a moving roof not two hundred feet above them. Hinton leveled the jet off and steered due north in the clear air.

"Saint George," he repeated, smiling with satisfaction as the vibrations became weaker and the wind wheeled again, shoving the Lear forward with a one hundred knot tailwind. "Except with this one sometimes he eats the dragon, but sometimes the dragon eats him."

Gloria looked at Dees thoughtfully as the clouds became thinner, finally dissipating into high, sheer wisps. Marco, in the seat next to her, had already started to snore lightly. Hinton consulted the compass and GPS readout and banked the jet to the right, heading almost due west. Dees was suddenly tired. He leaned his head against the cockpit canopy and began to breathe softly. Within five minutes, he was dreaming that he had walked into Theodore's restaurant and ordered one dragon patty to go with extra hot sauce.

CHAPTER 16

"Hey! Hey! Listen to this! Oh shit, man! Hey!"

Dees's right eye snapped open. He kept his left closed and squinted at Hinton, who was outlined by the bright blue sky. Hinton pointed at the control panel. "I punched in the all-news station in Miami. Listen."

A hiss of static with a voice trying to peek out from behind it crinkled in Dees's headset. Every few seconds a *whoosh* from lightning near the transmitter would obliterate the entire signal. "—news time is three-ten. Gales are still lashing Miami, but David is now moving west at five miles an hour, pounding the waterlogged Keys with even more rain and hurricane-force winds. The full forecast and live reports from Marathon in a minute. First, our top—"

A blast of static tore through the voice, which finally emerged, faintly, from the buzz and crackle. "—the body of one FBI agent, and another agent, alive but seriously wounded, near the plant. Turkey Point has been under guard by elements of the Florida National Guard because of the storm, and because of the recent heightened tensions with Cuba. We are attempting—"

An angry burst of lightning chopped the signal into sharp-edged squeals and pops. Dees glanced at his watch. Three-fifteen. They had taken off two hours and ten minutes ago. Adding that to the thirty minutes before Hinton had telephoned 911 meant that in just two hours and forty minutes,

Briscoe and Stevens had been found and the entire operation had been leaked to the media.

The jet eased down silently as Hinton pushed the yoke forward. The turquoise water came closer until it filled most of the cockpit window. Gloria stuck her head forward, between Hinton and Dees. "I am sure," she said, her voice vibrating slightly through the headsets, "that your religion frowns on suicide, so what are you doing?"

Hinton's laugh sounded breathy through the voice-activated mike. "Suicide is just what it would be to stay visible. Everybody is just too nervous, so we fly with the flying fishes since we're only about a half hour out, and we can keep everybody calm by just staying off their radar."

"Unless we end up in the drink," Dees said. "Several hundred miles an hour plus a little clear air turbulence divided by a few dozen feet off the water could equal us becoming a submarine unless we're lucky. Very lucky."

"Call it blind luck," Hinton said. "Call it faith. We have to believe in something, call it luck or fate or kismet or Jah Almighty."

The jet leveled off with a jerk. Hinton's eyes shifted between the control panel and the water rushing under them at almost three hundred miles an hour. Dees shook his head to keep from being hypnotized by the water flying beneath them. "Where are we, anyway?"

"Just southeast of Nassau, getting ready I think to go over Shroud Cay."

Almost as soon as he spoke, a spot on the horizon became a low lump, then a raggedly defined patch of green and tan, then a small island that appeared in their windscreen and vanished beneath them in the blink of an eye.

"Exuma Cays ahead," Hinton said, steadying the yoke in both hands against the bumping from the heated water beneath them. "We got a gas-and-go waiting in Georgetown in about twenty minutes."

Dees said, "You worried about getting palm trees stuck in the wings?"

Hinton laughed again. "When we go sneaking into Cuba, this will seem like we were flying at thirty thousand feet. Jah has provided the storm and the confusion between the Americans and Cubans to give us cover since everyone's attention is elsewhere. But I shall help the Almighty by flying as low and as fast as I can."

He switched the receiver back to the Miami radio station, but still heard nothing but static. He moved down the dial until another voice burst through the white noise. "—*el voz de Miami, noticias y más. Tiempo, cuatro menos veinte. Los totulares a esta hora, la tormenta en los cayes, cerca de Marathon. Un cuerpo de un agente federal en la punta pavo, y una espía cubana—*"

The voice faded, then broke through again in a blast of colloquial Spanish. "Cuban exile station in Miami," Dees said, straining to make out all the words. "Something about a body and a Cuban spy?"

"Shhh," Gloria said sharply. She pressed the headset more tightly onto her ears with both hands. By the time the voice again disappeared behind a wall of interference, her eyes had a tired look. "National Guard sources who were there when they picked up Stevens and this Briscoe? They say there is talk of the Cuban government involved in the murder. They are, as you say, going crazy all across Little Havana."

She looked angrily at Dees. "You had your video you took of this Briscoe. You could have left it behind with him telling the truth on it."

"No good," Dees said. "It shows him talking while you're cutting his toe off. That video's no good unless we use an edited version, something that shows him talking but doesn't make it obvious that he's being tortured. They have Briscoe's fingerprints on the pistol. They may even find some forensic stuff that's useful on Stevens's body. The Dade County M.E.

and the people from the FBI are no fools. They'll figure it out."

Marco looked down at his camera, with the tape still inside, then back at Dees, who turned and stared at him. Marco's look said he disapproved. Dees's return stare was expressionless. Maybe, Dees thought, we just canceled each other out.

The Lear started to lose speed dramatically as the wind whistled around the wings around the deployed speed brakes. A large green island loomed in front of them. Small settlements skidded under the fuselage and the plane shuddered lightly as the landing gear unfolded from the belly. The wheels kicked up small tornadoes of dust from the asphalt. Instead of turning left toward the tiny terminal, the jet slowed, rolled to the end of the runway, and turned right onto a taxiway. Two corrugated metal buildings, each about the size of a one-car garage, were perched at the edge of the asphalt apron that connected the taxiway with the runway.

An ancient fuel truck the color of a rotting pumpkin sat next to one of the buildings, balancing a large aluminum tank on its back, the offspring of a 1959 fire truck and an old milk tanker. A short black man with pomaded hair, wearing a suit that seemed to change from green to black in the sunlight, stood next to the tanker.

The jet rolled to a stop and Hinton shut down power to both engines. Dees stared out the window at the figure in the suit, then turned to Hinton. "Sharkskin?"

Hinton looked through the canopy and waved. The figure returned a lazy flick of a wrist. "Clayton fancies himself a bit of a dandy. His parents named him for the American congressman who had a home in the Bahamas, Adam Clayton Powell. You know of him?"

"Just from the old photos," Dees said as Hinton unbuckled himself and headed toward the fuselage door. "It looks like he copied the hair style, too."

Hinton chuckled as he opened the latch. "Clayton is too

much of a-Babylon to have the dreads, so his hair he gets from a bottle."

As Hinton got out, two men unrolled a hose from the side of the truck and plugged it into the underside of the left wing. As the aviation fuel gurgled into the fuel tanks, Hinton stood talking and laughing with the man in the suit. After a few minutes, the hose was disconnected and hauled under the nose to the right wing. Hinton was listening now, stroking his chin, first frowning, then nodding, then finally smiling. With a rattle and click, the hose was removed from the right wing, and Hinton and the man in the suit embraced. Dees checked his watch. The entire operation had taken slightly less than fifteen minutes.

Hinton climbed inside the jet and pulled the hatch shut. "Clayton has contacted an associate of ours who has allowed us to overfly and land in Cuba. He assures us if I can land on a certain highway and then leave quickly, there should be no problems, even now."

As the jet rolled toward the end of the runway, Dees looked sideways at Hinton. "And how much does keeping this graciousness on retainer cost?"

"Five percent of the gross value of whatever cargo we have, rather steep for a landing tax, I admit. This time—" He shrugged. "This time, we have agreed to wire a bit extra to an account in the Caymans. Headsets, please."

All four adjusted the headsets as the Lear's engines reached full throttle. Less than a minute after clearing the island, Hinton slowly brought the jet lower until, according to the digital altimeter, it was flying at an altitude of between twenty-five and thirty feet.

Gloria's voice popped through the headset. "There is actually someone in Cuba who takes your bribes? And allows you to fly out with drugs?"

"Merchandise," Hinton said crossly, keeping his hands firmly on the controls and his eyes moving along the altimeter, level flight indicator, and water ahead of them. "And there are several someones on your island with whom I have had, let us say, a passing association over the years."

"But this has been discredited for years," Gloria said quickly, "the drug smuggling I mean. The Americans have made charges, but there was never any proof, and if something like this was going on, then I would have—"

"Not known a single thing," Hinton interrupted. "Your socialist purity in Cuba is just another illusion in a-Babylon. You have your provincial party functionaries and your provincial Customs and military officials. All of them are hungry and restless about what may happen next and are taking care of themselves, and their families I would hope."

It was quiet inside the jet except for the seemingly distant rumble of the engines and the rush of air through the fresh air nozzles. Dees sniffed. "Smells like a new car in here. This wouldn't be a brand-new plane, would it? And you wouldn't be using this trip as a test flight, would you?"

Hinton cracked a smile. "Lear-45, only got thirty hours on it. Latest generation of every kind of technology I could want."

Marco leaned back in his seat. "Where're we landing, anyway?"

"A road on the coast near Caibarien," Hinton said. "Just turn left at the Camaguey Archipelago. I am informed we have a ten-minute window of opportunity. Normally, I would fly low after I dropped you off, cross Cuba, exit near Cienfuegos, and fly on to Grand Cayman. Given the, ah, tensions now, I will head back the way I came and gas up again on Great Inagua and then on to Kingston. I should be back in my own bed in Miami within twenty-four hours."

"Where's Caibarien?" Dees asked, turning to Gloria. "And how do we get to Havana?"

"About twenty miles from Santa Clara, one hundred fifty *más o menos* from Havana. I should be able to get us transportation with a little bit of persuasion."

Dees wrinkled his brow and stared out the window. Richie,

he thought, I haven't failed yet, but it's looking that way, and I hope Janie understands when I tell her I didn't find the killer but did screw around and let a nuclear bomb go off and let an asshole in a Soviet fighter bomb Florida. Nice live shot material: Sorry folks, but if I had managed to get this on the air sooner we could have stopped this war but it's a little late now. This live report brought to you by St. George Meat Patties, just the thing to feed your hungry dragon.

"Welcome to CADIZ." Hinton's voice crackled through the headsets.

Gloria had seemed to be asleep. Her head straightened. "You know about—"

"The Cuban Air Defense Identification Zone." Hinton laughed. "Actually we have been inside it for some time if they have the low-frequency radars on, which I would imagine they do. In my business, I have had a continuing education in your country's air defenses."

"Such as?" Gloria said suspiciously.

"Careful," Dees said. "Nothing hurts as much as finding out everybody else knows your secrets."

"Just things I found out from this man," Hinton said, nodding toward Dees.

"Such as?" she repeated.

"Such as your microwave radar," Dees said, turning toward her. "In normal times, they'll spot just about anything above three hundred feet. Easy enough to fly in a slow prop plane. Things get a little tense, they switch on the UHF radars. You know, the ones snuggled in the hills behind that Russian-made power plant about forty klicks east of Havana?"

Gloria's eyes narrowed. "Oh come on," Dees said, "nothing's secret much anymore, except maybe what we're doing here. Anyway, things get really tense and they switch on the low-frequency radars, which can spot just about anything flying above a hundred feet. That's not a serious problem if you're in a slow plane and the weather's dead calm. But as fast as we're going and as low as we're flying and as nasty as the weather is north of us? We need luck, faith, and insanity."

"Camaguey Archipelago," Hinton's voice hissed in the headsets, "and we're right on time."

A low line of lumpy land appeared to the left, and the jet, barely above the wave tops, made a gentle turn toward it. Within minutes, a faint ribbon of green was strung across the entire horizon. The engine's whine became a lower-pitched rumble as Hinton eased the throttle back. "Clayton told me our contact would arrange for our usual road to be completely clear of people. I'll pop up, land, leave you, and take off, assuming they have not moved the road or we have not been lied to."

Marco shot him a glance. "And if they lied, I guess we're fucked?"

Hinton shrugged. "Maybe. But we have been very profitable for this person in the past, and we have tapes of our conversations. If he double-crossed us, I would imagine he knows it would go very badly for him when his superiors receive the evidence. He knows General Ochoa was shot with less proof."

Gloria's left eye twitched. Dees noticed, and her face became an expressionless mask. Hinton said quietly, "Here we go." The jet nosed up and climbed to what the altimeter claimed was fifty feet. As the power was reduced to the engines, Dees noticed a strip of macadam cut through scrub and cane fields.

"All this over sugarcane," Dees said.

"More than that," Gloria said without inflection. "Raw sugarcane and raw power are much the same here, no?"

The jet swept slowly past the cane fields and banked to the left. There was a *thunk* as the landing gear folded down. The wind whistled through the speed brakes beneath the wings. The Lear leveled off, touched down gently, and shuddered in protest as Hinton jammed on the brakes. The plane slowed, then stopped.

"Out now," Hinton said. As Dees began to unbuckle his

harness, Hinton clutched his arm. "I love you like a brother, my friend, so do not do anything foolish. We shall pray for you."

Dees unbuckled and squeezed Hinton's shoulder. "Thanks."

The hatch swung open and Gloria scooted onto the pavement. Marco followed, then Dees jumped down. Hinton appeared in the doorway, started to say something, stopped, and held a clenched fist in the air. Dees returned the salute and watched as Hinton resealed the door.

Dees, Marco, and Gloria sprinted to the far side of the asphalt as the Lear's engines began to whine. The jet strained against the locked brakes, then jumped forward as the engines shrieked. The nose was already pointing toward the sky, but the rest of the plane looked as if the tires were glued to the pavement.

Finally, the wheels left the ground. The jet was barely ten feet above the cane when the landing gear folded into the belly. The Lear disappeared toward the north, ducking down below their line of sight within seconds.

Gloria turned to Dees. *"Bienvenidos a Cuba otra vez,"* she said. "Do you have anything that might replace this Navy flight suit?"

Dees reached into a large flap pocket of his photographer's vest and pulled out a wadded forest-green T-shirt. "It may be a little big," he said, "but it may match those uniform pants underneath—"

He stopped. Gloria had shed the flight suit. She still wore her olive-drab uniform pants. Dees's eyes ran up from her navel, across her stomach, to her breasts enclosed in a white bra. She held out her hand and said, "Well?"

"Well, well," he said, handing her the T-shirt.

Marco stared and muttered, *"Oye, mami."* She ignored him, slipped on the shirt and tucked it into the pants.

"Wait here," she said, looking down the road in the rough direction of Caibarien. "Hide in the cane and try not to be arrested with your bag of weapons."

Dees felt the clatter of Stevens's Uzi and his own .32 in the duffel. "Where're you going?"

She gave him a quick kiss on the cheek. Dees smiled, surprised. She continued, "To get us transportation. The DGI still outranks any provincial official who might want to keep his automobile, and this may take some time."

She looked at the edge of the road. "Wait in that cane over there by those two fence posts bent together in an X-shape. And please, be quiet."

Dees and Marco walked across the road and climbed over the fence, which was nothing more than a single strand of rusted barbed wire nailed to a series of posts. Dees turned before disappearing into the cane, and saw Gloria strolling north. He walked into the seven-foot-tall stalks, looked for snakes, didn't see any, and placed the duffel on the ground and sat on top of it. The only sound was the rustle of a lazy breeze and a pair of frogs croaking repeatedly in sharp, staccato bursts. Maybe, he thought, they're mating.

* * *

Dees's eyes snapped open. He looked around in panic. He rustled the cane stalks as he sat upright with a jolt and rolled into a crouch, looking in front of him, behind him, and to the sides. Nothing, although the combination of thick purple twilight and overlapping cane leaves made it impossible to see farther than six or seven feet.

He checked his watch, as he had twenty minutes ago. Gloria had been gone two hours and change. He took a deep breath through his mouth, blinked twice, and remained in the crouch, listening. A dog barked in the distance. He strained and thought he could make out a far-off truck or car.

Marco was awake, staring at him flatly. "I don't like this."

Dees looked confused for a moment. The cameraman's voice strained like a taut fishing line ready to snap. "I get my paycheck from GTV to cover the news, not to sneak into Cuba and maybe go to jail on some half-assed wild-goose chase. The desk'll have my ass, fire me even for going along on something like this."

"You volunteered," Dees said quietly. "You could've said fuck you any time. You knew we were sneaking into Cuba to find the bomb and try to stop this thing. You could've said no thanks and walked away."

Marco looked away absently through the cane, then back at Dees. "And what about torturing that guy back at Turkey Point, what about that?"

"What?" Dees said heatedly, keeping his voice at a whisper. "He's a murderer, he doesn't care if World War Three gets started as long as he gets paid, he's probably guilty of treason, being an FBI agent. You think I liked watching that? He helped plant an atomic bomb around here someplace, he killed Stevens, he may have helped kill Richie."

Marco snorted. "It's always personal with you, ain't it? You almost get both of us killed delivering food to those kids in Kosovo, we get arrested in Jakarta because you cold-cock a cop for beating up some woman in the street, you almost get yourself killed a dozen times finding out who sent chemical weapons to Iraq. What're you, God's little helper?"

Dees felt his stomach growl. He fished in his vest and pulled out two granola bars. He opened one, and offered the other to Marco, who tried to ignore it before he snatched it from Dees's hand and ate half in one bite. Dees chewed slowly and said, "So how come you keep volunteering with me?"

Marco finished the bar and wadded the wrapper into a shirt pocket. "I'm divorced twice, and neither one will let me see my kids much. You've almost got me killed four times and you saved my life a few times on top of that and you're the closest thing to family I got, asshole. So this is my life and ain't that a bitch?"

Dees smiled thinly. "You sure you're okay with this?"

Marco sucked a piece of granola bar from between his teeth. "Yeah, yeah, I'm okay. At least it beats the shit out of working in an office. Hey, can you see either one of us shuffling papers in a cubicle?"

Dees shook his head. He walked in a crouch toward the edge of the cane and paused, listening to the silence, before he gingerly poked his head out. Looking quickly right and then left, he saw a small cloud of dust approaching from the north, and ducked back into the field. Ten minutes passed, the darkness gathering quickly. The tinny clatter of a small engine grew louder. He could hear the asphalt and gravel clicking and humming underneath the tires. The vehicle stopped directly in front of where they were hidden, its valves clattering. Dees thought it either was a diesel or needed a tune-up.

A door opened with a creak. *"Oye, chico. Señores imperialistas."*

Dees walked out of the cane. Marco followed, holding the camera. The dark was wrapping itself tightly around the horizon as he saw Gloria standing next to the sputtering Lada. It was a dirty gray except for an electric-blue passenger-side door. He stepped over the fence and opened the blue door.

She nodded toward the backseat. "Lift up the seat and stow your bag and camera underneath."

Dees tugged the rear seat upward and it popped open. The compartment underneath smelled of mildew and grease. Marco, looking dubious, gently placed the camera on its side, and refastened the seat. He squeezed into the backseat, testing the springs with his butt, satisfied that the seat wasn't pushing against the camera. Dees got in the front seat, closed the door, leaned across the shift knob, and kissed her. Her eyes opened wide in surprise, then closed as her lips yielded. After a few seconds, he pulled away. He said, "Payback for patting my butt at the plane."

Marco snorted. "Get a room. Get one for me while you're at it."

She stared for a moment before a small smile crept across her face. Without a word, she ground the floor shift into first gear, and the clattering four-cylinder engine began to jerkily pull the Lada after it. She strained to see the blacktop illuminated by the weak headlights. The clatter settled into a steady hum as she shifted into second gear, then third, then fourth. She leaned her head forward and said, "*Adelante* Havana for a discussion with *Señor* Gato. Three hours, maybe four."

She turned left onto a narrow dirt road that ran for twenty yards before it intersected a wider, two-lane paved road. She barely slowed the car, turned right, and floored the accelerator. The car picked up speed slowly, the engine revving to over 6,000 rpm to push the car at forty-five miles an hour. "Clutch's going out," Dees said, glancing at the tachometer. "Think this thing will make it?"

She looked at him out of the corner of her eye. "Be grateful for what we can get. It is not easy in this country to procure an automobile, especially one with a full tank of gasoline."

"Gratitude is my motto," he said, looking at the muddy floorboards, cracked plastic dashboard, and rusted hole he could stick his finger through where the windshield frame met the dashboard in front of him. "How'd you get it?"

They passed a sign that read SANTA CLARA 20 KM. She seemed to consider something for a moment. Finally, she said, "Put yourself in the position of an official in a small seacoast town. You are sitting in your Interior Ministry office yawning when suddenly an officer from the Directorate General of Intelligence walks in. She shows her identification and while this official is trying to make out her nipples under the T-shirt, she begins asking him questions."

Marco laughed as she pressed her lips together and began a singsong parody of a disapproving schoolteacher's voice. "What do you know about a jet plane that landed and took off again from here? How long have you served here? What area does your jurisdiction cover?"

She laughed. "By this time he is looking down at his desk and then at the portrait of Che on the wall, and not at my chest. And he says, 'What plane? In the four years I have been here, I have never had any incursions by the *gusanos* or counterrevolutionaries.' So I just stare at him and he seems to be sinking in his chair."

Dees smiled wryly. "I've seen you have that effect on people."

"Just so," she said without irony. "I know that any arrangements your friend Theodore has made to land in this area over the years must involve several people, what with keeping both air space and ground traffic clear. It seemed to me this greasy little man at the Interior Ministry office is probably one of them, since this is, after all, a small town, and everyone would probably know the business of everyone else."

She turned right without downshifting at a sign reading LA HABANA 280 KM. The engine slowed, clattered in brief protest, and picked up speed again. She continued, "So I said to him, 'Havana is looking into this. Do you propose that I tell them the *campesinos* who have seen these aircraft are deluded? We will not have more of the Ochoa fiascoes against the revolution.'

"That, as you would say, got his attention. So now that his visions of my breasts are replaced with visions of a firing squad, I let him squirm a bit more. So he then says, 'Anything I can do to help you, I will do. I have no reports of this but I will defend *la patria* and blah blah blah.' So then he agrees to cooperate completely, including the use of his office. I took his vehicle instead, filled with gasoline, and told him his cooperation would be fully and favorably noted. I thought he was actually about to faint in gratitude."

There was a hole in the metal dashboard where the radio should have been. "So much for listening to Radio Havana," Dees said. He turned toward her. "So how did you end up here, anyway? What about your family?"

She looked at him quizzically and said she had two sisters and two brothers and that she was the youngest. Her mother was still alive, still eking out a living at the University of

Havana's sociology department, but without any hope of advancement because of her father's friendship with the late, disgraced and executed General Ochoa. She was thirty-one, a Pisces, loved soccer and swimming, and had once talked her oldest brother out of boarding a raft for Miami with the promise that someday things would improve. She had studied in Beijing for a year and a half.

Dees looked surprised. "Beijing?"

She shrugged. "Moscow is no more, and the few remaining Communists flock together, much like the last flock of dodos. We are much friendlier with the Chinese than you might suppose."

As they drove through Santa Clara, she was able to recite the details of Che Guevara's victory over Batista's forces there. She noted, with a wave of her left hand through the open window, that what was left when the Bolivian government returned Che's remains was buried over there, someplace, under a huge monument. She knew the history of every town, village, and crossroads.

When they saw a sign indicating Havana was seventy five kilometers ahead, she laughed. She pointed to the right. "Puerto Escondito is over there. Your CIA used it quite a bit in the sixties. My father once told me how about a year after the Bay of Pigs he led a commando team here, waiting for the invaders for forty-eight hours. Finally, they arrived and had barely gotten off their boat when my father sprang the trap."

In the darkness, Dees could barely make out the green and brown hills on the right, rolling to the ocean. To the left, cane fields stretched in a valley to the dark horizon. The Lada sputtered along the four-lane road into Santa Cruz del Norte. Marco stared to the right. "Havana Club?"

Gloria nodded. "It is the largest rum factory in the world, or so they say."

Ten minutes later, and the air smelled of a combination of rotten eggs and crankcase oil. Off to the left, a series of smokestacks belched flame into the sky. "The Russians ran

out of money before they could finish it," Gloria said, cough-
ing. "It runs on oil and it is filthy. But it keeps the lights
burning."

To the right, small oil wells, their arms rocking up and down
like piston-driven seesaws, sucked petroleum and natural gas
from the shale next to the ocean. The logo for CUPET—Cuban
Petroleum—was plastered across a pair of storage tanks. A
restaurant with a large wooden patio perched unsteadily on a
jetty past the oil pumps. "El Cayuelo," Gloria said. "It is almost
a national landmark. Your CIA used it as a checkpoint for infil-
trators in—"

"I know, I know, in the sixties," Dees said. "Since the CIA
spent so much time around here, any of them buy beach property and retire?"

There was only more silence for the next few miles. Finally, up ahead, Dees saw a cafeteria on the right side of the
road. Knots of men stood under its blue-and-white-striped
awnings. "El Rincón de Guanabo," Dees read from a roadside sign. "Think that place is open for coffee?"

"Checkpoint," she said, slowing the car and downshifting.
She looked straight ahead, her mouth a tight line. "Do not say
anything at all, you understand? Even if they speak to you, I
will talk. You are a Canadian, and you," she spoke over her
shoulder to Marco, "you are Italian, and neither of you understand a word of Spanish."

The car rolled to a stop. Two sawhorses made of metal
tubing blocked the pavement. A young soldier in green
military fatigues approached her door, while another, who
seemed to be even younger, stepped to Dees's side. A flashlight beam caused Dees to shield his eyes. It glared on him,
scanned the backseat, shone on Gloria's profile, and returned to Dees.

Before the soldier at her open window could speak, she
shoved a laminated photo ID at his nose. *"Soy Comandante
Gloria Bravo,"* she snapped, continuing in rapid-fire Spanish,
"and I have level one clearance. He is a trade attaché from the

Canadian embassy. And he back there is from an Italian investment firm."

The flashlight stayed on Dees as the soldier at his window asked, in broken sibilant English, "Jou're name esss whot?"

Dees reached out a finger and gently moved the flashlight down an inch, away from his eyes. "Gretzky. Wayne Gretzky. How're you doing, eh?"

"And we are part of a meeting at his embassy with the Ministry of Trade and the Interior Minister," Gloria continued in Spanish, "and we are coming from Santa Clara about possible Canadian and Italian tourist investment near the Che memorial. We are expected in Havana very soon, so I assume we may proceed?"

The soldier stared at the card, which she still held firmly in her hand. He straightened, saluted smartly, and motioned the other soldier to remove the barricade. She returned the salute lazily, put the car in gear, and drove forward without looking back. Marco finally exhaled and said, "Wayne Gretzky?"

"First Canadian I thought of."

Large, skinny casaurina pines lined the road. Buildings began to appear on both sides, the large stadium and athlete's housing built for the 1991 Pan-Am Games looming to the right. Half an hour later, they stopped at what was once a toll plaza leading into the tunnel running under Havana's harbor, and was now a military checkpoint. It took less than a minute for them to be waved through.

They drove down into the white-tiled tunnel, and emerged on the other side of the harbor near the Morro Castle, on the edge of the oldest colonial part of the city. Dees glanced at his watch. Almost ten o'clock. "Where would we find Juan about now?"

She stared carefully through the bicycles and pedestrians on Calle L, approaching the Havana Libre. She wrinkled her nose in distaste. "He would be home, I assume, over in San Isidro. A very bad neighborhood. But first we should stop by the GTV office at the hotel, where the equipment is stored and—"

She hit the brakes. The Lada rocked on its rusting springs, less than a meter short of three young women who walked languidly into the street. One, wearing a white T-shirt with a red silkscreen portrait of Che draped over a pair of spandex shorts, glared at Gloria, then looked at Dees and smiled. Next to her, a taller woman with hair the color of rust and a red tank top crushing her ample breasts walked over to Dees's window. Behind her, a girl who looked to be maybe fifteen wore a tight lime-green knit dress that barely covered her buttocks. Her small belly pooched at the fabric like a half-filled water balloon.

The tall one leaned next to the open window. Her breath smelled of peppermint and cigarettes. Her breasts were shoved against the car door. Dees noticed they were covered with freckles. She snapped her gum, looking first at Gloria, then at Dees, then at Marco in the backseat.

"Oye, rubia," Dees said, *"qué tal?"*

"You have dollars?" she asked. "The three of you want a good time?"

Dees looked incredulous. "All of us?"

She smiled. Her front teeth had small chunks of lipstick stuck to them. "We all three will go down on both of you and your girlfriend for fifty dollars."

"But what about the revolution?" Dees asked innocently. He nodded toward the T-shirt. "What would Che think?"

"The revolution?" Her laugh sounded like a bray. "Fuck the revolution."

"The revolution has fucked us, so we return the favor," the one in the T-shirt said, and giggled. She stared at Gloria. "So how about it? I'll stick my tongue inside you while your boyfriend fucks me, you like that?"

Gloria reached in her pants, pulled out the ID, and thrust it in her palm at the one leaning in Dees's window. "How about you *putas* getting fifty months on La Isla de Juventud chopping cane instead of the fifty dollars?"

The redhead shoved herself away from the window, turned without a word, and walked away quickly. The other two appeared momentarily confused, then followed. The one who looked fifteen turned, extended her middle finger toward Gloria, stuck out her tongue, then ran after the other two.

Gloria angrily ground the Lada's gears and aimed the sputtering car up the hill toward the hotel. Dees looked out the window and laughed. "Condemn me if you will. History will absolve me."

"What is that supposed to mean?"

"You know. Castro said it when they convicted him in the Moncada Barracks attack in July 1952, your glorious Twenty-Sixth of July Movement. And there goes history, in a skirt barely covering her teenage ass. No food, no money, no hope. Ask that piece of history if she'll absolve the revolution."

A faded green bus pulled in front of them, blasting out an exhaust cloud of sooty gray smoke. Gloria hit the brakes and said impatiently, "What do you want? Your Nike swoosh on everything in sight? McDonald's on every corner? Two hundred dollar sneakers that young people can murder each other over? Downsizing? Stock options? Good medical care only if you have money? Private schools for the rich and terrible schools for the rest? Pfah."

Dees grabbed the steering wheel, and jerked it to the right. He snapped, "Stop here! Pull over!"

The Lada turned sharply and barely missed a row of parked bicycles before she jammed in the clutch and hit the brake. "Are you crazy? That is one of the most stupid—"

"Look! There!" Dees said, pointing up the block, across the street. Gloria angrily turned to look, and saw Juan Gato standing at the hotel's entrance. He crossed the street from their left, dodged two bicycles, and paused on the center stripe as another ancient bus rattled past. He crossed the street, opened the door of the scabrous Chevy Nova and, with both hands, carefully placed an object inside.

The flickering streetlight glinted off a huge metal briefcase.

"Mierda," said Gloria.

"Shit," said Dees.

CHAPTER 17

It took them the better part of an hour to navigate the streets leading to the highway that ran east along the coast from Havana. The signs said they were on National Road 123, but Gloria said it was called La Vía Blanca and that she had no idea what white person or thing it had been named for.

The traffic thinned, then disappeared just past the sagging wooden shacks that defined the edge of the city, until the Nova and Lada were the only two vehicles on the highway. As the Russian-made car groaned around a traffic circle in Santa Maria Loma, Dees said, "Not the best way in the world to tail somebody, considering we're the only two cars for miles."

Gloria downshifted. "No problem. Even at this hour there are normally, how would you call them, autos for hire? Sort of taxis that may not be registered?"

"Gypsy cabs?"

"*Exacto,* gypsy cabs that may be carrying tourists out to Las Playas del Este, or further out to Varadero. So this could be just a car with just another drunken tourist coming back from the Tropicana."

They drove through Boca Ciega and Guanabo and Veneciana, past the slanted roofs and narrow windows of the tourist hotels and clubs that had been built in the middle fifties, modeled after long-vanished motels in Las Vegas. The signs that pointed toward the beaches and recreation areas—*las áreas deportivas*—became more and more infrequent until there was nothing at the edge of the road except scrubby vegetation and mangroves, and off to the left, the gentle *whoosh* of the surf, which could be heard even over the Lada's clattering valves. In the distance, the lights of Mantanzas glowed like the dying embers on a barbecue grill.

The Lada's tires hummed over the asphalt. Almost an hour later, the terrain became familiar to Dees. Ahead, the Nova's taillights suddenly turned left. "I'll be fucked," Dees said. "Isn't that—"

"Puerto Escondido." Gloria nodded. "It would seem history merely moves in circles after all."

About ten car lengths past the road, Gloria steered toward the right shoulder, and stopped. She put her finger to her lips. Dees nodded, gently opened his door, and got out. Marco removed the camera, and attached a small battery. The voltmeter indicated an almost one hundred percent charge. Dees pulled out the duffel, unzipped it, and reached inside. He withdrew the revolver and ankle holster, secured it on his left ankle, and slipped a handful of bullets into his left trouser pocket. He took the Uzi from the bag and handed it to Gloria, along with the taped twin ammunition clip Stevens had stored in the bag. Dees stared at it. It seemed like Stevens had put it there ten years ago.

Gloria took the clip, latched it into the Uzi with a soft click, and pulled the spring-loaded handle over the clip to rack a shell into the chamber. To Dees, it sounded as loud as a firecracker. He zipped up the bag and slung its oversized handles over his left shoulder, draping them across his chest and under his right armpit, securing the duffel to his back like a Civil War trooper's bedroll. Marco hoisted the camera onto his shoulder. Gloria slung the Uzi's strap over her left shoulder, and motioned for them to follow her. They crossed the highway and crept along the left shoulder until they reached the dirt road.

Immediately to their left, two rusted buses sat behind a

chain-link fence next to a pair of gas pumps and a white concrete building. Dees guessed it was the filling station for the buses that ran the local routes. He heard a rustle and tensed. A goat, tethered with a rope to a stake driven into the ground, munched on vegetation and eyed him with disinterest.

There was a small village of a half-dozen shacks on one side of the road, and on the other, a cliff rose to a plateau maybe twenty feet up, then climbed even higher. Hills obscured the sky in front of them. The road made a sharp turn to the right and then turned left again, opening up on a harbor, where they saw a one-story cement and cinder-block building. In front of it, a pier jutted two hundred feet into the water. Tall hills rose on all sides, giving the harbor the appearance of a dark bowl. Dees stopped as Marco fished inside the duffel, and silently withdrew the long night thermal lens.

A wooden boat that looked like a shrunken trawler was tied up just beyond the Nova, which was parked in the lot next to the building. The ship looked to be thirty feet long, with a high bow and an old-fashioned wheelhouse planted in the middle of the deck. Dees heard the soft growl of its diesel engines and could make out a pair of exhaust pipes sticking up on each side of the stern.

Gloria tugged on his sleeve, and whispered, "I suppose now we should find out if *Señor Gato* has a nuclear bomb or if he merely carries a briefcase with him when he makes night drives to the countryside."

Dees silently took the pistol from his ankle holster and slipped it into his right trouser pocket. He whispered, "Stay close and stay out of sight. If something goes wrong, be sure to shoot the other guys and not me."

"What are you going to—"

"Go in through the front door." He was already getting to his knees. "That way we know how many of them there might be. You're covering me, so we have the advantage."

Before she could reach up and pull his sleeve again, he was walking toward the boat. He walked twenty yards and paused.

Silence, except for the *pumbum-pumbum-pumbum* of the idling boat engine and the gurgling slap of water against the bow.

"Hey!" he yelled. His voice sounded as loud as a cannon in his ears. "Hey, Juan Gato! Hey, Juan! It's Dees! It's Peter Dees!"

He listened. Nothing. "Juan, goddammit! It's me, Dees! *Oye, Juan el Gato! Este es Dees. Soy Dees, un periodista grande, fuerte, y feo!* Hey asshole!"

He heard a rustle to his left, and nonchalantly stuck his hands in his pants pockets. Gato emerged from a path that ran next to the pier. Gato's head was cocked to the left, as if puzzled, and he carried what looked to be a large board in his left hand. As Gato stepped forward, Dees saw it was a double-barreled shotgun, the splintered stock held together with gaffer's tape.

Gato made no effort to raise the gun, and Dees said quickly, "Where the fuck have you been? I've been trying to find you. I saw you leaving the hotel and tried to catch up. You ever try to overtake a Chevy in a Lada?"

Gato took one step forward, then stopped. "You caught me at a bad time, *jefe*. I'm just getting ready to leave."

A man suddenly appeared at the boat's stern, standing at parade rest. "Juanito," he barked in Spanish, "shall I radio for air strikes?"

Gato looked at the trim man tenderly. *"Capitán,"* he said softly, "no need. Remember, you are on temporary duty with our navy. Please check the bow to make sure there are no UNITA frogmen in the water."

Captain Rafael Gato, late of the Army of the Republic of Cuba, snapped a salute, adjusted his eye patch, and walked toward the front of the boat. Gato turned to Dees. "My brother and I are preparing to do some fishing."

Dees glanced at the boat, then back at Gato. "Fishing? Maybe looking for marlin just off Miami Beach?"

"Something like that. But you'd better leave now."

Dees sounded tired. "Juan, I don't care if you run for mayor of Miami. But I do care people are getting killed all over the place, and I do care that war may be getting ready to start. I've been shot at and knocked cold and almost killed, and I'm hungry and sleepy, and I get irritable when cameramen start playing with nuclear bombs."

Gato's eyebrows arched. His head jerked, but the shotgun didn't move. Dees stared at it. "Come on, Juan, I need to know what's going on. Aren't enough people dead?"

Gato exhaled deeply and said, "You're an okay guy and I like you. But I don't have time to talk. I guess you found out all about it back in the States?"

Dees's right palm was perspiring against the pistol grip in his pocket. He tried to sound exasperated. "Just what did you do?"

"Young man," a familiar voice to Dees's right said, "the question is both what and why. The reason is always as important as the act itself."

Professor Fuentes was leaning against the metal rail that circled the boat. His face was wreathed in a smile. Dees didn't take his eyes off Gato and the shotgun, and said, "Professor, you want to tell me what's going on here?"

"My dear boy," Fuentes said with a chuckle, "you are entirely too bright to ask that question. We are obviously about to set off a small nuclear device and then, as you might say, get away and throw ourselves on the mercy of *el coloso del norte* and ask for political asylum."

Gato turned. "Professor, be quiet!"

Gloria stepped from the shadows, the Uzi held tense in her hands against the strap over her shoulder. "No! I will not allow it to happen!"

"Oh great," Dees said.

"Ah, a foursome," Fuentes said, smiling again.

"Make it five," Marco said, standing up. He held the camera by the handle on the top, like it was a suitcase, still rolling, keeping it aimed at Dees.

Gato began to raise the shotgun. Dees pulled the pistol from his pocket and held it in both hands, aiming in the general direction of Gato's midsection. "Stop! Everybody stop! Juan, put the fucking shotgun down, now! Gloria, don't shoot, it's okay! Pedro, stay out of the line of fire! Juan, put it down!"

"I've got nothing to lose," Gato said, pausing with the shotgun aimed at a forty-five-degree angle at the ground. "Radio Havana, my ass. *Tú eres una Fidelista, eh bebé? Socialismo o muerte, verdad?* She'll arrest me, and I'll join the rest of the Angola vets who became a threat six feet under."

Not taking his eyes off Gato, Dees said, "Nobody's arresting anybody."

Gloria started to speak. "But—"

"No buts," Dees interrupted. "Nobody's arrested, nobody's shot. Just go get the fucking briefcase and we'll dispose of it. Just go get it and we'll all get on your boat and we can turn it over to somebody when we get to Florida."

"Es posible por la mayor parte." Fuentes chuckled again from his perch on the starboard side of the idling boat. "But my understanding from Juan is that part of what you ask is impossible."

It was Gato's turn to chuckle. "Oh, what the fuck," he said, dropping the shotgun to the ground with a dull *thunk*. He looked at Dees and gave the shotgun a passing kick. It clattered about three feet. "Fucking thing probably wouldn't have fired anyway. Nothing else in this country works."

"Juan!" Rafael Gato said the name like a command. He was back on the stern, standing again at parade rest. "If you must surrender, remember, nothing but your name and rank. For *la patria.*"

Gato sighed and said, gently, "Raffie, it is not a surrender, more like a strategic repositioning."

Rafael Gato nodded once, as if satisfied, and walked back toward the bow, peering down at the water with his one good eye. Dees stuck the pistol back in his pocket. He bent over and clicked the thumb switch on the shotgun, breaking it open. Two shells dropped into his palm. He looked at them, and said, "You wouldn't have done much with these shells, anyway. Damp, probably rusted."

Dees glanced at Gloria, who still held the Uzi at waist level. "We're cool, Gloria. Put that thing down."

She didn't move. Dees repeated, "Gloria!"

She blinked once, looked at Dees, and slowly slung the Uzi back over her left shoulder. She glared at Gato. "The briefcase. Where is it?"

Gato glanced at his watch. "About forty minutes away from making one big fucking noise and a mushroom cloud the *gringo* navy won't be able to miss."

Dees was breathing through his mouth. "How do we shut it down?"

"We don't. They're set so that once you lock in the time and close the latch, they'll blow up if you even touch them."

"Show me!" Gloria snapped.

Gato just shook his head and jerked his thumb over his shoulder. "About fifty meters back there next to the base of that cliff. But you move it, shit, as far as I know, you even walk near it and it goes off. And we're down to about thirty-eight minutes."

Gloria started to step forward, past Gato, but Dees took two strides and grabbed her arm. "Don't."

"But I must stop it!"

"No," Dees said. Marco raised the camera to his shoulder, focused, and kept taping. "You have to make sure nobody gets hurt. That boat have a radio that works on it?"

Gato nodded. "Yeah."

Dees said, "Get me a flashlight." No one moved. "I said get me a goddamnn flashlight!"

Gato hurriedly pulled a flashlight from a rear pocket. He clicked the switch. Nothing. He banged the butt with his palm. The light flickered, then came on.

Dees said, "Gimme. Pedro, over here." Using the feeble sliver of light, Dees picked his way along the muddy trail, with Marco and Gato following, until he reached some brush near the vertical wall of a cliff. A metallic glint winked in the beam. Marco pointed the camera toward a small metal case that lay on the ground. Dees yelled over his shoulder at Gloria, "Get on the boat, use the radio, call your frontier guard or the coast guard or somebody. Tell them to get everybody out who's within five miles of here."

"Yeah," Marco muttered, not taking his eye from the viewfinder, "before I'm vaporized." He pushed the shot in until the briefcase filled the entire viewfinder.

Gato snorted. "Hell, there's nobody within five miles of here, maybe ten."

"Do it!" Dees barked. Gloria had climbed aboard the boat and disappeared by the time Marco shut down the camera. He turned to Gato. "Let's go. Do you have any idea how much of an asshole you are? You're going to get everybody killed."

"Not everybody," Gato replied, "just this fucking government."

Back at the boat, Dees tossed the duffel onto the deck and hoisted himself aboard. Gloria was in the wheelhouse, fiddling with a radio as Dees entered. She said with satisfaction, "There. This should be the standard marine frequency."

She keyed the mike and spoke in Spanish, so rapidly that Dees had a hard time following. "*Emergencia, emergencia. Guardia costal o guardia fronteras, este es una emergencia.* Come on, this is an emergency, over."

The radio crackled. "Come in," a voice said. "What sort of emergency do you have? *Guardia fronteras* station Guanabo, over."

Gloria took a deep breath. "Listen carefully. A large explosive device has been planted about twelve kilometers east of you. Repeat, a very large explosive device twelve kilometers east of your position. It is beside a cliff inside

Puerto Escondito. You must evacuate all people in this region immediately."

The radio hissed and popped. "Who is this? What is your position?"

Gloria said, "This is Major Bravo of the Directorate General of Intelligence. My reference number is five-nine-zero-alpha-romeo-two-two."

Gato whistled. "Motherfucker."

Fuentes pulled on his lower lip. "Most impressive. Not surprising, though."

"Ssshh," Gloria said angrily. She punched the microphone button again. "My location is classified. You must evacuate this entire area within half an hour or Havana will make sure everyone at your guard station will be punished. Over."

"We have a coast guard station on the cliff at the head of the harbor with a lighthouse," the radio immediately replied. "They can assist you. And I will verify this with my commanders in Havana before we—"

"No!" Gloria said. "Tell them to evacuate themselves immediately. If you take the time to contact Havana, it will be too late. If you do that and people die because of the delay I will have you shot."

"We can try," the radio speaker hissed. "Is this an American attack?"

"No!" Gloria said into the microphone. "This has nothing to do with the Americans! It is . . ." She paused. "It is one of our military exercises that has gone wrong. Cordon off the area between you and Matanzas. This is a level one emergency. Do it immediately or you will wish you had joined your cousin on that raft to Miami! Understand? Over."

The radio speaker was silent. Then, with another crackle, it said, "That is understood, but we need—"

She clicked the radio off. Her eyes had dark circles underneath them as she leaned against the wall of the wheelhouse. She looked at Dees, then at Gato and Fuentes. "I should kill these two."

"Not a half bad idea," Dees said, turning to the two men. "Who drives this thing?"

"That would be me," Fuentes said with a slight bow. "I have read everything there is on the nautical arts. Have you ever read Samuel Eliot Morrison's biography of Christoforo Colon? It is a wonderful—"

"So," Gloria said tiredly, "you have never actually piloted a boat?"

"In my mind's eye, Horatio," Fuentes said. "Juan, if you will haul in the two running anchors, I will move us to the open ocean."

"Not yet," Dees said. "We've got to get those people out of the houses along the road. Professor, the key to the boat. Juan, give me the Nova key."

They merely stared at each other. "Juan," Dees said through his teeth, "give me the fucking key to the car. Professor, shut the engine down now."

Fuentes sighed, shut off the diesels, and handed Dees the key. Gato fumbled in his pocket and dug out the Nova key. Dees said, "Gloria, Pedro, come with me. You guys can stay here or swim." Marco scurried after them as Dees grabbed Gloria by the arm and dragged her to the Nova.

The car tossed gravel in all directions as it skidded back down the road. Dees stopped in front of the shacks and leaned on the horn. Its sound echoed off the hills like an air raid alarm. "Get 'em up!" he yelled at Gloria. "Six houses, I figure maybe forty people, more or less. Head 'em toward the gas station. Hurry!"

Without a word, Gloria and Marco sprang from the car and began pounding on the doors of the nearest concrete shacks. Dees honked the horn repeatedly as he gunned the engine and drove down the road. He saw a pair of sleepy heads emerge from the shacks nearest to him. At the fueling station where the buses were parked, he made a looping turn to the left, snapped the wheel hard to the right, and accelerated.

The Nova's front end smashed into the chain-link gate, buckling the metal and sending a rusted chain and padlock flying into the night. Dees slapped the Nova into neutral and ran toward one of the buses. He stuck his head in the open door of the rear bus. No key. Swearing, he sprinted toward the second bus. A key dangled from the dashboard.

Hopping in, Dees slipped the long floor shifter into neutral and turned the key. The bus groaned lazily as the engine turned repeatedly. He stopped, pumped the gas pedal quickly, and tried again. The bus shuddered and belched to life. His hand fumbled along the dashboard until he felt a knob, then pulled it. Instead of switching on the lights, it turned on the emergency flashers. Another knob turned on the interior lights. Finally, the third activated the sickly front beams.

Dees shoved the gearshift up and depressed the clutch. The bus lurched forward. He jammed in the clutch, and ground the shift lever down. He let out the clutch, and the bus stalled. That's fourth, he thought. So maybe reverse is, yeah, right here. He started the engine again and shoved the shifter to the upper right. The bus crawled backward. He heard crumpling metal and tinkling glass, and figured he had smashed into the front of the other bus.

He wrestled the wheel sharp to the left, aimed at the fence, floored the accelerator, and let the clutch out. The bus shot forward, hit the fence, and slowed. Dees kept his foot on the gas. Finally, the aluminum pipes supporting the chain link bent. He drove the bus over the flattened fencing, and turned, aiming it out the gravel road and toward the highway, not fifty feet away.

He heard shouts behind him. A ragged line of men, women, and children stumbled down the road. Gloria, behind them, was shouting and waving her arms. Marco was helping an old man walk, unsteadily, toward the bus. Dees jumped off. "Hey," he yelled. "Get somebody who can drive this. Have 'em get it out of here now!"

Marco shouted a question in Spanish. No one responded. He yelled again. This time, one man raised an arm uncertainly. Marco motioned him toward the driver's seat, and herded the rest through the door. Gloria picked up a small boy dragging his puppy by a rope. She brushed his hair as he looked up at her, then put him down and gently shoved him through the door. She shouted at the driver and waved her arms.

The bus coughed again, and slowly moved down the gravel, turning left and sputtering east, in the general direction of Matanzas. Dees grabbed her arm and pulled her toward the Nova. Marco dove into the backseat. They roared toward the parking lot next to the harbor, where Dees locked the brakes as he stopped, and opened the door before the car had stopped rocking. All three of them sprinted down the pier and jumped aboard the boat.

Dees handed Fuentes the key. "Let's go, Professor. As fast as you can."

Gato stepped outside and began hauling on a line dropped over the stern. Dees turned to Gloria. "Where'd you get that about the guy on the radio and his cousin on a raft?"

She shrugged. "A guess. Everyone has a cousin in Miami."

"Since the storm's moving off, this could be when Diaz decides to use that jet. I need to warn the States."

Gloria shrugged. "This radio seems to be low-power and does not seem to have anything but the Cuban marine frequency. Since none of us has a telephone, and since even if we did I doubt any signal would get through the storm ahead, I think, *chico*, you will have to wait to do that."

As Gato turned his attention to the bow anchor, Fuentes expertly moved one of the two levers that stuck up from the console next to the wheel. The right engine and its propeller spun, pushing the boat hard to the left. Fuentes pulled it back, gripped both levers in his hand, and slowly moved both forward. The boat chugged down the harbor estuary. The cliffs opened. A lighthouse perched on a promontory on one side. To the other, a sheer cliff rose, sliced off flat at the top. Directly in front of them, waves foamed above reefs near the shore.

The boat jolted back and forth as the waves of the open Caribbean slapped the bow. The engine noise rose in frequency as the bow slowly angled up from the water. Fuentes clicked both levers forward, and the nose pitched upward before slowly lowering itself into the dark ocean in front of them.

Dees stepped outside and looked over the gunwale at the water rushing underneath, then came back into the cramped wheelhouse. "About three feet of freeboard. This thing isn't loaded, but it's not empty, either. What's stored below deck?"

Fuentes laughed. "About twenty cases of books and a suitcase with my equity from decades of reeducation and tips."

"Dollars?" Dees asked.

"All denominations. About sixty thousand, I believe, enough for a small position in Microsoft or Coca-Cola, perhaps both."

Rafael Gato, his hair neatly slicked against the wind and spray, appeared at the door of the wheelhouse. "I shall be at the bow to watch for mines."

As the elder Gato walked toward the bow, Dees rubbed the bridge of his nose. "How much time we have?"

Gato looked at his watch. "Twenty minutes more or less."

Abruptly, Dees gripped the front of Gato's shirt, balled the fabric in both fists, and lifted him, first to his tiptoes, then off the deck completely.

"My knees hurt holding you like this," Dees said quietly, his face inches from Gato's, "so I may be tempted to drop you over the side. Start talking about you and Cabrera before I drown your sorry ass."

"I would do so if I were you," Fuentes said, turning from the wheel. "Tell him, I mean. Since we will be on the edge of a hurricane, I will be very busy in a little while, so take my advice, Juan, while I have time to give it. This young man holding you has an overdeveloped sense of justice, and I believe he *may* very well drown you."

Fuentes turned his attention back to the wheel. Gato's eyes were wide. He looked at Gloria, who said, in Spanish, "Talk, *maricón*. If he does not kill you I will be glad to do it myself."

Gato nodded vigorously. Dees sat him down, and thought for a moment the cameraman might pass out from hyperventilating. The boat began to roll slightly. Dees realized Fuentes was humming the suite from Handel's Water Music.

Marco powered up the camera and nodded with satisfaction when Gato's face appeared in ghostly green and white in his viewfinder. He circled the index finger and thumb on his left hand and motioned toward Dees.

Dees said, "The night lens is working and the camera mike'll pick you up just fine. When did you first get in touch with Cabrera?"

Gato was breathing in ragged gasps. "Okay, shit. Okay. Some of us Angola vets, the really pissed-off ones, keep in contact with some of the *gusanos* in Miami." He smiled weakly at Gloria. "Including your old man, I hear."

Her mouth became a thin, tight line. She was lazily swinging the Uzi off her shoulder when Gato held up his palms again. "Okay, okay, it's what I heard. I mean how the fuck would I really know, I was just a fucking sergeant, okay? So anyway, this guy I know comes back from Angola with *la SIDA*, fucked around with those bush *putas* and got it. But check this out, no symptoms at all for five years, *nada*, then *ba-bing*, he gets open sores and starts losing weight and he's got AIDS. Oh, they give him medicine, all right, and they lock him up in a quarantine center like he's a fucking POW."

Gato gulped in a lungful of air. "His sister, she's pissed that her hero brother's locked up like an animal. So she contacts a cousin in Hialeah, who puts her in touch with Cabrera. I visit her brother once a month or so, and she knows about

Raffie, so she figures I'm okay, and she puts me in touch with Cabrera.

"I call him at some Miami number with the cash the sister fronts me, and I tell the telephone exchange assholes he's my uncle. The sister, she's given me a list of medicines, each one's a code name for weapons or money or something. We talk about some medicines Cabrera wants to send to a sick cousin here. He says tetracycline, and I know that means a timer of some kind. He says amoxycillin, and it's high explosives. He mentions a messenger service in Miami that ships parcels from exiles to relatives, and that means it's coming by air. He says he's planning to send specialized medicines for his cousin that'll end up costing twenty thousand, U.S., and I know that's my cut."

The boat pitched up over the crest of a wave, sending stinging spray flying out of the dark. Fuentes, humming softly, checked his compass and started the ragged wiper blade swinging back and forth across the streaked glass of the wheelhouse. Gato continued, "Then he tells me he has a message from my office, that I need to make sure I've got the right Customs forms for some equipment they're sending me. So hey, I figure, what the fuck, so he knows I work for GTV, okay, no problem. Then he gives me the flight number the stuff's coming in on. And then—"

He looked straight into the camera lens. "Then he gave me your name. He knew you were coming and knew what flight and when, and knew you'd be babysitting GTV equipment."

Dees growled, "Did he ever mention anybody named Briscoe? Or how he was going to get the briefcase in with the GTV equipment?"

Gato shook his head. "Nah. I'm just supposed to sit tight with it until I get the word the hurricane's starting to move west. The grapevine, it's got all sorts of stories about Diaz and some jet he's supposed to have. So I put two and two together and figure Cabrera wants to start something between the *gringos* and Cuba, which is no skin off my ass since I'll be out of here."

He paused and glanced between Dees and Gloria. The only sound was the *whoooossh* of spray across the bow and the creak of the boat's wooden spars. "So I get word through the sister, see, she gets a phone call from Miami that says not to worry about her family, that *la tormenta* is moving west. So that's my signal. But then . . ."

He shot Fuentes a sour look. The professor glanced down at the compass, then up, out into the darkness, picking up the story while staring straight into the black spray hissing over them. "Then I noticed that our friend Juan is more nervous than usual, even for him. I notice that he is very concerned about one small piece of equipment I help him unload. I hear he has been asking around about the availability of a seaworthy craft such as this. So I approached young Juan with a proposition. I will use part of my funds to procure a boat. In exchange for that, and for my silence, I will go along with him, and take his brother also."

Fuentes turned and flashed a smile at Dees. "The discussion did not last very long."

The boat paused in midair, shuddered, then dove into a shallow trough, its bow splitting the next oncoming wave like a sharp knife. "All this talk is distracting me from the job at hand," Fuentes said over his shoulder. "I have steered past the reefs, but need to concentrate since I do not wish to become like another old man and the sea, dead in his boat. Please continue without me."

Gloria looked like she had bitten into a rotten mango. In Spanish she said, "Did you ever think that this is what the people you hate most want also? *Los duros* create more tension with the *gringos*, thanks to help from this Cabrera. The threat of an invasion rallies everyone to *la patria* and they use it like they have used the *yanqui* blockade, to repress us even more. *Tú eres un tonto!*"

Marco lowered the camera and thumbed the power switch to Off. Gato looked at his watch and smiled. "Don't shut that off just yet. You got about a minute to get one hell of a light show."

The boat had stopped thrashing, and now rolled gently from one trough to another. "Twelve miles out," Fuentes barked. "Given my understanding of this device, more than enough space to guarantee safety."

Marco opened the narrow wooden door and stepped out onto the spray-slick deck. He grabbed the starboard rail, bent his knees slightly, rolling with the deck. He unsnapped the night lens, quickly replaced it with the normal lens, and jammed the longer, thicker lens into his pants pocket. Then he thumbed the power switch, aimed at the horizon, and focused on infinity.

After about thirty seconds, a small pinpoint of light appeared in the center of the wobbling viewfinder. Suddenly, a flash whited out the entire screen for an instant. Marco looked up from the viewfinder, and saw a roiling column of light that seemed to boil from the ocean's surface, punching upward through the black sky.

For fifteen seconds, the horizon was lit by a wave of light that pulsed from the fireball. Like a tree illuminated by floodlights at the base of its trunk, the rising pillar of fire and smoke was lit by the flash at the bottom. Finally, the vaguely mushroom-shape cloud began to fade into darkness, just as the noise caught up with the boat.

Dees could feel the air in his face, propelled by the force of the blast. By the time it hit him, it had diminished to an insistent breeze, ruffling his hair. The windows in the wheelhouse vibrated in their cracking caulk seals. The air itself began to vibrate like something alive, thick with sound, as if, Dees thought, he could reach out and rip off a chunk.

The pulsing subsided. The pillar of fire vanished, leaving only a low glowing mound of light straight off the stern.

Marco looked through the viewfinder. It was dark except for the glow at the bottom of the screen. A final sound from the shore, a ripping noise like cloth being torn, reached the boat. It blended into the hiss of spray, then faded completely.

CHAPTER 18

The boat's bow registration was faded but still legible: Fo-65523. Fo stood for folio, the registry for all vessels in Cuba. 65523 had been built twenty-three years before from oak and marine-grade steel in Manzanillo, designed for open-water trawling in the Cayman Trench as far out as Honduras. When the hard-liners had taken control of the Cuban Central Committee for most of the eighties, 65523 had been pressed into service as a coastal patrol craft. The navy men who took it over had appreciated its refusal to wallow in heavy seas and the power from the mammoth Soviet diesel below deck.

Professor Fuentes only knew that it had been used for fishing along the north coast. But his reading told him the solid feel of the wheel in his hand and the deck beneath him was a good sign, even as dark waves the size of small buildings slapped the deck with a sound like cannon fire. The blunt bow would dive into a trough and then climb, edging up the side of a huge roller before nosing down again. All the while, the 900-horsepower Minsk-made diesel would grind along, spinning a single propeller at several thousand revolutions per minute.

If Hurricane David hadn't picked up forward speed dramatically, moving away from them to the west, all six people huddled in the wheelhouse would have died from towering waves slicing off the decktop enclosure like a knife splitting an apple. But the winds on the southeast edge of the huge storm were down to forty knots, and the waves, even at their worst, were now no more than eighteen feet, well within the limits of 65523's tolerance. The wheelhouse shuddered, groaned, and vibrated, but remained in place.

Gato, sitting on his heels in a corner with his head buried in his arms, whimpered every time the deck rattled, moaning as the boat seemed to be held motionless in the ocean's palm before the propeller bit into the churning water and shoved it forward again.

Rafael, in contrast, stood erect just over Fuentes's left shoulder, staring into the spray-soaked darkness as if his eye was locked on something three thousand miles and fifteen years away. A rolling wave unexpectedly hit the boat from the port side, causing it to heel violently to starboard before it righted with a series of groans, creaks, and snaps. Fuentes looked at Rafael as his knuckles turned white on the wheel.

Still at attention, Rafael placed his hand gently on Fuentes's shoulder and clasped the fist of his other hand on the wheel. Bending his head forward slightly, he said, "Be strong, Admiral. The lives of many people depend upon us. Duty, eh? Duty and *la patria*."

Fuentes glanced up gratefully and said, "I am not a superstitious man, but this could be a propitious time to cross myself. Since I cannot remove my hands from this wheel, I shall do it in my mind and hope the Lord, should He exist, will forgive my hypocrisy."

Marco stood with his back braced against the rear wall, clutching the camera like it was an infant. He had draped it in a blue rain cover, then sealed it inside a thick, clear plastic waterproof bag sealed with Velcro. He glared down at Gato, cowering in a corner, and said, in clipped Spanish, "Hey, *primo*, stop your damn whining. Be a man. Your brother's nuts, and he's standing like a real Cuban."

Gato looked up, his hair plastered to his skull with spray and sweat. "Maybe," he croaked, "*mi hermano* is being brave because he *is* nuts. Me, I'm sane enough to be shitting in my pants. You're a little crazy yourself, *gusano.*"

Marco thought about putting his camera down and planting his fist on the top of Gato's head. He decided against it and just glared. He glanced at Dees, who was staring at the water trickling slowly under the caulk of the Plexiglas windows surrounding the wheelhouse.

Dees lurched forward, to Fuentes's right, and jerked open the doors of a small wooden cabinet tucked underneath the control panel. Fuentes said, without looking down, "I am afraid a boat from the people's paradise will be a little short on crucifixes."

Before Dees could answer, the boat seemed to pause, shaking only from the engine's vibration, before it pitched forward to the bottom of a deep trough. Dees was thrown to his knees, his forehead banging off the cabinet's wooden frame. He was rocked backward almost immediately as the boat wrenched upward and a wave Dees could have sworn was the size of Mount Everest buried the vessel, bow to stern, under churning water.

Dees tried to shake off the dizziness as 65523 poked its bow out of the froth and continued to plow forward. The back edge of the right rear window had popped loose from its caulk, bowing inward. Water poured through like spray from a garden hose. Jerking open the small door, Dees dived head first into the compartment, feeling with his hands. He dug through clutter that included rusted pliers, a hammer, an unopened can of beans, and a pile of oily rags before he felt a pair of rubber straps.

He pulled on them and withdrew two scarred diving masks, one with a crack running diagonally across the faceplate. He clutched them as he forced himself to his feet. Grabbing at the slick rail on the control panel, he stood next to Fuentes and yelled across to Rafael in Spanish, "*Capitán,* you are relieved. Your brother needs you."

Rafael turned his head, slowly, blinked the water from his

eye, and looked at Dees. He turned on his heel, silently walked to the rear of the pitching wheelhouse, and bent down, balancing himself expertly on the balls of his feet, to spread his arms tenderly around Gato's huddled figure. Rafael's broad back shielded his brother from the spray now pouring through the sprung window.

Maybe that's what it takes to be kind and brave, Dees thought. Maybe you have to lose your mind. He fitted one of the masks tightly across Fuentes's face, yelling in his ear, "We're going to need these! The windows are going!"

"Then I must breathe through my mouth, I suppose!" Fuentes shouted back.

Dees adjusted his own mask and grabbed the violently vibrating wheel. He had just looked down at the bouncing compass ball, and saw they were still heading north by northwest, vaguely toward Key West, when the windows bowed, rattled, cracked, and exploded inward, flooding the wheelhouse with a rush of roaring water that seemed as black as the night in front of them.

* * *

The normally clear Gulf waters between the bight and the Mallory Dock looked like a floating lumberyard. It had been less than an hour since the last of the howling winds passed Key West, replaced by gusty breezes. The white vessel with the diagonal orange stripe on the bow was actually thirty-eight feet long, but everyone called it a forty boat, including the lieutenant at the helm and the four crewmen on the cramped, narrow deck.

The lieutenant swore under his breath as he steered, engines barely idling, through undulating wood and metal. The storm had moved through rapidly. The Coast Guard even had reports of two rust-bucket Haitian freighters on David's lee side that had wallowed in the waves but were still chugging toward Miami.

"Hey," he yelled through the open window of the small enclosed bridge that perched above the deck, "off the port bow! Gaff that!"

He pointed, squinting to make out an object that looked to be the size of a small car, bobbing just to port. Two sailors dressed in dark blue shirts and pants, mummified inside orange life jackets, scrambled to hook whatever it was with gaff poles. The sun was still a pink glow just below the horizon. The lieutenant couldn't tell what it was they were approaching until they were fifteen feet away.

He finally made it out, and quickly pushed the twin throttles, first to idle, then bumped them once, twice, three times in reverse. The boat stopped just short of the object. It was a battered red Toyota sport coupe, barely floating, its windows sealed tight. The hood and trunk bobbed just below the surface. The gaff poles screeched on the roof as the sailors nudged it out of their path.

Off to the left, half of the Mallory Dock had disappeared under a jumble of debris, including corrugated metal roofing, shards of aluminum siding, piles of wood ranging from two-by-fours to splintered sections of telephone poles, three small cars, two sailboats, and several dozen bicycles and motorbikes that had been sucked from a tourist hotel's garage and then tossed, twisted and broken, onto the concrete dock. A row of five royal palms that had been uprooted from a new housing development floated side by side. Their fronds hula'd in the water like green grass skirts.

The debris on the water thinned out past the end of the dock, scattered as far as the lieutenant could see between Key West and the small private scrub islands huddled near the big island's tip. The sun finally crept over the horizon. The entire expanse where the Gulf met the Atlantic, resembled a huge swimming pool recently abandoned by a party of giant children and left filled with floating toys. Looking to the west, the lieutenant saw the backside of the hurricane retreating behind a wall of onyx-black clouds that hugged the horizon.

Dees saw the Coast Guard ship bobbing in the debris field.

He shoved himself out of the wheelhouse, his shirt and pants soaked, his hair plastered to his skull. He walked to the rear deck and used the increasing light to help him see where shattered Plexiglas lay sparking like ice shards around the hatch.

Fuentes slowly moved past Dees, bending over, forcing the hatch cover open. Dees looked into the wheelhouse. Rafael held the wheel, steadily staring toward the Coast Guard cutter. The professor placed the cover on deck and looked down. The only water in the hold seemed to be what had run inside when he cracked it open in the first place. He seemed satisfied, and placed the fiberglass hatch cover back with a clatter, pushing hard until he felt the rubber seals grip and the latch click.

Marco sat on the bench attached to the rear of the wheelhouse and checked the camera. He looked up at Gato standing over him, looking over his shoulder. "*Coño, la guardia costal.* I'm fucked."

Without a word, Marco turned the camera on and took a variety of wide shots, pans, and zooms of the battered coast. Satisfied, he put the camera back into the duffel. Dees and Fuentes walked inside the wheelhouse. Dees took the wheel, gently, from Rafael, who took three steps backward and stood, silently at parade rest, at the rear of the wheelhouse. Dees noticed the red ring around the professor's eyes and nose where the mask had bitten into his translucent old man's skin. "Professor," he said, "a favor?"

Fuentes looked puzzled. "How may I be of service?"

"This is for everybody," Dees said loudly, steering through the increasingly thick debris. "Listen up. Professor, please go below and bring up three thousand dollars for Juan."

Fuentes merely stared. Dees cut back on the throttle so he wouldn't impale the bow on some sharp piece of flotsam and spoke again, quietly this time. "Here's what we do. We're a GTV crew. Just let me do all the talking. When we dock, Professor, you stay on the boat. Sleeping quarters may be hard to come by, considering the damage. Juan, you take the three thousand dollars and your brother and disappear. You can bribe your way to Miami and probably do just fine with some Spanish-language TV station shooting propaganda pieces. I'll help you pull some strings and get Rafael some treatment, or at least a safe place to stay. I don't want to see you again."

"But he must go to jail!" Gloria said heatedly. "He needs to be punished!"

"He will be," Dees said. "He gets to live in Miami. Gloria, stick close to me. I need to tell that Coast Guard boat to radio somebody to be on the lookout for Diaz and the jet. We need to get this shit on the air before something else happens. Then we find Cabrera and ask him some questions. Professor, I'll repay the cash within two days."

"I know you will," the old man said, and chuckled. He was surprisingly agile as he stepped past Dees, removed the hatch cover, and lowered himself into the hold.

Fuentes emerged within a few minutes. "Here," he said. He held out a cylinder of bills secured by a rubber band. "Twenties and fifties."

Gato eagerly grabbed the roll and stuffed it into his pants pocket. Dees slowly steered the boat toward the mouth of the harbor. "Okay," he said to no one in particular, "the Coasties'll probably hail us in a couple of minutes. Just agree with whatever I say and look like an overworked news crew."

He turned to Rafael, and said, in Spanish, "*Capitán*, please crouch low. Just stay there until we tell you otherwise."

Rafael crouched, balancing himself on the balls of his feet, as he had during the storm. His expression never changed.

Less than a minute later, a megaphone-amplified voice ricocheted off the water. "Vessel ahead. Where is your Florida registration? You have Cuban registration numbers on the bow. This is the United States Coast Guard. Stand by to be boarded."

Dees waved and maneuvered the boat nearer. Gato said, "Oh shit."

Dees smiled and waved again, and said, through clenched

teeth, "Shut up." He smiled some more, put his hands to his mouth and yelled "Media! We're a news crew! With GTV!"

"Who is aboard?" the lieutenant yelled. He was close enough now to not have to use the loudspeaker. "Where is your registration?"

"I'm Peter Dees, I'm a reporter." Dees saw the lieutenant nod. Good, Dees thought. Name recognition. "I have my producer and cameraman and soundman and Dr. Fuentes from the Hurricane Center. We rented this tub in Marathon to get video of the storm. Guy there said it was used by some rafters a few weeks back and he kept it. We worked our way down here. I need to get the video to GTV immediately."

"Shouldn't be a problem," the lieutenant yelled, maneuvering his vessel closer. "There are five satellite trucks on Duval Street alone, a few more other places. TV crews are all over, what with the hurricane and trouble with Cuba."

"What's the latest on Cuba?"

"You didn't hear? A nuclear explosion near Matanzas. They're claiming it was an American attack. Rumor is Castro's croaked. They're ferrying a fighter intercept squadron to NAS Key West once the runway's cleared of debris. And you've got a boat with Cuban registration."

Dees cupped his hands to his mouth. "I need you to make an emergency radio call!"

The lieutenant looked sour. "What? Why?"

Dees took a deep breath. Keep it simple, keep it calm. "A fighter jet may attack someplace in Florida soon. It's—"

The sour look was replaced with anger. "What? We're going to board you now! Stand by!"

Dees yelled again, "Radio somebody! A fighter jet may attack someplace in Florida shortly! It's flown by a Cuban exile lunatic! We need to contact somebody now!"

The lieutenant gunned his engines in a short burp, moving closer to Dees in the littered harbor. "Keep your hands where I can see them!"

"Use your goddamn radio! Warn somebody!"

The lieutenant ignored him and sidled the forty boat closer to Dees. Fuentes gripped the wheel. His hand rested, briefly, atop Dees's. "Young man, it seems to me you have too much of the Don Quixote in you. Remember, the Quixote died brokenhearted and quite mad."

Dees felt a shiver pulse up his spine. He smiled at Fuentes. "I intend to die just like you, peacefully in bed, just another rich old reprobate surrounded by his mistresses."

Fuentes smiled, tiredly. "My lovers are my books, and I plan to sleep with all of them this night."

Marco powered the camera up and took a wide shot of the Coast Guard boat as it moved closer. He pushed in tight on the fantail, then slowly pulled back. In the viewfinder, he saw a small speck moving from the left of the screen.

He looked up and felt his jaw sag. It was a familiar jet, with straight wings, a red star insignia on each one, executing a gentle dive. Flashes of light pulsed from the plane's nose at the same time small twin geysers began erupting in the water in front of the forty boat.

"No!" Dees yelled. One of the sailors had time to look up, in Dees's direction, before the geysers stopped at the orange diagonal stripe on the bow. The vessel was suddenly engulfed in spinning debris.

A sailor on the bow was almost cut in half by the thirty millimeter cannon fire, his body shredded at the waist. He folded in half like a closing pocketknife before toppling into the water. The whining shriek of slugs hitting metal filled the air, along with a scream that grew louder, then abruptly stopped. The wheelhouse seemed to explode from the inside, metal and glass bursting outward as it disintegrated. The white-hot ammunition penetrated the fuel tank, and a white fireball roiled from the ship's bowels before engulfing the boat in black smoke.

A second explosion, sharper than the first, blew a chunk of the stern straight up in the air. Before it landed, Marco saw through the viewfinder that the forty boat was almost completely underwater. Marco jerked the camera upward, and caught a profile of the jet and its tailpipes as it swooped back up and went into a sharp right bank, across Key West.

It seemed to be picking up speed as it turned, engines howling, standing on its right wing, so Marco had a perfect sweeping shot of the top of the plane. It snapped level again and headed straight for the bridge of Dees's nose.

"Get out of here!" Dees screamed. "He's coming back! Get overboard!"

Fuentes's head jerked up. "I must go below. My savings."

"No time!" Dees yelled. "Over the side!"

Gloria dove, arms extended over her head, as the winks of light appeared again on the plane's nose. Marco shot five seconds worth of video, jammed the camera inside the waterproof plastic pouch, managed to seal it and stuff it inside the plastic-lined duffel. He eased himself into the water, feet first, and gently dog-paddled behind the floating duffel, pushing it in front of him. The air inside the sealed waterproof bag counteracted the weight of the camera, so the bag floated uneasily in the choppy water.

"My money!" Fuentes repeated, lurching from the wheelhouse and walking unsteadily toward the hatch cover.

"I can't swim," Gato said, panic in his eyes.

"Shit!" Dees yelled over the increasing noise from the jet engines and concussions from the cannon. "Both of you just jump to me! I'll be in the water! Just hang on to me and we'll all make it!"

"It's too far!" Gato screamed as wood, bits of metal, and shards of concrete exploded from the dock.

Dees, poised on the stern, turned to Fuentes. The old man had stopped, and sat heavily on the hatch cover, facing the plane and the *blopblopblopblop* from the geysers of water and flotsam erupting closer and closer to the boat.

He looked at Dees and shook his head. "Too old, too far, too late. Give the money to a charity, eh?"

Rafael suddenly emerged from the wheelhouse and strode to Gato. He placed himself in front of his brother and faced the jet. Water exploded in pinpoints from the space between the boat and the dock. As splinters of wood began to spiral up from the stern, Rafael drew himself erect, snapped a salute at the nose of the Sukhoi, and shouted, *"Soy Capitán Rafael Gato! Viva la patria!"*

Dees had time to make out the crunch of wood splintering as he threw himself head first into the water. A second before his head went under, he heard what sounded like a series of water-filled balloons bursting. Sunlight filtered through the debris-mottled water. Dees opened his eyes to the sting of salt water and saw a yellow glow spread across the surface, outlining each piece of wood and fragment of metal as sharply as if it had been etched on glass.

A rush of bubbles caught him from behind, shoving his head down. The concussion lifted his legs and shoved them forward, spinning him end over end. His lungs aching, he shoved the surface litter out of the way and burst to the surface, sucking in air with a gasp.

Looking up, he saw the twin glow from the jet's engines climbing up and banking hard to the right. The jet snapped back into level flight as two trails of smoke burst forward from under each wing. Dees had time to follow the flight of the missiles before they disappeared in the distance, to his right. A tower of black smoke rushed skyward. From where? He tried to think. The answer hit him about the same time he saw Gato's body, floating facedown, his left arm missing. Diaz had just strafed the Trumbo Annex, the old Naval Air Station now used for training and military housing.

Dees could hear voices yelling in the far distance. He dog-paddled toward the dock, careful to keep his head high to avoid gulping in any of the water now filled with debris, diesel fuel, and body parts. He paddled toward where Gloria had climbed a rusted metal ladder to the top of the dock. Marco stood next to her, examining the camera. It was still dry.

Dees pulled himself up the ladder unsteadily. He threw himself face first onto the dock, gasping for air. Gloria sat next to him.

"Welcome to hell," she said quietly. "It seems this Cabrera and *los duros* have the war they wanted."

"Not yet," Dees said with a wheeze. He glanced toward Marco, who looked down at the camera, then at Dees, and flashed a thumbs-up.

"Come on," Dees shouted. He paused and stared at the harbor. Fuentes's body floated, facedown, arms outstretched, surrounded by floating books and hundred dollar bills gently rolling on the oily surface. Next to him, the torso of Captain Rafael Gato floated facing the sky, his eyes open. The rest of his body bobbed in a clump of smoking debris twenty yards away. His face had a puzzled expression.

CHAPTER 19

"You got it, New York?" the producer shouted into his cellular phone. He used his free hand to cover the other ear. "It's a fucking Cuban jet! . . . Yeah! What? . . . Yeah, it's attacking Key West! What? . . . *What?* . . . Yeah, Key West is in the United States!"

The five satellite trucks sat nose-to-tail in the middle of Duval Street, the hum and sputter of their generators forming a layer of white noise underneath the shouts of technicians, reporters, and producers.

"Track it!" a producer with jet-black, brush-cut hair yelled to a stocky cameraman wearing a Panama Jack T-shirt. The cameraman was balanced on the roof of a satellite truck whose paint job advertised UPLINK WORLD. He was bracing his back lightly against the metal arm that supported the satellite dish, aimed southeast at a seventy degree angle. The cables running from his camera to the side of the truck skittered over the metal as he panned, following the flight of the jet, left to right.

At the next truck in line—"Channel 13, *Your* News, Florida!"—a raven-haired reporter wearing jeans and a khaki shirt with the top two buttons strategically undone was in the middle of her live shot. ". . . bombing Key West. As you can see from the videotape we just shot, the Cubans have already fired into a military facility here. Key West is still reeling from Hurricane David, so it's hard to tell what damage was caused by the storm and what's been caused by the Cuban attack. I'm told we're now going to ABC's Art Jackson, live at the Pentagon."

She paused, looking straight into the camera until a producer stuck his head out of the combination edit bay and control room inside the truck and shouted "Clear!" She exhaled, and seemed to sag, holding the microphone to her side, her hands shaking.

No one noticed Dees, Marco, and Gloria emerge from behind the broken glass and shredded awnings of the Ocean Key House, at the head of Duval Street. The street was filling with people. Most were young men whose eyes darted from place to place, searching for opportunities. Two of them, shirtless, had stepped through the opening left by the Ocean Key House's vanished windows and plywood sheathing, and were stepping out again, carrying stacked wicker chairs from the lobby. Another, still inside, pounded at the padlock that secured the bar's liquor supply until the eagle's head on his Hog Rider from Hell tattoo was glowing red.

He wound up and smashed the hasp again with a hammer. It fell away. He jerked the cabinet open and filled his beefy arms with mostly full liters of bourbon, gin, and scotch. Stepping outside, he shot a threatening look at Dees, and walked quickly down a side street.

"Bienvenidos a los Estados Unidos," Dees muttered under his breath. He walked carefully through the broken glass and twisted metal.

Gloria just stared after the waddling biker until he clinked around a corner. "And what do we propose happens next?"

"They're all feeding their networks," Dees said, nodding toward the trucks. "It looks like this is going out live, and most of these stations are affiliated with at least two of the nets. See the truck from Uplink World? I recognize the guys in front of it. They're from Channel 8. Too cheap to buy their own truck, so they rent them. They're a GTV affiliate, and CBS, so they're feeding both. Channel 13's ABC and CNN. I imagine that Channel 9 truck's feeding NBC, CNBC, and

MSNBC. If Channel 5's here, they've got Fox News covered. Add that to the Spanish language trucks feeding TeleNoticias, Univision, Telemundo, and Christ knows who else, and my guess is every TV set in the Western Hemisphere's carrying a live attack on the United States about now.

"So if I can get this stuff to the Channel 8 truck and get it on the air . . ." As Dees stepped away from the building and toward the Channel 8 truck, he looked to his right. Abruptly, he extended the back of his left arm across Gloria's chest, and shoved her back against the building.

Dees jerked his head to the right. "Down there. In front of the Channel 44 truck. Take a look."

The truck, smaller than the others, was painted orange, yellow, and red. CANAL 44, the letters painted on the side read, ¡NOTICIAS Y MÁS! In front of the truck, a tall reporter with a bushy black mustache was staring into the camera, gesticulating with one hand while holding the microphone in his other. A taller man stood next to him, his slicked-back hair glistening, his blue button-down shirt freshly pressed.

Gloria's eyes widened. "Come on," she said, stepping in front of Dees. "We can get closer and hear."

They walked past an old bank building that had housed a Planet Hollywood on the second floor. The large globe that had been the restaurant's logo lay crumpled in the street. They edged to the outside of a crowd of about two dozen people, mostly Hispanic, who were listening intently to the Channel 44 report.

"*Este ataque desde Cuba continúa, un altraje comunista,*" the reporter was saying. Dees reached down, and picked up a sodden Tampa Bay Devil Rays baseball cap off the street. He jammed it to his ears, pulling the bill low over his nose. Marco powered up the camera, and looking down at the viewfinder, struggled to translate as he shot. "We will hear from the White House in a moment about this outrage. For now, we have with us the noted anti-Communist and patriot,

Manuel Cabrera, who has come to Key West with relief supplies. But you come with more than that, true?"

"Es verdad, amigo," Cabrera said.

Dees tugged on Marco's sleeve. "Get closer."

Marco hoisted the camera on his shoulder and blended into the crowd, arrayed in a ragged semicircle around the live shot location. He pushed in for a close-up of Cabrera, who let a half smile pass across his face before he locked his mouth into an appropriately solemn frown.

"En este momento, nosotros enfrentamos un día nuevo en la patria," he said, turning every few words to face the camera directly. "This new day we face means freedom. The Communist beasts have set off an atomic bomb on our island and have blamed it on America. Now they use this as an excuse to attack this country, as we have all seen on live television.

"America must react! This outrage must not go unpunished!" He paused for a smattering of applause from the crowd. Marco took a step backward, framing the tableau in a wide shot. Cabrera straightened his shoulders. "But we cannot have chaos in our fatherland! The beast of Cuba is dying! We must have order until free elections are held in Cuba! We all know of the San Carlos Institute here in Key West. The great José Martí spoke from its steps to rally the Cubans here against the Spanish. The building, as you all know, is technically Cuban territory."

Dees wondered if the old Spanish colonial building two blocks down Duval Street was even standing after the hurricane. After Cuba's independence from Spain, the United States had given the building and land to Cuba, conferring on it the same status as an embassy. Once Castro seized power, the state of Florida had set up a commission to oversee the operation of the San Carlos Institute, decreeing that the building would return to Cuban control when a democratic government was installed. A few years back, after an ugly political fight that lasted almost five years, the hard-line anti-Castro exiles from Miami had wrested control of the commission from the moderate exile faction that still lived in Key West. Cabrera was on the commission.

"This building is free Cuban soil!" Cabrera shouted, grabbing the microphone from the reporter, who was nodding approvingly. "America cannot negotiate with these Communist animals! But once there is retaliation, it can negotiate with an interim government. I am going to the San Carlos Institute now, humbly, as nothing more than a servant of my country. We shall rally there and wait."

Except for two dull-eyed men with stringy hair and missing teeth who were looking for TV equipment to steal, the crowd burst into applause. Cabrera, still solemn, nodded, and held up his palm. "I offer myself as a point of contact for the United States government and the resistance forces in Cuba. I will negotiate an end to this once the Communist bandits have been punished, so we may all return to Cuba to our families and properties that were stolen from us."

The crowd began clapping again. Cameramen, producers, and reporters sprinted from their trucks, shoving through the crowd, sticking microphones in Cabrera's face. Marco shut down his camera and nodded to Gloria, who was hovering at the edge of the rapidly growing crowd.

Dees, standing next to her, whispered, "We have to get this on the air now. Follow me."

The cameraman and producer from the Channel 8 truck were running toward them. Dees shouted, "Sammy!"

The producer broke stride and turned, while the cameraman kept running toward Cabrera. "Peter," he said, looking at the small mob around Cabrera, then back at Dees. "Where the fuck have you been? Your desk in Phoenix is going nuts. Our reporter's been providing coverage until GTV can get people here, which may be a while. The way the desk sounds, man, you're in deep shit."

Dees said, "I've got video of the A-bomb going off in Cuba."

The producer froze. *"What?"*

Dees said ironically, "Got your attention. It's a better story than that. Cabrera's behind this attack. The jet's his, not from Cuba. I've got video."

The producer furrowed his brow, looking first at Dees, then at Gloria. Dees said, "Sorry. This is Gloria Bravo. She helped us get the video. Gloria, Sammy Grazak. He used to work at GTV until he discovered the money was better in local TV."

Grazak smiled. "And until I got tired of being shot at with these assholes." He pointed a finger at Marco, who grinned. "So what's up? Talk to me."

Dees walked toward the Channel 8 truck. "Come on, I'll explain. I need to do a live shot ASAP. I'm willing to declare a field pool with all this video. Everybody can get it but everybody has to take the live shot."

"Huh?" Grazak said. "Sounds like a great exclusive. Why a pool?"

Dees stopped and gripped his arm. "Never thought I'd say this, but screw the exclusive. We get this on the air on as many networks as we can and we might stop a war. Here's the *Reader's Digest* version."

Dees sketched a bare outline of the past week, eliminating all references to guns, knives, and torture. Grazak shook his head. "Shit. Shit. Darrell's in the truck. Let me do the talking to John. He's a little touchy."

"John?"

Grazak snorted. "John Camponella, the reporter. Lazy fuck with an attitude. Great hair."

The uplink truck looked like a large moving van with a satellite dish on top. Grazak stepped on the bottom of three metal steps that led to a door in the side and opened it. Inside, two men sat at a familiar editing console, two videotape machines and three monitors built into the wall in front of them. Behind them, an arm's length away, were arrays of switches, buttons, and gauges that controlled the operation of the truck itself, including the satellite dish.

"John, Darrell, " Grazak said. "We need to talk."

"Talk about what?" the man in the chair nearest the door said. The shoulder muscles straining against his blue blazer showed the effect of regular workouts. He was clean shaven, and a thick shock of dark auburn hair was swept across his forehead. Dees thought it made him look like a small mammal was asleep on his head. In back of him, a man in a dark blue T-shirt, his hand on the knob of one of the editing machines, looked at Grazak over the top of a pair of half-lens reading glasses.

"John, Darrell," Grazak said again, "This is—"

"Hey, Peter!" Darrell said, smiling. "Good to see you again. Hey, Pedro. What's up, man?"

Darrell started to extend his hand when Camponella swatted it away.

"You're not going to bigfoot me out of this story," he said. The veins in his neck were standing out. He looked Dees up and down, and smirked. "You may be a network big deal, but this is Channel 8's truck. Besides, I'm reporting for GTV on this since they haven't been able to find you. So I guess you're S.O.L. Call our newsroom in Miami and maybe they'll reserve some time for you when I'm finished, maybe tomorrow. Darrell, shut the door."

Before Darrell could move his hand, Grazak gripped the door. "I don't need your shit now, John," he said smoothly. "Besides, we need you to interview the next president of Cuba."

Camponella looked puzzled. Grazak continued, "Ben's down there with the camera. This Cabrera guy's at the San Carlos Institute."

"Cabrera?" Camponella said. "Manuel Cabrera?"

"The same," Grazak cooed. "We need you to get him for us. You're the only reporter I know who can do it, John."

Camponella nodded. "He likes me, you know. He told me after his news conference about tightening the trade embargo a few months back that I'm the best reporter in Miami."

"That's why we need you. Get us that one-on-one with him."

"Right." Camponella heaved himself off his chair, walked down the steps, and turned to face Dees. "Don't touch anything in this truck. This is my story. Oh, yeah, you look like shit, too."

He sauntered off in the direction of the human maelstrom swirling around Cabrera. Darrell said quietly, "Y'know, he ever shoves me like that again, I'll break his neck."

"Stand in line," Grazak said. He turned to Dees. "What d'you got, what d'you need?"

Dees ran his hand through his bristly hair, drying fast in the increasing heat. He tossed the wet baseball cap to the ground. "I've got digital video. First, I need it transferred to tape in sections. I'll do a live shot, and just give you voice cues to roll the inserts. Sammy, get with the other producers, fast. Remember, they get video of the explosion, and the rest of the story, but they have to take our live feed. Tell them—"

Grazak held up his hand. "I know what to tell 'em. You call GTV."

He walked off. Darrell took the camera from Marco. "Digital, hm? I had one digital deck but the damn thing crashed and I've been too busy to fix it. No transfer facilities here, but, lemme see. . . . I play the video straight from the camera, maybe, run it through the time-base corrector? Could work. Let's see what I can do."

Marco climbed inside, Dees followed, and Gloria squeezed in behind him. Two of the video monitors above the editing machines were blank, but the one on the left had an image of a shoreline, water, and more land in the distance. Dees looked up. "What's that?"

"Shot from the microwave truck," Darrell said as he fumbled in a cabinet and withdrew a handful of small cables. "It's over by the bridge, looking up toward the Naval Air Station on Stock Island. You know how hard it is to find enough hurricane-proof garage space on this rock for uplink trucks and microwaves?

Pretty damn hard. I paid off a guy at one of the new condos to let us park in—"

"Excuse me," Gloria said. "What is this? It looks like smoke?"

"Huh?" Darrell said, jerking his head up. The camera had pushed in tight to a column of black smoke rising from the strip of land on the horizon. It pulled back to follow a jet's flight as it swooped down, then back up. "Shit! I turned the audio down so it wouldn't bother me."

He turned up a wall speaker. "—more explosions now. The Cuban jet is making another pass, and—there! There! You can see it launching rockets. Another explosion. We can't get any closer because the bridge between Key West and Stock Island is closed due to storm damage. But we believe the Cubans are attacking the U.S. Naval Air Station near Key West."

Darrell flipped a switch, and all three monitors popped to life. The same picture was on all of them, except that on the right monitor, the familiar GTV logo was in the lower right corner, with the words LIVE COVERAGE beneath it. The camera unsteadily pushed in toward the far horizon. The image flickered, then stabilized on two dots, trailing smoke behind them.

"You can see in the far distance what we can only assume are jets," the voice said through the speakers. "We don't know for sure, but we guess they're American, since they're coming from the north. They could be from Homestead Air Base."

The image flickered again, and pulled back to a wide shot. Three plumes of dark smoke now rose from the horizon. A white trail appeared in the sky, moving away from one of the jets approaching from the north. The camera jerked as it hunted for the Sukhoi, then stabilized again once it located the plane. The pencil-thin trail of smoke approached it with amazing speed. Suddenly, two bright balls of light appeared as Diaz stood his plane on its right wing, banking hard right and losing altitude rapidly. There was a flash where the jet had been just a moment before.

"Flares," Dees said. "Used them to fool the heat sensors on the air-to-air missiles and then juked out of the way. Talk about balls."

The shot pulled back even wider. A missile leaped from underneath the Su-25's right wing. By now the twin tail fins of the approaching jets were plainly visible. One banked hard to the left, the other to the right. The missile seemed to hesitate, then slowly looped toward the jet that had veered right. "F-16s," the voice said through the monitor's speaker, "we're told these are a pair of F-16s from Homestead."

One of the F-16s climbed until it was almost out of sight, the missile following. Dees squinted, trying to follow the twin contrails, a fat one from the jet's twin engines, a thin one from the missile. The jet suddenly reappeared, diving down rapidly. The missile followed until the jet's nose snapped upward and climbed again. The missile skidded past where the jet had been seconds before, plowing into the ocean and erupting into a geyser of water.

The Sukhoi had banked left and seemed to be heading east, in the general direction of the Bahamas, when missiles bloomed from under the wings of both F-16s. They approached the Su-25 like the twin legs of a V, both seeming to meet at once on the tail of the Sukhoi. The jet vanished in a pair of explosions that tore it apart and sprinkled the water with debris.

The camera pulled back to a wide shot that showed the two F-16s zipping past and disappearing in the time it took to blink. A young anchorwoman, with Asian features and dark, flowing hair, appeared on the screen. She paused. "We have never seen anything like this, apparently an attack by Cuba against the United States. GTV's Abby Crutchfield is at the White House. Abby?"

The screen filled with the image of a blond reporter, an oval dark blue seal over her left shoulder. In the middle of the oval was a picture of the Executive mansion, with the words

THE WHITE HOUSE underneath. "Judy, the President is due here in the White House briefing room momentarily. Administration sources claim the Cubans have been, quote, uncooperative and bellicose, close quote. The sources say the Cubans deny having anything to do with this dramatic jet attack that much of the world has seen live. But these sources say Havana is blaming the United States for the nuclear device they claim was detonated near the city of Matanzas early last evening."

She paused as the words, "Ladies and gentlemen, the President of the United States," came from the press room speakers. She pirouetted to her right and disappeared as the screen filled with the grim figure of the President stepping to the podium. Dark circles seemed to throb under his eyes, and his long, straight nose was framed by two deep creases.

"Ladies and gentlemen," he said in his famous nasal voice, "there will be no questions. We have all been shocked by the televised attack on our military facilities at Key West. We have reports that twelve American service personnel have been killed, five from the United States Coast Guard, seven from the United States Navy. No American aircraft have been destroyed, since the Naval Air Station at Key West removed all planes to be out of the path of Hurricane David.

"A Coast Guard vessel has been destroyed, along with fuel storage facilities at the Naval Air Station. All the Navy personnel killed were in fire brigades attempting to put out those fires."

His voice quivered with anger. "All those killed were unarmed. I have just been informed that the attacking jet, a type called an Su-25, was destroyed by two American F-16s from Homestead Air Base. The Su-25 apparently used the hurricane for cover and appeared suddenly over Key West as the storm cleared. The plane came from the direction of Cuba.

"Our task force in the Florida Straits, led by the aircraft carrier *Harry S Truman*, has reported an attack within the past hour from three Cuban patrol boats against vessels of the *Truman* task force. All three vessels have been sunk."

Dees said, "Oh shit."

The President looked down at papers in front of him on the podium, and continued. "The government of Cuba claims its vessels were responding to an intrusion of American ships into its waters. That is untrue. American vessels have not violated Cuban territorial waters. The government of Cuba also claims the United States is responsible for a nuclear explosion on its territory. That is also untrue.

"And finally, the government of Cuba denies it is responsible for the attack on our facilities in Key West." He paused, staring directly into the camera. "We point out here and now that the United States considers this to be an act of war."

Gloria whispered, "Like you say, *chico*. Shit."

The President took a deep breath. "I have ordered the aircraft carrier *John Stennis* to join the *Truman* on station off the Cuban coast. In addition, I have ordered the reenforcement of our base at Guantanamo Bay, Cuba, with five thousand Marines. Thank you all, and God bless the United States of America."

The press room erupted in shouts of "Mister President! Mister President!" as he turned from the podium and disappeared through a rear door. Dees picked up the phone hooked to the wall and punched in the number for the GTV foreign desk in Phoenix. He began talking rapidly. Gloria could hear the voice at the other end responding to Dees, even across the small edit station.

Dees cradled the phone between his chin and shoulder as he scrawled edit notes on sheets of his reporter's notebook, and handed them to Marco. "No," he said. "No. Look, you can fire me later. I would've called but I've been busy. I've been in Cuba. . . . Yeah, C-U-B-A. I've got video of the nuclear explosion."

Darrell, Marco, and Gloria all looked up as the voice from the phone began screaming. Dees held the phone away from his ear. It sounded like an angry mosquito on steroids. "Oh my God! Oh my God! Call the board! We've got tape of a nuclear explosion! Oh my God!"

"Hey!" Dees shouted into the phone. "Get me Ricardo O'Bannon now. What? . . . No, Ricardo. Now, please . . . Thanks, I'll wait."

After a brief pause, Dees said, "Ricardo. Thank God. Listen to me. . . ."

He told O'Bannon about the explosion, and the rough outlines of Cabrera's plan, including the attack on Key West.

"Yeah," Dees said. "A live shot. Half an hour at, let's see, seven-thirty Eastern, call all the other nets. . . . Tell them they have to credit GTV throughout the live shot. Tell them they have to kiss our asses. I don't care what you tell them, okay? . . . Yeah, I know, I know. What's the worst that can happen besides losing our jobs and living under an overpass? If we want to stop a war, we've got to get this on the air everywhere. Thanks."

He hung up and turned to Darrell. "I know roughly where all the stuff is. Pedro, here's how we edit. We open with the explosion and, yeah, right there. Open with three seconds of darkness, then the bang, yeah, all the way through."

The door jerked open. "What the fuck?" Camponella shouted.

"Shhh," Dees said, not looking up. "Okay, we go to this bite here."

"Get out!" Camponella balled his fists. He reached out to jerk the cable connecting the camera to the back of the edit machine. Gloria put her palm on his arm and shook her head. He pulled his arm away, and spat, "You get out, bitch! You're not supposed to be in—"

With one hand, Gloria grabbed his hair. It crunched slightly from the hair spray. Before he could react, she slammed his head into the metal door frame. His head bounced back. Keeping her grip, she twisted her body, putting more force behind her arm as she crashed his head into the frame again.

Then she released his hair and brought her right elbow down sharply where his shoulder met his neck. Camponella crumpled in the doorway.

Darrell looked up briefly, over the top of his glasses. "Cool."

Dees glanced up. His eyes met Gloria's. *"Una bolsa de basura para llevar, por favor?"*

She smiled. "One sack of garbage to go."

She stepped over the crumpled body, grabbed Camponella's feet, and pulled him down the steps. His chiseled chin bounced off the metal. She dragged him to the rear of the truck, and plopped him on the pavement, immediately under the belching diesel exhaust from the truck's generator.

For the next fifteen minutes, Dees, Marco, and Darrell transferred video from the camera to tape as Gloria watched. Some of the images were ragged, but all were acceptable, and some were almost as good as they would have been if Darrell had the proper equipment. The door opened and Grazak stuck his head inside. "What d' we have?"

"Live shot in about ten minutes, at seven-thirty," Dees said, staring at the screen as Darrell played the transferred video. "You?"

"The Nobel Peace Prize, if negotiating counts for anything. All the trucks have agreed. All the locals'll take it and they're calling their nets. You look like shit. Face is dirty, shirt looks like you wiped your ass with it. If you want them to pay any attention to what you're saying and not be laughing, you need cleaning up pronto. Where's John?"

Gloria started to speak, but Dees cut her off. "Said something about feeling woozy. Wanted to lie down someplace."

Grazak shook his head. "What a piece of work. He's got his suitcase in the cab. Nice starched denim shirts so he looks like somebody who actually works in the field for a change. They may fit you. I'll get his shaving kit and some soap."

Ten minutes later, face scrubbed, Dees positioned himself in front of the camera. The damaged Duval Street storefronts stretched behind him. The starch in the dark blue button-down denim shirt made his shoulders itch.

Marco looked up from his viewfinder. "Cheat a little to the left," he said. "Good. Light's a little funky but we can live with it. You got IFB?"

Dees turned up the volume on the small switchbox clipped to his belt. In his right ear, he heard a tinny voice saying "—but apparently the first C-130 of Marine reenforcements was able to land safely at Guantanamo Bay despite some reported small-arms fire from Cuban territory. We're taking you now to GTV Special Correspondent Peter Dees with what we're told are some amazing developments on this day of amazing developments."

Dees heard Ricardo O'Bannon's voice from the Phoenix control room. "Coming to you, Peter. You're in a split with the anchor. It's Judy Chan."

Dees heard O'Bannon say, "Take the split. Peter, you're hot."

If this doesn't work, Dees thought, it'll get a lot hotter pretty fast. He took a deep breath.

CHAPTER 20

Dees's face appeared, simultaneously and suddenly, on all five monitors tuned to the all-news channels in the Pentagon's Public Affairs Office. He popped up in Des Moines, where a housewife had tuned in to the *Today* show, and in Caracas, where a businessman was starting his day with Univision's financial report. The Cuban foreign affairs ministry was monitoring GTV, the new king of Jordan was watching CNN, and a young couple snuggled under a comforter in Cleveland had flicked on *Good Morning America*. A colonel in a counterintelligence office in Beijing had just accessed MSNBC's video web site. All found themselves looking at Dees.

Dees paused, giving all the nets and the locals time to join with their own anchor lead-ins. He counted to himself, one thousand one, one thousand two, one thousand three . . .

Finally, he nodded, and said, "An astonishing development in this story that's led to the brink of war. We have learned that this attack on American facilities here in Key West did not, and I must repeat this, did not come from Cuba."

He paused a half beat to let the opening line sink in. "We have also learned that the nuclear device detonated in Cuba did not come from the United States. Both the fighter jet attack and the nuclear explosion have been orchestrated as part of a plan to cause tension, and possibly war, between the United States and Cuba."

That was Darrell's first cue. He hit the Play button on an

edit machine, and Dees's image was replaced by darkness for two seconds, followed by video of the mushroom cloud erupting in the night sky over Cuba. As the fireball spread, Dees voiced-over the video. "This is last night's nuclear explosion. It was detonated in an unpopulated area east of Havana using a one-kiloton, Soviet-made device, left over from the Cold War, contained in a briefcase."

Dees flashed back onto the TV screens. "The briefcase was obtained on the black market in Serbia, and then smuggled into Cuba. It was purchased, and detonated, on the orders of this man."

Darrell picked up the cue cleanly. Slightly wobbly video appeared on the screen, showing Cabrera at his Duval Street TV appearance less than an hour before. "This is Manuel Cabrera, millionaire Cuban-American sugar baron and owner of Gold Cane Sugar. Cabrera's plan is to raise tensions between Cuba and the U.S. to the point where the United States would take military action. Cabrera's plan calls for him to step in and buy control of Cuba's lucrative sugar industry. Cabrera announced a short time ago that he will wait here in Key West until the U.S. attacks Cuba, willing to be a go-between."

Dees was back on camera again. "Cabrera's plan was to detonate the nuclear device and make it seem that the U.S. was somehow responsible. This man actually smuggled the atomic device into Cuba."

Gato's face appeared in a freeze-frame. "Juan Gato was a cameraman for GlobeStar Television in Havana. Gato was killed this morning in the jet attack on Key West. Before the attack, Gato told us he smuggled the nuclear device into Cuba and was paid to do so by Cabrera. This video is green because it was shot with a night lens, off the coast of Cuba, moments before the bomb went off."

The freeze frame of Gato became animated as Darrell rolled the sound bite from the truck. As Gato talked about Cabrera and the money he was promised, Dees looked down the line of live trucks. Small knots of reporters and producers had gathered around the TV monitors at each truck. "Stand by," Darrell's voice said in Dees's ear, "ten seconds."

Dees looked into the camera again. He heard the sound bite end, and immediately continued, "Cabrera's involvement goes much further than that. While Cabrera purchased the nuclear device in Serbia, he also purchased a Soviet Su-25 fighter jet, plus weapons for it. Cabrera arranged for the plane to be flown by Orestes Diaz, a former Cuban Air Force pilot who had defected to the United States. Cabrera and Diaz launched their attack on Key West from an old drug-smuggling airstrip in the Bahamas, using Hurricane David as cover. Even before the attack on Key West, Diaz had killed members of the American military."

Video appeared on the screen again, this time the smoldering wreckage of the Navy helicopter in the Bahamas. "This video was taken two days ago in the Bahamas. A U.S. Navy helicopter had gone to investigate reports of a jet on this small island's unused airstrip. Diaz shot down the unarmed helicopter, killing the two U.S. Navy officers inside, the pilot and copilot."

The video flickered again, and the scene shifted to debris flying off the deck of the Coast Guard boat in the Key West harbor. It ended with the explosion as the forty boat disintegrated. Dees continued, "Diaz then completed Cabrera's plan by attacking American facilities in Key West, including this Coast Guard vessel. Five unarmed Coast Guardsmen died."

Dees reappeared on screen. "To keep all of this secret, Cabrera also arranged for the murder of Ramon Vargas, a Cuban exile leader who had staged a commando raid on the Cuban coast. Cabrera also bribed an American FBI agent to be part of his scheme."

The screen flickered with an image of Stevens's body, grainy in death. "This is the body of FBI agent Curtis Stevens."

Dees felt his voice begin to crack. He cleared his throat.

"Pardon me. Agent Stevens was murdered by the FBI agent who had been bribed by Cabrera, John Briscoe."

Briscoe's sweaty face appeared in a tight close-up. Dees had been relieved to see that, in the sound bite where Briscoe talked about Stevens's murder and Cabrera's payoffs, Briscoe merely looked like he had a bad case of the flu. After Briscoe's sound bite ended, the video wobbled and Cabrera's image from his Key West interview filled the screen.

Dees paused one beat, and continued. "Manuel Cabrera is responsible for setting off a nuclear device in Cuba. He is responsible for the attack on Key West. He is responsible for the murder of an FBI agent, and the murder of a leading exile figure."

Dees paused again, and heard O'Bannon's voice in his earpiece from the Phoenix control room. "On-camera. Go."

Dees looked straight into the camera lens. "The United States government believes this attack came from Cuba. That is not true. The Cuban government believes the nuclear device was set off by the United States. That is not true. What is true is that a scheme for one man to take over Cuba's sugar industry, and possibly take over Cuba's government, has brought the United States and Cuba to the brink of war.

"Manuel Cabrera has conspired to commit murder and cause a war to serve his own ends. Cabrera has violated the laws of both the U. S. and Cuba. And both countries are now mobilized because of the greed of one man."

He paused a half beat, suddenly exhausted. Marco looked up from his eyepiece with a puzzled look. Dees discovered he had run out of things to say. "This is Peter Dees, reporting live from Key West, Florida. Back to you."

He stood, staring into the lens, as he heard the anchor say, "GTV Special Correspondent Peter Dees with an amazing story. GTV's Carl Rachlin is with us live from the Pentagon. Carl?"

"Jackie," a male voice said, "jaws literally dropped here as

Pentagon officials watched this live report. Moments ago, Defense Secretary—"

The voice went dead with a *blip* in Dees's earpiece as the IFB line was disconnected, and Dees heard O'Bannon's excited voice from the control room. "Shit, man! Shit! The phones are nuts! The Pentagon's calling! The State Department's calling! What? What? Jesus, man, the Cubans are calling! From Havana! Shit! They all want to talk to you!"

"No time," Dees croaked into the microphone. "I need to get to Cabrera."

"Great TV, Peter! Great entertainment!"

Dees's brow furrowed. "Who is this?"

"Jack," the voice in the earpiece said. "Jack Dunlap. Remember me? You were a little touchy the last time we talked on the phone, remember? So this time, let's keep it positive, okay? Say, this Cabrera guy kinky?"

"What?"

"You know, Santeria, voodoo, sex with boys, like that? I want more sass, more sizzle. I'm getting together a great graphic, 'The Mad Cuban Bomber.' Anyway, great TV, man. Remember, make it sexy. *Ciao.*"

Dees just stared at Marco. He looked down at the microphone. "Ricardo?"

After five seconds, O'Bannon's voice crackled in his ear. "Yeah?"

"What was that?"

Another five second pause. "Big changes here, Peter. The *Global View* show at night? Now it's *Global Gossip. World Press?* Now it's *Papparazzi Globo*, the world's tabloids. I'm being transferred."

"To what?"

"New show. They're shows now, by the way, not programs. Shows. Focus group research shows distrust of government is hot. We've got a new daily show, right after the morning one. *Conspiracies and Cover-Ups.*"

Dees sighed. O'Bannon continued, "We're getting calls

from the board. They're mighty pissed that we shared this. They say you're paid for exclusives, not pool material."

Dees put his hand over the microphone. "Pedro," he said to the cameraman, "break down. Cabrera's supposed to be down the street. Grab what you can. I'll be with you in a couple of minutes."

Marco nodded, unsnapped the camera from its tripod, hoisted it on his shoulder, and trotted, rattail bobbing, toward the San Carlos Institute. Dees uncovered the mike. "Ricardo?"

"Yeah?"

"Tell the board they can always advertise that GTV stopped World War Three. Hell, use a dove as the new logo and call it the 'Network of World Peace.' Or they can fire me. Like they say in Palestine, same-same."

Dees thought he heard O'Bannon laugh. "Got it. Y'know, I'm thinking of going back to Chile, buying a vineyard, making wonderful cabernets."

Dees smiled. "Save a bottle for me. *Buena suerte,* pal." He clicked off the receiver box clipped to his belt, unfastened it, unplugged the microphone, and walked to the uplink truck.

Darrell bounded down the steps and grabbed him in a bear hug. He squeezed Dees, then held him at arm's length. "You know sometimes, not too often, but sometimes I'm proud to be in this business."

He gave Dees another hug that forced the air from his lungs. Gloria stuck her head through the doorway. "*Chico,* this telephone in here keeps ringing."

"Let it," Dees said, freeing himself from Darrell's embrace. "Probably just my employers telling me where to pick up the severance check."

"No, could you grab it, please?" Darrell said over his shoulder. "They may be calling me to drop the signal and come down off the bird."

Gloria emerged seconds later, holding the phone in one hand. Darrell reached for it, but she shook her head. "No. The call is for him."

Dees looked unenthusiastic. "Who?"

She cracked a half smile. "They claim it is your White House. Your President?"

"Very funny," Dees said. He trudged to the truck and took the phone. "Yeah?"

"Peter Dees?"

"Last time I looked. Who's this?"

"Stand by for the President, please." There was a pause. The next voice was familiar, even through the cell phone's static. "Peter? It's a pleasure."

Dees cleared his throat. He tried to talk but his voice sounded more like an asthmatic frog. He tried again. "Thank you, Mister President."

"How accurate was that story you just did?" The voice was friendly enough but, Dees thought, carried an undertone of accusation.

"One hundred percent accurate," Dees replied, pointing to the legal pad lying on a shelf. Gloria handed it to him, with a pen. He flipped to a blank page and began scribbling, *POTUS—'Q'—how accurate story?*

"I've respected you as a reporter since the wife and I followed you from the Gulf War to Bosnia and Kosovo. I was on the Senate Intelligence Committee, you know."

"I remember, Mister President." Dees waved the pen impatiently in the air with a get-on-with-it circular gesture.

The voice said, "So I know that when I tell you up front this conversation is off the record you'll stop taking notes." Dees looked at the phone like it was a piece of rancid liver, but put the pen down.

The President continued, "Some people here doubt your story. I'm going to put you on a speakerphone."

There was a click, and the President's voice sounded suddenly hollow. "Peter, I'm here with, ah, a number of other people. Tell us what you know. Please."

Dees talked for five minutes with no interruptions. For a

while there was only silence on the other end of the line. "And that's it," he concluded. "So are you going to stop this?"

Dees could only make out muffled voices. Finally, the President said, "We're getting in touch with the Cubans. But there are a lot of people here who still think the Cubans are behind this."

Dees tightened his grip on the phone. "Mister President, off the record now on my part. You've got people in D.C. and Miami who'll blame the Cubans for global warming. Foreign policy shouldn't be dictated by a bunch of fanatics with deep pockets."

The voice on the other end was clipped. "Where is Cabrera now?"

"Down the street in a building, waiting to help negotiate peace."

"Thank you," the voice said hurriedly. "We'll be picking him up, and I think we can defuse this. Good-bye."

Dees clipped the phone back into its wall-mounted cradle and looked at Gloria. "What about you? Maybe we can call your people and tell the hard-liners to back off."

"Too late," she said quietly. "They have already won. They never wanted a war with the United States that they would lose. Now they have American ships off their coast and they have a *gusano* who set off this atomic bomb on Cuban soil. Even when your government calls its reaction off, *los duros* will say the exile lunatics not only attacked Cuba, they attacked America as well."

She sat in the small chair heavily. "So the hard-liners will blame the exiles and the Americans for all of Cuba's troubles. They will blame us reformers for being too friendly with the Americans. So now it would seem they have won, whether Fidel lives or dies."

Dees felt queasy. Grazak stuck his head through the door, out of breath. "Ran back here. Damn. Every reporter in the world's after your ass. It's a pig fuck at the San Carlos Institute. Camera crews out the ass and a small mob of Cabrera's fans who want you hung by the balls. Marco's in that crowd, trying to find Cabrera. Phoenix wants more live shots."

Dees felt a wave of exhaustion wash over him. He slumped against the carpeted wall of the truck's edit bay. His arms and legs felt like they were encased in cement. His eyelids had small bricks hung from them, pulling them shut. His voice sounded like it belonged to somebody else. "Sammy, can you tell 'em to rerun the first live shot? I haven't slept in a billion hours, I need to check my house, and I probably have meningitis from swimming in the water. And I just guaranteed a few more years of dictatorship in Cuba. I need a vacation."

Behind Grazak, Marco appeared, wheezing, at the bottom of the steps, soaked with sweat. "No Cabrera. We went through every room in the place to find him and he just fuckin' vanished."

Dees felt like he was listening to someone speak Turkish. "Huh?"

Marco looked sour. "I said he's gone. He's not around any-place, or maybe he sprouted wings or maybe somebody snatched him. Shit, I need some water."

Dees forced himself to stand up. "Sammy, just beep me in three hours or so and I promise I'll be back. I just need some sleep and a pair of pliers."

Grazak looked puzzled, then pointed toward the back of the truck. "Storage area in the rear has a couple of cases of water in liter bottles, just take all you need. Toolbox, too."

Dees walked down the steps. Gloria followed him to the rear of the truck.

Camponella was still lying on the ground, but moved as Gloria stepped over him and unfastened the storage area door. She removed four bottles of water. Dees rummaged through the compartment, found a small tool kit, and took out a pair of pliers, a screwdriver, and three more bottles of water.

They fastened the door and turned to leave. A faint voice said, "Hey."

Dees looked down. It was Camponella, who looked around, seemed to be trying to focus, raised his head, and stared at Dees.

"Hey," he said. "That's my shirt."

CHAPTER 21

In some places the water was almost knee-high. In others, it barely sloshed over Dees's boots. A block behind him, roof trusses, tiles, and plywood filled the street. A block ahead of him every house was intact, with only a banyan tree in the street as an indication that anything had happened at all.

Dees's front porch and its sheltering bougainvillea had been sheared off by a sedan-size fragment of someone's roof. The slab of wood and its gray asphalt shingles formed a mammoth front step leading to the front door, which was still securely sealed behind the bolted hurricane shutters. The ficus hedge that had shielded the cottage from the street looked like a scrawny row of leafless Montana winter saplings that had found themselves transplanted in the tropics.

Dees circled the house warily. Gloria walked behind him, surveying the house. "Where are the others?" she asked.

Dees had reached the rear of the house and the cinder-block attachment he had cemented together the year before. He reached down and pulled a thin metal safe deposit box from the space where it had been wedged between the wooden house and the blocks. He took out a key and opened the large padlock that secured the thick metal lid, painted white. He swung it open with a grunt, resting the top edge gently against the house, and turned to Gloria. "What others?"

"The others living here."

Dees reached inside the storage area and pulled out three neat coils of heavy orange extension cord. "I'm it."

She shook her head. "One person for all this?"

He laughed. "You've been in the worker's paradise too long. Two bedrooms, one bath, a kitchen, a living room. Not a lot of space."

Gloria seemed to be considering the idea as Dees turned the key on the generator. It growled, sputtered, and started with a roar. He nodded with satisfaction and shut it off. Handing Gloria the socket set, he said, "You take the shutters off the windows. I'll get the back door."

Half an hour later, sunlight poured into the kitchen, bedroom, and bathroom. Dees plugged in a double-eyed hot plate and the office's window air conditioner. He made sure the generator's tank was topped off and that the three five-gallon cans of gasoline next to it were all still full. He turned the key again and the generator roared. Within five minutes, the hot plate was heating three liters of water in a pair of saucepans, and the damp, closed air in the house was freshened with a cold blast of air from the window unit.

A water stain started on the front room ceiling and ran down a wall where a section of shingles had blown away. Otherwise, the house was dry. Dees removed various items from the waterproof bags inside his duffel. The clothes were soaked and sour, so he went outside and hung them in the bright sun, spread out over the top of the spindly ficus. Two of the three batteries for the small cell phone were ruined. He put the third in a battery charger, along with the phone itself, and plugged them in. He swabbed off the pistol and the Uzi with a towel, removed the clip, and thumbed out the shells, spreading them on a dry towel next to the cartridges from the Smith & Wesson.

As the water heated, Dees got a small gun-cleaning kit from a closet, swabbed, dried, and oiled the pistol, and loaded it with fresh shells from a box in a kitchen drawer. He then oiled, dried, and cleaned the Uzi as best he could, dried the shells, reinserted them in the clip, and snapped it back into the weapon. He walked outside, made sure the hole punched in the cinder blocks as an exhaust port for the generator was clear, closed the metal lid, and locked it.

He walked into the kitchen. "Let's set the alarm for four o'clock. That'll give us five hours before I have to gas up the generator again."

His pager hummed and beeped two hours later. Dees got up, groggily, brushed his teeth, washed his face, and put on a fresh black polo shirt from the closet. He went back to the bathroom, stared in the mirror, and opened the medicine cabinet. He pulled out a makeup compact, smeared the powder underneath both eyes, and evened it out with his fingers so the dark circles under his eyes almost disappeared.

Back at the truck, Sammy told him Camponella was driving back to Miami. He thought he might have a concussion, and planned to both sue and get Dees fired. Marco was curled up comfortably on the bench in the truck's smaller editing bay. He opened one eye and laughed. "A-bombs can't kill this guy, so how's a ferret in a sport coat gonna do it?"

Marco stretched and ambled outside toward his tripod-mounted camera. In the next hour and a half, Dees did four live shots for GTV, fed a new voice track for a fresh package using the tape from the live shots, and did a closing stand-up for the package. When he finished, he invited both Darrell and Marco back to the cottage. Darrell thanked him, but said he had plenty of food and water and needed to do some maintenance on the truck. Marco said, "*Gracias, jefe,* but I'm going back to sleep here."

Dees returned to his house and made sure the air conditioner was still running and the windows and back door were locked. He kissed Gloria lightly on the lips. She didn't stir. He thought of moving his hands across her breasts and thighs, but decided it would be too much like necrophilia. Her snoring was as loud as the sputtering generator, and besides, what would she think of his performance if he fell asleep in midstroke? He closed his eyes and was out cold within a minute.

Two hours later, the alarm buzzed for five minutes before Dees rolled out of bed, threw on a pair of shorts, stumbled outside, and refilled the generator. He checked his beeper. No calls. Good, he thought, the story's shifted to D.C. and Havana. He reset the alarm.

When it buzzed again, it was black outside. He got up and flipped on the table lamp he had plugged in next to the hot plate in the kitchen. He grabbed two granola bars from a cabinet, fed one to Gloria, and made her take several sips of water. She smiled and fell back asleep. After two bites, he decided he wasn't hungry.

Dees walked outside, checked and filled the generator again, and took the bag of quicklime and the small shovel from the generator enclosure. He sat them inside the kitchen near the back door, so that when the urge finally came, he would be able to dig a slit trench in the soft earth without too much fumbling. To make sure, he tore open the top of the lime sack and dug a coffee cup into the corrosive powder. He figured the twenty-five-pound sack should be more than enough to neutralize buried body waste until the water and power came back on, and set the alarm for two-thirty.

All the cottage's interior doors were open so the window unit could cool the entire house. Dees was dreaming about being aboard a boat in the middle of a dark ocean, surrounded on every horizon by billowing, glowing mushroom clouds. Abruptly, his eyes snapped open.

He felt himself squinting as he strained to listen. All he could hear was the friendly hum of the air conditioner and the generator's dull roar. He put his hands behind his head and nestled in the pillow, then raised his head again when the sound from the generator became louder, just for an instant, and faded again. He heard a faint creak. He was sitting straight up now. Someone, he thought, had opened the back door and just stepped on that squeaking floorboard in front of the sink. He heard a soft sound of metal clinking that lasted for a couple of seconds.

He turned to Gloria, shook her, and put his hand over her mouth. She awoke with a start, but he held his hand tight. He whispered, "Get out of bed. Quiet. Get over by the door. Somebody's in the house. They've got the guns in the kitchen."

She nodded. He released his hand and pointed to the door. "Over there. I'll get on the other side. Take the alarm clock. You can use it like a club."

She silently crept from the bed, wearing a T-shirt and a pair of his old swimming trunks she'd put on before falling asleep. She took the large, wind-up alarm clock in the palm of her right hand, solid brass with two hemispheres on top that clanged like a fire alarm. She thumbed the alarm switch off, hefted the clock in her hand, and pinned her back flat against the wall next to the open door.

Dees felt under the bed and clutched the end of a baseball bat, a thirty-seven-ounce Gary Sheffield autograph model that had been gathering dust since it was purchased as a souvenir of the Marlins '97 Series win. He scooted across the floor in his bare feet and paused behind the open door, straining to listen. He could make out the sound of breathing, and a faint squeak from the floorboards in the hall.

Suddenly, a tongue of flame flicked through the open door with a *pbbhht* sound. Dees heard the *thunk thunk thunk* sounds as bullets tore into the bed. Each created a white flash in the room despite the flash suppressor and silencer, spinning several grains of lead alloy at several hundred miles an hour into the rumpled covers, pillows, and mattress.

His eyes had barely recovered from the throbbing flashes when a figure stepped through the open door. Dees planted himself and swung, extending his right arm and turning his wrists in a motion designed to power a line drive between short and second. Instead of making contact with soft flesh, he felt the vibration of wood hitting metal. The figure doubled over, pitching forward, as Gloria jumped from the shadows along the wall and drove the clock down with her right hand.

Dees heard a soft *thump*, and Gloria staggered, tumbling

into him. He was pushed backward into a wall, and barely managed to both keep his balance and hold onto the bat. A bright light stung his eyes, and he heard a familiar *crack*, followed by glass shattering. The mirror over the dresser, he guessed.

"My own gun," Dees said, shielding his eyes from the light with his free hand. Gloria was turned toward the light, body tensed, next to him. "You really willing to risk the death penalty for stealing a generator and a couple of guns?" he said loudly.

He heard a familiar voice from behind the light. "I am afraid, Mr. United Nations, that we want a good deal more than a generator. Although, as you might say, power is the end product of both."

*   *   *

A large arm holding the Smith & Wesson moved aside, and Cabrera stepped past it. "Into the kitchen now or my friends will finish this job here."

In the splinters of light that skidded across the bedroom floor from the shattered mirror, Dees could see that the figure with the flashlight was small, wiry, and dressed in black, head to foot, including a ninja-style hood pulled down over his head. The figure behind him also had a hood, and a narrow waist that spread upward in a V to wide, sloping shoulders and massive upper arms. He walked into the kitchen, reached behind him, and clicked on the table light.

In the harsh glare, Dees could see a lumpy outline under his long-sleeved black pullover. Body armor, he thought. Must've hit him right in the metal chest plate.

Another ninja, medium height and build, stood next to the closed back door. He held what looked like a Glock aimed at Dees's midsection.

"Here we are." Cabrera chuckled as he gestured toward his three hooded companions. He turned to Dees. "You have cost me more than you will ever know. You have heard, no?"

Dees shook his head. "No."

"It seems your government has pulled in the fangs of its aircraft carriers, and the Cubans. . . ." His voice trailed off and he sighed. "The Cubans are flying their foreign minister to the United Nations tomorrow with the intention of meeting your Secretary of State. The crisis is cooling like an old passion, and I, I am afraid, am now a man wanted by both governments, on paper at least."

"More than on paper," Dees said, taking in the barrels of the revolver, the silenced semiautomatic pistol, the Glock, and the Uzi. "Murdering a dozen American servicemen, paying for a jet attack, setting off an atomic bomb. I think you're a perfect candidate for the Federal death penalty. And the Cubans would probably make you wish you were dead."

Cabrera smiled. "*Qué ingenuo,* as you might say. How naïve. My money has bought me more than photo opportunities over the years. It affords me a certain immunity from these things, or at least enough time to leave this glorious country and continue my work through other means.

"Besides, I have many friends of all political persuasions. That is why it may seem I am being hunted for right now, but I can move very freely. I do not think your government is searching for me as seriously as they pretend."

He looked behind him at the man by the door, then at the other two hooded figures. "Please remove those ridiculous masks. A surprise before dying for our friends here."

Cabrera swiveled the pistol toward Gloria's head. "And Mister Dees, do not move or this one will die first. If you please."

The one by the door peeled off his hood first. About thirty-five, Dees guessed, with a thick mustache and a five o'clock shadow on his skull where his shaved head had started to sprout hairs. Hispanic. The hulking figure holding Dees's pistol removed his hood. Hispanic ditto, Dees thought. He was clean shaven, and his thick black hair showed the sharp edges of a recent, and probably expensive, razor cut. The smallest figure peeled off the hood in a swift motion. "Hello,

Peter," Janie said, keeping the silencer pointed toward his midsection.

Dees felt the air go out of his lungs. Cabrera chuckled again. "What, no flip conversation at this moment? I am most disappointed. I also know her only as Juanita. Maybe she will tell us her real name, then?"

Janie's mouth was a thin, tight line.

Gloria said, *"Tu nombre en actualidad es la tortuga, verdad?"*

Janie moved the pistol a fraction, aiming it at Gloria. *"Silencio, puta."*

"La tortuga?" Dees said. "You? Shit. Shit."

"A nice name, la tortuga," Cabrera interrupted. "I have not heard it before. I only knew of her as being with the Interior Ministry, Department Tres-quatro, I believe?"

Dees asked, "Department Three-four?"

"Counterintelligence for religious affairs," Gloria said quietly. "Keep religious fanatics under control in Cuba, although not as active as they used to be since the Pope's visit a few years ago. This would seem to be outside that realm."

"All sorts of duties fall inside the Interior Ministry," Janie said without emotion.

"Los duros," Gloria said bitterly, "use the Interior Ministry as a playpen."

"All the better to keep an eye on traitors," Janie said, smirking.

Dees looked thoughtful. He looked at Cabrera. "The island's crawling with Federal agents and troops now, and you're a wanted man and everybody knows what you look like. They're probably searching everywhere, including cars. Except maybe government cars?"

Janie's expression remained flat. Dees studied the tiny curling fibers on Cabrera's wrinkled white dress shirt. There was a small spot of what looked to be grease near the monogram just above the right cuff link. Dees shook his head. "You've been riding around in the trunk with an INS agent at the wheel of a government car. These other two, let me guess. Her assistants?"

"Prisoners, actually. She rides in front, they are in back handcuffed." Cabrera snapped his fingers toward the hulk in the T-shirt. Cabrera nodded toward the pistol and snapped his fingers again. The big man handed over the Smith & Wesson. Cabrera studied it as he spoke. "They are stopped and she is an INS agent and these are some illegals she has rounded up for questioning. Just one more Federal agent among all of the Federal agents here. And me? I am actually very comfortable in the trunk. The Crown Victoria, what a car. Such roominess." He exhaled. "Juanita, or whoever you are, take the Uzi. Give the silenced pistol to Ramon here."

The big man took the pistol with its silencer from Janie, who slung the Uzi strap over her shoulder and held it, waist level, in a firing position. Cabrera motioned toward the bedroom. "Come, Ramon. Let us set the stage so when the police arrive hours from now it seems our friends died in a burglary."

Ramon walked toward the bedroom. Cabrera followed, grabbing one of the drying towels off the kitchen table as he walked past. Janie's thin black leather gloves muffled the soft *click* as her thumb moved a switch on the Uzi's trigger guard from the three-shot burst setting to single fire. Here it comes, Dees thought, and pivoted his body between Gloria and the Uzi just as a loud cough came from the bedroom. Janie pumped two quick rounds into the mustache of the man by the door at the same moment the hallway was lit twice by flashbulb pulses of light. The combined noise from the terrycloth-wrapped .32's barrel and the percussive Uzi was no louder than someone banging a hammer into a nail twice.

Cabrera strode out of the bedroom as Janie turned her gun on Dees. He folded his arms to keep his hands from shaking. "So what the cops find is two guys with records. I assume you made sure they both have records?"

Janie's expression didn't change. Behind him, Cabrera

laughed. Dees continued, "Yeah, two guys with records. They're dead, shot with my pistol and the Uzi, and we're dead, and we just shot each other up because they broke into our house looking to loot, I guess."

Cabrera covered them both as Janie put down the Uzi and took the silenced pistol from Cabrera. Dees looked at the sugar king. "What's in it for you to pay off a Cuban agent like her? Your plan to take over in Cuba is shot to hell."

Cabrera clucked his tongue. "To a point. Even if I take over, as you put it, one still needs an internal security apparatus. Batista had one, and Grau after him, and Prio after him, then Batista when he came back, now Castro. Ideology may change, but function does not. Assassination, for example."

"Shut up," Janie said with sudden force. "You've got a big mouth."

"And a big *pinga*," Cabrera said. "But since they are dead anyway, it cannot hurt for them to know that you—"

"One more word," Janie said, leveling the gun at him, "just one."

Cabrera stared calmly at the silenced pistol. Dees made a sudden move to his right, but had only gone a half step before her pistol was level with his chest. "Clumsy try, Peter."

Dees stared down at the pistol, then at her. Their eyes locked. He said, "I can guess. New butch haircut. Agent Victor Fleming? Briscoe was already paid off. So you killed Vargas, right? Your hard-line bosses would want him out of the way, and Cabrera wanted him dead because he knew too much."

Dees laughed. "Jesus, I finally get it." He turned to Gloria, nodding toward Janie. "She's how the two guys with the beards at the *Habana Libre* knew I was trying to find whoever killed Richie. She told her friends back in Havana I was coming. Ain't life grand?"

He turned back to Janie. "Nice. You fooled me, you fooled the Bureau wives, and you fooled your friends. What about Richie? You manage to keep espionage from a pretty savvy

FBI agent? Maybe he was just too busy to notice he'd married a spy? Or maybe he found out? Maybe he found out."

Dees kept his eyes on Janie. "Richie wasn't the type to easily be fooled. Maybe he gets suspicious. Cabrera pays for the Vargas raid on Cuba. That works for Cabrera because it pisses off the Cubans. But Cabrera can't have Vargas surrendering peacefully on Cudjoe Key because Cabrera needs something to turn up the heat and piss off the Americans. He knows Emilio is a schitzy doper and may cause an incident, but he can't be sure, so—"

Janie's expression was still a flat mask. Cabrera said, "Most impressive, Mister United Nations."

Janie shot Cabrera an acid look. Dees absently stroked his goatee with a thumb and forefinger. "Cabrera needs some way to guarantee the surrender on Cudjoe Key goes south," he said. "What better way to have an FBI agent shot dead? He knows his boy Emilio well enough to know if he's supplied with some meth to snort, he'll do something crazy and provide confusion, at least. And for argument's sake, let's just say Richie was picking up a few hints and getting suspicious of his wife?"

Janie's face was still frozen in a blank stare. Dees dropped his arms and seemed to sag. He looked around the kitchen, at the flickering lamp on the counter, at the thin pencil marks he had never painted over on the door, where someone who actually lived a real life had marked their children's growth. He felt as temporary as the shadows that streaked across the walls, walls that seemed cheerful in the tropical sunlight but were now the color of jaundiced skin.

"It was you," he said to no one in particular. He turned his head toward Janie. "Richie marries a Cuban mole. Great cover for you. Maybe he gets suspicious. Or maybe you and your handlers just figure it's time to move on. Cabrera needs an incident. So you kill Richie in the confusion. Both your problems solved. Nice shot, considering it was a secure government facility on Cudjoe. I'm guessing either from the

Overseas Highway Bridge or from some boat bobbing around that nobody would even notice."

The only sound was from the generator, which was starting to vary its pitch, running normally, then faster with a higher-frequency roar, then slowing again. The table light grew brighter each time the generator raced.

Cabrera stifled a yawn. "I see your generator is running out of petrol, which is just as well since you yourself have run out of time. For a man who knows a great deal, you know next to nothing."

Dees rolled his eyes. "Tell me about it. I never heard Janie speak Spanish, so no wonder I didn't recognize that other voice at the shack out in the swamps. It was her. She was up to speed on the whole thing, including the attack."

Cabrera seemed bored. "A very important asset, this young lady."

"Will you be quiet?" Janie said through clenched teeth, never taking her eyes off Dees.

Cabrera smiled. "You make five hundred pesos a month from your Communist superiors, no? That is, what, twenty dollars?"

Janie's eyes flashed. Cabrera smiled. "I am paying you thirty thousand times that much, so you will keep your temper, Juanita, or *la tortuga* or whatever it is you are called. In a few hours we will no longer have to do business together, but for now I want Mister United Nations to know something, since he has caused me so much trouble and expense."

Janie, without expression, kept her pistol leveled at Dees. "Good," Cabrera continued. "Mister Dees, you have injured me financially, and you have effectively killed this plan. So of course I will kill you. But first do you know how I will get away?"

He smirked again. "It is because my dead presidents, as your country calls them, have many friends, and because no one will look inside an official car with United States government license plates."

Dees folded his arms again, staring at her and the pistol. "INS know the car's missing?"

This time Cabrera laughed out loud. "If you ever checked your facts rather than your suppositions you would find the vehicle is registered to your Department of State. And we, the two of us, shall simply vanish with a little help from the friends of my friends."

He turned to Janie. "Now that this fool knows he has done all this for nothing, we may proceed."

The generator was racing and slowing more rapidly now as the fuel pump sucked up a combination of gasoline and fumes at the bottom of the tank. The table light pulsed in counterpoint, growing brighter, then dimmer. Janie switched on her flashlight and jerked the silencer toward Dees. "Move. Over to where I stood."

Dees paused. "Did you ever love him? At all?"

"Business," she said without emotion. A thin smile appeared, then vanished. "The fool wanted to have kids. Can you imagine? Move."

As Dees walked toward the counter, the generator coughed, then backfired with a *baanng*. Cabrera and Janie both jerked their heads toward the door. Dees straight-armed Gloria in the chest with his left arm. With his right, he reached into the sack on the floor, closed his hand around the coffee cup of powdered quicklime, pulled it out, and, swiveling, threw the powder in Janie's face. If he had been close enough, and if it had been perfectly quiet, Dees might have heard a barely audible sizzle as the corrosive powder began eating into the soft tissue of her eyes, nose, and mouth.

She made a gargling sound, followed by a scream that sounded like an injured cat. She gasped for air, sucked bits of the lime into her lungs, and shrieked again. She made a motion as if she was washing her face, faster and faster, trying to brush the powder from her nose and eyes. Dees sprang from his crouch and easily twisted the pistol from her hand.

Gloria threw herself forward, driving her head into Cabrera's midsection. With a *whooff*, Cabrera was driven back two steps before he brought the pistol down on top of her head. As she fell, Dees turned and fired. Janie's pistol made no more noise than a clapping hand. The bullet entered Cabrera's left leg. He fell against the door jamb with a *thunk*.

Dees turned. Janie was writhing on the floor, spastically slapping her face with her palms. Her mouth was open, but the only sound was a rattling *whuaah whuaah whuaah*. Gloria shook her head and got to her feet. "Here," Dees said, tossing her the pistol. She caught it fluidly with her right hand.

Dees stepped to the doorway, put his knee on Cabrera's chest, and grabbed the Smith & Wesson off the floor, inches from Cabrera's reach. He slapped his left hand over Cabrera's mouth. "Shhh. Just keep quiet and I won't have to—"

He heard what sounded like two quick handclaps behind him. He pivoted on his knee and aimed the snub-nose with both hands. The generator raced and began to die for the last time. As the kitchen light pulsed, growing brighter than usual, he saw Gloria facing him, pistol at her side. It became bright enough briefly for him to see one of her eyebrows arched, ironically, before the generator coughed and died, and the yard went black.

"*¡Ayúdeme!*" Cabrera yelled.

Dees slapped his palm across his mouth again and stared at Gloria. "What the hell did you do?"

Her voice came out of the darkness, quietly. "Her face looked like a rotted fish, so I put her out of her misery. A professional courtesy."

Dees was breathing through his mouth. He sat heavily on the floor, his right hand still across Cabrera's mouth, the pistol in his left. He shook his head. "No more. As much as he might deserve it, you can't kill Cabrera. No more."

"Then what?" she said almost tenderly. She knelt next to him. "Then you turn him over to your justice system so he can become a martyr in court? So that everyone finds out the truth about the wife of your friend? So his reputation gets worse in death because he married a Cuban spy? So I can be arrested as a spy?"

Dees jerked his head. "Feel under the sink. I've got a roll of gaffer's tape I keep for repairs."

She stepped over Cabrera and returned a moment later. Dees shoved the pistol toward her and took the tape. "If he makes any sound at all, shoot him."

He removed his hand from Cabrera's mouth, peeled a six inch piece from the roll of gray, cloth-backed tape, and secured it across Cabrera's mouth.

Dees looked up at Gloria. "Sit. Here, beside me. Tell me if this makes any sense."

As they talked for the next ten minutes, Cabrera's eyes grew wide. He kept shaking his head violently, side to side. Dees stared at him.

"Come on, Manuel," he said in a whisper. "You always wanted to go back to Havana again."

CHAPTER 22

Dees pulled the cellular phone from the battery charger and handed it to Gloria. "I've got some errands to run. You have a New York number to call."

Dees spent an hour in Bahama Town, negotiating by flashlight. When he returned to the cottage, the sky was growing lighter. There were three orange tarps next to the back steps, each about six feet long and cigar-shaped, wrapped in gaffer's tape every couple of feet, and wrapped again several times lengthways. They looked like reefed sails dropped from the boom of a passing schooner.

The generator had been filled with gas and started again. Cabrera sat in a kitchen chair, shadows from the countertop lamp playing across the tape on his mouth. His hands were taped behind him. Gloria poured hot water from a pan on the hot plate into two coffee cups. She handed one to Dees.

"This instant coffee is convenient," she said, "but other than an emergency, I do not see how you can drink it."

"I hardly ever do," Dees said, taking a gulp of the hot, coffee-flavored water. "What d'you know?"

She shook her head. "It took me half an hour to convince this fool on the telephone in New York. Perhaps it was because I had to speak carefully since this is an open telephone line. But we finally had a meeting of the minds. My United Nations mission is contacting our embassy in Nassau. They will receive us, but they need to know where they should be, and when."

331

Dees sipped his coffee. "Jacob, the guy I told you about? He has relatives on Bimini. He doesn't like to be awakened after a hurricane, so he was cranky, and greedier than usual."

"And you know him how?"

"Business associate of Theodore's. Helps keep bundles of import items from becoming waterlogged after Theodore dumps them out the door of the plane. He's the boyfriend of another friend of mine. He's dependable."

"Ummm," Gloria said.

Dees ignored her. "So tell your people to be waiting at Paradise Point on North Bimini around noon. You'll be sailing away from Cuba and all the brouhaha, so there shouldn't be any trouble. And if everything goes okay, you and *Señor* Cabrera should be in Havana by, say, suppertime."

Cabrera began to shake his head wildly again. Dees said, "Careful, you'll hurt your neck."

Gloria opened the cellular phone and punched in a number. She paused, and said in Spanish, "Your family will be there around twelve noon, all three of them. They are very anxious to see their loved ones after this terrible storm. Paradise Point I am told is a wonderful spot for a picnic on North Bimini. . . . Yes, yes, everyone is fine. Our love to Father."

She clicked the phone shut. Dees looked at her. "You know what might happen?"

She nodded. "I could end up in jail or executed. But I think I may be a Hero of the Revolution instead. Cabrera will tell his tale, willingly or otherwise. I bring them the bodies of the spies. And perhaps, perhaps maybe, the reformers can take some measure of control and discredit the hard-liners."

Dees heard an engine stop on the street. "I think we're ready."

Dees and Gloria, Cabrera limping between them, walked out the back door. A thin black man with a fringe beard stood in the backyard. A figure a half a hand taller because of a piled-up bouffant was beside him, wearing a pastel print dress in a Monet pattern. "Peter, honey, if this is the one you told me about, then o-lay. *Oye, guapa, qué tal?* Welcome to the States, homegirl."

Gloria smiled uncertainly and raised an eyebrow in Dees's direction. Dees nodded an introduction. "Gloria Bravo, Tequila Mockingbird and Jacob Williams. Tee and Jacob, Gloria."

Jacob nodded gruffly. Tequila walked to Cabrera with an exaggerated wiggle of his hips. He bent down and whispered in the old man's ear, "You're the one, huh? You be good on our trip or I'll show you why they don't like he-she's in Havana."

He stuck his tongue in Cabrera's ear. Cabrera recoiled, stumbling against Dees, who gripped the back of his shirt with a fist and pushed him upright. Tequila blew Cabrera a kiss over his shoulder and sashayed next to Jacob, who just nodded again and said, "The deal, then."

Dees said, "Cash when you return, since I have to get it and the banks'll be closed for a while. Five thousand premium for the delay."

Gloria whispered, her voice almost catching, "Five thousand? Dollars?"

"Listen, missy," Jacob growled, "I wouldn't even do this at all for anybody else, and even if I did, I sure as shit wouldn't do it without money up front. This one I can trust, and besides, he's well-off. Ask about his portfolio."

"Not as well-off as a few minutes ago," Dees said. "What now?"

Jacob jabbed a forefinger at Cabrera and Gloria. "These two, under the tarp in the back of the truck."

He looked past Dees, toward the orange bundles on the ground. Dees followed his gaze. "Jacob, help me load them. Tee, help Gloria and our guest into the truck."

"Come on, honey," Tequila said, taking Gloria's arm. "You know, this is the first *vacación* Jacob and me've had in years. Spend a few extra days in Bimini and spend some of this money. May even do me some bonefishing, if you know what I mean," he said, rolling his eyes lasciviously and laughing.

Dees turned. "Jacob? Would you and Tee mind giving us a

couple of minutes? I need to have a private conversation. It shouldn't take long."

Jacob nodded gruffly and stomped away. Tee followed. Dees and Gloria moved Cabrera back into the kitchen, where Dees ripped the tape from Cabrera's mouth with a sharp tug. He immediately slapped his hand over Cabrera's mouth.

"You need to talk some more," Dees said. "This young lady's pretty skilled at cutting off people's toes. But I'll make you a deal. You want to hear about a deal?"

Cabrera shook his head up and down vigorously. Dees seemed to think for a moment. "A deal. First part. You don't make a sound when I remove my hand. One, it won't do any good, and two, I'll turn her loose on you. Understand?"

Cabrera shook his head again with undiminished gusto. Dees removed his hand. Cabrera smacked his lips and looked as if he was about to say something, but Dees put a finger across his lips. "Shhh. That's part of the deal. Now don't speak at all until I ask you a question."

Dees straightened and folded his arms across his chest. "There's a chance you won't have to go back to Cuba. That's what you can get from me. All it takes is simple, honest answers. Edward Davis from the United States State Department. Have you been working with him?"

Cabrera took a gulp of air in through his mouth and looked as if he would speak, then stopped, blinked his eyes, and said, "Could you do these things for me?"

Dees pursed his lips. "There's a chance. Edward Davis."

Cabrera nodded. "This Davis has been an, er, associate of mine for several years. Like you, he is a surprising man. He has helped me funnel—that is the correct word?—yes, funnel my influence. He has also helped with this affair. Did you know? Of course, you could not. You do not know, then, that he was with the great Vargas the day you two met?"

"How come?"

"In case, ah—" Cabrera paused. "In case you needed to be dealt with. I paid him very, very well to help facilitate policy, but I paid him a premium for his other talents, including persuasion. He is a most persuasive man."

Dees scrunched his eyebrows. "Davis is on your payroll? And you use him to get policy made *and* for muscle?"

Cabrera nodded. "Just so. I have the sense he actually enjoys the enforcement portion of his job as much as the other. He gave me the car we are driving."

Dees leaned close to Cabrera. "State Department policy types don't moonlight as enforcers."

Cabrera shook his head in agreement. "My feeling also, but when the gentleman has been so useful for a number of years in Washington, and when he has helped me resolve some more immediate problems, then I do not question him too closely, no matter how much money it has cost me."

"Who're your other contacts in Washington?"

Cabrera actually laughed. "You would need much more time for me to list them. But they are all friendly on an official level, in exchange for my generous contributions to several political campaigns. I have friends, very, very good friends, on the House International Relations and Senate Foreign Relations committees, the House National Security Committee, the House Appropriations Committee, the Senate Intelligence Committee, in the National Security Council, at the White House. My goodness, so many, so many."

He paused again. "But Mister Davis, he is the only one who works for me instead of with me. The only one."

"How much does he know about all this? Richie's murder? Your plan to attack Key West? The atomic bomb in Cuba?"

Cabrera smacked his lips. "I could use some water."

"Later," Dees said. "Keep talking."

"Mister Davis," Cabrera continued, "knows all, much like a soothsayer. He is even the one who told me your friend the FBI agent had married a Cuban agent and that she could be useful to us."

Dees whistled, low. He walked to his office and returned with a microcassette tape recorder. He held it in front of

Cabrera. "When I turn this on, state your name. And repeat the entire story about you and Davis. Okay, we're rolling. Begin."

Cabrera talked nonstop for ten minutes. When he finished he looked imploringly at Dees. Dees turned off the recorder, slipped it in his pocket, and went to the kitchen counter. He returned with a small bottle of water for Cabrera. "Go into my office," he said to Gloria, "and find the radio by the bed. It's on batteries. Push the little button on top that says 'Weather.' I need to know the marine forecast."

She disappeared into the office as Dees fed Cabrera sips from the water bottle. Dees placed the bottle back on the counter and tore off a six-inch-long strip of gaffer's tape from the roll.

Gloria came back into the kitchen. "They say fair skies and calm winds. The weather between here and Bimini looks almost perfect."

Dees stood in front of Cabrera and looked at Gloria. "What's the chance of rain today?"

She shrugged. "Almost none. Ten percent at most, they say."

With a fluid motion, Dees slapped the tape across Cabrera's mouth. "You know I told you there was a chance you could avoid going back to Cuba?"

Cabrera nodded. Dees smiled. "It was like the rain, only about ten percent at most."

* * *

Twenty minutes later, they arrived at the Key West Bight. The harbor was still a sea of debris. Several boats had been ripped from their moorings and sunk, but none in the channel. A forty-two-foot sport fisherman at the end of the pier, *Junkaroo*, was undamaged except for a cracked windscreen.

Jacob and Dees carried the orange bundles to a large locker behind the bow. Gloria helped Cabrera limp aboard. A tourniquet made from a towel secured with gaffer's tape was above his left knee. Jacob, without a word, started the engines, stalked forward, and gathered in the bow line. Tequila tiptoed to the stern. Cabrera sat, bug-eyed, strapped into one of the seats used by tarpon anglers. Dees and Gloria were locked in an embrace.

Tequila bent over, shook the stern line loose from the dock cleat, and turned. "All ashore that's going ashore, loverboy."

Dees continued to kiss Gloria, hard. He played his lips about hers as the boat began to sway underneath their feet. She pushed him away, lightly. He returned, kissed her again, and said, "You know where to find me."

"Here," she said, placing his hand on her breast. "I can always find you in here. But it will be easier if you return to Cuba and find me, okay?"

Dees kissed her again, mouthed the word "Okay," and jumped as the *Junkeroo*'s engines gunned. He landed on the dock and turned as the boat pulled slowly away from the dock in a haze of blue exhaust. Gloria wiped her eye with a fist, and clutched Cabrera by the arm, helping him walk unsteadily from the chair to the wheelhouse. Jacob was up the ladder, above her, on the flying bridge, carefully scanning the water as he steered toward the harbor mouth and the Gulf.

Dees watched until the boat was out of sight. He walked back to the cottage, and found crews from the Florida National Guard and Key West Street Department shoving debris out of the streets, using growling front-loaders to dump metal, glass, and wood into a line of idling dump trucks. As he picked his way toward his house, he saw a dark blue Ford sedan parked at the corner of his block. He stared at the white United States government plates.

Looking inside, he saw the keys still in the ignition, and tried the door. It was unlocked. He got in, started the engine, and slowly drove through the littered streets. He finally arrived at the easternmost point on the island, bounced over a couple of large limbs, and parked in the littered asphalt lot at Smathers Beach. The orange sun seemed to spout steam as it slowly came up out of the Atlantic. He scanned the horizon.

Several pleasure craft were already out, as if the storm and the attack had never happened, except on television.

He squinted until he saw the vaguely familiar shape of a fishing boat come into view, moving diagonally away from him, toward the Gulf stream. He put on his sunglasses and pulled the cellular phone receiver from the cradle bolted to the floor. Looking at the languidly rolling boat, he punched in the number of the GTV desk in Phoenix without looking at the phone.

"Yeah. Dees here . . . Whoa, slow down, slow down. I'll file an update when there's something to file on. . . . Yeah, I got some sleep. . . . Twenty minutes? I'll be at the truck. I have a couple of new items to add. . . . Well yeah, there's no war, but Cabrera's just taken a powder. It's like he disappeared. . . . No, *Conspiracies and Cover-Ups* will have to get by without me. No conspiracy here as far as I know. But I have audiotape of Cabrera implicating someone from the State Department. At least I think he's with the State Department. . . . What? . . . Yeah, yeah, yeah. If the tabloid segments want this, they can use somebody else's voice and face. I'm just one of those hard-news dinosaurs that's wondering where all the little mammals came from. . . . Huh? . . . Nothing. Just a joke . . .

"What? Who? . . . Oh, yeah. That Camponella guy seems to have a drinking problem. . . . Yeah, no shit . . . He what? . . . All I know is he fell down drunk. . . . Okay, twenty minutes. Before that, do me a favor. What's the State Department duty desk number in D.C.? . . . Yeah. Okay, got it. Thanks."

He beeped off the phone and punched in the 202 area code and number. The boat receded slowly. A pair of wave runners cut across the horizon, tossing up fishtails of spray. Someone on the other end answered.

"Yes, I need to speak to a Mr. Edward Davis, please. . . . I know, but this is an emergency. I'm calling from the FBI in Miami. . . . Davis, Edward Davis, common spelling. He'd been on temporary liaison with us in Miami. . . . Agent John Briscoe. I'll wait, thanks."

The boat had almost reached the horizon. If Dees squinted, he could barely make out its outline against the angry sun. "Hello? . . . What? . . . But I met with him. . . ."

He stared at the dashboard as the voice on the other end continued. "You're telling me there's no one at the State Department named Edward Davis? Anywhere?"

There was another pause. "And he was the only one recently? . . . He worked in Tokyo? . . . He died in 1979. . . . I see. No one at all assigned to work with the FBI in Miami? . . . No, no, I understood you the first time. Thanks."

Dees hung up and stared through the windshield. All he saw was the sun, rising slowly, and more than a dozen fishing and pleasure boats already dotting the water near shore. He got out of the car and left the keys in the ignition. Twenty feet away three unshaven men, one whose massive arms were completely covered in tattoos, huddled near the trunk of a banyan. They stood over a dozen half-full bottles of off-brand rum, cheap bourbon, and cheaper tequila.

The one with the tattoos darted his eyes at Dees as he walked toward them. "Get the fuck away," he slurred, wiping his mouth with the back of a hairy arm. "Get your fucking own."

Dees stopped. "Pickings good on Duval Street?"

A short man with dirty blond hair and two missing lower front teeth stared belligerently. "You a fucking cop?"

"Nope," Dees said. He nodded toward the Ford. "That car's unlocked. The keys are in it. I'm leaving now."

Dees walked slowly away, toward the center of town and the satellite trucks on Duval. He felt for the tape recorder in his pocket. He touched it, reassured, and wondered if Darrell could dub it to videotape. He snapped his fingers. Computer sketching. He'd feed the information to Phoenix on his laptop, and they could whip up a rough facsimile of Davis's face.

He squinted and removed the walls and ceilings from every building between him and the cottage. He could see it, quiet as still water, the air conditioner keeping a house full of electronics cool, nothing breathing, nothing alive except for electrons pulsing through random wires.

He picked up his pace, and began whistling "Guantanamera." The sun felt warm on his face. He heard a door slam, an engine start, and tires screech. He kept walking, without looking back.

DON'T MISS THE MOST AUTHENTIC
THRILLER OF THE DECADE!

REMOTE CONTROL
by Andy McNab

A former member of the Special Air Service crack elite
force, Andy McNab has seen action on five continents.
In January 1991, he commanded the eight-man SAS
squad that went behind Iraqi lines to destroy Saddam's
scuds. McNab eventually became the British army's
most highly decorated serving soldier and remains
closely involved with intelligence communities on
both sides of the Atlantic.

Now, in his explosive fiction debut, he has drawn on
his seventeen years of active service to create a thriller
of high-stakes intrigue and relentless action. With
chillingly authentic operational detail never before
seen in thrillers, REMOTE CONTROL is a novel so
real and suspenseful it sets a new standard for the
genre.

Published by Ballantine Books.
Available in bookstores everywhere.

AN AMERICAN KILLING
by
Mary-Ann Tirone Smith

A bestselling true-crime author, wife to a
Washington insider, Denise Burke knows the facts
behind the rumors, the stories behind the scan-
dals. Now Owen Hall, a charismatic congressman,
urges her to investigate a triple murder case that
may have led to a wrongful conviction. But as she
begins to penetrate the fateful events surrounding
the years-old homicide, Hall suddenly begs her to
stop. Yet Burke is in too deep. The stakes reach a
deadly level when Hall dies suspiciously with a
D.C. call girl—and Burke uncovers a chilling connection. Desperately pursuing a story of secrets,
sex, and blood—not for profit, not for fame, but
for her very survival—Burke exposes the terrify-
ing truth about the most monstrous crime of all.

Available now in bookstores everywhere.
Published by The Ballantine Publishing Group.